SEEKING HAKKA BAKKA

हक् का-बक् का

Bebe Lord Gow

iUniverse, Inc.
Bloomington

Seeking Hakka Bakka

iUniverse books may be ordered through booksellers or by contacting:

iUniverse
1663 Liberty Drive
Bloomington, IN 47403
www.iuniverse.com
1-800-Authors (1-800-288-4677)

ISBN: 978-1-4759-1734-5 (sc)
ISBN: 978-1-4759-1735-2 (hc)
ISBN: 978-1-4759-1736-9 (e)

Library of Congress Control Number: 2012907264

Printed in the United States of America

iUniverse rev. date: 9/11/2012

"'Tain't what you do, it's the way that you do it."
—Sy Oliver and Trummy Young

ACKNOWLEDGEMENTS

This story is a work of love. It was inspired first by my dad and mom, and then my kids, all of them, who eventually tired of my questions about the title, whether or not it had a good storyline and if a certain character was too wimpy. And so then I left them alone and took on another group, my friends, until they stopped taking my calls and averted their eyes at the sight of me. Finally, I crept up on the blind side of anyone who looked sympathetic, whether in a movie line, reading a grocery list or waiting to see a doctor and said "excuse me, may I ask you a question?" And then I pounced.

And so this book is for all of you, especially three generous friends for their time and invaluable suggestions and my loving family who received most of the brunt. Thanks and enjoy.

PART I

1.

In the Beginning

SHE REALLY REALLY LOVED her dad. He was brilliant. She wanted to be just like him and whenever he was home she did her best to impress him.

Early one Sunday morning she called to another room. "Hey Dad! Did you hear those bells pealing? That's what tintinnabulation means. Are you proud of me?"

There was no reply. He never slept much, probably already deep into another book. With a raised voice, she called again. "Guess what? I woke up singing that song you taught me—the one you learned when you were my age, remember?" She sang 'taint what you do, it's the way that you do it, that's what it's all about, hey!' What does it mean exactly?"

Her question met silence and then more church bells. "Come on, Dad, wake up. It's time to talk and I have a really cool idea. You know how you always ask 'what shall we do today, love bug'? Well, you're leaving on another business trip tomorrow, so how about if we skip Sunday school and church and you teach me more about tacking into the wind. I'm getting better. Right?"

Shoot! Still no answer. She moved in the bed; it squeaked. *Weird,*

3

she thought. Where was her hammock? More bells with various tones sounded outside, while inside unfamiliar voices from somewhere below jerked her tiny body upright. What was going on? She was very very cold which she almost never was and the dismal room destroyed her enthusiasm. Only two things were recognizable, a beat-up copy of *Huckleberry Finn* on the bare floor beside her emptied backpack and her ever-present scratched yo-yo, a major comfort during times of loneliness.

She picked up her yo-yo and called. "Da-ad? Where are you? I don't like it here. You didn't forget about me, did you?"

Gray light through a crack in the heavy drapes beckoned. When she pulled back one side, and looked out the window, the only window, there was more grass than she had ever seen. Was it a golf course? And who was the tall man driving a big machine up and down, up and down with one arm. She studied him and discovered saw his other arm was kind of withered, hung loosely and didn't seem to bother him. That meant he was brave like her dad. Cool! He would be her friend.

She pulled the drapes further back to see more when one side landed in a heap at her bare feet. Immediately to control her shivers, it became a wrap she called a *pashmina*. Some of her friends' parents called it a *rebozo* and since being grown-up was her goal, she resolved to always wrap in a *rebozo*.

On her way back to her bed, a clap of thunder triggered a nerve and part of the curtain tripped her. A tear fell…not because she hurt herself or anything like that, but because something wasn't right. In fact nothing felt right. Her bottom lip quivered and then salty tears poured forth, mimicking the heavens which had opened up.

She and her Dad liked the same things. He would never pick a depressing, dusty place like this for a surprise adventure. They liked rooms with many colors or all white with accents of very bright colors. This place looked like the pictures in those well-worn decorator magazines she found at the CLIP JOINT… a crazy-fun sort of hair salon her dad went to. No one had to tell her when her dad was not making money because his hair hung down his neck and he looked like a woman. She hated that and praticed cutting her own hair so that one day soon, she could cut his and save him money.

Where they were now was neither crazy nor fun. She felt like the poor cuckoo that once got trapped inside her favorite clock, a birthday present from Norway when her dad sailed there. Would they ever have the money to fix it? Not knowing answers bothered her. Her head swiveled. Hold on.

A large off-kilter painting of a young boy strangely dressed in velvet shorts and a girlie-girl shirt, hung on a puke green wall. He looked about her age, nearly eight, with a cute smile, auburn hair and eyes that were big and blue. Her dad believed a person's soul shone through his or her eyes. She didn't get that but was trying because he thought she was "sharp as a tack." In addition, he believed that souls, God, Heaven were real and she was supposed to believe in all that. She didn't. The caricature she had drawn of her dad with only a few lines took no belief. It was right there, in your face.

A doorbell chimed, a door slammed, another opened and then she heard footsteps. Yes! Her dad was back! She could ask about the portrait. Holding back her black hair to see through the rails of a long winding stairway, a uniformed woman with fiery red hair entered a huge atrium. She stopped beside an antique sleigh like Santa's. Weird. Why was a Santa's sleigh inside a house three months before Christmas, or anytime? And why was the woman wiping her eyes with her clean apron? Was she worried that she couldn't give her kids all they wanted? If so, Mandolin could comfort her. She almost never got what she wanted and it wasn't so bad after all. Not knowing the whereabouts of your Dad was far worse, but happily as soon the apron lady got to the door, he could answer many of her questions. Mandolin removed her yo-yo from her jeans' pocket and performed 'the rock the baby twirl,' her inclination when patience was obligatory or trouble came her way.

Her reverie was interrupted by an antique clock that chimed twelve times. Twelve? Holy Pig! If this old clock was right, it was the first time in her seven and three quarters years she had slept 'til noon—like teenagers do. Mandolin knew a lot about antiques because her dad collected them when he had money.

The apron-lady dragged herself past a gigantic room decorated with patterned material with assorted amoebas in hues of dull colors from what she could see. Yuck! She was young but not without opinions—strong opinions. Then the apron-lady finally opened the front door and greeted a stylishly-dressed man with a large roll of paper under his arm. He shook his umbrella, set it on the porch and the air that rushed up the stairs warmed Mandolin's bones. Holy Pig!! They had air conditioning here. That's why her bones were so cold. But immediately out went her yoyo. This man was not her dad.

"Morning Fanny," greeted the entering guest.

"Mornin' Mr. Pizza—Pizzatola," came a cheerless response in a deep Texas accent.

"Wait a minute. When you found out my first name is Antonio. and you were going to call me Tony, right?"

"How about if ah call you Mr. P? Suits a country gal lahk me better."

Mr. P. agreed, looked at his watch restlessly and Heather understood.

"Mrs. Mac was expectin' you at noon, but things are not exactly the same today. She won't be meetin' with ya'll after all." She wiped her eyes with her apron.

"Is she having a bad day, Fanny?"

"Ah'm called Heather now and we're all sufferin.' If today was a fish, ah'd sure throw it back."

Heather caught sight of Mandolin at the top of the stairs and asked

Mr. P. to step into the living room with her. He followed and she burst into tears. He tried to comfort her; she tried to talk but the tears kept falling. He turned to get help, she grabbed his arm and explained what she could through her sobs. Neither she nor the rest of the staff had been told the full story but after Mr. Jim dropped off, Mandolin, the bosses' granddaughter the previous evening, Mr. Jim and Mr. James had gone off on a deer hunting trip. She could barely choke out the rest. They would never be returning "cuz of...cuz of the fatal accident."

Mr. P. was shocked by the news. Mrs. Mac's husband, James MacDuff was a well-respected and entertaining man with many friends. He had not seen their son in years or known they were grandparents.

"Sure hate to say this but...but ah'm supposed to tell you two things. First, Miz Mac can't see the big oak in her yard because of where you put the window, and second you... you won't receive the rest of your money until you fix it."

Mr. P. gulped his way through the next question. "When's the funeral, do you know?"

"She's leaving shortly to make arrangements in New York."

"My condolences to you all. I enjoyed working with Mr. Mac."

"We all loved that man to death." She realized her gaff and covered her face.

Still on the stairs, Mandolin's curiosity had sent her step by step almost to the bottom to hear better. Heather and Mr. P. appeared and she let him out the front door. Immediately Mandolin blurted.

"Have you seen my dad?"

Heather couldn't deal with the question and escaped into the kitchen. Mandolin sighed, guessed she had chores to do, when she suddenly smacked the side of her head. Of course! Heather couldn't tell her because her dad was playing hide and seek, a game they often played. He was in the living room and like a hound dog on a scent, she sniffed around downstairs...without success.

Back in her gloomy room, she twirled her yo-yo around her head and then pulled herself up to a yoga position on her head to help collect herself. When she heard noises outside the door, she opened hers and peered into a room with a canopied double bed draped in lace, a closet full of elegant clothes and shoes, plus a solid wall of hats. Holy Pig. What a cool place to play dress-up. Then a snappish voice full of anger and frustration became clearer. "This child and then this! Why did it happen to me? Me, of all people!" The sound of a receiver hitting its cradle was followed by clomping heels approaching on a wooden floor. Mandolin ducked back into her room.

All at once a hot human blast with a hammer in hand blew in. Without a glance in Mandolin's direction, a wrinkled stick-figure with loose skin under her neck in a black dress entered in a furor. Why was she draped in lacy scarves when it was hot outside? She marched to the portrait of the boy and removed it angrily. Mandolin felt like she was in trouble, just like back home. Whenever her nanny, Valentina found globs of jelly on the counter, the remains of a PB and J sandwich, she punished Mandolin by hiding the jelly *and* the peanut butter for a whole week. It made Mandolin mad because Valentina was not her boss. She only came to stay with her during the week while her dad was gone.

Trying not to laugh at the lady's lopsided hat stuck up with black feathers, Mandolin spoke with her usual candor.

"Who are you?"

Frustration straightened the old lady's spine, as far as possible. "What? You don't *know* who I am? Why do you suppose you were brrought here? I am the owne*rr* of this estate and you may call me Hopscotch," she stated in a strange accent, rolling her r's.

"What a weird name."

"Not a-tall. If you knew anything about originality or the worrrld, you would think it quite clever as my many frriends do."

"Oh! Do you and your many friends know *the world is full of magical things waiting for out wits to grow sharper?* A lady named Linda Rence wrote that on a poster and I think she is very smart."

"Magic? Poof! We Scots are rrealistic but I am too distrraught to even mention that Russia honored me with an icon because of my importance in the worrrld." She began to cry, caught her breath, spun to the wall in annoyance and hammered a nail into it as if she wanted to kill it. Mandolin couldn't help smiling when she missed. Now with more fury, she attacked the nail and hung a framed photograph of a woman with dilapidated features. Mandolin sidled up, pointed and shuddered.

"Yuck! That lady needs a facelift."

Hopscotch's swung around. "What do you know about facelifts, child?"

"I know they fix up funny looking old ladies. By the way, I like the portrait of the boy much better."

Hopscotch whimpered and then shot her a comment that stung worse than a stone from a slingshot. "Did anyone ask for your opinion, idiot child?"

"My name is Mandolin and I…"

"Mandolin?!" A sour chuckle followed. "No mother in her *rr*right mind would ever name a child Mandolin. That is the name of an outdated musical instrument. Arrround here, you will be called Madolin and never forrrget it."

"That won't work. I've been Mandolin ever since I can remember and my dad told me I look something like *his* mom, and he thinks I'm pretty like *my* mom."

The old lady rolled her eyes, waved her arms with major frustration, burst into tears and screamed. "I don't care to hear another word about that woman my son ran off with."

Oh no! Was this her dad's mom? Mandolin watched her gramma's hammer beating the wall and thought of Valentina. She was strict, but this was the true wicked witch from the West or East, all dolled up in

9

'*fahncy*' clothes. *How can she talk so ugly when she doesn't even know me? What makes people mean?* Where was her dad? She had to know. She took another look at the replaced photograph and thought of the way the woman had thrown the hammer across the room. She was scary and dangerous.

"She's not...she's not my mom, is she?"

"Your mother?" Indeed not! This is Eleanor R-r-roosevelt, the wife of a former President of the United States, a photograph I have saved since I arrived in this country in 1948. Eleanor Roosevelt was a Civil Rights activist and an admirable woman, not a disgrace like your mother."

Mandolin was confused and defenseless. All she knew about her mom was that she had one somewhere and down went her yo-yo into the 'sleeper' mode.

Hopscotch blew up. "Put that ridiculous thing away."

What was wrong with yo-yoing? If it was bad manners, her Dad would have told her instead of asking her to look up its history. What was a disgrace? Was her name actually Madolin? She felt dizzy until she remembered her dad. He was good at straightening things out - like he always coiled the lines of his boat neatly and looped them around the winches while she practiced her square knots. But for now, curiosity about a civil rights activist trumped that. This felt more like civil wrongs.

Mrs. Know-It-All forgot her hammer, turned on her high-heeled sandals, and wobbled. She caught herself on Mandolin's shoulder, acted as if she had touched the devil and Mandolin wanted to giggle. But right then, she had the answers. This woman was born a grump like Cinderella's wicked stepmother. She wanted a fun gramma like Dorothy to take her over the rainbow. Or maybe even someone like old William in *Alice in Wonderland* who was still playful enough to stand on his head.

Valentina was not always fun either. She swore a lot, but compared to this woman, she was a saint. Not much was going right, and now it seemed that her Dad had been called away on one of his boat trips again.

Escape! That's what she should do. She could take the hammer and bash her way out! And yet climbing back into her bed to save her soul seemed best. *"If I should die before I wake, I pray the Lord my soul to…* No God! No! Don't let me die. I'll believe in you if you bring back my dad right away to find me. We love each other more than anything. Please! In case you've forgotten I want to remind you of the fun we had on our mystery trip yesterday and the day before that. Please let me know where he is."

She cuddled under the covers, closed her eyes and whispered memories to God.

2
The Past Comes Forward

TOO EXCITED TO SIT still, Mandolin loosened her seat belt, looked up and watched her dad remove a messily folded road map from behind the visor.

"Guess what, Dad? When I look up your nostrils, I can see what's on your mind."

His deeply tanned, weathered face creased into a smile as he spread the map across the steering wheel.

"Okay. What's on my mind, love bug?"

She brushed her long hair aside and snuggled up to his lean muscular body. "That I'm so looking forward this trip with you...our mystery adventure as you call it."

"That's my girl. And I have news for you. I can look right through those pearly green eyes of yours and see a brain that never stops working."

"That's because I'm nearly as big and as smart as my best friend Fawiza. And one day I'll be as smart as you, promise."

His sideways glance challenged the wisdom behind her comment. His defiance and rejection of discipline had caused many years of anguish for his parents and he now knew he wanted much more for his daughter. He was puzzled about how to respond. Mandolin saved him.

"In three a half months, my booster seat goes. Yes!"

"Being small is not all bad. Napoleon was small and became the fearless leader of France during the Revolution."

"What's a Revolution?"

He focused on the map. "Remember the question and ask me again when we're on the road."

"I know it has to do with standing up for what you believe and I will."

"I'm counting on you." He started his 1999 Jeep, and handed her the unfolded map. She made a face, tried to refold it, then threw it on the floor.

"Crap! It takes hours to fold it right."

Her dad held up his hand in a stop position and spoke in the tone she hated more than anything. "Man-do-lin."

She knew exactly what he meant. Bad words were "not appropriate" and he expected her to work on the map until it was neatly folded. She obeyed and waved it in his face. He accepted the map, slipped it into his door pocket and looked down at an exceedingly plain, yet curiously fetching seven, nearly eight-year old.

"One day I'm going to invent an automatic map folder, just wait."

"A great idea. And away we go!"

He pulled out, jammed on his brakes and exclaimed. "Watch it there, you dumb bunny."

"Da-ad. Slow down. When you put too much juice on the tensioner, you can burn up the conveyor belt."

Highly amused, he wanted to know where she had heard that.

"On Valentina's car radio. And it could be dangerous, the man said."

He collected himself. "Righto. I see you brought your hammock, but you're ready to sleep in a real bed, right?"

She sighed as if this had been an issue. Adjusting his dark glasses, he checked the side view mirror, sped out quickly onto the highway and began to hum.

"You always hum that tune. What's it called?"

"It's an old tune by Steve Allen." He sang: "*You're looking in someone eyes, you suddenly realize, that this could be the start of something big*"… da-da de-da-da…Now what other news do you have for me?"

"Did I tell you that I'm on the last chapter of *Huckleberry Finn?*"

"Really! Has Valentina been reading it to you?" he asked.

"No, silly. I've been reading it to her. When can I read the rest to you?"

He had been unaware of his daughter's accomplishment, and his expression was surprise mixed with shame. All he could say was "soon."

"You'll like Huck, Dad. He's really really brave and popular like you. When you surprise us on the beach, people who don't even know you always gather around. I can sit in the middle of a sofa in hopes others will join me and no one does.

"Funny you should say that. Just last night while on my trip to New Orleans, a friend invited me over to watch a video and…"

"A…girlfriend?" she asked with a tremor in her voice.

Stymied, he turned serious. "You're interrupting. Do you want to hear about the video or not?"

"Sorry. Tell me."

"It's about *hakka bakka*, a Hindi term that implies you've finally found your place in the shade."

"But I like the sun."

He laughed. 'Shade or sun, it means to find joy and where you belong in life."

"Is it hard to do that?"

"Harder for some than others."

"*Hakka bakka*. That's really cool because guess why. Ivar says in

Norway kids from all over meet in a forest and have a blast dancing, singing and acting out fun animals. They call it *hakkebakkeskogen*."

"There you go. You see Mandi, if we open our hearts and minds, there's no telling what will happen." He laughed "Who knows? We might even learn to fly over the rainbow."

"I love your laugh, Dad. Some grown-ups grumble over the weather or the president or the war and you never do."

He hid his anxieties and reached for her hand. "*Te amo, muchisimo.*"

She nestled close. "Love you more. *Mucho mas.*"

"Good. Between Huck and *hakka bakka*, we'll never be bored, right?"

"Except for last night. Fawiza and I had to sit at Beach Burger and listen to Valentina talk to her friend about how stupid boys are. That was worse than boring."

"You weren't rude, were you?"

"Oh no. You once told me that when I'm not having a good time it's my own fault, so guess what I did?"

"What."

She giggled. "I knocked over Valentina's glass of water so we could change the subject, and it worked. But like always, Valentina gave me this eyebrow anger thing. I can't wait to be grown up and do everything I want."

He wiped his face to cover his anxieties. "Tell me about Fawiza."

"She's older and my best friend and teaches me lots of things."

"Good. "We must always stand up for our friends."

Mandolin tried. "It's not easy in the car."

He smiled, and reached for her hand. "It means to defend your beliefs."

"There's just one thing wrong with her though. She doesn't know that when a man puts his peanuts into a woman's virginia, a little peanut grows inside it."

He did his best to keep a straight face. "I'm…I'm so happy you explained that."

"But, Dad, it doesn't make sense. Peanuts grow in the ground."

"It's complicated. Tell - tell me more about Fawiza."

She frowned and loosened her seat belt. "Da-ad! Do you want to hear more about virginias and peanuts or not?"

"Sorry. I interrupted, didn't I?"

'You certainly did, young man," she teased, "and please don't do it again."

He liked this. "You got me that time! Now do me favor and fasten up."

Her shoulders fell. "You noticed." She tightened the seat belt reluctantly "Fawiza is Muslim and they must not know about peanuts and virginias."

A shock of red hair fell over his glasses. He pushed it back and disappeared into his own world. That's what grown- ups do when things bother them, was her thought.

"Da-ad? I miss you."

"Oh. I—I was thinking about you, love bug?"

"Listen, I have to tell you something, I'm big now, and this 'love-bug' thing has got to go."

His bit his lip. "How about 'my little maid of the seas'? Does that go too?"

She nodded. "Mandi or Lizard are good."

"Okay Lizard, now where were we?"

"Talking about Muslims. Where is Muslim anyway?"

"Muslim is not a country. It's a religion they call Islam that supports one God called Allah."

"Dad! Stop!"

A fat bumblebee landed on the window right next to Mandolin's face. "Help! Dad! Help! There's a bee in the car."

She buried her face in his side. He pulled to a stop and gently flicked the bee out the window.

"You're so-o brave."

"My Dad, your grampa was a beekeeper and taught me about fear. When bees sense it, they sting and then die. So we have to just hum along and stay calm."

"I'm never going to die. Can we raise bees when we get back home?"

"It all depends on what kind of a job I get. A lot of equipment is needed. We'll need a beehive, white bee suits, bee masks and a smoker."

"Cool. Maybe Fawiza can help. She says the Byzantine Empire was named after bees. Get it? Bz-z-zy Bees. Byz-z-zantine."

"I get it. Bees are b-z-z-z-y like you."

They bounced over a bump. "What's a tope?"

"You know that word."

"Oh yeah. A bump in the road to slow down fast drivers through these little towns. Fawiza says I'm lucky to have lived in so many places with you and catch on to languages, but I mess up in Spanish a lot... like yesterday when I mixed up *boda* with *soda*, which reminds me, let's get a...?"

"Now Lizard, remember we've had to reduce our spending habits lately."

"Oh yeah, but no prob, Dad. When I get bigger I'm going to write a story about our adventures and we'll be really really rich."

"Good girl. I'll be your first customer. Now, what made you talk about a *boda*?"

She recognized the tension in his voice and regretted her words. *Boda* meant wedding and ever since her Dad took her out to a special dinner and explained the sad story of her mom and him not working it all out, his expression gummed up whenever she asked about her mom. She hated to upset him and knew that one day she would meet her mom. And then for some reason, her dad reached for her hand and kissed it. Weird! But he did that a lot.

Minutes passed. Mandolin got fidgety. "It's time I started school, right?"

He gasped. "I'm sorry I had to be away last year. We'll look into it as soon as our trip is over."

"Trr-*iffic*! Pinky swear?"

He nodded convincingly. She looked up into his eyes.

"Why don't we have black eyes?"

"God gave you exceptionally beautiful green ones. Why would you want black ones?"

"Fawiza's are the best."

"It's more or less a culture thing. Daddy's family is Scottish and many of us are fair-skinned and freckled with red hair and blue eyes. You're an exception."

"Your hair is not red like strawberries, Dad. It reminds me of ginger snaps or yummy butterscotch drops. *Chingados*! I left my whole bag of gummy bears on the kitchen table."

Here it came again, the look she hated.

"*Chingados*? Do you know what that means, Mandolin?"

She didn't know but knew he was really angry because that's when he called her Mandolin. "Valentina says it when she's really really angry."

"Are you really really angry Lizard?"

"No, and don't you be, either. In church on Sunday, we sang about a wench and that's a bad word too."

"It sounds as if you were singing *Amazing Grace and the word is wretch*...a miserably unhappy soul which neither you or I are, right?"

She hugged her dad.

"I'm happy Valentina takes you to church. She's a good Nanny."

And then he stopped talking which bothered her because it meant he was thinking again and she wasn't learning anything. She cleared her throat loudly.

"Sorry, the same woman with the video has a beautiful voice and interprets words for the deaf."

"I want to do that too."

"I can remember a few letters she taught me."

They stopped at a light. He demonstrated an I I with his left hand and stuck two fingers out to the side. For the B, he held up his right hand in a stop position. She practiced. Her fingers would not cooperate and frustrated her. Then her stomach squealed like a siren and they laughed.

"Now it's your stomach that's making signs, so watch for a place to eat."

Suddenly she hummed her thoughts to him "I know where we're going! "I know where we're going, either to Egypt, Israel."

"What makes you say that?"

"Remember when you read me about the land of milk and honey in the Bible?"

"Good for you, but how can we possibly get to the Holy Land in our Jeep? It's way across the ocean."

"So - we should have gone in your boat."

"Too dangerous. But someday we'll take a cruise together."

"Awesome. And meet kings and go to Timbuktu and think of lovely things to do like we read in that kid's book of my grandpa's... you know the one... by A.A. Milne. It's about Christopher Robin and Pooh Bear."

"I'm surprised you remember all this, especially the author's name."

"I hate forgetting things. Remember the drawings inside the book? I copy them on scraps of paper."

He pulled into a McDonalds.

"Oh please! Not another McNo. I really don't like the Happy Meals anymore or all the princess toys…or being treated like a baby. How about Chinese? Eating with chopsticks is fun."

'Wait a minute, Mandi. McDonald is a Scottish name and we Scots have to stick together, right?"

She shrugged. He parked, opened his door, indicated for her to come out his door and jump into his arms. He then whirled her around and set her on his shoulders.

"Oh! My aching back," he teased. "You're getting too big for this."

"I know, in only three months I'll be only two numbers younger than Fawiza."

"I'm pleased you have good friends, sweetheart."

"Me too, but do you have to be married have a baby?"

The question threw him. "Is—is that what Fawiza told you?"

She nodded.

"Having a baby when you're married is best, Lizard, although it doesn't always happen that way."

They skip-raced up the sidewalk to the restaurant and of course she won. A dog was tied up outside the door. She fell on her knees, hugged it, sat up like a dog and looked imploringly up at her dad. He shook his head. It was always the same, "not until I get a steady job."

"But Dad, I get lonesome when you're gone. The kids on the beach are not interested in what I am. They argue with me and dogs never do. They wag their tails and never care where their mom is."

He pulled to a stop. "I…I thought we were over all that."

She tightened her long hair at the nape of her neck to release tension. "Sorry. It just slipped out."

Just before they entered the restaurant, he took her hand and they joined a line inside.

"Do you have to pee?" he asked her.

She flinched. "No, I'm good. And besides me and Fawiza don't like that word. It sounds like a word that boys have and girls don't."

A smile defied his will. His expression brightened while he wondered how much they knew about sex and when he should discuss it with her.

"Okay then, have a look at the luncheon selections on the wall. Various packets of colored sweeteners in a bowl attracted her more. Her dad ordered a burger, rare. The waitress glared at Mandolin, drummed her fingers on the counter and in a snippy voice asked if she had made up her mind—yet.

"My daughter will have chicken McNuggets and fries please."

The waitress typed her order on the screen and turned to the next in line.

Mandolin countered. "Da-ad! That's not what I wanted. I was going to try—"

"Sorry, my mistake, Lizard."

"That lady was rude to me."

He took her hand as they moved along. 'Maybe she has sore feet, or a sick daughter or …"

"Maybe so but…" Mandolin looked again at the menu. "Why do some stores charge $2.49 and not $2.50 and others charge $19.99 instead of 20 dollars?"

He explained that it sounded like less money, and by the time they finished discussing how to earn and save her allowance, it was almost dark and time to leave McNo's… with half of her Happy Meal untouched.

Back at the car, he helped his tired little girl fasten her seat belt. Then as he climbed into his side, he pulled his door to close it and caught his leg. He never winced nor cried aloud, took out a clean handkerchief and stopped the blood with pressure.

"See. I told you this present from you and Valentina would come in handy."

"Fawiza is brave too, Dad. Have you seen how she removes her fake leg and hops happily down the beach and into the water?"

21

"I have, and it takes guts to be like that."

"Do I have guts?"

"Sure you do. You like to take chances, right?"

Mandolin nodded, then yawned, inched closer to him. A late afternoon sun that filled the sky with brilliant swirling of cerulean blue reminded her of the dichroic glass pendant Valentina's boyfriend had given her.

"I hope I find a brave boyfriend some day," she mused aloud.

"One of these days, a good guy will find *you*, Lizard. Just you wait! You've got "*it*"!

Her little body fell limply against him. He looked down with pride, wondered if she would ever be aware of her uniqueness, and when he could give her the life she deserved.

When Mandolin rejoined the real world, her first thought was that her dad said she had guts. And that meant she took chances. She looked around her familiar dismal room and focused on a square box as well as a slim package marked *fragile* on the floor. Both were tied together with a rope. When her dad put them in the Jeep, she didn't have the guts to ask what was inside because he was busy and she had already asked too many questions. Now was her chance to find out. Recalling her dad's lessons in untying ropes tied to piers, she finally loosened the tight knot and separated the packages. A noise outside her door distracted her. Was it her gramma? She listened, it went away, but the photo of that ugly lady on the wall, had to come down. With all her might, she shoved the heavy box under it, climbed on top and pulled it down. Whoosh!

She then tangled with a stuck top drawer, lost her patience and slipped the picture and a fragile package under some sweaters in the bottom drawer. A bunch of white smelly balls rolled out onto the floor. Why did they smell like toothpaste? She crawled around the floor, recovered them and returned them hastily. Totally stressed, she took to her lotus position on the bare floor.

Was she in hell? Every part of her begged for help. "Dad! There's no one to play with and your mother is even meaner than the boy who kicked over our sand castles on the beach. Where's our *hakka bakka*? There's no joy here like we know about and besides we belong together. Right? We belong together."

Under her pillow was a mangled box of crayons. She sat back on her bed and cheered herself by drawing colorful animals and fish on the pukey-colored wall with bright orange, then Kelly green, pink, blue, and purple. These bright colors were like those the Africans used. They lifted her spirits and inspired her. Creating something, anything original thrilled her, but was her work actually original? *When the world is so big, how can anyone be sure the same thing is not being done at this very moment someplace else? Or if it has been done before?*

She was remembering her few pieces that sold in the Saturday markets back home when the voice that sounded like confused chickens made her flinch. Her grandmother was back!

"What are you doing? Get up from that bed! There is work to be done."

And then she viewed the damage. "Upon my soul! What have you done to my beautiful drapes? And the walls? You can begin by scrubbing away all those scribbles. F'r the luv of God, lass! I should be disgraced if anyone should see a room like this during my house and garden tour."

She slammed the door and heard her gramma's door click. Why did she always lock her door? Was she hiding something? Did she think Mandolin would steal from her? *Da-ad? Help me. I'm trying to be happy and tough like you but...but...*

Huck. What would he do? She opened the book to her marker and counted the pages to the end. She hated endings, of anything and everything. They made her sad. Her dad was always leaving her for his trips. Had she stopped reading Huck because of this? Does something bad happen when the King joins the slave on the raft? Had her dad ended their lives on the beach and brought Mandolin back to his home town to start a new project? *Please, Dad, not here in this Dragon Pit.*

Mandolin took another look at the backyard and saw a swimming pool. A swimming pool in a yard? Holy Pig! Back in the cushion-less window seat, she wound and rewound her hair around her finger. The rain was over; she drew a dog in the foggy window and then used her hand to wipe it away. The sky reminded her of a blank canvas that she so wished for, and once again it was time to improvise, a trait she had learned by herself because her dad couldn't afford them…yet. She unrolled toilet paper and on each of many squares drew animal ears and peoples' ears of all shapes and sizes, even meercats and porcupine. Why didn't her drawings cheer her as usual?

Her dad had forgotten her eighth birthday and she stuck and alone like in a labyrinth. Why? Had she done something wrong? Was this trip some sort of a punishment? What would Huck do? Would he try to remake himself to change the opinion of his gramma? Of course not! He had guts and so did she. She pounded on the wall so hard it caused the picture to fall to the floor. Fine! She hated that stupid picture. Then she heard voices downstairs, flew to the back stairs, leaping two-at-a-time to the bottom where she heard a TV.

A newsman was talking about *Grease* and when her eyes absorbed Heather's actions in the large kitchen, she understood. Heather was making soap out of grease for Hopscotch like Valentina did for her and her dad back home.

Heather and Mandolin exchanged smiles.

"Hi! You seem really nice. Are you?"

"Sure hope so, but this news about Greece and the world is real bad."

Heather turned off the TV. "So you must be Madolin."

"Mandolin."

"It's none of my business, but m' boss is real fussy about names. From what ah understand, she wants us to call you Madolin and if ah were you, ah'd go along with it."

"I don't get it. What's wrong with her?"

"Mrs. Mac lost her husband and her…she's forgetful at times and…" Heather sniffed and collected herself. "Ya'll like to cook?"

"Not sure. Back home, we eat out. Is it fun?"

"It sure is for me. When ah meet folks, ah like to figure out their favorite foods. Take you, Madolin. Not the cupcake type. They're for girls in fancy petticoats, raht?"

"And ones who always hang up their towels."

Heather got a kick out of this. "Me and you are gonna have a real good time. We're kinda plain vanilla."

"With nuts on top!"

"Coming right up. How about helpin' me cut up some walnuts?"

"I'll try. So my grampa is dead?"

Heather parodied. "Some folks use blenders to chop nuts but Mrs. Mac likes them all exactly the same size, so ah'll teach you…"

"I think she's a giant nut.'

Again, Heather parodied. "Be sure to keep the sharp end away from you."

"I know. I talked my dad into giving me a Boy Scout knife for my seventh birthday and he taught me all about them. Like he's a neat freak. I can clean my fingernails with it, whittle a stick into a point to spear a snake, and how to splice ropes on his boat."

"You're way ahead of me, but listen a minute. Tidy and quiet are the rules here."

"Quiet?! My gramma, if that's what I'm supposed to call her, screeches at me at the top of her lungs."

Heather tried not to smile. "Back in Dahm Box, we call it a screech whenever a cow crosses the train tracks and the engineer has to pull up fast."

Mandolin thought that was funny. "Why is a small Texas town named Dime Box?"

"We got lots of crazy names in our state. There's Muleshoe, Turkey, Cut 'N Shoot and you can even drive up ta Paris. But gettin' back ta Dahm Box and your question. In 1877 before a Federal Post Office opened up, when folks wanted to deliver a letter to a nearby town, they put a dahm in a box in the one and only grocery store."

"Interesting. And if anyone was going that way they took it along, I suppose."

"You got it. People were good ta one another there but ah was lookin' for more excitement. Jeez m'beez! It's been close ta ten years already."

"Wow! "I've never seen a train. Will you take me there sometime?"

Heather said she'd like that and continued. "Before you came to live with us, Mrs. Mac hired a real expensive decorator to make this new home of theirs the showplace of Houston. She wants us to keep it lookin' good all the time and she means all the time. An invitation to the showplace means you're special and "*in*.""

In? Mandolin wanted *out*. Any place would be better. Maybe her gramma's inside-out view was totally charming, but from the outside, it was absolutely terrifying. She turned back to Heather.

"I heard you talking earlier. So being called Heather is okay with you now?"

"Sometimes you gotta let things flow on by, like one of your sticks in a stream. No sense gettin' your panties in a knot over it."

Mandolin's face reddened with temper. "But I like my name."

Heather silenced her with a stare, until she thought it over.

"O-kay. If you can do it, so can I. Call me Madolin until my Dad comes back. Then I'll be Mandolin. He'll never go for a change."

A noise at the kitchen door startled her. When it opened there stood the machine man. Determined not to look at his arm or long legs that seemed more like stilts, she blurted, "Hi up there. You look like Abraham Lincoln and that's good."

A forced smile brightened his shiny black face.

"Be with you in a second. Gotta wipe off the Grasshopper first."

Mandolin giggled. "You call that big machine out there a Grasshopper? Are you always funny?"

He picked up a cloth with his weird arm. "No one ever called me funny before."

"And you have guts as well. My dad will like you. Have you seen him around here? He likes to be outside and...do you know where he is?"

The machine man's smile disappeared while he thought how to answer. "Tell you what, darlin', I got work to do and we can talk later."

"Like what kind of work?"

"Well Miz Mac likes her gardens weeded, her cars shined up each day, and taking care of this big estate, helping in the kitchen and all them problems that come up, keeps me real busy."

"So are you like a...a slave?"

"Oh, my no. They freed the slaves long ago. But I been in her *employ* forever it feels like, and plannin' on stickin' with her long as she lets me."

"Don't you think she's mean?"

"Tell you what. Big Mama and my girls been wantin' to meet you. How 'bout comin' over to our house for supper tonight?"

Mandolin jumped up and down with excitement. "Can I be your friends?"

"You sure can doll-baby, I'll tell Miz Mac what we're doing, and I'll betcha she gonna be real happy for us all."

"And I'll bet you're wrong."

He looked down at her. She looked up and up at him. "Wow! I think I'll call you Sky. Is that okay?"

He gave her a sweet almost sad smile, and she asked. "Heather's making some good stuff inside. Will you come in with me?"

The voice of Hopscotch on the intercom interrupted his reply.

"My travel agent called and I want you to pick me up at the front door in exactly five minutes. I must be in New York in time for… in time…" The sound of a nose blow followed. "And don't keep me waiting." A click.

"Yuck! I don't get why you work for such a mean lady, but I'm glad to meet *you*." commented Mandolin.

"Don't know how much longer they plannin' on you being around here, but sometimes it's best to ignore folks who got meanness inside 'til you know 'em better. Then you find they got a fair side after all. Think on it like this. If it wasn't for her, me and Heather would be out of work, and no way for us, you and me, to be friends.

Her dad! He had no job. She hung her head which troubled him.

"An' please, you can call me Sky if you want. Suits me good."

This soothed her. "You're good to me, and while I wait for my Dad to come get me, I need other friends more than anything in the whole world. Do I have to dress up?"

Big Mama makes the girls shower before dinner, but you can do as you pleases."

"What time should I be ready?"

"Prob'ly around seven, Miz Mac puttin' the mansion on tour next month and we got lots of preparin' ahead of us."

Sky put Hopscotch's bag in the car but she had left her purse somewhere. Sky found it and off they rushed to the Hobby Airport.

Mandolin was excited. Maybe his Mama knew something about her dad.

3
New Friends

SUPPERTIME WAS THE BIG event of the day at Sky's house. His usual place, empty for now, was set opposite Big Mama's at one end of a painted wooden table in the kitchen. Big Mama was Sky's mom, a kindly soul with a lumpy body dressed in one of her hand-made flowered "frocks," for which "she didn't need no more patterns." A string of colored beads hung over it and a ribbon held back her white hair. Sky had two girls, Lillian, named for Big Mama, was twelve and skinny, with frizzy black hair and eyes. Tina, eight, had lighter skin, a sweet smile and small bones. They flanked Big Mama with kitchen cutlery, odd glasses and paper napkins in front of all.

A late afternoon sun in Lillian's eyes bothered her like most everything when teenage years are about to strike. Between the open kitchen/dining area and the 'parlor' as Big Mama called it, an old upright piano was wedged in. The piano had become the focal point of the house, with its yellowed keys, a missing black key, several sheets of music open on the rack, and a box full of used sewing patterns on top. Beside it, an early Singer sewing machine with a curled-up, yellowed mail order catalog faced down over the top. Flowers were everywhere... big red maroon and pink ones printed on the curtains, orange yellow and blue ones on the kitchen chair pads and bunches of dried, faded ones tucked in a bookcase.

Big Mama proudly jingled her silver bracelet while punching a branch of fresh crimson crepe myrtles into a Ball jar on the kitchen table. Drawing attention to the silver charms her family had given her through the years was no accident.

"Now then, I knows better than to eat before your Daddy and Madolin gets here, but my stomach's growling at me. Hand me them biscuits, Tina." And then she chuckled. "One thing good about gettin' old is the battle of the bulge is over. You kin just let it all hang out." And it did.

"What's the magic word?" asked Tina.

Big Mama slapped her own hand. "Shame on me! All these years we be teachin' you manners and now you is teachin' *me*."

"Remember the day you asked us to tell you when your chin hairs got long again?" asked Tina.

Big Mama rubbed her chin. More chuckles. "We waited too long, darlin'."

"Why don't you just shave them off?" was Lillian's curt question.

"No Missy. We might just find me a brand new beau soon and I sure don't wanna be scratchin' up his face with my whiskers."

She handed the tweezers to Tina with a wink and a grin. Lillian saw nothing amusing about chin whiskers, and showed it while Big Mama recounted another story of her past, a favorite topic.

"Maybe my recall needs an overhaul for today's e-vents, but goin's on back in the sixties be comin' real easy. We use-ta honky-tonk and run loose wherever we wanted."

"I wish I lived in the olden days," reflected Tina.

"At them outdoor drive-in thee-yaters, we sat in the car, pretended to watch the movie and necked up a storm with one of our boyfriends."

"Neck?"

"That's right. We smooched and pawed around."

"*You* did that?" Tina asked.

"Heavens to Betsy. Course we did. An' a lot of other funny things back then too. Them was good days. Did your Daddy ever tell you about Marvin Zindler and his Eyewitness News show?"

The girls shrugged.

"Ooo-ee! He lived on and on, face-lift after face-lift, uncoverin' bad doin's aroun' town— like dirty restaurants with slime in the ice machine."

Of course Lillian rolled her eyes and then complained about her homework. Tina knew that Big Mama's heart was warmed when she told stories of the past, and hugged her tight.

"We have so much fun with you, Big Mama. We're so lucky you live with us and not our own momma or that Hopscotch lady. She's really mean."

"Mighty glad to hear that, but it's not good to talk bad against nobody. Somethin' makes 'em do like they do. Could be with Miz Mac don't have no upstairs maid no more cuz they is hard to find and kinda outta the loop like they says. And remember, Hopscotch is what other folks call her. But *Miz Mac* is what we calls her. Ever'body unnerstand?"

Lillian countered "That's what *you* call her, Big Mama. She's 'Cruella' to me and Tina."

Big Mama could not hide her laugh and pretended to swat both of them on the rear causing her bracelet to jingle. "Tell Big Mama something, girls. How long your Papa been working for the MacDuff fambly now?"

Too long, thought Lillian.

"Seems like yesterday when things got all changed up around here. Was that like right after Christmas?"

"No Big Mama," corrected Lillian. "Mr. Jim arrived back here, in June. We had just gotten out of summer school."

"Only a month ago? Well I'll be." Big Mama pulled a story down from somewhere up above. "I remember it was that real hot night in August up in the high nineties."

"It's still July, Big Mama." Lillian corrected.

"So what," alleged Tina. "Let her talk."

"I wasn't there at their old house at the time, but your papa was and he says you both were sleepin' when Mr. Jim burst in. He was real excited to show off his daughter to Miz Mac and her grampa for the first time. Yes ma'am. After all those years, I knows Mr. Jim was sure happy to be in Houston agin."

"Papa said he really wanted to go on that pheasant hunt up in New York."

"You right Tina, and things sure have a way of workin' out. Mr. Jim was meetin' a buddy at the huntin' lease and there was no room for anyone else in the car."

"Jeez," declared Tina. "I can't imagine what it would be like without Papa."

"Me neither," alluded Big Mama, "I done had him when I was fifteen and we been best friends ever since."

"Fifteen!? That's three years from now for me," argued Lillian. "Were you nuts?"

"People today think so, but back then, it was kinda normal. I got me a good man who took care of me long as he lived."

"Does Madolin know about her dad?" Lillian asked.

"Don't think so. Miz Mac got some sorta secret goin' on about not sayin' nothin' to her yet. Nobody knows why. What we do know is her Daddy sure took chances in his life and 'specially in cars. When they found the wreck, his body was… "

Tina interrupted. They had agreed to forego all remarks about the accident. Lillian paid no attention. "If she won't talk about the accident, I'll bet she had something to do with it."

"Now Lillian, darlin'. You been readin' too many a them misery stories."

"*Mystery*! Mystery stories," Lillian corrected.

"The important thing is get the correct facks to Madolin. Miz Mac's got her all confused. We needs to make sure she knows her daddy was a good man with lots of friends. 'Fore he left outa here, they all use-ta say Mr. Jim was a Man's Man."

Lillian kept digging. "How come you called him Mister when you're way older than him?"

Big Mama pulled herself up with effort. "You does what the boss lady wants," explained Big Mama. "And mind you, that's the way it's gonna be when you all big and gits a job. You does what your boss wants or else you git fired or git outa there 'fore they fire you. Now, while we waitin 'on your Papa and Mandolin, I'll teach you a song we used to dance to. Weren't no dance really, it was called Truckin.' We played it on the victrola and it went like this."

Big Mama shuffled her feet, and swayed her body while her charm bracelet jingled. Sky opened the door. Mandolin followed, listened to her sing and dance to the beat. '*Taint what you do, it's the way that you do it. And that's what it's all about. Hey!*'

So that's where that song came from, thought Mandolin.

Big Mama welcomed her warmly. "How come you smilin', darlin?"

"Because my Dad and I think that when you feel good about what you do, it's called *hakka bakka* and that fits you. Now it's your turn, Big Mama. Please tell me what 'the way that you do it' means, exactly?"

Big Mama's eyes grew wide. She had no answer. Mandolin frowned. "When people don't answer my questions, I think it's about sex and stuff, like that."

Lillian was totally embarrassed. Sky stepped in. "Naw. It's about how you treat folks. You can treat 'em good or you can treat 'em bad. We don't hate nobody here. We jes' not fond a some."

Big Mama spoke and danced around. "If folks don't like the way I do it, I feels sorry for them. They missin' out on the fun. So come on and join us, Madolin."

"I like to dance, but compared to my friend back home, I'm horrible. Fawiza is like a hummingbird. She can hover in the air."

The girls were intrigued with Mandolin. Sky explained they were late because he had been preparing for the house tour.

"Your Dad works hard like my Dad."

Lillian commented. "Miz Mac treats you bad, Papa. She raves to others about her fantastic gardener, and yet when no one's around, she blames you for everything."

"Me and my friends call her bossypants and a snob."

"Now, now, Tina. that's enough of that. We got Madolin with us. Let's show her a good time. Set another place and let's use the crystal goblets tonight."

"Awesome. We never use them except to…"

"…to make an impression" concluded Lillian sourly.

"We use jelly glasses when we eat at home," Mandolin admitted.

Lillian needed the facts. "Your real name is Mandolin, right?"

"Madolin or Mandolin. It's okay 'til I see my Dad. Just be my friends, *please*."

Big Mama broke in. "That there is Lillian and…"

"Hi, I'm Tina, the youngest and I wish I were you. Papa says you can do everything, like draw animals with funny faces, and funky clowns and…"

"No. Not really. My gramma laughed at the two faces I drew for her as gifts and I never saw them again."

Big Mama frowned. "You kin draw my funny face any time you want darlin,' and I'll set it on the pi-ano. And too, you is welcome to live with us any time you pleases."

"And read *Huckleberry Finn* to me. I'm not the best reader," urged Tina.

Mandolin nodded willingly and performed her flying saucer trick with her yo-yo while she explained that she wanted to be a psychologist and an anthropologist."

Tina spoke up. "What do they do?"

"They try to figure out why we're all different. What makes people commit crimes, make you feel uncomfortable and act mean for no reason. I think that's important."

Lillian snatched the focus away from Mandolin. "You and Tina have time to talk, but not me. My assignment over the *weekend* is to write a school paper about race tensions."

"I love races, especially when I win," Mandolin admitted.

Lillian looked at her as if she was stupid. "Not that kind. It's about the color of our skin."

Mandolin didn't get it and began to feel she was painfully behind her peers on her trek to adulthood and blurted . "I'd love to have your color skin. Mine is pasty."

The girls looked at Big Mama for the answer. "Pass me them biscuits, will ya, precious?"

"Whatever happened to those big fluffy pancakes we loved?" asked Lillian.

"Well, they come in a box with a pitcher of Aunt Jemima in a head scarf until they changed her pitcher. This po-litical crackness business messin' things up. PC! PC! PC! That's all I hear. Seems like they tryin' to blend the blacks and whites like we a mix in a box."

Tina scowled. "I guess we don't see color like you do, Big Mama."

Mandolin's eyes darted from one to the other like a windshield wiper until Big Mama spoke up. "Salt is salt and pepper is pepper." Tina changed the subject.

"Madolin can help write your paper, Lillian. She's real smart."

Lillian rolled her eyes at her sister.

"You right," concluded Big Mama. "From what I hear 'bout you darlin', you kinda like a three-ring circus all wrapped in one and gonna fit right into our fambly."

Sky put his fit arm around Mandolin's shoulder. "This girl is a real good sport, she entertains herself and me too. She tryin' to teach me to yo-yo, do a pig grunt, pick things up from the floor with my toes and then drop them on a table. We can all learn plenty from our new friend."

Mandolin was excited to see a computer. "Cool. My gramma forbids all electronic equipment in the mansion because she's afraid of losing all her money and going broke like my Dad almost is. She has Heather saving potato peels and lint from the drier just in case."

"In case what?" Lillian asked. "So she gives fancy parties and saves drier fuzz? If you ask me, Miz Mac has nothing but fuzz in her big fat head."

Big Mama giggled "Maybe she need to see one a them shrinkers. I hear they kin shrink up your head real good."

Sky stepped in. "Now, now! We goin on about nothin' here. It's gettin' late. What we got for supper, Mama?"

Big Mama pulled a casserole from the oven to the tune of her jingling bracelet her kickshaw, she called it proudly. Sky asked Lillian to carry it to the table and invited everyone to stand.

"Tina darlin', will you please say the blessing."

"Good food, good meat. Good Lord let's eat. Amen."

Sky added "and let's all remember to eat humble pie."

"Excuse me. If I don't like it, do I have to eat it?" asked Mandolin innocently.

Lillian giggled. Sky shot her a look of disapproval.

Mandolin remained confused until Tina explained. "Dad's afraid we'll get big heads cuz we got more than most. He says it at the end of every blessing."

Mandolin thought that over as they ate. Sky asked her to tell them what she had learned on TV with Heather.

"Oh yeah. Me and dad are Scottish and some terrorists caused a plane to crash in Scotland. 270 people died."

"Where's Scotland?" Tina asked.

"Look it up in World Book, Lazy. Or else listen to the History Channel on channel eight," Lillian suggested arrogantly.

"Don't bother now. It's across the Atlantic next to England and Ireland."

"No tellin' what this world is comin' to," interjected Big Mama. "We got a nuclear power station blowin' up out there in Ukraine and troubles in the *Fucklands* wherever that is. People is never satisfied, always wanting more and causin' trouble. Seems like them terrorists out to kill us all."

"We just have to get smarter than they are."

"That's right Madolin, and you set me wonderin' about who's smarter than who. In all the years Sky been workin' for Miz Mac, she only raised up his salary one time. Now that's telling me she got your number, son."

"Some folks are greedy Big Mama, but me? Long as Miz Mac pays me enough to support you all and keep Miss Madolin around, I'm happy."

"Why did you come here?" Lillian asked Mandolin.

Sky took the question. "That's a long story. We'll talk about it one of these days."

"I hate it when people say that," countered Mandolin. "But when I ask Hopscotch questions like wher emy dad is , she looks away like I'm stupid."

Everyone looked away except for Lillian. "Stupid is dumb. She probably doesn't know the answers, herself," was her reaction.

Tina's reached out to Mandolin; certain she would enjoy Galveston.

"Where's Galveston? Is there a beach there? I love to dig in the sand and collect shells and watch the pelicans. My Dad knows an awesome verse about a pelican…"*who can hold more in his beak than his belly can.'*"

Big Mama chuckled aside. "And who knows how the *hell he can.*"

The girls giggled.

"First we gotta get Madolin enrolled in school," said Sky.

"You thinkin' of askin' that lawyer friend of yours to help, son?"

Sky nodded to Big Mama. Mandolin explained that they need not bother because "as soon as my dad and I go back home, I'll start school there."

Doubtful and nervous looks were exchanged by the girls, unnoticed by Madolin because she was busy trying to untangle her hair messed up during the car ride. "My friend Fawiza and I promised never to cut our hair. We love how the wind swirls it."

Tina poked Big Mama and whispered behind her hand. "She thinks her Dad is still…"

Big Mama purposely interrupted Mandolin "You lucky your hair ain't all kinky-like."

Mandolin felt comfortable with Big Mama. "When you were young they called you 'nigger', right?"

Eyeballs jumped out of their sockets and rested on Big Mama who was undaunted. She nodded slowly while pulling out a man's long black sock from a basket.

She began to darn it "You sure right about that, darlin. Oftentimes I tells the girls to let ugly talk fly by. We got a past same as everyone else. Some of it's good and some of it's bad. Sometimes we was treated good and sometimes not, but I'm real proud of my folks and what we done. Too, they be callin' some white folks white trash and that's the same as when some black people useta be called niggers."

Mandolin was confused. "I don't get why Huckleberry Finn got in trouble for saying nigger."

Sky spoke up. "Best thing is to let bygones be bygones."

"Why, Sky? What's wrong with learning what niggers used to do?"

Lillian and Tina squirmed and looked at Big Mama for guidance. Mandolin didn't notice. "I found a book in Hopscotch's library called

"*How Come Christmas.*" It begins with a fun reverend entertaining a group huddled around a pot-belly stove. He is saying that 'back in de days of kingin,' all de folks wantin' to stay on the good side a de kaing so dey heaped up presents on de po' little baby Jesus. They brought gold and franklin cents and fur, so de kaing stop choppin' dey heads off.'"

Tina liked the story and started to laugh. Mandolin moved close. "My dad says newspapers write about wars and murders and death. Fawiza's favorite subject is history and she says the past wars are all the teacher talks about. That's worse than talking about niggers, right?"

Big Mama stopped sewing and addressed Mandolin squarely. "We got lotsa good stories that don't pass PC no more *like Little Black Sambo, Uncle Tom's Cabin* and more. Come to think of it, one a my gent'men friends told me somepn' he read 'bout us which done made me laugh. It says in the ol' nigger days, white folks ignored most of us black people, and if I remember it good, it's kinda like this. When we born, we black, and when we in the sun, cold or sick, we black. Now I been noticin' when I get skeered I stays black. And you know, I betcha when I die, I still gonna be black."

"You're funny, Big Mama."

"He read me 'bout you white folks too. 'You pink when you born, and from then on keep on changin'. Out in the sun, you gets red, when you cold, you turns blue, when scared you is yellow, when sick you green, when you bruise up, you purple and when you die you looks gray.' So he says to me, I is happy bein' black and I stayin' black—But fo' shore, Madolin, that's enough talk about niggers, we won't be using that word aroun' here no more."

Mandolin hugged Big Mama. "You're awesome. So what's the big deal about all that?"

Tina and Lillian giggled. Sky turned to them. "When you girls come up with some answers of your own, how 'bout cluin' me in?"

"My Dad and I never argue. We call it discussing, but I got it! Some whites are trash and some blacks are trash."

Big Mama added. "And we all got work to do on ourselves and that's that."

Mandolin sat back silently with frown.

"Did I upset you, darlin'?" asked Big Mama.

"No. I'm missing my dad and I'm worried."

Silence. Dead silence. She looked around the room and everyone was looking at the floor sadly. Something was wrong, really really wrong. Then her stomach clutched, she gasped, and looked up to heaven. "God, are you there? Remember our little talk?"

Tina moved beside her. "That's really cool Madolin—the way you talk to God."

Mandolin stared, first at Tina and then her eyes moved around the room. When she saw Lillian poke Tina and put her finger to her lips, she knew it was over. She had tried not to admit the truth and now it was out. She knew it! So did everyone. He was dead. ***Her Dad was dead! What had happened?***

Emptiness, total emptiness turned her body into mush. She stared at the floor, her eyes burned and the room became dark and blurry. She forced back tears, looked desperately around and a voice inside called. *No, no, no! Please Dad. Please Dad. Dad*!

Struggling for breath, Mandolin lowered her head, tears stung her eyes and began to fall. She had never lived a single minute without the love of her dad. What would happen to her without him? He had not always been there and when he left, he always came back. Now he was gone and she had nothing, absolutely nothing to look forward to.

In a choked voice, she asked the floor "wh-what am I supposed to do now? What happened?"

Big Mama felt for her and rushed to hug her. "There was an accident, darlin' after your papa dropped you off." Sky followed and led her to a lounge chair, adjusted her beside him and wrapped his good arm around her. With touching empathy, he slowly related the story of a car accident in New York, how her dad and her grampa slipped off the road and—and then a crash and sirens. Other words faded into nothingness. She sobbed in big heaves for a long time while he rocked her gently for almost an hour with the girls close by.

"Madolin's hurtin' but with our love she's gonna be OK."

Mandolin looked up at him, tried to smile but her usual optimism was trapped by pain. Sky looked down at her and squeezed her tighter. "You know, Mandolin baby, each morning I wake up and ask God to help me do what he wants, but I'm never sure if I'm gettin' it right. The way you looked at me and how you staying close in to me, makes me feel I done good this time. We all loves you around here."

Mandolin could not remember anyone else ever holding her except for her dad. And then a vision of his infectious smile flashed in front of her. He would not want to see her cry and she knew he would love Sky for being here for her. She had to be brave. She had to, for him and for Sky. She knew right then at that table that she was part of something good and would never be alone. Her eyes began to clear. Sky loosened his hug. Mandolin looked around and knew these people were now part of her life. They were going to be her family.

Tina touched Mandolin's arm and met her glassy eyes. She nudged her again and said softly into her ear, "It's dessert time, Mandi and you're with *us*."

Big Mama's hands fluttered nervously, her kickshaw jingled and she took her cue. "Lord Almighty! This here home made Angel Fool cake been waitin' on us for a long time tonight. Come on everybody and serve yourself a piece or six."

Big Mama set a piece in front of Mandolin who looked at it and then disappeared into her thoughts again.

On the way home in his truck, Mandolin's head fell against Sky's side. He looked down and assumed she was quieted…until he felt the thrust of her sobbing body and her tears beginning to soak his shirt.

4

Back at the Mansion

WHILE BRUSHING HER TEETH, she tried to find something other than death to fill her mind or she would never stop crying. Her Mom. She leaned down, picked up the toothpaste cap and popped up with a new memory…a silly song about zippity-doo-da her mom once sang.

So her mom was happy, or at least acted happy. But how could she find out? How would it feel to have a mom? To help, whenever she saw moms and daughters with arms around one another or laughing, she stopped to hear what they were saying. That made her want to know even more and when she found her, they would talk and talk and catch up. Each night pangs of emptiness caused tears to sting her eyes and soak her baby pillow until she finally disappeared behind her eyelids.

When dawn finally broke, she was glad. She could at last ask Sky what to do.

"Seems like diggin' in your past, and findin' what turns you on gonna send you in the right direction…kinda like that yo-yo a yours. You send it out or down, spin it and when you bring it home again you feel good about yourself. Right? Same thing gonna happen when you put a bit of that brilliance you talk about into that head a yours. You gotta look into future 'stead a the past."

She stayed in her room the entire day and thought over what to do. She had to find her mom. She had to, starting at that moment. Did all Moms get incensed when their sons had fun with other women? Was her Mom crazy or maybe a whore? No. Her dad would never tangle with those types but she had to know for sure. Had Hopscotch removed the portrait of the boy because it was actually her Dad? If so, why? And what had become of the two packages she had slipped in the middle drawer, the fragile one and the smaller one? Did Hopscotch remove them? What about school? No need to ask her gramma. She had little interest in anything except chasing social status and belittling her own granddaughter. But it was okay. At least Sky and his family watched over her as well as Heather.

Let's face it, she told herself. Her gramma would never be her friend. But at least she traveled a lot. Funny, how she used to dread the times her dad was gone and left her alone with strict Valentina, and here it was the same. Life at home with Hopscotch always headed towards a battle of wits. If she could find answers to her questions her heart would feel less turbulent.

Sky's voice followed a knock on her door. He and Heather were worried about her. She assured them she was not hungry, remained curled in the window seat, listened to the grandfather's clock ticking loudly in the atrium and watched a waning moon. Later that night, she wandered around the mansion, looking again for color to cheer her room and herself. In a hall closet, she found a bright pink can of room deodorant. She loved bright pink and by the conclusion of her search she had found a bright pink apron, a brighter pink towel, a roll of pink ribbons, a bag of candies in a pink wrapper, a can of pink lemonade and a book with a pink dust jacket. When she placed them around her room she slept well and could hardly wait to see her pretty room in the daylight.

She awoke with a smile and felt impish for the first time in weeks. She spent the day following Sky around and that night, after

Hopscotch's party, she entertained Sky and Heather in the kitchen with an impersonation. Remembering that her dad had called a Scottish accent a burr, she burrred her worrrds. "Yes indeedy. Everryone with prrrominence and in the know calls me Hopscotch. Don't you agrrree it is the perrrfect name for a native Scot who hops frrrom this charrity to that and voluteerrs hourrs and hourrs of her prrrecious time?"

They were all giggling at her rendition when suddenly the door opened. It was "The Snapdragon" with her hand on her hip wearing one of her dreadfully unpleasant expressions. "What, may I ask, is so funny?"

Heather took the blame. "It's…it's all my fault Miz Mac, I ate so many leftovers I nearly fell off the stool."

Mandolin thought of her dad. He would have taken the blame that same way. Why would anyone want to ruin a good time? Did her gramma preclude fun purposely or was she just plain sour? Her dad had taught her so many fun things, and now Heather was in charge. Yay, Heather!

During a "safari" to the Houston zoo with Mandolin and Tina in early August, Mandolin spotted a sign on a city bus. It read: "Back to School Sale." She gave Sky a nudge which reminded him that vaccinations and immunizations were needed to enroll in school. A serious talk with Miz Mac was on the docket which was never easy.

The meeting was not the best. After all, Hopscotch was "a busy woman" and told Sky to get "that girl" into a better school and out of her hair.

"Sure Miz Mac, but…"

"Please, Brrrown. You are to handle *all* of her school matters. *All* of them. I have nothing furrrther to say on this topic."

"Sorry, Miz Mac. The thing about school is they be needin' a few things like… "

"You hearrrd me, Brrown."

Mandolin learned about their visit one afternoon when Sky

brought Big Mama her blood pressure medicine and took her along for entertainment. It was always a special treat to be around Big Mama. She played old piano tunes, her favorites like Ray Charles, Lionel Hampton and Sarah Vaughan, and show tunes from the musical *South Pacific.* Perry Como was her favorite and she squeaked out a tune about "*hot diggity, dog ziggity*" and a boy who held her tight.

O-o-o-! How would it feel if a boy held her tight, Mandolin wondered.

When Big Mama sang "*in the mornin', in the evenin' ain't we got fun,*" Mandolin clutched up again. Somewhere she had heard that tune. Could it have been her mom? No. she remembered it was her dad.

While she picked out the tune on the piano, she heard Big Mama questioning Sky in the background. "She's eight now, time for third grade, and we gotta make up for lost time, So how you figgerin' on gittin' Mandolin into a better school without a birth s'tificate, son?" She looked at Mandolin.

"Where was you born, darlin'?"

"Malaysia. I thought you knew that."

"No, Missy," said Big Mama. "Once Mr. Jim took outta here, he never did keep us up on any a his doin's"

"Poor Dad," and then she followed with a story that sounded well-rehearsed. "We lived near a beautiful island where they have world-wide sailing competitions."

"Well I'll be, how you knowin' all that?" asked Sky kindly.

"From my dad," she said proudly. "He knew how to read the wind, won races all over the world and I promised him I would too one day."

"And we'll be helpin'," said Sky. "But first Miz Mac aks me to see about a new school for Mandi."

"Y'r sure gonna call that law man Judge Baker, right son? He did a good job settling with y'r ex-wife."

"Good thinking there, Big Mama. I got it going already. Judge

Baker gonna git a birth certificate from Malaysia. Then he gonna aks them to transfer it here to the River Oaks *Ema - emalentry.* Never can say that word too good."

Mandolin raised a fist. "Yes! "River Oaks Elementary. That's where Tina goes and she loves it there."

"Things sure is easier these days," said Big Mama." Use-ta take months to do things like that and it cost more money for long distance than my folks ever had."

"I know. I know," giggled Mandolin. "And you had to walk five miles to school every day with heavy books in your book bag even when Northers hit and rain poured down and…"

Big Mama reared back, slapped herself on the head and laughed heartily at herself. "You hit it right on the old noggin, darlin'. My mama said the same thing to me." Mandolin asked what her real name was.

"Me? They called me Lily but nowadays they not usin' nicknames hardly and Lillian don't suit me. Now about this schoolin', son. We only got one month to make it happen and we'll take the judge to school with us for a refrence if we got to. We gotta make sure they knows how good you do over to Miz Mac's."

From that moment on, events unfolded rapidly. Sky received the birth certificate confirming that Mandolin *was* her given name and that James Elliot MacDuff was her father. Her Mother's signature was not to be found. Sky registered her in school before Labor Day, and saw that Mandolin was "happy as a puppy dog with two tails." She couldn't wait for new friends and a new start.

Each day, Sky drove Mandolin and Tina to school in Miz Mac's Town Car. When he saw Tina black as the ace of spades and Mandolin nearin' the color of curry powder, blendin' in with all the kids, it tickled him pink. He couldn't be with them in class, but for the first few weeks, watched as closely as he could from the car whenever possible. When the bell rang for outside activities, Mandolin was first out the door, followed by Tina, and they raced to reach the playground. before the others. He was real proud of their enthusiasm.

But Mandolin was different and often ignored by other kids for reasons she didn't understand. When Hakeem Kwarteng joined the class, they became friends because he was from Ghana and didn't know anyone either. Hakeem didn't catch on to games fast enough and so she and Ginger became friends. Ginger was smart and liked to laugh, but when Ginger made fun of Mandolin for trying to beat her into the restroom and being first out, Ginger called her weird and another relationship ended. What was wrong with wanting to win when it made her feel better? No one answered her.

To make an impression, she pumped a swing very high and then jumped farther than any of them. They all walked off and whispered. Even when she promised to share her Gummi Worms and taught them how to jump higher, they paid no attention. Didn't they want to be the best? Was she so different?

This resulted in abandonment, that horrid feeling of not belonging anywhere. She longed to ask her dad about her *hakka bakka*. No one else understood what it meant and she felt worthless. Even Tina looked at her strangely so she played alone.

One day at school she pumped the swing the highest ever, jumped out and landed on her nose.

"Aye-yah-yie!"

"Hey bean-pole," a girl called. "Hurt yourself?"

Another comment. "Oh it's her. She's a big show off."

She refused to allow tears to reveal her hurt feelings and so she stuck up her bloody nose, headed inside, and yelled something she hoped would hurt right back.

"Well, I think *you're a vagina*."

She was sent to the Principal, a scary man with whom she definitely did not want to discuss vaginas or Virginias, whatever they were. Nor did he. She was put on probation for two weeks without recess and given a note to give to her parents. Hmm. She had none and tore it up. Should she have lied to avoid punishment? Finding answers was difficult whereas studying sign language and learning about the upcoming elections for the class Fire Chief was far more rewarding.

While waiting for Sky to pick her up, she wandered into a room with four empty computers, learned how to turn one on and was having a blast when she looked up into Sky's smiling face. On the way to the mansion, she asked him about compassion. He couldn't put a word to it but would try to help ease her emptiness and fit all the pieces together. Somehow she liked doing things *his* way. But when she asked if he thought her gramma would buy her a computer, his shrug upset her. Her gramma had so much. Why not a computer? It took all she had not to cry.

In the following weeks, while Sky worked around the mansion, they discussed other disturbing issues. Why did the contest for Library Helper bring only one vote for her? Hers. Why did kids call her a 'Richie Rich' when she came to school in a black Town Car, and why was she teased about the hotel she lived in? Was it bad to be rich, better to be poor?

Sky didn't think so but felt he was not the one with whom to discuss the rich versus poor dilemma. He advised her to have a happy heart and to overlook things that upset her.

"That's not easy, Sky. Tiffany, a girl at school said my dad had mooched off his parents and then tried to make up for it by doing free favors for others."

"That's not all bad, Mandi. At least he had a conscience."

"Do I have one?"

"You can't see a conscience, you feel it. I just betcha yours is same as mine, big as your school."

"That's another thing. Kids ask me why my mom never comes to any of the school functions. Should I say I don't have a mom, or I don't know where she is or what?'

Sometimes Sky had answers and sometimes not, but he was always there ready to hug her real close, which felt so good.

"Big Mama and I thought Mr. Jim be inheritin' some money one day, but—"

Inherit? Not knowing all the meanings of things, frustrated her and bothering people all the time with her questions seemed wrong. It was best to work them out alone.

One afternoon Sky asked her to join him in the Grasshopper. She entertained him by making up a story as they went along.

"From deep in a hedge of ligustrum, a young boy sneaked away with a computer screen under his arm, tripped on the edging around the garden and escaped into the street. A woman watching from a window across the street clapped her hands joyfully and shouted out. 'Good, he got away! The old lady who lives there keeps a bucket of boiling water ready to throw at dogs or kids or anyone who rings her doorbell"

"You got me all mixed up, Mandolin. What's goin' on?"

"Lots of things, Sky. I'm trying to write a novel for grown-ups titled "You Were Young Once Too."

He knew. He understood her urge to be understood; to eliminate her abandonment frustrations, and suggested she write a 'misery' story like Big Mama called them.

"Perfect! I'll learn how on a computer. Or else I'll learn to play the mandolin."

"H-mmm, *h-mmm!* You jes' like one a' my sisters. She always wantin' to do somep'n new and different."

"*Chingado*s. Sky! I'm not like anyone else in the whole world not even that Greek Goddess called Pro—Promethea or something like that. I'm original and if you compare me again, I'll run away. Everyone is different with their own ways of talking and moving and laughing and thinking, not like a bunch of sheep in a big field. When people copy each other and dress alike and speak one language, they're big fat bores. Everyone I know wants to be a famous movie star or an author or a model. Not me. First I'll invent a secret code, called a "crode" to detect criminals and terrorists and then—and then something else."

Sky had to think. "Growin' up is woeful but one thing for sure, you gonna make us all proud, doll-baby."

Mandolin wanted that except for the times her fighting spirit catapulted. She had arrived here full of confidence and after the intimidating explosions of her gramma and her dad's accident, she often wimped out. Peace and quiet only happened when she was with Sky or with Heather in the kitchen. Both were fair and she knew they would help re-build her self-confidence.

Heather taught her how to braid her long hair and thread Big Mama's sewing machine on her day off. Mandolin wanted her to know that she was hoping to be one of the smartest and most fascinating people on the planet that her "interesting words" book defined lissotrichous as having straight hair.

Heather chuckled. "Dadgummit! You're way up over my head a hair, darlin'."

"No, I'm not one bit better than anybody. We may have different skin colors and backgrounds and that's what makes us interesting. Do you like Peanuts?"

Heather puzzled.

"The comic strip," Mandolin clarified.

"Oh. Ah lahk Charlie Brown, but Lucy is real mean."

"No she's not. She has spunk and that's what my dad says about me."

"Spunk? That good to eat?"

"Never mind. How about if we watch the History Channel and the news together, okay?"

"Sure but ah like the replays of *NICSI* and *Law and Order*."

Mandolin was excited. "Me too. I'm thinking of doing detective work because of Olivia Benson."

Heather smiled. "I wish I was smart like you."

Yes! Heather was with her. But her teacher ignored her. Was it because her she never had the answers or what? Her dad had always encouraged her to stand up for what she believed. She was sticking with what he said no matter what.

Gradually her grades improved. She made more friends and one day in history class she asked why people like Hitler wanted to kill other people. Her teacher accused her of interrupting the class with too many questions and Mandolin argued.

Mandolin shouted "*chingados*! No I'm. not. My dad taught me to ask questions to learn; my Muslin friend Fawiza is smart but too far away to ask and you're my teacher and are supposed to know the answers."

Back she went to the Principal again where she sat in anticipation of another punishment. Was *chingados* a bad word or was she sent there because she found her teacher stupid? Maybe she would try *sheet*, another word Fawiza used when frustrated.

Heather sympathized as always and explained that since the beginning of time, the need for power caused craziness. She bought her a brand new world globe to study the location of Islam and other countries which sort of offended Mandolin. She and her Dad had traveled a great deal and he had taken time to show her his map of ports. This gave her an understanding of the inner and outer countries of the world. But she never let on to Heather that she totally preferred her first gift, a waterproof watch with a bright pink pig in the middle and its pink band which she named "Pink Oink. "Nor did Heather let on that she noticed the globe gathering dust in her room.

"You know what, Mandi?" Heather began one afternoon "Me and you have lots in common. I lost my Papa too. He was a highway patrol officer and during a chase was shot by a criminal. Even today sometimes I feel lost. But you're bright with a good heart and you can find the answers, like your Dad wants you to."

Mandolin's eyes welled up with sad and happy tears. Heather got it! She understood how she and her dad when they were together.

5
School daze

FOR A WHILE LONGER Mandolin continued to get in occasional trouble in school, and never at home unless "Big Squaw Maw-Maw" was there, which she rarely was except when cameras and reporters were around filming the mansion as a promo for another House and Garden tour.

Mandolin loved books especially grown-up ones and always led her classes in reading. She read some to Heather and many to Sky like *The Hound of the Baskervilles,* while he polished the cars.

One day, three pages from the end of a *Sherlock Holmes* adventure, she stopped, knowing full well she could write a better ending than Sir Arthur Conan Doyle. *Her* characters would be more adventurous and creepier and set in scary jungles fighting off beasts, or else on the turbulent seas fighting wild storms. Only the brightest of all would solve the mystery and win the award for bravery.

At party times, she often stood at the front door beside tuxedoed Sky and greeting guests. She never minded irritating Hopscotch in her off-beat garb, this time her dad's huge sea-blue t-shirt which read, *"my other shirt is on my boat."* She worshipped this shirt and wore it over a bright skirt and Pink Oink, both Heather's gifts. One look at her and Hopscotch turned away. She swirled around the room in an obvious effort to attract the admiration of her guests with *her majestic* party choice.

At later parties, Mandolin had put her dad's shirt to rest and often heard comments about how she had grown and how lovely she was becoming. Yuck! She would never be 'loverly' like Eliza Doolittle, nor did she care. She only wanted to find where she belonged and have a friend or ten. For some reason, Hopscotch seemed against the idea. Whenever she heard praise about Mandolin, a vitriolic reaction was attached. "My granddaughter appears as a delicate rose but inside she is sharper than a thorn," and then she was outta there with a swishing backside.

It was okay. Mandolin didn't like to be talked about. She thought it was childish and unnecessary and never knew how to answer anyway. Mansions were confining and she longed for the outdoors and the adventures she knew with her Dad.

After a very late dinner and while guests were leaving, Mandolin stood beside Sky and play-acted Hopscotch under her breath one more time." *Indeed. And do it immejetly Br-r-rown.* When the Snapdragon appeared from behind them, they froze and stood straight at attention.

"Where have you been, Brrrown? We need more glasses on the barrr, now!"

She moved on. Mandolin giggled and Sky exhaled.

"Now, now, Mandolin, we can't be doin' that kinda thing no more. This be the only job I got in the whole world. I knows you wanna be your own girl but still and all you, Lillian and Tina gotta learn respect. What I'm gettin' at is all three of you gotta get it in y'r heads that you got plenty to be thankful for and quit takin' too much for granted. Millions of kids got nobody to tend to 'em. They out roamin' the streets with nobody to love or take care of 'em. Miz Mac, she does the best she can, but even when she can't show you love she still puts a roof over your head and food on your table…and ours too."

Mandolin swallowed. She saw fear in Sky's eyes for the first time. It was her first time to compare her life with his and some others. What would happen to her if she had absolutely nothing, lived on the streets and feared for her life? That night she stayed awake, absorbing until she began to understand. Of course Sky and Big Mama had bad times just as she did, a new issue to consider. Somehow Sky and his family were starting to respect her, to look up to her in more ways than one. It was time to think about them for a change. Was that what Heather meant by responsibility?

Routine kitchen activities began to change as well. Heather explained that Miz Mac had 'too much on her plate' to worry about planning meals, that her grandmother was getting old and was less able to lead the household. Entertaining was what she "adoahed" and could no longer be bothered with interruptions to her daily schedules and social obligations. Heather was now in charge and her original menus wowed many guests, new and old. Mandolin stuck close to her side and tried to learn. Heather and Sky, it seemed had become vital parts of the Mansion and assumed Miz Mac wanted Mandolin to learn to be a good hostess and understand the rights and wrongs of arranging formal dinner parties.

At her first one, Sky found her shivering with intimidation on the bench in the hall while *Night and Day* by Frank Sinatra drifted through the air waves over and around the crowd in the den. Why? Why had her gramma snapped her exposed bra strap in front of several guests and mortified her? Why bother with learning to hostess dinner parties? Why grow up? How she wished for her Dad.

When Sky found her, he led her into the kitchen where he and Heather jostled her out of the "sulks", that spot she often drifted into when wishing she was having fun on the beach. Heather led off. "You're much better with these party people than ah'll ever be, Mandi. Back up in Dahm Box, I grew up with country folks. A party to us was an outside bar-b-kew. Here in the city at these fancy-dress parties ah notice how good you speak up and make folks laugh. That makes 'em forget their troubles. Now stand up and show folks that being a good hostess is raht up your alley."

That did it! Gangly Mandolin was torched and soon learned to twist her mouth around and say *hors d'oeuvres* like the French. At the first sniff of bacon, she was ready and eager to serve Hopscotch's guests "very carefully" on a tray with napkins. Eavesdropping on their conversations was the best part.

"Your granddaughter reminds me of her father," announced an East Coast columnist to Hopscotch at a party. Hopscotch smiled the faintest of smiles and immediately turned to another guest.

Mandolin gasped. The familiar hollow feeling of memories of her dad and his sudden death attacked the pit of her stomach again. On her way out, she identified with a very tall spiritless man. He was all alone looking through thick lenses and a large plate glass window out to the back lawn.

She hoped to pep him up as well as herself. She approached him quietly with a nervous giggle that preempted her words.

"Hi. I'm from *Farlandia*. Are you lonesome like me?"

No answer.

She continued "You're like Sky, my best friend. He's very tall just like you and I'm catching up. I used to be up to his waist and now I'm even with his shoulder."

Dead silence.

"Do you bump your head on the shower head like he does?"

A polite smile came her way until he turned his gaze outside again.

"When he's not inside, Sky takes care of the estate and makes all those gardens out there the best in Houston."

More silence. Had she said something wrong again? Did he want her to leave him alone or what? Speaking up had always seemed the best way and this silence when trying to be friendly made her weepy. And yet she had a hunch he would speak eventually if she kept on smiling. Even Hopscotch smiled when guests were in the house. Pushing herself between the sad man and the window, she then pulled on his sleeve.

"Are you okay? Did I hurt your feelings? Am I in trouble?"

He raised his eyebrows and cupped his ear. Oh that's it! This sweet man is deaf, hearing challenged or whatever pc had decided to call those who can't hear diddly squat. Diddly squat. That was one of Big Mama's words and Mandolin loved it. Where did the expression come from? She would have to find out some day.

"Hi I'm Mandolin," she shouted, both relieved and curious. "You look like an intellectual. Are you a big thinker?"

He thought she was funny. "A big drinker? No, but as a matter of fact I could use a drink. Sky makes a wicked grasshopper."

She thought *he* was funny. "No," she shouted. "He cuts grass with a grasshopper."

He smiled knowingly. "Oh, at times the noise of these big parties and everyone talking at the same time is hard to take."

"I think so too," she yelled.

He asked for her name.

She felt like having fun and raised her voice. "I said it before. It's Puddin Tane. Ask me again and I'll tell you the same."

He frowned. She was sorry to upset him. Of course he didn't know the silly verse by William Allen White that her dad taught her.

Then she watched his frown become a grin as he quoted

"...I was walking on a bright and sunny day, a bright and sunny day
I met a sweet little girl, a sweet little girl
Who chanced to walk my way, my way..."
Mandolin was ecstatic and joined in.
"I asked her name, her name and here's what she said,

Puddin in tane. Puddin in tane. Ask me again and I'll tell you the same."

Mandolin threw her arms around him and exclaimed. "I can't believe this."

"Nor can I, sweet girl, My Mother read this over and over to my younger sister when I was a boy. Now tell me your name and we'll stop our game."

"You're a poet, do you know it? Do you know it?"

With his arm around her, he looked into her eyes and spoke. "I misjudged you. You're not only a sweet girl, you have a good sense of humor and a head full of brains."

Mandolin was touched. "People *can* be nice," she thought.

"Hi I'm Mandolin and I live here."

"Oh, so you're Jim's daughter." He smiled and offered his hand. "Another member of a fine family, and a beautiful young lady at that. Mandolin MacDuff. How do you do?"

"I do fine. Did you know my Dad?" she asked eagerly.

"Of course I'm not mad."

She quickly realized mad and dad sounded alike. She moved directly in front of him and shouted. "If you like music, I have a treat for you."

"And I have a treat for you." He reached in his pocket and pinned a small American flag on her shirt.

"The United States is the greatest country in the world and do me a favor. Wear this wherever you go to remind yourself and others of this fact."

"Holy Pig! Am I lucky. I now own two pieces of jewelry, Pink Oink here on my wrist and your flag. Thanks. I'll never take it off because you gave it to me. Now about my treat. Do you like music?"

Aha! He warmed to the question like a cat settles in a lap. "Music! Let me tell you something, sweetheart. I may be the only one you'll ever know who jumped from chopsticks to a pianist in a jazz band just like that." He snapped his fingers.

"Awesome!" Her desperation for friendship took another upward bounce and she extended him an invitation.

"Hopscotch doesn't own a piano but Big Mama does. If you'll come over to her house some night, I'll learn how to cook Chinese and we can play chopsticks together and eat with chopsticks. How about it?"

And then out of the blue, in one of her designer cocktail suits, came the antagonizing voice of her nemesis. "Madolin! Shame on you! I was the far end of the living room and heard your shrill voice."

"No worries, Hopscotch," said Mandolin's new friend." I can hear *you* perfectly, but I'm to blame for the shouting. You see, I thought I had met more people than I need to know and never struggled to hear others…until I met this precocious charming young lady. Now I've changed my mind. I don't want to miss a thing. Without realizing it, she has convinced me to look into new hearing aids first thing tomorrow."

Mandolin slipped her arm into his. "I hope precocious means something good because I've changed my mind about you too. You're not the least bit spiritless. You're my newest best friend."

"Madolin, you have stayed way beyond your welcome. Please excuse yourself and go upstairs to your room *immejetly*."

She did not go upstairs *immejetly*. Little Miss Muffet sat on a tuffet hoping to frighten the ugly widow spider away. Instead, she listened to Hopscotch malign her.

"Plucky, this one! Morre that a bit off the mark she is, Edgarr. So bewarre."

"Did you say off the mark? Aren't we all?" came his curt reply.

Hopscotch was gifted at ignoring remarks that irritated her and steered her tall guest by the elbow into another room. His wink back at Mandolin helped, but not enough to ignore another put down.

"I'm afraid I have been a wretched hostess, Edgarr. I have allowed you to be trapped by my granddaughter for so long. You were good to take it so well and now you and I will join the others for more interesting discussions. May I get you another drink?"

"You gave me this one a few minutes ago and that will do it." He turned to Mandolin. "May I get *you* anything, sweetheart?" She wasn't sure why, but she couldn't say a word and patted the pin he gave her.

On Saturdays when Hopscotch was at one of those affairs she simply had to attend with her cup of "latte-da" or cappuccino, Mandolin often sneaked into her gramma's huge off-limits library and studied. This time she began with animals, then grotesque birds and sea creatures and then back to anatomy. Discovering her breasts were filling out and other developments in her own body was awesome.

Another day when Sky walked by, he saw her reading. "Mr. Mac collected most of them books all by hisself. He be proud to see you in there readin' and gatherin' idees for your story."

"So this is not Hopscotch's collection?"

"She brought home a few, but she like me. Never does read much."

He smiled his usual encouraging one before leaving, and complimented her flag pin.

Mandolin found an English dictionary, discovered that precocious was an okay word for being young. Then she located a French-English dictionary beside the encyclopedias and read a section on pronunciations and the conjugations of verbs. *Boire*, to drink. *Je bois*=I drink, *nos buvons*=we drink and *ils boivent*= they drink. She also read a few simple sentences. I like you= *Je t'aime* and the pronunciation=juh tem. *Tête-à-tête* was now generic and pronounced tet a tet, meaning an intimate or private conversation.

She found a book called *James and The Giant Peach* by Roald Dahl that sounded naughty and adventurous. When she discovered it had been given to her dad from his dad, she put it aside for later. After all it sounded a little juvenile and the pictures in *Prehistoric and Primitive*

Man. were far more intriguing. Most all the figures in the book were of animals and lumpy looking people and drawings. She learned about masks that were funny or scary and from places all over the world like Alaska, New Guinea, Nigeria, Indonesia and China. Heather would be pleased to know she found them on her globe where she hoped to find her mom unless she found her elsewhere. Pictures of body parts excited her, especially *pendulous* breasts of young girls with babies sucking on them and others with *impregnated* tummies modeled in clay or wood carvings.

Wow! Sex was everywhere and it interested her. A lot.

Next, she found a series of Shakespeare's plays and opened Macbeth written between 1606 and 1611. She didn't understand it too well but inside a newspaper write-up was clipped to a page that made sense. "At the time, Jacobean people believed that the men were stronger than the woman. They believed that when married, the husband was in control and the wife who would have no choice but to do what her husband demanded. Macbeth and Lady Macbeth's relationship was every different."

She wanted to be like Lady Macbeth until she read that she was evil, witchlike, seductive, power hungry and thought nothing of killing King Duncan. That sounded like Hopscotch. Would her grandmother ever kill anyone…like would she kill her Mom? Is this why she avoided talking about her? The thought freaked her out; she slammed the book shut and found a novel called *Pepper*.

When Fawiza gave her the same book back home, it disgusted her, but not now! She was more than ready to read and learn all about sex. Does a guy ask a girl if she is ready? What if she or he isn't ready" How do they get together? Whoa!! Had her dad ever read *Pepper*? Would a man want to have sex with Hopscotch? No way, but maybe not with her either. If not, why not when she was so ready.

Without electronics in the mansion, whenever Hopscotch was gone, the Library it became her own internet. An unsuccessful search for her mom was followed by pictures of Venus and David *that* turned her insides out and made her squeal.

Had Hopscotch caught her hovering over these pictures, a severe case of panic would have set in. But why? Her gramma had been an adolescent once. Did she know what having fun was all about?

She shut the book, resolved to return to it at night "when no one was stirring, not even a mouse." For now she cuddled up in one of the big, red leather chairs and began again to follow the alphabet through the dictionary. Afghanistan was a mountainous country of many complex societies struggling for control and enduring many military casualties. Australia was the land of kangaroos, a famous opera house, sailing and where the hot movie *On the Beach was filmed* in1959 starring Gregory Peck, Ava Gardner, and Astaire. She had watched Heather's tape over and over and learned to be sexy like Ava and Gregory. She liked Fred, but he was not sexy, just a nice guy and a good dancer.

Next, in case she ever got to Europe, she jumped to the Celtic countries where Winston Churchill had been Prime Minister. Prime? She imagined Winston to be very very important. How would that feel? He had once commented that among the smaller nations, only the ancient Greeks had contributed as much to the world as Scotland. She learned that the great Scot scientist Alexander Fleming had discovered penicillin, and that Adam Smith was the Father of Capitalism. He wrote about individual enterprise and the benefits of free trade, whatever that meant.

Scotland's royal history, and its magical kings and queens intrigued her, especially Queen Mary because she was a Hopscotch look-alike, with her long nose, weird hairdo and plain face. Plus she was nasty like Hopscotch. Why do people need to interfere with the happiness of others? Why did Bloody Mary as they called her, violently destroy Protestants who rejected Catholicism and why did Hitler destroy Jews? She tried to understand the mean nature of people, well aware that her Dad would want her stick with it.

At the age of five, Mary was *betrothed*? Five? Why would anyone want to have sex at five, she asked herself? She had once thought fifty-five would be about soon enough, but now that she was twelve, she was curious. Very! The changes that had occurred in her in just a few years were mind-boggling. When she learned that Mary had lived in many countries, and never minded demeaning her elegance with an occasional dirty laugh, she wondered exactly what a dirty laugh meant. Fawiza had taught her the facts of life. Was that dirty? Do Queens have sex? After reading about *psychology* and then later finding a new word, *cacophonous*, which reminded her of the mansion when her Gramma was 'in session,' she smiled. The library was a peaceful, learning place.

Then one day, while sitting in the big chair with an open book by a library window, she took Sky's suggestion to dig into her own life. From then on, whenever she was thinking hard, she took the position of Homer's "The Thinker" with her hand curved under her chin and resting on it. Homer had to have been brilliant and associating with him gave her a boost. For the first time she realized that Hopscotch discussed her mom and her dad only when forced. How could that possibly be? Flesh and blood. Dad and Hopscotch. The question kept recurring. Why wouldn't a mom want to talk about her own son? What had gone wrong? Why would nobody tell her *anything*? A new thought. If she went to Scotland, could she find out more about her dad *and possibly* her mom?

She focused on Scotland. Would Hopscotch ever take her there? Probably not but maybe something magical were to happen. She liked to believe what that poster said, something about magic that happens when your brain accepts it. Maybe a gentler manner with Hopscotch would give her an impetus to teach her about Scotland. A trip with her gramma to her native land might just lead to her mom. It sounded crazy but it was possible that her mom and dad could have met and lived there before they came to the States. Everything was possible she had read somewhere.

From River Oaks Elementary, Mandolin moved on to Lanier Junior High where she made many Hispanic friends. She and Tina remained "best" friends even though Mandolin skipped the third grade. In addition, Lillian was dating an *Iranian* pre-med student, Big Mama's joints were deteriorating and Sky worried about how and where to care for his mama. He decided to stay where they were because it was close to "Terror" her name for the Mansion. Gone *with the Wind* had made a deep impression of her and she decided to call there she lived Terror instead of Tara and laughed when she thought of it.

For two years Mandolin excelled in school, Hopscotch continued with her endless dinner parties and talk of a trip was not broached even though she asked many questions about the country. On occasion she asked Sky what he knew about her mom and dad. He had known her dad growing up, but neither he nor anyone else was much help. He did not know if Mandolin looked like her mom, whether or not she read much, listened to music, liked games or Trivial Pursuit or *anything*.

Mandolin was young to graduate from Lanier, recognized she was bight but her self-confidence had been kicked into gutter by her arrogant gramma. Summer vacation began and frustration set in again. There was nothing to do. Friends were dating but boys mostly skipped over her. Sky saw her sitting alone in the kitchen staring blankly outside and quietly put his arm around her. "Sure do wish I knew a way to help you find your mom, Mandolin. You got a real big pursuit ahead of you, and we all know you gonna find her."

Without warning, she screamed wildly, raced up the stairs and shouted down. "You think it's all so easy, don't you? Well it's not! I've been trying to learn more about what went wrong with Hopscotch and my Mom and you won't tell me. I hate this place! I hate my life, I hate Hopscotch and I hate you!"

Sky knew her like his own daughters, but she truly startled him this time. After a few moments he collected himself and slowly followed her, stopping at the doorway to her room where she sobbed face-down on her bed.

"I know you don't mean that, Mandolin."

"Maybe I do. How can I learn more about myself if you're a wimp and won't ask Hopscotch to tell me anything about the past?" Sky pulled back. After a moment of silence, realizing he had reached the end of his helpfulness, he painfully put his head down and walked slowly down the stairs.

She could not see the hurt in his eyes, yet her mistake was obvious. Her only true friend was suffering. Fighting her way back into his affections was her next goal. Would he allow it? She would succeed. Somehow she had to. She could not stand more abandonment.

The next morning brought another concern about the gifts in the middle drawer in her room. They still hadn't turned up. And where was the portrait of her Dad as a boy? Sky was sure to know and if she could convince him to help her look, they would be working together again.

The sound of a car leaving the garage distracted Mandolin. This time it was a vintage VW convertible with 'a stick shifter' driving to the front of the Terror with Sky behind the wheel. He loved this car apparently almost as much her Dad had. She always got emotional when he drove it around the circle of undisturbed growth a few times before stepping out and waiting for his boss lady. Through her window, Mandolin watched Sky receive his daily orders from the Commander-in-Chief, responding respectfully with *Yes Ma'ams* and *No Ma'ams. The only thing missing was the salute.* He carefully tucked this pretentious Scarlett O'Hara and her huge red flounced skirt into the tiny car and swung the door closed. It was Thursday, time for her gramma's weekly color touch-up job which meant a long visit at the salon. Sky leaned towards the car window and spoke to his boss.

"No! No! Absolutely not! And neverrr speak of this again or you shall be firrred on the spot."

Mandolin had no idea what it was about but hated this for Sky. La Grande Dramma revvedup her engine, started off and then jammed on the brakes. Sky went to her car window, got the message, ran inside and reappeared with her glasses.

"Sorry to take so long Miz Mac but they were on the toilet tank in your bathroom".

How was it possible that nothing ever bothered him? She ran downstairs, out the door and told Sky she loved him and wanted to be just like him. When he hugged her back, it made her day. She was so happy she almost flew up to her room when she heard a gear strip. Out the window, she saw the car lurch, and then her gramma finally drive off in her Dad's sputtering treasured VW convertible out the long winding driveway.

Was it mean to laugh when this 'perfect woman' made a mistake? Sure, but today all that mattered was that Sky and she were friends again and Hopscotch would be gone for awhile.

Down the stairway she went again with no danger of breaking another one of Hopscotch's stupid rules. Rules. The only ones she believed in were the ones that stopped murders and robberies and telling secrets. Living with so much secrecy caused her constant anxiety.

Wait a minute! Was that a sign toward the front of the estate? She squinted fiercely. Beware of Cat. If it was supposed to be funny, Hopscotch had a sense of humor after all. Beyond the sign, way down the driveway, a blob was approaching fast. Was it a boy? She hoped so because the boys in her school were becoming more interesting and less *persnickety*, a new word her teacher emphasized.

The figure drew closer and closer and shaped into a tall boy on a bike. He was taller than any in her school and she already liked him because he had dared to ride his bike beyond the PRIVATE PROPERTY sign at the entrance to the drive. In a flash she imagined big possibilities. Maybe he could be her friend and they could race to the gate and back, or play her made-up game called Crime and

Punishment. No. They were both too old for that, but the good news was he was very cute. As he reached the house, he swirled around in a tight little circle, stopped, and climbed off his bike, the most beautiful one she had ever seen. It had gears and a place for a water bottle on the support bar.

"What kind of bike is that?"

"A *Vamoots*, a special custom titanium bike made in Colorado."

"Holy Pig! That's cool. A Colorado mountain bike. How much did it cost?"

"Over three thousand dollars. You can buy one at the West End Bicycle Shop not far from here."

"Are you kidding? My gramma would never..."

He pulled down his Baylor t-shirt over his tight riding shorts, and she totally forgot her gramma. Her eyes landed on his waist, then his legs and then...she felt one of those weird feelings inside that occurred more and more often these days.

"Hi I'm Mandolin. M-A-N-D-O-L-I-N."

"You sure don't talk like a Texan."

Her spine straightened. She was about to ask what was so good about being a Texan when she became rattled. He was s-o-o-cute. And so she told him he looked like *Alice's* flamingo with his pink skin. Then she raised her hand like a stop-sign.

"No. I think you look more like a beautiful big stork with long skinny legs."

He took offense and eyed her book. She pushed her copy of Alice *in Wonderland* in his face. He said he never read girls' books.

"You'd really really like it."

"It's childish. I know the story. A little girl like you uses big words, is bored with her sister, sneaks off and then falls down a rabbit hole."

Then he yawned which bothered her a lot and she shifted the topic.

"My most favorite book is about Huckleberry Finn. He's really really big. Why did you ride up here anyway?"

He ignored her question. "Huckleberry Finn!? Sorry, I'm into the classics now, stuff like Homer's *Odyssey*."

She froze for a moment. Who was Homer, she wondered. Then she decided he should know that only exceptional readers with a bit of brilliance understood *Alice* and the craziness of the Mad Hatter's Tea Party. When he laughed again, she spouted her knowledge of The Boston Tea Party of 1773, about the anger of the colonists at the British government and the monopolistic East India Company. How well she enjoyed informing him of their control over the tea coming into the colonies and the refusal of the Boston officials to return three shiploads of taxed tea to Britain.

He started to interrupt and she continued. "So a group of colonists boarded the ships and destroyed the tea by throwing it into Boston Harbor."

"Well, aren't you the clever one. You act like one of those smart Asians in my senior class."

Stork, her unspoken name for him looked her over in a strange way. She squirmed and by the time she pulled out of her thoughts, he was already half way down the drive.

Over his shoulder, he called "Hey kid, if you see a little white dog running loose around here, let me know."

She was stunned and hurt when he called her 'kid', but hid her reaction. "Is his name Toto?" she asked quickly.

He spun back around, raced up beside and answered "No. stupid. It's Adam, like in *Adam and Eve*. Have you ever heard of them?"

"Of course. Your dog must be chasing a bitch in a garden somewhere."

She hoped he would think this was a grown-up remark, but with a toss of his head, he dismissed her in this rude way. "Hey, kid, If I were you, I'd quit trying to impress people. Showing off with all those big words will get you in a lot of trouble when you grow up."

Tears filled her eyes until he swung his leg over the bike seat and her gaze drifted down to his crotch. How did it feel down there when he rode a bike? She decided it had to hurt from the sculptures of men she had seen. She looked at his face and found new growth on his chin and young hairs on his upper lip. "Oh My God! You are really mature."

He liked this. "I'm staying with my Dad down the street for the weekend at Number Eleven. E-O-Leven! Let us know if you see Adam."

Crotchy peddled away. She ran ahead to get his attention. "I wish I had a bike like that. Please come over and see me again. Please?"

He turned quickly without a word and she choked up again. Why were kids mean to her and to one another? With the exception of Hopscotch, grownups were good to her. And then her temper flared. Watch my words? He was the one that used strange words like E-O-Leven. Once her Dad used the same word when he came back from Las Vegas, but why?

She watched Cotchy disappear along with her spirit. Her goose bumps disappeared and she screamed after him. "Off with your head! My dad and Huck are much more fun than you. So what do I care about you? You're just a dumb bunny!"

And yet she did care about him. The good looking brute was embedded in her memory. *Sheet!* The urge to strike something took over and when she passed the scrubby looking circle, she knew what to do. She would ease her frustrations, and please Sky and her gramma at the same time.

With a shovel and clippers she worked her heart out, clearing out as much of the growth away as possible. She felt better. It looked neater and Sky could now plant beautiful flowers. Meeting Stork and losing herself in work had provoked a new challenge and new questions. Unless she found some answers and confidence away from Sky, his family and Heather, and unless she learned how to deal with funny feelings in funny places in the night that woke her up sometimes, she might never understand what was going on. She might never turn out to be cool and a pretty lady like she was sure her mom was. She just *had* to stop getting teary, keep busy and find out more about herself, her mom, boys, grandmothers and life!

She ran to the kitchen and plunked herself down with a troubled expression.

"Can I ask you something, Heather?"

Ready to listen, Heather sat on a stool.

"I'm really really confused about so many things and want the truth, okay?

"Ah'll do my best."

"Okay. Why do think my gramma is bothered by my questions and why doesn't she have a computer, a calculator or even a cell phone?"

"Many of us like me have troubles with the new tech stuff."

"Gotcha. Another question. Why does she sleep 'til noon every day when she doesn't do anything except on Tuesdays when she goes to the Guild Shop?"

"You're wrong about that. She goes to charity luncheons and to late-night parties."

"Oh, so she... there's something else. Your place is attached to the garage. Do you ever hear her rattling around in the kitchen in the early hours?'"

"Maybe once or twice. Why?"

"Well, the bar area is under my room where she keeps all those bottles and I'm forever hearing glasses break. My Dad told me about a crew member on a boat who drank all the time. He had hangovers and got kicked off as a crew member for sleeping on the job. This morning I checked the trash and saw two empty bottles labeled "Grasshoppers." If they're full of whiskey or something...maybe that's why Hopscotch sleeps so late...to get over her hangovers."

"I don't know about all that, but she's been through a whole lot in her life. Remember she lost her husband and…"

"…my dad at the same time. I know that, but…"

"It takes some of us longer than others to get over things."

"I know. I'll never get over my dad's death."

"Anything else on your mind?"

She thought of Stork but wasn't comfortable sharing her anxieties about a boy yet. All she was sure of was that she had spilled out of the training bras Heather brought her, liked the way Crotchy's jeans cupped his rear end, and that any mention of sex stimulated her and sent her imagination spinning.

"Actually Heather, I do have something else on my mind. I'm twitchy. When you feel like you've been in a place too long, my dad called it cabin fever."

"Funny, I've been feelin' the same way lately. It's past time for my two week vacation and since you all settled in now, think I'll ask Miz Mac to let me go to Isla Mujeres to visit my sister. She and her boyfriend Bubba broke up and she moved down there to start over .Her name is Choc."

"Choc? A guy in my art class from Yucatan sculpted a reclining figure and called it Chac–mool."

Heather smiled. "Not her. Sis has been a chocoholic since she was born."

"Isla Mujeres. I've heard of that before. It means the island of women. Maybe my Mom lives there. Take me with you. Please? I'll bring Choc a couple of Hershey Bars. Maybe she knows my mom."

The back door opened and here came *trouble with a capital T* like the song from *The Music Man* except not in a melodious voice.

"Where is Sky?"

"Upstairs waxing the floors like you said Mrs. Mac. Is something wrong?"

"Wrong?! The centerr island in front the house has been destroyed.

The house can be seen from the street! I shall now have to withdrraw my estate from one of the most exclusive house and garden tourrs in Texas!"

Sky appeared on the scene. "Sky! Call the chairman right this minute and tell the committee I cannot…"

"No use, Miz Mack. The phone is dead."

"Dead? Well fix it."

"I tried but the line ran through the center circle and I could see the phone line had been cut. He has contacted the buried desk and is sending someone out first thing in the morning."

"The buried desk?" Did someone die out there?"

"No ma'am. Not that bad, not that bad at all. You got nothing to worry about."

"How can you say such a thing? My beautiful place will not be on the tour."

"Oh my God. Oh my God!" Mandolin confessed in tears. "I did it. I thought it would…"

"You! Of courrse. It had to be you! Ever since you came we have had nothing but one disaster after another-r."

Mandolin eked out a wee "I'm sorry."

Heather spoke up. "She was trying to be helpful, Mrs. Mac."

"Helpful? She doesn't know the meaning of the worrd."

Mandolin started to protest. Heather reached out. "Ah got somethin' to ask you Mrs. Mac and it's this. Ah haven't taken my vacation time yet and you know how travelin' alone puts the fear of God in me. Ah'd sure like to take Mandolin along with me for the week."

"Go! And take this numpty with you!"

Mandolin was sure numpty meant a pain in the butt but she didn't care. She was about to get away from the *Queen* of Numpty for a few days.

Early the next morning while Sky was taking Heather and Mandolin to the airport, the doorbell rang. It buzzed upstairs in Hopscotch's room through the intercom and she answered. Ii was the phone company and her thought was that he could fix the line it and all would be well. Dressed in black lace panties and a black top, she advised him to stay right there and she would be down to have a talk with him right away.

As fast as possible she descended her stairway, opened the door, and greeted him most pleasantly. He took a look at her and apologized for bothering her.

"How can you possibly think you are botherrring me when I have rrrun down the stairrs to welcome you?"

"Sorry ma'am." He indicated that her outfit was a surprise.

She looked down and then up at him immediately. "Well shame on you for starring at me. Now get on with fixing my line 'immejiately.' My contemptible granddaughter cut it and it must repaired in time for my house and garden tour. "

6
Isla Mujeres

DURING HER FIRST PLANE ride, Heather was pleased to see Mandolin so relaxed and happy. The minuteness of the houses and trees down below amazed her as did the flight attendants who served free snacks and a choice of all the free fruit drinks she wanted. When Heather quizzed her about her past, Mandolin remembered a huge silver cup on top of the fridge in the beach house where she grew up in. She remembered it because her dad had won a sailing race to or around Isla Mujeres which meant island of women. Why would only women wanted to live together on an island? Weird! Was it still that way?

While waiting for a ferry to the island, the sight of actual sailboats tacking into the wind excited her. She had had two lessons before... before her dad's accident...and finding someone here to give her more lessons might just happen.

Finally the ferry arrived and women and *guys* raced for seats. Phew! Not only women lived on Isla Mujeres. She wanted to sit up top to see *everything*. Heather slid their one bag into a back storage area along with the others and then watched Mandolin, now prematurely budding climb to the deck. Her long legs and hair, green eyes and innocence wowed the Mexicans, particularly men of all ages. Heather wished she was still young enough to attract boys until she felt the heat and disappeared to the air conditioned deck below.

The horn sounded, Mandolin checked her flag pin to make sure it was still on her shirt and found a seat along the side of the boat. Once they were on their way, two very young boys charmed her. They were full of pep and seemingly impossible for their dad, a middle aged guy in very short trunks, a red sombrero, and a multi colored Hawaiian shirt to control. She sat on the floor of the deck near him and walked her fingers towards the boys ala creepy mouse. They giggled. What a treat it was to have escaped the labyrinth, to mess around with kids and to act herself again.

They played tag. They touched her and she jumped in surprise each time. Fun was being had by all when the dad sat beside them. The howling wind and the boat's engine made hearing difficult but he seemed interested in her whereabouts and even more interested when he heard she was from Houston. Heather came up to join them and chatted with him while the boys tugged on Mandolin's short skort. All three wanted more games when the dad told the boys to sit still.

Within seconds, she convinced the boys to sit on either side of her and chat with her. Mark explained he was almost six, that Mason was almost four and never behaved. Mason punched Mark. He hit him back and Mandolin took control. The dad sat across the ferry, appeared intrigued by her way with kids or was it with Mandolin herself? She played many games, one called slap my hand. The game was to slap her hand before she pulled it away. They swung and missed most of the time and when she let them win, they loved it.

She pointed to the boats, big and small out in the water when passengers began to gather by the stairway. Their dad approached, thanked her for taking over his kids, asked her name and where she was staying. All she knew was that Heather's sister sold silver jewelry in a stall on one of only three shopping streets *al centro*.

Mandolin hugged goodbye to the boys, met Heather at the foot of the stairs and they disappeared in the crowd on the way to meet her sister. Neither of them noticed the dad pulling his boys quickly along to catch up with them or that Mason fell and screamed with pain.

Instead Heather was listening intently to Mandolin. "My dad never liked me to complain, but since living with Hopscotch, I...I..."

"Ah know what you mean. You've lost you snap, crackle and pop like in Rice Krispies. But like we say back home you're startin' to smoke it out. And you will, angel. You will."

Heather continued to bolster Mandolin's spirits like she imagined her Mom would. She had a flashing sense of hakka bakka as they held hands and walked along to Choc's *casita* (small house) *al centro*. Choc, a well-rounded, kind-faced woman in her fifties and her cat Tigre, welcomed them, as well as the Chocolate bars.

"*Habla espanol?*" Choc asked.

"*Un poquito*" was Mandolin's reply. She hated Spanish and yet because of Houston's huge Hispanic population, her teachers had encouraged her to at least learn the basics.

That night, Heather, Choc and she shared a room. While the sisters caught up with one another, Mandolin cuddled *Tigre*, the new born kitty and took notes on their trip thus far.

Too excited for sleep, Mandolin was up early and ready to go. Heather was not. She chose to sleep in, and so Mandolin joined Choc for a breakfast *of huevos, muy picante* (spicy) sausage, *frijoles, arroz* and *tortillas*.

Afterwards, she followed Choc to her silver stall where three silver bangles gave Mandolin a serious case of the "I wants." But since Heather was paying for the trip, she let it go, to concentrate on speaking to people in Spanish.

On Hidalgo Street, the merchants had a way of stepping out of their shops when Americans went by and she was definitely an attractive target. People wanted to help her. She tried to be polite and struggled to speak their language. Choc suggested ignoring most of them, that they liked her looks, but she was carried away by a multi-colored hammock. From her previous experiences with the poor south of the border, she knew families often shared hammocks. She adored the colors in a particular one. Choc offered to buy it. Mandolin refused because she knew Choc had left Dime Box to make a new life and like her dad, had to struggle. Plus, she learned that the value of the *peso* changed almost every day.

Each day was filled with activities, a thrill because she had only a few days to enjoy before the challenge to out-hop the Scottish witch began again. There was much to absorb, people hanging on to billowing spinnakers and jumping into the water; wind-surfing, fishing trips; snorkeling lessons, and when an awesome guy offered her a free lesson, she was psyched. She so wanted to do it but once again it was a lesson in discipline. She was afraid to get hooked before she could enjoy luxuries like that.

In the afternoon, she and Heather checked out a new hotel under construction as well as fabulous beach houses and *palapas*, straw tent-like structures used as sun shades. Even in the hot weather, cool breezes made it possible to have a margarita or two and dine outside. If only her mom lived in one of these. Mandolin had come from a beach and yearned to end up near water again some day.

Mandolin accepted a ride on a killer guy's moped. Heather took his name dutifully like a mom and instructed him to return Mandolin to the same spot in fifteen minutes. Her emotions were mixed. In one way she felt like a baby. In another, she felt that Heather really cared about her.

During the thrilling ride, she learned that taxicabs were about to strike because mopeds as well as golf carts were stealing their business. It was even more exciting to be invited to wrap her arms around killer's waist to hold on. Holy Pig! It felt so-o—good and better yet when he placed his hand over hers. His name was Jose and just before he pulled up to the curb beside Heather, he asked if she could join him somewhere later on. Goosebumps popped up and quickly disappeared when Mark, Mason and their dad approached in a golf cart from the opposite direction. Crap! She liked those boys, but not too well at this moment. Their Dad wanted to chat. She introduced them to Jose who looked at his cell and said "I have duty to go now." And they were off. It was time to take her back to Heather, and that was that... except for the unforgettable smile sent Mandolin's way by Jose at the end.

Heather and Mandolin trekked to the Punta Sur, the highest point on the island. Choc joined them for lunch and explained the reason the island was called Isla Mujeres. When the Spanish expedition landed, they found many female shaped idols representing the goddess Ixchel, and then in 1517, when Francisco Hernandez Cordova arrived there, he called it Isla Mujeres.

The fresh fish *ceviche* with fresh lime juice, made its way into Heather's recipe notepad. Mandolin ate little while visions of Jose's smile floated through her head as well as his invite to hang out.

That night, they were tired and stayed home. Mandolin opened her cell, wishing for a message from Jose, but of course they had not exchanged the necessaries. She then studied her Spanish dictionary and just before Heather turned off the light, she congratulated Mandolin on her improved Spanish. The compliment caused her to hop out of her bed and kiss Heather's available cheek. "Thanks Mom, and you should get to know Jose. He's really really cool."

Heather sat up and wiped away a tear.

Little sleep came her way once again and when morning came and Choc was preparing to leave, Mandolin slipped into a typical embroidered Mexican dress and followed her to her stall. The silver was okay but across the busy street was a colorful hammock that intrigued her. Off she went for a quick minute to search through them when that pest dad approached her.

"Hey there, cutie. I've been trying to ask you something ever since the ferry ride."

"Oh! You look better in your hat. I didn't recognize you without it."

He was not put off. "My boys took to you right away, and I'd like you to seriously consider taking a weekend job as their *au pere* back in Houston."

"Thanks. I need the money, but I'm not sure I can. My gramma… I'm too young."

"That right? You look at least seventeen or older."

"I do? Really?"

"Absolutely. I'm Gregory and this is my lucky day."

"Why?"

Stunned by her question, he laughed insidiously and his words dribbled out slowly. "Because…because my life has been a mess without a nanny and I feel a change coming on."

"My life changes all the time. Do you live near the water?"

"Let's don't worry about that right now. Here's fifteen *pesos* for the hammock."

She protested. He insisted, gave the pesos to the delighted vender. He then asked for her phone number in Houston. She gave it to him while hugging the hammock and he jotted it down. A ferry back to Cancun was due shortly, his last words were "Thanks cutie. Like I said, this is my lucky day." He grabbed his two boys, left her and took off with a jaunty step.

When Choc heard the story, she repeated it to Heather. And then the fireworks began. Running off without word and giving away personal information to a complete stranger was wrong. Mandolin tried to explain with a bit of wit. "Strangers in Mexico?! No way. They're *mooey seempatico*!"

Heather was not amused and took issue. If Mrs. Mac found out what happened, she could be fired. Mandolin's eyes shut. A lump mounted in her throat. She had always believed that once you were an adult, you got your way. She never suspected a woman in Heather's position could be fired. She begged for Heather's forgiveness and to please not tell her gramma. And then her eyes shot heavenward. "I really goofed up, Dad. Sorry."

On the way back to Houston on a night flight, she worried what would happen if somehow her gramma found out. Giving away the address and phone number of the mansion on top of clearing out the brush was bound to put her in deep doo-doo. So what else was new? She was far more concerned about Heather's job and apologized again.

When she awoke in her own bed, it was quiet. No horns honking. No shrill voices or whirring vacuum cleaners inside. No churning grasshoppers outside or machines whipping them up inside. It felt ominous until the motor of her gramma's vintage VW sent her to the window. Holy Pig! The center garden was filled with tall trees and bushes in pots.

She dashed down the stairs and Heather filled her in. The Garden Club members had donated enough plants to hide the mansion and the house tour was on. Then she heard Hopscotch's car roaring down the drive and remembered it was another Tuesday, her day at the Guild Shop and she would be gone...gone again to this mysterious place. Where was it and what actually happened at the Guild Shop? Mandolin had so worried herself about seeing Hopscotch, but the Garden Club had saved her from more misery and she felt brave.

7.
The Guild Shop

HOPSCOTCH'S DRIVE TO THE Guild Shop was slow and irritating to many on the road. Honks or crazy drivers who drove too fast never bothered this day because she was trying to remember something. Her cell phone, a birthday gift from Heather and Sky tooted "Ah-oo-ga. Ah-oo-ga," and then again. She pulled to the side of the road, fished into the bowels of her large satchel and finally found it. She punched this and that and complained into the phone that cell phones "are controlling minds, destroying the art of conversation, and promoting poor vocabulary and grammar and unless the hellish contraptions became simpler to operate, no company would get one more dollar from her."

She pulled away from the curb, concerned about the whereabouts of her diamond watch until she discovered it on her wrist.

"Good gracious! Leave me be, Mr. Alzheimer! You are not allowed in this car or anywhere near me."

She drove away slowly until attracted by a long line of customers of many sizes, shapes and backgrounds outside the door of The Guild Shop. All apparently awaited the chance to unload donations, to pick up checks from past consignments or find bargains.

Many watched La Grande Dramma maneuver into a space where only fools would dare to tread. Some cheered, others smiled at the bumper sticker. *Caution: Redheaded Scot at the Wheel.* The Devil made Mandolin put it there and thus far no accusations from Senora Scrooge had reached Mandolin. After many efforts to parallel park, the little old driver who meant to be so lively and quick pulled herself out painfully. With a hand graced by a fine ruby ring, she patted the hood of her vintage car and walked a few steps to the shop.

"Natural r-redheads are diminishing rapidly," she announced to all around and so don't be left behind. Wear-r- reds of all shades and heads will swing in your direction." She waved her fuchsia pashmina, and then dramatically wrapped it around her shoulders. "Houston's habit of turning on the AC the minute the outside temperature falls to 70 degrees is costly and freezes my bones."

Then this unnatural redhead passed those waiting to enter with a bit of a jig. She rang the bell and pointed to the sign over the entrance, *The Best Little Charity Shop in Houston.*

"Many of you may not recall the movie *The Best Little Whorrrehouse in Texas* but that's where I got the idea for the sign."

"Is a horse's house like a stable?" asked a young girl in the crowd.

Never one to miss a chance to educate anyone in sight with her own take, Hopscotch explained the word was whorehouse, not horses house. "Ah child, when I was y'rr age, Mae West was one of those whores. She was a peroxide blond and swiveled her hips, like this."

Hopscotch never noticed the horror on the mother's face as she swung her hips in and out in a suggestive way and then patted the child's head. She waved her nametag 'Jewelry Lady' in the air. "Look for me in Jewelry. People tell me I'm the best saleswoman of us all."

Gilbert Gonzalez, the security guard and friend to everyone opened the door. At the sight of Hopscotch, his grin spread so broadly that even the disgruntled were cheered. The shoppers filed in, he drifted into his playful mode and welcomed Hopscotch.

"Bless your cotton socks, Hopscotch. Lovely to see you this fine day."

"Hopscotch embellished her burr. And you. Arrre you behaving yourrrself, you handsome devil you?"

"Behaving me lady, you ask? Why I haven't behaved since meeting you."

"You are a trrrue delight, and let me tell you Gilbert, if you werrre white I'd be chasing you."

Gilbert, a bit shaken, forced a smile. "Thanks for the compliment ma'am, but I'm already taken."

"A pity. So come now, move aside and let me in."

He winked with an exaggerated flourish ala Sir Walter Raleigh and chatted with the first customer.

"She's one of our favorites. But let me warn you, it's best not to ask her age; better to suggest you have a male friend you'd like her to meet and watch her become the flirtatious gal she once was.

Inside her jewelry booth, a squared off area near the front door and cashier's counter. "Annie," Hopscotch's name for her volunteer-in-training was dutifully wearing her red apron and unlocking the cases. Gretchen, a furniture volunteer also in a red apron stood outside the area looking at bracelets through the glass case.

"Do you like working with Hopscotch?" Gretchen asked.

Annie nodded slowly as if unsure.

"I never did. She tries to be another Lucille Ball and misses by a mile."

Annie indicated Hopscotch was approaching.

"Did I hearrr my name?"

Gretchen scurried away.

Hopscotch joined Annie. "How arre you, Annie?"

She waved her had in front of her face as if hot. "Doin' good in this weatha for a gal from Vermont."

"Each of us has an interrrnal thermostat and complaining is not what we do herrre. Now then I see you finally rememberred to wear the vintage pin I gave you. But you in jeans? Why would you want to wearr those hot and heavy things that stick in your crrotch and make you look common?"

Annie was irritated and Hopscotch recognized it, atypically. "What I mean is, jeans were orriginally made for gold and coal miners and their diggings, not for a lovely volunteerr like you."

Annie checked herself in a mirror and relaxed. "Jeans make me feel and look younga. They bring out the culla of my eyes." She leaned down presumably to show how well they matched.

Hopscotch tsk-tsked, dismissed this discussion in favor of one about her granddaughter. For many, she had cramped her style with an unending surprise visit.

Annie overlooked the cruelty of the confession "So you were in a hurry when you left home this morning were ya?

You're wearing a pearl stud and a gold clip."

"I was not in a hurry a-tall. 'Tis my creative touch and the verry reason they put me in charrge of jewelry on Tuesdays,"

Annie shot her a look of surprise. "Well I'll be a one legged roosta!"

Hopscotch ignored the remark and unclipped the gold clip earring. "I chose these on purpose. You see when I found the man I wanted to marry, I wore one silver earring that read 'yes', the other said 'no'. And believe it or not, the night he actually did prropose I became flustered, and pointed to the wrrong earr."

"So then what?"

"Just before he dashed away, I rrealized my mistake, rraced after him, thrrew my arms around him and we werrre marrried."

"For how long?"

"For…for too many years to count until…" audible sniffs set Annie's eyes on her. Was Hopscotch actually distraught, or was she acting? This woman was complex and Annie was left to "pondah" while Hopscotch took her coffee break.

Heather and Mandolin entered. Heather was crossing her heart to prove she would never discuss Mandolin's stupidity in Mexico with Hopscotch. Gilbert introduced Mandolin to Annie who was delighted to meet this girl about whom she had heard so much. Immediately, Annie thrilled Mandolin with an invitation to assist inside the booth with her assurance she'd take full responsibility. Her instructions as to the locations of all the various categories and how to use the intercom for the high-end jewelry were easily understood. Mandolin was eager to get underway.

Gilbert led a young couple first-time visitors, to the Jewelry counter. He knew Mandolin would take good care of Sandra and Fabrizio which pleased her, just as he was pleased to be greeted by his good buddy dressed in scrubs. Kris chatted briefly with Gilbert with an eye on Mandolin and moved closer.

Fabrizio spoke softly, asked where the lockets were and Annie pointed to the case. Mandolin took over and admitted she had always wanted a locket herself to keep a picture of her dad, but so far…The couple looked at one another and Sandra nodded. He appeared to be the spokesman.

"We…we recently lost our child. She was six days old and we're hoping to find a plain locket for her ashes."

Mandolin was deeply affected, ran outside and around the counter, hugged them both with all her might and ran back inside the booth. The couple sensed her compassion and looked at more trays with Mandolin's help.

Kris was intrigued by this gal Mandolin, and moved to the other side of the counter for a better position and listened in to Fabrizio's words.

"Look *mi amore*, here is a locket with an eagle on it. Perfect, no?"

Sandra agreed. Fabrizio saw the look of delight in Mandolin's eyes and took her into his confidence. "A friend of ours sang *On Eagles Wings* at the ceremony, and we think this an excellent pendant for her ashes."

Mandolin wiped her tears, unsure of what to say. Kris wanted to help her out when Fabrizio turned to her. "Perhaps you know about eagles, but we were not aware of their, how do you say, their mothering instincts."

"Tell me more. I love to learn."

Sandra opened up. "When an eaglet leaves the nest, sometimes it falls and the mama eagle flies under it, catches it on her wings and returns it to the nest."

Mandolin was touched by the story. Sandra clutched the locket to her heart, thanked her, admired her flag pin and asked if she had found it here at the shop. "No, but it has a story that almost matches yours and the locket."

Annie put the locket into a small tray and guided the couple to the cashier's counter. Kris followed when the highly agitated voice of her gramma burst forth. "Why is there no coffee? It is certainly not *my* job to make it."

Gilbert returned to the front, found Kris lingering and approached him "Is your divorce final yet?"

Kris nodded. "Two months ago. She's gone back to her mother and I stopped by in hopes you and I can remain friends."

Gilbert put his arm around him. "I've gone through this too, man and it's tough stuff. Just be glad there were no kids involved. As you know I'm happy to help any way I can."

"Thanks." Kris had more on his mind. "Does Mandolin work here every day?"

"No. This is her first time with us. She's the granddaughter of a volunteer whose voice you just heard. She's going through a bad time from what I gather."

"Really," stated Kris. He responded to his beeper, thanked Gilbert and left.

An announcement over the intercom. "Quintus, please open the back doors. We have a delivery truck waiting there."

Mandolin scurried off to find Heather when she accidentally bumped into a cool-looking guy. He asked about a lady named Hopscotch who works in jewelry.

"You must be talking about my gramma."

"Really? Is she here?"

"Somewhere. Want me to find her for you?"

He liked what he saw. "Maybe later. She waited on me once and told me all about how she rode horses in Scotland. As it turns out I've been accepted to Napier U in Edinburgh and have a few questions. Actually. I'm also looking for some things to represent Texas. Would you show me around?"

Mandolin was more than happy to show him. On the way to the back they introduced themselves. He was Achilles.

She guessed he was Greek by his name and profile. She was impressed.

Hopscotch returned from the kitchen area and was approached by a customer. "I understand you have everything here. Where will I find bones?"

Mandolin skipped in from the back alone and in high sprits. She had sold Achilles a Texas flag and he had taken her cell number. Yes! A colorful striped body shirt in Ladies Casuals attracted her when the voice of Hopscotch distracted her.

"Bones? Bones? Woof! Woof! We are not a pet store. We do not sell bones here."

Holy Pig! Was this the same Hopscotch she lived with? "Hi Hopscotch. We're back."

"Oh, so you're here to upset me?"

"Oh no. This has been a great day in many ways. I'd like to thank you for telling me about the shop and to say you were awesome a minute ago when you were you played like a dog. Woof! Woof!"

"That customer is a pest. She's always here and has no couth."

"Couth?"

"Of course you wouldn't know about that. Those with your background are…"

"What do you mean by my background? I'm your granddaughter, right?"

"This is nye-ther the time nor place to discuss this and I am busy. Now go find Heather."

Mandolin let her tongue loose. "Are you ashamed of Heather and I?"

"Heather and *me.*" Hopscotch turned rapidly, wobbled slightly off-balance and moved on to her booth.

Quintus a burly employee approached the Jewelry Booth. He was waving a red apron.

"Here you go, Hopscotch. Minnie, the day chair wants you to wear it *now.* That's the message."

Hopscotch dropped it on the center counter as if it stank, and clipped her long newly colored cinnamon hair on top of her head.

"Is that volunteerrr sufferring with Alzeimers? Will she never rememberrr? I do not like aprons. I do not wear aprons, especially this vomitous shade of rrred. They are messy and detract from my display of jewelry around my neck and wrrrist which I model to make a sale. In fact, I shall tell her myself. This aprrron is to-do is much about nothing."

At lunchtime, working customers scurried in to check out furniture, clothing, china, silver, books, kitchen or glassware sections while those who were retired ambled in to chat or find something recently added. Heather carried a waffle iron to the check out, and listened to Hopscotch with a customer. "Is it Carolyn or Angelica?"

"I'm Rosemary."

"In any case, let me try this lovely ring on you. In Edinbur-rgh wher-re I come from we never see the likes of these beautiful gems at these pr-rices? Neverr!"

Mandolin joined Heather at the cashier's desk and watched Judith check her out with her winning personality. "I see you found the bargain of the day, sir."

Mandolin wondered if Achilles had bought the flag and asked Gilbert if he knew. He was uncertain but thought so and as he saw them to the door, he was thrilled to hear Mandolin singing:

"What a day this has been,
What a rare mood I'm in
Why it's almost like being in love.
There's a smile on my face for the whole human race
Why it's..."

It was another one of those happy tunes Big Mama had introduced her to, this one by Lerner and Lowe.

As soon as Heather dropped Mandolin off, she ran to the library and caught her breath. She had learned many things but mainly how much she loved people. She would meet as many as she could, somewhere, somehow.

Then she looked up the location of Napier University so that when she talked to Hopscotch about it, she would not appear stupid. Next, she found words to *On Eagles Wings. She was in the process of* memorizing them when Sky and Hopscotch entered the hallway. She was in one of her dramatic states.

"What a day! I am positively exhausted after waiting on hundreds of customers all day long. And why in the world did that ungrateful and rude granddaughter of mine come to the shop?"

Mandolin remained in the library. The phone rang. Sky picked up the phone at the foot of the stairs. "The MacDuff Residence...Yessir. Hold please."

Hopscotch's voice. "People never leave me alone." And then in a saccharine sing-song tone came her greeting. "Good ahfterrrnoon. I beg your parrrdon? You wish to speak to Mandolin? Who is this?" Mandolin appeared and asked to take the phone. Hopscotch held on tight. "Grregorry?...Well, I do mind. I am her grrrandmother. What is it you want?"

Mandolin reached for the phone. "I'll speak to Gregory, Hopscotch. He's a guy I met in Mexico. He has two adorable boys and wants me to..."

"Mexico!" Hopscotch glared at the phone and then spoke into it. "This girl is only a child and you are not to call again." She hung up.

"Shoot, Hopscotch! Heather and I had a great time there together. Her sister is awesome and I met people who seemed to like me. Why did I ever come back herrre? Why? Why arrre you so mean?"

Once again, Hopscotch had no answer, Mandolin felt her chin hit her chest listened to the tin goddesses' heels echo up the stairway *click clack, click clack* until she slammed her bedroom door.

Slumped in a chair, Mandolin recalled her moped ride with Jose, and then Crotchy and his bike. Sex took over her mind as well as a book called *Pepper* that Fawiza had giggled over before Mandolin understood why. She rolled the library ladder along the shelves, past a collection of Agatha Christie books, most of which had already tested her detective skills. Her mind skipped forward to a writing assignment. Miss Hughes, her "fave" teacher at Lanier Junior High believed Mandolin could do "anything she set her mind to." She had asked to be called Jenny outside of class, and honored her by assigning her the chance to write a unique detective story to read to the class.

Right away she knew the title. "A Brilliant Mystery Man Finds The Missing Link." And then she decided to make the mystery man good looking and really really sexy. She moved past a few paperback books when Yes! There was *Pepper* at the end of the row. Learning more about a real sexual relationship and how they pair up was more paramount now than ever. How had her mom and dad paired up and what happened? She drew the book in close, held it tight and jumped off the ladder.

"Ouch!" She hit herself on the arm of a chair and here it came again, blood from her nose dripped onto the Oriental rug. A few drops also landed on the jacket of *Pepper*. She took "The Thinker's' position and thought of her future. Was there more misery and punishment ahead. Why do I live here with a snapdragon who wants me dead? How can I be as brilliant as my Dad when Crotchy says I'll get in trouble if I'm smart like the Asians?

Sheet Dad and Mom! Why can't we all be together on one of your sailing races to Bermuda? You taught me how to raise a jib, remember, Dad? At that very moment, Mandolin's urge to escape became her goal. Her day at the Guild had shown her that being with interesting people made her happy. Somehow she had to find a way to be happy most of the time.

After wiping up the mess, she went back to her room, crawled into her thinking place, the window seat and made an attitude adjustment. Yes! *"I know what to do! First I'll finish my detective story that Jenny will love. Then we'll find a publisher and after that my mom will hear about it and know how to find me."*

Finally in her bed, she visualized her book's hero, an awesome hunk in a hammock making love to a beautiful woman. His strong arms held her close. O-o-o-o! And then a dream. A struggle with a key until it finally slipped into the lock. From then on she knew she was in paradise. Instead of just one, a series of familiar sensations down below caused her to pant faster and faster until she felt something absolutely sensational for the first time. She then fell happily onto her back and like magic, drifted off down the yellow brick road.

8.
Dating

THE DIFFERENCE BETWEEN BOYS and girls had become clear...clear and powerful...and yet so far none of her *heart-throbs,* met her dreams. No one reminded her of her dad, and lately when she asked each one if he was a virgin, the question drove each away. One, however, sold her a more advanced cell phone, cheap! She loved how she could talk to those outside the Mansion with no danger of her gramma listening in and catch up on old friends. Maybe she'd meet new ones too.

Then one afternoon, Tina who was more sophisticated it seemed, included Mandolin and some friends at "Sprinkles" for cupcakes. Ray was there. He was eighteen and plenty cool and invited her and Tina to stop by his home later that night...for a party...and to bring a date if she wanted. A date? The closest she had come to having a date was accepting one from a box at Big Mama's. In any case, Gregory was too old, Crotchy had skinny legs, Jose was too far away and Achilles... well she didn't dare ask a guy that cute to be her date...yet. He might refuse, she'd feel rejected again and everything would be spoiled. This was her chance to find a guy she could like and turn into the hero of her story.

Preparing for the party was a blast. Tina thought they would both look awesome with streaks in their hair. "It's the style, girlfriend. Want to?"

Of course she wanted to and Tina pursued. "As you can see, I've already had my ears pierced in many places and you know what? We should get tattoos."

Mandolin frowned. "I'm sure my dad would never have agreed to that. Will yours?"

"You know him. He cares what we do, but gives us space."

They rode bikes back to Terror, found peroxide in a kitchen cabinet, went upstairs, when the house phone rang. Mandolin ran for it with hopes it was some fantastic guy who had spotted her somewhere, some time and tracked her down. Heather took the call. Mandolin listened from the top of the stairs.

"Mrs. Mac's residence—No sir, she's out this afternoon—Yessir. Ah got it. You're J-a-c-q-u-e-s, your plane from Paris got delayed and soon as you arrahve in Houston you're takin' a taxi to the house."

She hung up, looked up the stairway and saw Mandolin. "Ah've never in my lahfe heard of anyone flying from Paris down here to Houston and then taking a taxi. He could drahve here direct in less than three hours."

Mandolin smiled. She was excited. "No Heath, this guy must be from Paris France. Did he have an accent?"

"An accent? Seems like everyone got accents these days."

Mandolin returned to her room and addressed Tina. "So Hopscotch knows a Frenchman? "I'm really really surprised."

"Not me." said Tina." She's into everything."

"You can say that again."

Mandolin was carried away with the peroxide bottle. They giggled because her hair had an attitude prob. Orange was what it took to and Tina assured her it was perfect. They enjoyed their togetherness and proudly faced a new and more colorful world with a party coming up and a Frenchman coming to visit. She had read about French men and their mistresses in novels. She knew he would be old and yet she was still curious...always curious...about everything.

Hopscotch returned and ordered supper in her room. Mandolin and Tina were too excited to eat. Mandolin was not about to tell Heather anything about the party after her performance in Mexico. As for Sky, they had kinda-sorta convinced one another that he would always want them to have fun. Tina primped while Mandolin sat by the window looking into a mirror along with developing the hero of her story. It was well after dark when the arrival of a taxi down at the front door interrupted her progress. From what she could see, a man who had to be Jacques, paid the taxi driver, waited for him to leave, and found the key hidden behind a bench by the front door.

He read a note attached, let himself in and climbed up to Hopscotch's room. Mandolin peeked out but he never turned around and then Yuck! The thought of her old gramma greeting a man in a fancy nightgown repulsed her. Why else would *she* not greet him at the door? But the good news was that he could be a brilliant artist or writer or... the following day she would have the answer... if he was still there.

Ray's old pick-up truck chugged up the drive. Mandolin and Tina ran quietly down the stairs, and were waiting outside before he reached the front. They hopped in and away they went into the wild black yonder!

A full moon lit the cow pasture. OhmyGod! Achilles was there. Incredible! He was on the other side of the fence in a crowd of mainly girls. Shoot! She was not one to show him she cared by leaping a fence to be with him. He seemed to be totally enjoying himself and so she played hard to get. But how long should she wait? It seemed that whenever she thought she had found *hakka bakka*, her dreams went backwards. And then the thought of disturbing sleeping cows began to bug her. It was mean and she had suffered with more meanness than she wanted to remember.

This was her first time to be in a crowd of her peers where beer, whiskey and pot abounded. Frankly, it unnerved her. Not so for Tina. She was enjoying the whole bit and so Mandolin with the help of only a slug beer gutted up and followed suit. Her panic evaporated and she felt totally comfortable perched beside Ray on a fence under *la luna de* silver. He reached for her hand and she lost almost all her breath until he leaned forward like…like he wanted to kiss her. *OhmyGod*! She absolutely lost it when all at once their lips met and then she felt his tongue. She had read about Eros, the Greek God of sexual desire. Was he responsible for the pulsations that ran all through her body? She wanted more…much more Holy Pig! This had to be hakka bakka.

"You bring condoms?" he asked.

"Excuse me?" She hopped off the fence in a panic and did her best to sound cool…"Um,..um…up 'til this moment, it 's been awesome but I'm…I'm so not good at what you want to do."

"How do you know?"

"I don't and yet I'd love to see you again. My e-mail is naughtynauticalnut@hotmail.com."

"Right. Sure. I'm no good at all with nuts or those hung up on morals if that's what your problem is."

"I…I don't plan to always be this way, Ray…just for a few days or more…and then maybe…"

He gave her two thumbs down and on the way home, his one word answers to her questions made her feel rejected again. Why couldn't she relax like Tina and Ray who were having had a blast discussing the party? Mandolin sat alone n back trying to figure out answers. Were these overpowering sensations with Ray, normal? Would others want her? What would they be like? She hoped so because her experience with Ray had added a new dimension to her life, even though they never went all the way. Did pregnant teen agers miss out on the fun? Should she always kiss and hug and stop there Or was it impossible?

Mom, she asked the space around her. Do you ever miss me or look for me? I've so needed you many times but never more than now.

She wanted to discuss her new experiences but at the moment all she could think about was that a boy had actually wanted to have sex with her, one that wasn't half bad.

Sky had been there for her, but discussing sex with him was definitely out. Sky was a *man*, had raised two girls, and Big Mama... all of a sudden, she stopped and thought back.

Sky had called to say her Big Mama was sick and she had never gone to see her. Shame gave Mandolin's heart a huge wallop. Big Mama had been there in a big way for all of them. She had helped her through the death of her dad, listened to her many problems, taught her all the songs of the sixties and seventies and when she became sick, Mandolin had neglected her. Undoubtedly she would have advice about adventures in sex, but now it was unfair to take advantage of her. Best not to call, to practice sincere apologies and to see her in the morning.

As for Hopscotch, discussing sex with her was absolutely out! By process of elimination, Heather was the one to make her feel normal. She remembered Heather's quote from an old timer in one of her Cowboys and Indians movies. *"Sex at my age? Why that be as useless as a milk bucket under a bull."* Mandolin now felt secure enough to ask what that meant and they talked for hours until Heather finally wound it up. "So these days they all doin' it but if ah were you ah'd trah to be different. Hold off 'til you got a keeper in love with you, and then you can surprahse him with all kinds of new tricks."

Mandolin fell asleep knowing it was up to her to stick to her guns and be a good girl. Laughter in Hopscotch's room woke her. What? Hopscotch could actually laugh? Were she and Jacques doing it? Yuck! Then another thought grabbed her. Maybe Hopscotch's French *ami* and she could have a productive adult conversation with a man to get his perspective. In other words, a tête-à-tête, about sex-à-sex.

Next on her to-do list, was a visit to Big Mama. Sky had prepared her for a wheelchair, and yet Mandolin was stunned to see her condition. Sky had explained that her over-strict devotion to a diet for her diabetes had caused her to lose weight too fast. Her limp body reminded Mandolin of a cooked strand of spaghetti and yet when she looked at Mandolin through a cracked eye, a smile spread across her creased face and she talked with a faint voice.

"I is real happy to see you, darlin'. Sky tells me you and your gramma goin' off to a Scotch place."

Mandolin took her hand and put her chin on the bed so as not to miss a word. "Her and you had your troubles, but let 'em go. Life too damn short to hang on to 'em."

In a weaker voice, she added "'Member them old tunes we used to sing together, specially the one by Englebert Humperdinck? Dunno if it was his funny name or the way he sang—um—what was—?"

Her eyes closed." Our favorite was *Our Way*, Big Mama. Remember we liked it because we like to do things..."

A tiny smile softened Big Mama's strained face and a wee voice "our way" came through.

Mandolin began singing another of her favorites, *On the Sunny side of the Street.*

"Seem like way back in the past I heard a voice, not near as pretty as yours, but..."

"Where Big Mama, where?"

"I's tired darlin'...so tired I can't get to it. But I never gonna forget that song we likes the very best." She croaked. "'Taint what you do it's the way that do's it.' So you go on and do's what you gonna do on your trip...and be sure to do it real good and make Big Mama proud."

Mandolin knelt by her chair, hugged her for a long time, and thanked God for putting this great lady into her life. She then said good-bye and turned to find Sky behind her. His loving eyes brimmed with tears...more than enough for both of them. He squeezed out the words. "Big Mama sure a tough act to follow but she not going no place right away. I got a hunch Mama gonna wanna hear about your trip when you get back."

"I hope you're right. Not just because she's too good to lose but by then Big Mama might recall the song her mom had once sung that could lead Mandolin to her. It might be one that would help me find my Mom."

Sky smiled down at Mandolin. "You always hopin' and that's good. Real good."

PART II

1

And Away We Go

MANDOLIN LAY ON HER bed the next morning picturing her mom. She saw her as Julie Andrews singing "The hills are alive with the sound of music," when Hopscotch barged into her bedroom without so much as a knock. She was dressed to the nines, tens and even the elevens. Mandolin sat up in her usual casual threadbare jeans and body shirt, took a deep breath and clamped her teeth over her tongue to avoid a temper explosion.

"I have plans." announced Hopscotch without so much as a hi. "It is time to examine your rrroots."

Roots? What roots? Nonplussed by Hopscotch's oversight of her wide streak of peroxided hair, Mandolin relaxed a bit and listened to her gramma's burr.

"Prreparrre yourrself child, we shall be taking to a trip to Eurrrope aboard the Queen Mary 2 to visit Scotland, the birrthplace of your dear, dear grr-randfather and myself."

What was going on? *Dear* grandfather? Had the impossible wretch suddenly become soft-hearted? Was this Jacques there for the trip? Was he her beau? "Oh My Gosh!—Really?—Europe?—Scotland?— Awesome, Hopscotch, do you really mean it? That's incredible."

Incredible it was…and much more than just the trip. This was the first time Hopscotch had ever mentioned her grandfather, or anyone else in her family in a kind way. The fact that her gramma was including her in this activity was as unbelievable as President Kennedy's murder. A replay on the History Channel had taught her that millions of really good people die tragically. Possibly if she brought up the subject, Hopscotch might be affected and start sharing stories about her son, Mandolin's dad.

No such luck. That was it! Hopscotch added no clues and her cryptic manner returned. "I have made reservations for three, and you must be ready to leave for New York by nine tomorrow morning."

Reservations for three? This meant…this meant…Jacques had to be coming. She crossed her fingers. Please let him be interesting and fun, *please*?

In her gramma's encyclopedia she learned that Queen Mary was considered a mean Queen. Curious, she thought that a ship would be named after her, but knew she could find more information aboard the ship. So it was really going to happen—her first opportunity to grow as a family member…a chance to look for her mom and learn more about her grandparents' country and her heritage. Her dad was gone, but if she kept on believing in *hakka bakka* she would find her place with her mom.

And yet she seemed never to be without an issue, or two hundred and ninety nine. Who was paying for Mandolin's trip? She had heard that Hopscotch could afford two or three mansions, and yet she had scolded Mandolin for tossing out a used tube of toothpaste. Even her dad never cut the tube in half and squeezed out the very last dribs. What was the deal? This ambiguity confused her and to make sure who was paying, she bravely approached Hopscotch.

"I've made a little money stocking at Kroger's and HEB after school and selling a few of my crazy animal sketches, but there's no way I can afford the trip myself."

"Of course not!" Hopscotch answered impatiently. "All you have to do is drrress like a lady, behave like a lady and f'r the love of God, get rid of that revolting white streak in your hair. What on earth were you thinking?" she said slamming the door.

Phew! *Earth, Wind and Fire* had left the room. The hair patrol had waited before launching her surprise attack on Project Peroxide, and Mandolin's edginess had been aroused. To plead her case for streaks, when they met in the hallway, she related a tale about Alfred Hitchcock, an impressive British director of her gramma's era whose camera shots maximized anxiety, fear and empathy. His wife had blond streaks and had their bacon flown into Hollywood from Denmark daily.

The tale fell flat. It only kindled more imperious comments as well as affording Hopscotch the chance to list the famous people she knew in Hollywood and elsewhere. And so what remained was crediting her gramma for the cruise of which she and her dad had dreamed; eliminating her white streak and dressing like a lady.

But hold on! Hopscotch had bought her an old-fashioned wardrobe that even a freezing homeless person might reject. Clearly it had not dawned on her gramma that styles for teen-agers now had a sexual twist since her days as a bonnie lass in Scotland. Mandolin's concern? If she complained at all, Hopscotch, the one *paying for absolutely everything* might cancel her ticket and leave her behind. Staying with Sky and Heather would have been cool except giving up a free trip made no sense.

That afternoon, Mandolin painfully, yet obediently, modeled the outfit her gramma had chosen for the trip. First she slipped on a wool coat with big brass buttons and played the game that determines your future mate. She pointed to each button one at a time until there were no more. "Rich man, poor man, beggar man, chief, doctor"... she stopped and held her head in her hands "I'll marry a doctor? No way. They're way too smart." Next she slipped on her knee socks and her "sturdy walking shoes," when a gentle knock startled her. Always warmed by Sky's smile, she invited him in. He surprised her with a farewell gift from Big Mama and the girls: a brand new backpack. Crap! He was not included on the trip. After an emotional hug, she visualized their separation and her adventures ahead.

To keep him around as long as possible, she convinced Sky to help her pack up his awesome gift with books, a notebook, a scrapbook for mementoes and comfortable clothes. How she wished he could come with them and after he left, she dropped the hint at Hopscotch's door.

"Completely out of the question, Madolin. What would people think if we were to take a servant on a trip like this? He will take you and all the luggage to the airport where Jacques, my *Parisian* beau and I shall join you. And then he shall return "immejiatly" to the mansion to perform his duties. Mandolin almost lost it. First, because many books had been written about the old days when the wealthy actually took ladies-in-waiting aboard with them and adding if he came, other guests would be the luckiest people in the world. But more importantly because Hopscotch had a beau. She couldn't imagine an old lady in the dating world.

"How old is Jacques?" she asked.

Up went Hopscotch's nose as she huffed out the door.

At the airport, the International one, Sky drove up to the drop-off area and began unloading the luggage. Eager sky-caps appeared to help. Mandolin watched him wave them off graciously until a way too familiar staccato voice crackled though the din of the traffic.

"Over here, Brown. Over here, and be quick about it."

Mandolin, dressed like a British lass and yet proudly displaying her American flag pin, put her well-developed muscles to use. The books inside her bag weighed a ton but helping Sky carry hers and others to the sidewalk check-in made her feel good. Then came her first glimpse of Jacques, a marshmallow sort of a guy kind of like Hot Diggety, the puffy cheeked order-taker at Denny's where she and her dad liked to eat. She knew better than to laugh.

Jacques was nowhere near "as high as an elephant's eye," an *Oklahoma* favorite of Big Mama's. He was far younger that Hopscotch, she thought him about her dad's age with thick wiry hair, in which she imagined birds could frolic. She had never before seen hair in ears or a pewter-hued handle-bar moustache and was impressed with the leather patches on the elbows of his tweed blazer. She and Valentina had often watched Robin Williams as a professor in *Good Will Hunting* which gave her hope that the little man, le petit homme would be intelligent and she would learn about France and other things he knew.

Sky returned with the tickets and baggage claim stubs and Mandolin threw her arms around her best buddy's neck, as if she would never see him again.

"I'll miss you so much, Sky. Give Big Mama a hug, and Heather too."

"Sure. You be good, write to us and have a safe trip."

Sky signed an H and a B. Since she and her dad first heard of *hakka bakka*, she knew the H sign for hakka and the b for bakka and he remembered her showing him. He had a way of touching her heart. And then she heard the voice that had a way of crushing it.

"Where have you been, child? Why must you always be late?"

Mandolin pointed to her watch, proof that they arrived before the designated time which evoked a reproving glance from Sky that said let it go. She watched him disappear through the crowd on his way to the limo.

"And what is this? Your hair! Why, pray tell did you color it red?"

"You complained about my white streak and I thought you'd be pleased if me and you have the same color hair."

Hopscotch tsked-tsked, rolled her eyes and looked away disdainfully. "Really, Madolin. Such poor grammar! How could you say me and you when your father spoke with elegance."

105

Another first from Hopscotch. Never before had she mentioned her dad in a complimentary way. Mandolin resolved to hear more, but not until later, when all had settled in and they were on their way to Scotland.

At the La Guardia airport in New York City, Hopscotch insisted that they all ride the bus to their hotel on West 59th Street in the city, their three-day home while *she catches up with the city once again*. Mandolin was blown away by her first visit. The horns were deafening and taxis weaved wildly through the traffic. Mandolin studied the buildings scraping the sky. She sat alone and called to tell Sky they had arrived and that she loved him, but held off discussing Achilles until she actually got to Scotland. What would happen when Hopscotch discovered they had a mutual friend? Or was it because she was afraid he would never call. She was sure this cutie had many girlfriends at Napier.

The next morning in a crowded subway car on the way to Radio City Music Hall, Mandolin stood at a pole, an irresistibly tempting one, and twirled around and around it until she heard Hopscotch's stinging command. "Sit down and behave yourself, Madolin. "You are acting like a child."

"I'm dressed like a weirdo, so why can't I act like one?"

"You heard me Madolin."

Madolin! Why was her gramma unable to call Mandolin by her proper name?

"Sest intendoo," Jacques commented in a low gargly smoker's voice.

She wished for her French-English dictionary since if he was trying to say he agreed, it should be *c'est entendu* pronounced '*say awntondu*'. But if Mandolin wanted to see *Wicked* on Broadway she had to let it pass as Heather said, like a stick in a stream. And she did, far easier than she had imagined this time.

The theatre and the play were unlike those at school and she wished for someone to discuss it all with. The tunes had sexy words that turned on her "wicked" streak. She opened her lungs, sang along, tapped her feet, moved in her seat to the beat, and roared with laughter at Elphaba, the future Wicked Witch of the West. So unlike Hopscotch, she was honest with herself. *"I don't cause commotions I am one."* Mandolin tapped her gramma on the shoulder and whispered "I love Elphaba's directness, don't you?" Hopscotch put her finger to her lips. "Don't you know better than to talk in the theatre?"

Another "repuke" from the wicked witch in front seat. "Were she to write a synopsis of her gramma's modus operandi at this stage, she would use these words: "A perpetual effort of a cowardly old bag, on and off her rocker, with zero intellect and sex appeal, struggling to impress others with her youth." If only her nerve to speak the truth had not been destroyed by this real-life bitchy Elphaba!

For a couple of days, the threesome walked and walked along Park Avenue, Fifth Avenue, toured the Metropolitan Museum and frequently sat on benches in Central Park so Jacques could have a smoke or tend to a blister on his heel. The ever-observant Mandolin, with her ever-improving detective skills was positive there was no blister, especially when she noticed Jacques's efforts to squeeze out goofy smiles at her between his tobacco stained teeth.

Each day secured her conjectures. These daytrips were all about Jacques and Hopscotch getting to know each other. Hopscotch responded to his every desire and he to hers, i.e. providing him the opportunity to puff away because *he* wanted to, and stopping in at all the boutiques along Fifth Avenue because shopping was *her* favorite activity. When she asked Jacques if they had met through a dating service, he reached for his pack of cigarettes and went outside. Had they lied about thier ages? Had he looked for an older woman because she was more likely to be a rich widow and she because being seen with a younger man was considered a coup? Instead of coping with Hopscotch's demands and waiting for salesclerks to make yet another big fuss over her, Mandolin joined Monsieur Jacques outside the shops.

"Hey Jacques, has my gramma ever talked to you about her son?"

"She has a son? I mean to say, we do not deescuss zees kind of theeeng."

"I see. Then I am sure you wouldn't mind telling me how you met."

"Why you want to know thees?"

"Because I'm writing a love story and…"

"Your gramma, she weel tell you these an-*swers*"

He stamped out a cigarette on the pavement, and offered her a piece of gum. She declined while thinking a strong breath mint might do more for his breath and cough.

"Thanks anyway. My dad said people look gross when they chew gum."

Jack missed her intended insinuation and discussed their up-coming afternoon excursion in his husky, huskier, huskiest tenor voice. "Ah, *mon petit et belle Mandoleen*, do you know that in 1763 my coun*tree, it* gives to your coun*tree* the Statue of Liberty, a symbol of freedom?"

What? 1763? Impossible! That was the year The Treaty of Paris ended the French-Indian War, surrendering Canada to England. Thus her desire to upgrade his behavior from peculiar to normal was losing ground. "You see een France, where I was born either twenty-two or three years ago," he said with a wink apparently trying to impress her with his strange humor, "we enjoy much to theenk of the foo-toor and nothing of the derriere."

"So you've never cared about seeing the Mona Lisa or drawings on walls of the Lascaux Caves?"

"I do not know Mona and we are without caves een France."

She was seriously trying to like this *beau* of her gramma's but ignorance and a peculiar French accent kept blocking the way. Unaware of the caves… maybe, but not to know Mona? Not! From Marie, a girl in her sophomore class born in Paris, she had picked up many French words and knew derrière meant ass and not past. The recurring message to "let it go" was about to beat up her brain.

Another surprise. Four hours of shopping had loosened the strings of Hopscotch's purse which resulted in an atypical taxi ride to a sightseeing boat around New York Harbor. They toured Ellis Island where early immigrants landed in America. Mandolin got goose bumps and tears formed. The thought of their bravery in sailing to a strange place all the way across the Atlantic Ocean reminded her of her dad and his dangerous adventures through storms at sea.

And then she wondered about her mother's heritage. Mandolin had been born in Malaysia. But was her Mom born there as well? Where did she meet her dad? What was her family name? Did her ancestors arrive on a ship at Ellis Island years ago as well? She felt closer just thinking about them.

She and Jacques had spoken a few times with confusion each time. Could she and her French-English dictionary convince him to talk naturally and smile from the heart? Oops. Neither her dad nor Sky approved of quick assessments. *Okay, Dad, I'll try. He's at least someone new, a huge distraction from Madame Supérieure and her derrière.*

2
All aboard

THEIR TRIP ON THE Queen Mary 2 was upcoming and Mandolin slept little the night they were set to sail. A frantic morning followed. Hopscotch packed and repacked a dozen times to squeeze her purchases into her luggage. At last they all arrived at the wharf. The ship far exceeded her wildest dreams. It was huge with an outside deck to walk around. Mandolin's anticipation was leaping freely while Hopscotch barked orders to the porters about the placement of her bags. Finally they crossed through security and entered over a gangplank. She felt as if she was heading for a new world, and thought of Christopher Columbus and his first venture to a new world. She had a blast waving down at the people remaining on the dock and squealed when the porter opened the door to her cabin.

When the ship's horn sounded *oo-ooo* and they set out for Southampton, England, shivers of excitement startled her body, as well as the hot breath of Jack in her ear.

"I see you have goose bumps, Madoleen. Did you know that in my coun*tree* some of the little goosies, zey honk louder than thees horn or than doggies bark?"

"Is that right?" She replied sweetly, but wanted to gag at his behavior and baby talk. Goosies and doggies?

Her dad had often talked of giving another the benefit of the doubt and she needed his help at this moment. It was obvious this guy lacked a feel for Mandolin's maturity and faked another blister to have a smoke. How she had hoped for an intellect or at least good sense of humor and look what she got. "Ah *Madoleen* how about Mother Goose herself. Did she not have bumps and lumps when she had all her little goosies?

Mandolin winced while Hopscotch thought him "brilliant and quick-witted" and lavished the old fogey with another kiss, this time a long one on the lips that made Mandolin blush. Not only because of the smooching but rather his habit of cupping his hand around Hopscotch's rear, to her delight. Had Hopscotch forgotten her age?

The worst was the night they were invited to sit at the Captain's Table. The ship's cocktail waiters were attentive and Hopscotch too soon gulped "tee many martoonics." Mandolin watched in amazement as her gramma pinched the Captain's "chubby little cheek" and giggled at everything he said. In addition when music wafted in from a nearby piano bar, Hopscotch squealed like a teenager. With no compunction, she feigned a Mic, and cast her blinking eyes and fake eyelashes at Jacques while crooning a regenerated Elvis tune *I Can't Help Falling in Love with You.*

Mandolin felt like she was in a time warp and way out of place. She wondered how all this would affect her mom until she heard a loud theatrical smooch from the undaunted duo. "Yuck!" she said to the waiter, who himself made a face and stepped away from the table.

Act like a lady? Mandolin was struggling. She was fifteen and had a strong urge to dump her feelings on her gramma like *"F'r the love of God Hopscotch, behave yourself and stop getting steamed up by a marshmallow. Monsewer Jack is not so nimble, not so quick with a breath loaded with gar*lic- *ick."*

She wanted to unload, and yet a stronger impulse stopped her...

maintaining her dad's respect as well as her gramma's seniority. It was difficult to believe that Hopscotch had borne her dad, but she had. Her optimism again burst forth with another positive idea that surprised her. Being able to practice detective work with a candidate like Jacques the Rip-off was a real stroke of fortune…and she was comforted by her belief that this was an opportunity to learn more about her mom.

Mandolin met some other kids her age group who invited her to meet up in a lounge the first night. She felt awkward, uncomfortable with their small talk and parental problems and diverted their attention with word games ("How do you spell annihilate, how do you spell symmetry, fuchsia, guerrilla and others."). Games were her bailiwick, her defensive tool along with her yo-yo.

Unhappily, sly glances like those from her earlier school days were still in evidence and she had to accept that these kids were total conformists. They were the kind who never stepped out of the box, hung with their peers full-time and never asked outsiders questions. Did they ever think for themselves? How did they learn about the real world?

And yet this was an opportunity to learn more about boys and talk booze and pot. Would getting stoned or making out with any one of these elite guys ever be worth it? What about Achilles? And what would Sky think?

A self-imposed smack against the side of her head brought her back to her senses. She offered a polite but early exit.

"Have fun you all. See you around."

"So what's with you?" one boy asked. "Why are you heading off?"

"Been there, done that." It was a lie, but for a moment she realized that acting bored and sophisticated gave her an edge. She bet that none of the others had the courage to walk away like she did. And she knew her dad would be proud she had.

Once again aware that she was unlike the norm. But who was

normal? The dictionary in the ship's library described it as average, common, ordinary She hated the sound of all those words. She wanted to be extraordinarily bright but after scanning several history books, she sadly realized the tiny scope of her knowledge. Would she ever be as smart as—as Charles Darwin, Einstein, Freud, Bill Gates, Shakespeare, Mark Twain or a guy near her age named Steve Jobs? She had so much to learn but for now, her only desire was to be as imaginative as Agatha Christie. She would focus on developing powers of observation like Sherlock Holmes as well as his craftsmanship in writing detective stories. Why did Sherlock have a good relationship with Doctor Watson, a detective at Scotland Yard, even when he disliked their methods? Why was it called Scotland Yard when it was in formed in London in 1829?

She was scouting the library when her eyes landed on a biography of Eleanor Roosevelt which she grabbed and opened. Maybe now she would understand more about the woman whose portrait Hopscotch substituted for her young dad's portrait. Where was it anyway? Suddenly she wanted it more than anything.

Cozy as a cat in a comfy chair, she learned that Eleanor Roosevelt, the wife of President Franklin Delano Roosevelt was a woman of great wealth. She considered herself homely, as did Sara Roosevelt, her Mother-in-law, and Sara had nicknamed Eleanor "Granny" because she found her uninteresting and boring. Sara also promoted her son's affair with Lucy Mercer, a pretty and vivacious woman, not serious like Eleanor who wrote columns and delivered speeches on Human Rights and social causes.

What? Did Hopscotch really admire Eleanor or feel sorry for her? Could this mean her grandpa was having an affair when he died? Was Hopscotch actually one of those women who pretended all was well when really in a bad place? Why else would she hang a photograph of a woman who had suffered with her husband's affair? Or had all the mystery stories she had read caused her imagination to run rampant?

Jack sauntered into the library in striped boxer shorts, sat opposite her, crossed his legs and picked at his hairless legs, an ongoing habit.

"What ees this you read?"

"Nothing really. It's a history book about a famous woman. It's a kind of chick-kick."

"Um-m. I like thees kind of book. In general they are much about love and sex, no?"

Mandolin held her ground. "You're French, and so you might not understand. This is about Eleanor Roosevelt. She wrote a column called *My Day*. Have you heard of it?"

"Nintendo."

"Nintendo? That's a game. What do you mean?"

"This means 'of course' in my language."

"Oh? I thought it was *bien entendu*."

"You misunderstand," he quickly countered. "We speak fast. What did thees lady write about?"

"I thought you just said you knew about it."

"Ooey, Ooey, ooey." She knew he was trying to say the French word for yes, oui. He continued, "I am interested in how you theenk."

"I am interested in how you theenk as well. Who was Eleanor's husband, I forget?"

"Everyone knows ze anzair."

"Many do. Do you?"

He had had enough. It seemed that the interrogation was temporarily suspended as was the repulsive view up his shorts. He left, thank God.

Presidents and their wives. Men and their lovers. The more she thought of the many books about the subject the less she trusted Jack. And the more she read about romance, the more doubtful she became of her gramma's weird relationship with this creeper! Are they lovers? How well did she know him? The whole bit disgusted her. Why couldn't she let it go?

Mandolin looked through the books and quickly found a Sherlock Holmes adventure: *The Hound of the Baskervilles.*

"After all my dear Watson, all this is elementary and there is no point in wasting time. We must plan for the job ahead."

Mandolin thought it sounded sort of James Bondish, a character she wished to emulate one day. She read on. *"We cannot afford only to observe but to see around us and keep our noses to the ground."*

Nose to the ground. She smiled. Of course that's what hounds did in order to catch the fox. She thought herself quite clever, though hardly modest. But her satisfaction was short-lived. Her nostrils filled with cigarette smoke mixed with heavy cologne.

One of her common hunches told her Jacques had hung around. She felt nauseous but not enough to escape to the fresh salt air outside. Her hunch paid off. She cuddled in a chair and hid behind *The Hound* while watching the mix-scented intruder reenter. Seemingly ill at ease, Jacques returned two books to the shelf on the other side of the room, mashed his cigarette butt into a coffee cup, pulled out some gum and took off.

Detective Mandolin determined then and there to win the case of Hop vs. Flop. She noted the exact location of the books he had been reading, checked to make sure he was gone, and pulled them out, one at a time. One was called *Conversational French* and the other: *One Hundred and One Sex Positions.*

She stood in shock with *Sex Positions* in her hand, when an evening squall with lots of thunder caused the ship to rock, and with it came a stumbling Hopscotch in a long too-tight sheath clutching a satin shawl and struggling with her balance.

The book! Mandolin sat on it quickly. Her gramma struggled with the rolling of the ship as well as criticizing Mandolin for wearing "frayed jeans, a man's sloppy shirt and sitting in an unladylike position." Hopscotch took a firm hold of her arm, pulled her to her feet and spouted vitriol. Mandolin slyly reached her leg up to the chair and kicked the book under it.

Hopscotch continued her tirade. "Your generation is known as the whiny generation. You expect instant gratification as demonstrated at lunch when you interrupted Jacques with some sort of a ridiculous question. And now I find you here with a book you are reading for your own pleasure with no thought a-tall of the ship's superb shed-u-ling of bingo and other games for those your age. How ungrateful you are for this luxurious cruise. It costs a fortune. Are you aware of that?"

Was she finished? Yes. With the courage of an impressive Navy SEAL, she held her ground against her grandmother for the first time in her life. In measured words she went after her.

"You are so wrong, Hopscotch. I am grateful but it is difficult to show it because you've have never shown any interest in me. You talk bitterly about me and around me, never directly to me with any sort of a meaningful discussion. You've never so much as given me a hug or asked me a single question about my feelings or even tried to understand life of a teen-ager. So how could you know what goes on in my life or in my generation? *Your* generation is called the booze generation, and as a result, you have left me alone and I have had to find my own way…with thanks to the kind and loving people who work for you. If it weren't for them I'm not sure where I would be today."

"Do you mean to tell me you talk to them about personal matters?"

"Why not? They have become my friends."

"Shocking!"

"Why? Is it because people can't relate to those less fortunate or poorly educated?

Her gramma's expression was poisonous but discouraging. "I'm not wasting my time in this library. I'm discovering all kinds of historical and significant facts. They happen to be important to me but not you. What is important to you? Parties and more parties. No wonder you find fault with whatever I do or say. You don't offer a thing, I'm your granddaughter and you treat me like a total stranger with leprosy or something. You're more thoughtful to your guests than to me."

Hopscotch's shock was visible as she tried to regain her composure.

"Tsk! Tsk Tsk! As I have said, you are an impossible child, just like your father."

"My dad? Don't say or even think that he was impossible. He taught me about love, to believe in people and myself. He taught me to be happy and to believe the world is beautiful with possibilities all around us."

Hopscotch panted heavily, tried to collect her thoughts, started to leave and changed her mind.

"There is a teen-age crowd here and there around the ship. They appear to come from wealthy families. Is there any reason you don't talk to them? Or are you determined to act like an old Granny and be a recluse with no friends?"

"Excuse me, did you call *me* an old Granny? My dad was your son and I doubt he would agree. You won't discuss either him or my mom with me. So is it my fault I don't know much about myself? Neither you nor Jacques include me or introduce me to anyone. I may not be like other kids and that's no reason to criticize me. Maybe I like being alone with my thoughts and books and to learn online.

Hopscotch recovered without missing a beat. "Now that is indeed a surprise. A line? Who would have thought that a young girl with no style at-all would have *a line?* Upon my soul, my friends will be so impressed that my granddaughter has her own line."

Was it possible to be any more out of touch with the real world than her gramma?

Suddenly Mandolin felt the start of an eruption inside like from some kind of a weird volcano. It started with a tiny smile, then grew into unbelievable laughter. Yes! Mandolin had shaken up her gramma's well-anchored perspective and now needed a tension release and giggled.

Not surprisingly, what she heard next was "Stop that ridiculous childish giggling, and get ready for dinner. In exactly one hour, I want you to appear in your finest outfit at our table in the dining room with some drawings from this line of yours. Perhaps someone aboard will be interested in promoting it. Those aboard are among the most influential in the world and when they learn we are related, they will undoubtedly move things along.

Aha! Influential people. If Hopscotch could impress others with a relative of hers, then she would wield some influence among those aboard. Was that it? Mandolin found this pushiness obnoxious, just as bad if not worse than Jack's eye that wandered readily down her cleavage and around the *callipygian* parts of all the younger women aboard.

What fun it was to have full use of the web, to fuel her favorite topic, words, and learn that *callipygian* meant well-shaped buttocks. Unloading her repressed emotions onto her gramma had felt really good and if she could just avoid mustachioed, pop-up Jack-in-the Box, another show-down with Hopscotch would never happen. Patience. Wherefore art thou patience?

Still in the library Mandolin found *Sex Positions* under a computer table and returned it to the shelf beside *Conversational French*. Just outside, she heard Hopscotch telling Jacques to go back to the room and she would be there shortly. Mandolin held her breath in hopes she would pass by but no. Hopscotch blew in just as the ship heaved, fell and ripped a seam of her dress. Mandolin tried to help but her help was rejected adamantly. Mandolin sensed her embarrassment at being seen out of control while keeping a death grip on her mission of the moment. "You *must* wear your finest outfit for dinner and to be on time…or else."

Actually Mandolin had little choice of outfits since Hopscotch's formal "gifts" for the trip consisted of a totally boring and classic shirtwaist dress, and a flouncy, bouncy long dress with a high neck. Then she remembered the glittery top that Heather had bought for her. Would it fit? She had no idea.

3

Dinner

SHE WOULD BE LATE. How could she help it, when to impress her gramma, she was replacing one of her turtle neck shirts with her glittery v-neck top and trying to fasten it to her jean skirt with safety pins. The fabrics were uncooperative for what seemed like forever.

In the dining room, she found her group across the room seated around the Captain's Table. With a prayer that her outfit would stay together, she stood tall and walked sedately to join them. The Captain pointed to a seat between a handsome, fit traveler and Jacques, both standing behind their chairs awaiting her arrival.

Phew. She made it. Her handsome seatmate pulled out her chair and Jacques remained behind her breathing his familiar garlicky breath down her neck. Affected by his abominable scents and her wicked sense of humor, Mandolin tossed her long hair back and bingo! When she turned around Jacques had stepped back as if wounded by her hair. But only for a moment because almost "immejetly" his eyes popped and danced down and around her cleavage. She shot him a withering look, and turned to the Captain who was "charmed to have this beautiful young woman dressed in one of the latest styles along with them."

Mandolin blushed at his unexpected attention. It was not easy to look older than she was, to deal with older men and…and their attention as well as Hopscotch's ridiculously proud claim as her grandmother. When Jacques finally sat down, he pulled in so close to her that his nervous knee asserted itself and caused both bodies to shake simultaneously. She inched away. He inched closer. She spotted a tray of hors d'oeuvres on the table and pointed.

"Will you please pass those to me?"

He stood up, reached way across the table and looked them over.

"What ees thees?"

Yes! This could be the test, Mandolin was excited. "They are called something I can't pronounce."

A woman with French accent spoke up. "We call these *hors'd-oeuvres, ma cherie.* H-o-r-s d-o-e-u-v-r-e-s."

"Aha! said Jack. "Horses hooves. My companion, she knows *muchissimo* about horses."

Eyeballs met eyeballs around the table. Mandolin tried to meet Hopscotch's but her gramma's nose was deep in a wine glass. Mandolin gave Jacky boy a literal cold shoulder and decided to have fun with her other dinner partner.

"Hello. How did I get lucky enough to sit by you? You are from—from…"

"I om from India, though I have lived in many countries."

"India!" came her excited response along with strong palpitations under her jean skirt when this gorgeous man with bronze skin and dimples looked directly into his eyes. "May I ask you a question?"

"Of course."

"My dad and I once watched a video starring Kishore Kumar. Have you heard of *hakka bakka* or seen the video?"

He thought for a few moments and then politely acknowledged that he had heard the name. It was Hindi. His answer disappointed her. And yet it was a beginning. She had connected with an Indian.

"Your dad is proud I om sure, to hov a beaut-i-ful and intelligent daugh-ter."

Instinctively she clutched, especially when his eyes took off into her cleavage. Did her gramma stare at her because she noticed, or because as soon as a waiter refilled her wine glass as fast as she downed it? Mandolin shifted her attention to an older gent in a wheelchair right behind her and at another table. His tales of a knee replacement, deteriorating joints, and round-the-world travel experiences evoked her sympathy.

"Aw. Poor you. "If I were you I'd be angry about all my ailments."

He chuckled. "I am, sweetheart. When I can't tend to my own personal needs, it pisses me off and I'm sure they can hear my reactions anywhere in the world." He tried to roll his wheelchair backwards and it got struck. "In addition, this damn wheelchair constantly pisses me off."

Mandolin helped her new buddy. If this dear man gets pissed off, then she felt okay to say her gramma pissed her off constantly. Just the idea gave her a boost.

Waiters were now serving dinner. They were dressed like Sky when he served formal dinners for Hopscotch, although these waiters wore red bow ties, white shirts and blue pants. A smile crept across her face as always when she thought of Sky, then her dad and imagined them there at the table.

"What is so amusing, Madolin?"

Oh God! How she wanted to say "It's not you who amuses me, Hopscotch. Hell no! You piss me off." But when it came to actually vocalizing the words she hit a blockade. Instead Mandolin turned to *Jacques* and hurled a zinger at him.

"If you grew up in Paris, I can't help wondering why you are studying '*Conversational French.*'"

Jacques developed a "dreadful" cough and glowered at Mandolin through bloodshot eyes. She had read that looks can kill, and his look could. She swung around in her seat, her glittery top separating from her jean skirt, grabbed at it, excused herself and raced to the exit. As she left, she heard Hopscotch announce to the group that her granddaughter was young and too shy to show them a scrapbook of her original dress designs. She was sure that all who looked them over at it were certain to find many treasures.

O-o-o kay! She was now sure Hopscotch was deliberately lying to impress others and this time by exploiting her granddaughter. But at the moment, her concern was her outfit. Her room! She had to get thee in a hurry.

The key! She reached inside her bosom where she had put it for safe-keeping. Holy Pig! It was gone.

At the front desk was a sign: *Back in ten minutes. Ten minutes before she could get another key.* Desperately gripping both sides of her skirt she remembered reading a verse by Confucius. "Pain makes man think; thinking makes man wise, and wisdom makes life tolerable." Tolerable? Crappito! How long was she supposed to tolerate *this* predicament?

The ladies room? Empty. The library? Empty, and for the few minutes while waiting for the attendant she escaped into it and picked up *The Hound* where she had left off. It was an exciting part. Sherlock was in Scotland Yard investigating a bank president whom he hoped to handcuff more than any criminal on his docket in years.

Inspired by new ways to be on the alert for Jackie Boy and to keep her hound-like pursuit on his multiple scents, Mandolin became engrossed...until she felt another tension release coming on. How about enlivening these boring dinners by asking how many sex positions each had enjoyed. Did she dare? No. Her dad would flip over in heaven if she did and then...and then. Oh no! Oh no!

Here came a revised Jacques, a man with a determined stride stemming from fury. He marched past her to the shelf, found both books he had returned earlier and discovered her. That did it! He dropped his accent and confronted her.

"You are far more trouble than your grandmother even knows! You seem to think you are some sort of a wormbook!"

Wormbook? Before she could ask, he shook a fist.

"If you think that a kid is going to ruin the relationship between Hopscotch and I, you're wrong, *dead* wrong. And I mean **dead** wrong, kid. You are playing around with fire! I'm taking both of these books, and leaving no proof that they were ever here. You are never to discuss either the books or this conversation. Get it?!

Mandolin only stared.

He moved into her face, "Do you understand me?"

Her nod came with difficulty.

"Remember! Not a word of this to *anyone*, or else."

"But may I have a word with you?"

"What is it?"

"I just wanted to tell you that I know one French word and it describes both of us. We both like to be *dishabille, n'est-ce pas?*"

"Ah may wee."

He appeared content and left the room. Yes! Mandolin was absolutely positive he was not French, but had taken a big chance by using a French word that meant undressed to check him out. It had worked, but what if he looked it up? Would he find out and come after her? She was terrified once again, then angry, and finally tears fell freely. What would Sherlock have done in her case? More importantly what would her dad have done?

One of his stories shot forward, the one when his boat was stolen. The police and a detective who found it stirred up her will to keep on point. She would not allow this miserable snip Jack or his machinations to detract from her efforts to apprehend him or from locating her mom.

The attendant had now returned to the desk, handed her a key and after dressing casually she returned to her search on the web for females named Mrs. James MacDuff, paid off. Yes! There it was—a marriage to James MacDuff in 1943 in Edinburgh! Along with it came a list of necessary info. From a routine exam, she knew her blood type was O. Finding her mom's DNA was more difficult although one site reminded her that interracial marriages were becoming quite common. Wow! This meant her mom could be as cool as Big Mama and Sky and…and all the rest. Yes!

Other sites were helpful, especially Neanderthal Man and one about genomes. She learned that millions of chromosomes and genes comprise humans, animals, and every single species in the world. But how could she find out more about her genetics without cooperation from her gramma, the only living relative she knew?

Wild thoughts played tag in her head. What made her think her Mom was Scottish when Mandolin knew she was born in Malaysia? A hunch and a wish. Years ago, at the Big Bad Mac, her dad had said that Scots had to stick together which pleased her since her skin and eyes were light like his. And besides, she *wanted* to be like him. He was a sailor, a traveler and would of course want to visit Scotland where she imagined that he fell in love with her Mom, a Scottish lass. That made sense. If only her grandfather were alive she was sure he would help. And then the horrendous possibility that her grandfather might be like Jacques or President John Kennedy hit her. Supposing he had other women in his life.

If only she could stop second guessing and settle her thoughts. From visits to Sky's church, she remembered that God made us all equal and had sent his son to prove his love for the world. Had God sent Mandolin to live with Hopscotch for some special reason as well? These questions rolled round and round in her brain like an empty Ferris wheel, as did the whereabouts of her Mom.

And then she lay in bed and made new plans. She would play nice, tactfully ask Hopscotch to share information about her mom, explain what attracted her to Jacques, and learn Sherlock's tactics for locating missing souls. She resolved not be intimidated by Jacques but to be clever, remain silent, keep her eyes on him and never allow herself to be alone with him.

Almost immediately, angels danced by, sheep leapt over rainbows and the angst of the day was alleviated.

4
London

WHEN THE SHIP APPROACHED Southampton, Mandolin fondly bid farewell to the crew and her new friends and then waited while Hopscotch packed and repacked. Memories of the past evening haunted her.

Where did this slime ball find the nerve to invite her, a fifteen year old to the discotheque and act as if all was well? When he said he wanted to have a little 'tit-a-tit' she was sure that was exactly the case. Yuck! It made her skin crawl. She wanted his explanation of *tête-à-tête*, which he pooh-poohed and when she asked him to describe a faux pas he answered "Fo Pa? You are too old to talk baby and quickly escaped.

What would happen in London? They were booked into a hotel near Harrod's, which became a favorite haven for them all. The variety of items sold there fascinated Mandolin particularly the display of honeys from all over the world and a continuous film on bees and bee-keeping. She learned how different flowers produce a variety of tastes and how to extract it from the hives. She so wished for her dad to share the fun.

In his honor, she paid fifteen dollars for a Loch Ness Noggin

Wrap which jazzed up her staid wardrobe. Stories about the Loch Ness monster intrigued her. Convincing her gramma to take her was another thing.

In Hyde Park at the Speakers Corner, Mandolin and THE BIG TWO joined many others who had gathered in the rain. Some had serious issues and Mandolin vented hers from under an umbrella.

"Can I learn about my mother without her full name or her DNA?"

"Come now, Madolin. We have no time for this."

A male voice spoke out. "Not-a tall, Mum. She comes from the United States and may not know we gather here to help one another."

Hopscotch noticed her flag pin for the first time. "Where did that come from?"

"A very nice man at your party gave it to me."

"Who?" she demanded.

A clock bonged twelve. "Is that Big Ben?"

Hopscotch was exasperated. "You can certainly learn the from that from the guide book without bothering us with these questions. Now tell me who gave you…"

"I was not trying to bother either of you, Hopscotch. Here we are in London, there's so much to see and learn that I thought *you* might help me."

Hopscotch's comment? "Each and every time I think you are maturing, you disappoint me."

Mandolin turned away, mouthed a hearty *sheet* and felt better.

The following day, their guide drove them to Piccadilly Circus. Hardly a circus, it was an entertainment and shopping paradise for Hopscotch and Jack. A roundabout for traffic fascinated her. It described Jack. Around and around he went, always ending up where Hopscotch beckoned. Charlie Chaplin came next. The guide explained that he was famous mime back in Hopscotch's day. Unconsciously, Mandolin imitated him which brought her applause and embarrassment.

Jacques spoke to Hopscotch "You said your husband was a mime, nest pass?"

Hopscotch shunned him. The news thrilled Mandolin. "Yes! If grampa acted crazy, then I take after him. Cool!"

"Come along, Madolin."

She wanted to stay longer because it gave her more ideas for her future life, but Hopscotch wanted Jack to see the art at the Tate Museum. Mandolin's artistic sense got a boost by an exhibit by Rousseau. It inspired her to cut more crazy animals out of colored tissue paper and then sell them to decorators for kids' rooms. Jacques found it it "trez magnifeeca."

The next day, Hopscotch determined that a guide was unnecessary and she would be their guide. Near Parliament they passed Whitehall, "a group of buildings inside the complex," Hopscotch explained, like an experienced, arrogant travel guide.

Mandolin was excited. "Scotland Yard is there just as in Sherlock Holmes stories. How odd they call it *Scotland* Yard when it's in London."

Hopscotch perked up once again and shared more of her knowledge. "When the Scottish kings visited British royalty, they were put up in this complex and thus it became Scotland Yard."

"Let's go there. And after that let's ride the London Eye. It's a perfect day for it."

"What on earth is the London Eye?"

Mandolin breathlessly explained it was the popular Ferris Wheel, 443 feet high with 32 seats in each of the 32 glass capsules and was on the Thames "and you can see—"

"Do you not understand that Jacques is anxious to visit the London Bridge?"

"Wee, wee. We like ze song." Jacques tuned up. "London Breedge is falling down, falling down...where did it fall, thees breedge?"

Mandolin found the angel of tongue-control was with her and, without a word followed the leader and joined a long queue for tickets on an old-style red double-decker bus. The sign read *free* for those 15-16, but when her tight-fisted gramma fussed unpleasantly to the attendant that although her granddaughter was not quite fifteen she should ride for free, it drew an argument which she eventually won.

At Marilyn Tussaud's Wax Works Jacques introduced himself to Marilyn Monroe and commented that Marilyn found herself too famous to speak. They passed Buckingham Palace, still occupied by the Queen, and when bored by too many cathedrals as "magnifeeca" as they were, Hopscotch led them off the bus. Mandolin asked to visit Stratford to see Shakespeare's birthplace. Hopscotch stared at her.

"Why do you want to go there, Madolin?"

"Because I have read almost all his plays and since you own so many books of plays, I was thinking that some of them might have been my dad's or my granddad's…or else come from my mom. If my granddad was a mime, chances are that some cared about the stage. Did they?"

Hopscotch sent daggers. "Your *father* liked many things, too many things, and we are not going to Stratford. You have had your way too many times… a trip to the Tate and Speaker's Corner. You simply must learn to think of others. "

Huh? *She* must think of others? Okay then. She was sure they all would enjoy following the route of Winnie the Pooh along the Thames River. Hopscotch made fists of both hands and shook them in her face. The battle of wits and wills continued and Mandolin ended up the underdog…again.

"We shall leave London tomorrow for Scotland, where I shall give dear Jacques a tour of God's Country, a land that escaped his viewing before he arrived in the States."

She took his hand and kissed it. "Thank God you came, my darling. You have given me relief from this child and enhanced my life immeasurably."

"And you mine, moan pet-it"

The next morning, Hopscotch was actually cheerful at a continental "breaky" of toast and orange marmalade. While Hopscotch checked to see if the tiny Ford Fiesta had arrived at their hotel, Jack had a riddle for Mandolin. "What deed the baby chick say when the rooster looked into ze nest?"

Mandolin loved word games; she had heard this one many times before, politely played dumb and asked the answer.

"Look at ze orange marmalade."

Jacques was enormously pleased when she asked him to explain it. "Aha! When I say marmalade, eet means 'mama laid. I repeat for you. 'Look at ze orange mama laid.'" Mandolin survived his proud and uproarious laugh and was not a bit sure she thanked her tongue angel this time. Tongues. The bible said to speak in tongues. Was did that mean?

5

Home Sweet Home for Hopscotch

At last they arrived in Scotland, Jacques was the designated driver and often forgot to stay on the left side of the road. There were no seatbelts in the rear and when his swerves threw her from one side to the other again and again, she was sure he meant to hurt her. The suspicion gathered credulity when she caught him with a grin in the rearview mirror.

"Watch out, Jacques, We're—"

"Madolin, please. My Jacques will protect us from all misfortune; will you not, my dearest?"

So Jacques the Bumbler, who reminded her of a pear-shaped fretted mandolin, would now be their shield and protector. Kaboom!

Hopscotch was in charge of their tour and seemed to enjoy herself, a surprisingly recurring event. She took pride in every part of her country and her enthusiasm for the Royal Edinburgh Tattoo was impressive. The event occurred every August and consisted of marching military bands from forty countries around the world. Review stands were set up in front of Edinburgh Castle a thrilling sight and venue for all ages.

"Never forget, both of you, that bagpipes stir men's souls" said Hopscotch with a warm smile and a sentimental glisten in her eye.

In their seats in the huge stadium, Hopscotch explained that those performing for Scotland are not given the choice of participating, and often called on to perform in only a few hours notice.

"This is Scotland at its finest and includes our hymns to God."

Mesmerized by the many regimental colors, drums and bagpipes, plus a spectacular fireworks display, Mandolin felt a patriotic spirit. But nevermore than at the end, when a lone piper stood high above the huge castle complex over the city and the Scottish War Memorial and played a hymn to Scotland's fallen heroes. Her eyes watered as she pictured her dad in his kilt. Amazing, she thought. Memories of her dad before five were few but this one had stuck as would the sound of taps at the end of this Spectacular. When the lonely echo rang high above the huge castle complex and over the city, she wept like a baby. How she wished for her dad, that he could have been there to show her see this part of her heritage.

The show was thrilling and as always, she hated endings of anything and did not want to leave. For the first time ever, she felt she belonged somewhere, and as they were leaving she decided to be bold and ask Hopscotch more about the name Tattoo. Mandolin was not sure what to expect but Hopscotch put her arm around her and explained.

"During the seventeenth and eighteenth centuries, a common saying in the inns around the country was "doe den tap toe" which meant 'turn off the (beer) taps.' The last two words sound like 'Tattoo' when said quickly by a true Scot. Thus, the word Tattoo took hold and has remained to this day."

They watched silently and happily together as the stands emptied.

"Doe den tap toe. Doe den tap toe." Mandolin thought it all was awesome, while Jack, relieved at last to be able to have his smoke, finally led them away. The more Mandolin knew this guy, the more trouble she had calling him Jacques. Jerk, Jock, or Jack were far more appropriate.

That night in her bed at the hotel, Mandolin replayed the events that had shaped her thinking. Asking questions gave her confidence. Issues with Hopscotch would always be prevalent, but at last she knew somewhere down deep inside there was a heart. As a result, she was now positive that a career in detective work and psychology was her destiny. Perhaps when Hopscotch and Jerk understood her goal they would be there for her? If he had feelings for her family, it was not evident, at least not yet. All she could do was hope for the best.

The next day, Hopscotch again insisted the mysterious Jacques wear the bowler she had bought him at Harrod's. "You must protect your handsome face from too much sun, my darling." In all honesty, Mandolin was convinced it was no gift but her method of improving his image among the highbrows. It proved to be the case. In Craigie's Village, a small elite area and their next stop, two teenagers passed. One pointed at him and they both giggled.

The threesome strolled through this village farm shop loaded with fresh veggies and milk products. Hopscotch was reminded of her family's farm on the Isle of Skye where she grew up. Mandolin begged to see it, was ignored but was blown away when she learned that Hopscotch had milked cows there as a child. Jerk's reaction blew her in another direction. He wanted a demonstration of teat-squeezing.

Mandolin turned away with disgust when Hopscotch removed two cucumbers from produce and demonstrated the art of teat-squeezing. Jock's suggestive remark to Hopscotch embarrassed her even more. At times she wondered who the adult was, and how Hopscotch could possibly overlook the ridiculous appearance of her man in the bowler in black socks and white tennis shoes and revealing striped boxer shorts.

At lunch in the café, the waiter was quite taken by Mandolin especially when she greeted him with a friendly "Hi."

"Hi back. You'r-re an all American gir-rl, rrrght?"

She rubbed her fingers over her pin. "I am. But my grandparents and maybe my mom were born here."

Mandolin adjusted her Loch Ness Noggin wrap. The waiter smiled.

"Looks good on ya, and since the bus tour is takin' you to Loch Ness, you'll find many other mementoes, as well."

"We're actually going there? Yes! This lake is miles long and 400 feet deep. Did you guys know that sightings of a snake-like monster in it trace back to 565 AD?"

Of course Hopscotch knew. She also assured them that *she* was their guide and would be driving wherever she chose. Mandolin thought it wise to take the opportunity to thank her for the trip. Her reply, "you are welcome" amazed her.

Her gramma ordered wine for herself and Jacques, and the waiter offered Mandolin haggis, the traditional dish of Scotland. Naturally she wanted it. She wanted to try everything and experience anything new and unusual. Even Jerk's disgusting gag did not deter her order. She chose a "bevy" (beverage) and her Hopscotch ordered scones for all..."awftah" they finished their wine. Crap! Enough please, of their shenanigans.

The service was slow, and it seemed even slower for Mandolin as she watched squaw Maw-Maw and her flunky drink their lunch. With each glass of red wine, Jack's 'stash grew redder and when they acted lovey-dovey, Mandolin left the table. On her way to the loo, she bumped into a guy and when he turned around she was elated. "Oh my God! Achilles! I can't believe it's really you!"

Hopscotch swung around. "Of course it's Achilles, Mandolin, Hi my darling. Come right over here and join us. How lovely to see you. Do you know my Jacques?"

She gave Jacques a quick glance, informed him of the long bond between her and Achilles and then threw a possessive arm around Achilles. "How's school, my darling? Oh silly me! I know you are in some sort of a universary, a university and..."

While Achilles shook Jack's' limp hand, he assured Hopscotch his life was great and asked to borrow Mandolin for a minute. Mandolin totally forgot the loo and was outa there in a second with Achilles' arm around her. She was ecstatic. Not so for Hopscotch who glared, obviously upset by the triumph of youth—especially Mandolin's.

"Jacques, Jacques! We simply cannot allow a young girl to go outside without a chaperone. Go get them and wearrr your hat, my darling, unless of course you wish to be one of us Brits. Rremember that old saying, "only mad dogs and Englishmen go out in the noonday sun.""

The marshmallow shrugged stupidly. The waiter served their drinks and assured them their customers were a health-conscious young crowd who hung together.

Hopscotch blew her irritation in his direction, never took her eyes off the action outside the window until Mandolin returned alone in high spirits. How could she help it? Achilles had asked her for a date and given her his number which she glued on her brain since neither had a pen. One look at her gramma's sour expression and she felt sad for her in a strange way. Only a few years had passed since *her* questions had been ignored. Was a pay-back a cure? Her response was considerate.

"Achilles reminded me that you rode horses to the hounds in your day."

"What do you mean in my day? I could still do it if I had a horse. Now tell me what else you and Achilles talked about."

The waiter was ready to take their lunch order and Hopscotch waved him away. "Did you hear my question, Madolin?"

"I did but first I need a pen. Does either of you have one?"

The waiter passed. Hopscotch hailed him. "Never mind, I'll ask the boy here."

A disgruntled, desperately curious Hopscotch watched while Mandolin jotted in her journal. Jack had a coughing fit and as she opened her mouth to speak, *the boy* politely urged them to make their order because others awaited the table. He suggested eating dinner near Loch Ness since drive through "the lush heatherr-covered Highlands. was a tr-r-eat." Mandolin returned the pen with thanks not only for the pen but for diverting a situation similar to the Spanish Inquisition. Hopscotch was forced to order rapidly and pulled out her glasses to study the menu so they could order and get the… outta there.

After a few minutes on the road with Jack behind the wheel, Hopscotch searched for her glasses to study the map. Back to the restaurant they went, "the boy" had her glasses and they continued their journey along the beautiful Firth of Forth. Mandolin was in high spirits due to Achilles' invite and felt frivolous. "Is this the first of fourth?" she asked Jacques.

"No, no," he answered. "Thees ees the fourth of August."

Mandolin was relentless and became sillier. "Are you thure? I thought it was the fifth of Thep-tember, cloath to my birthday."

He was clueless. And then she asked if he knew why all the cows faced north into the wind. Of course he knew.

"Eet keeps the hair out of their eyes, eh?" With a glance at Hopscotch for approval, he laughed like a hyena, drove them to the side over a bunch of rocks and bumped to a stop.

Jack remained motionless, as if to ignore the problem, flicked open an old Zippo lighter, filled his lungs with smoke and blew it out towards the back seat. Mandolin's shackles rose, she feigned a deep cough…a useless effort…and half-way out of the car, an old truck pulled up and Jacques took off to the bushes.

A man with a smiling face, a few wispy strands of red hair across his balding head and a piece of grass between his teeth, leaned out the window and asked with a sing-song Scottish brogue "Got a flat, do ya? Need some help?"

Mandolin opened her window. "My dad taught me pretty much about…"

"You'rre in luck, Miss. You got troubles rrright here in this ditch near my grandson's job. He tends sheep forr the landownerr here, got blessed with my name and so I'm K-one and he's K-two. I'll wave him down for ya and with a push from us all, we'll get you out of this fix quick as you can say supercalifragilisticexpialidocious."

Jacques reappeared pulling up his zipper and adjusting his hat. "Mercy. Mercy" said he.

K-one looked him over more carefully and chuckled. "A bowler in the sheep country? You're a funny one. Hats are big arround here. Bet you could make a worrrld of money if you started selling 'em and calling 'em Ma*hat*mas."

Jacques was lost. Mandolin giggled and oddly enough Hopscotch cracked a smile. K-one reassured them his grandson would be right back and floored his accelerator.

"You see, Jacques? This is Scotland. We are delightful and always ready to help."

Mandolin got goose bumps. Not only from being part of a bucolic scene unlike anything she had ever seen but from hearing a pleasant attitude from her gramma. She went over to hug her and Hopscotch screamed. "Ouch! Watch what you're doing! You put your dirty bare foot on my little toe."

Accustomed to her off-putting comments, Mandolin became capricious once again. "Doe den tap toe. Doe den tap toe. So-rry! Was it your pigeon toe upon which I tread?"

"I do not have pigeon toes."

"A shame. Then they must be hammerr toes. Or prrrehensile, perhaps?"

Jack confessed he knew nothing about *thees* kind of toe nor did he have the vaguest idea how to fix the flat tire.

"You have talented toes," Mandolin explained still trying to distract Hopscotch from her toe. "And Jacques, I'll bet I can teach you to pick up a pencil or perhaps one of your cigarettes with your toes."

Sure she was acting ridiculously, but K-one had set her off. Hopscotch frowned and Mandolin kept her conversational edge." I'm confused by your reaction, Hopscotch. You said this was Scotland where you have fun. I was having a blast."

This time Hopscotch did not pursue it. "Very well. But we will save more merriment until the repairs are made and we are underway."

Merriment. At least Hopscotch knew what it was.

Hopscotch grabbed on to Jacques and they walked down the road where he lifted her on to a fence and strained his back. It was clear that No-Jack Jack had come up with a clever excuse to leave Mandolin in charge of repairs in the mud. Unfazed, she proudly jacked up the car. Her dad had taught her how.

How could her grandmother have a son like her dad and fail to see beyond the facade of the phony pursuing her? Enough please of running her hands though his thick hair, overdosing him with praise for his 'virile physique,' and pretending that his bloodshot eyes were "as blue as deep still waters." How could she not see that his accent was *manufractured,* that his clothes recked of cigarette smoke, that his dumb jokes were sick and all for her benefit?

The minute K-one returned in his truck, Hopscotch helped Jack limp back to the ditch where K2, a wiry redheaded youth about Mandolin's age waved his sheep through a gate. Jacques called to him. "*Gar-kon! Gar-kon!* Are you leetle Bo Beep's brother?"

And then a strange sound, like a car sputtering out of gas caught her attention. It was Jacques laughing at his own joke.

Mandolin's strong aversion to mispronunciations, inspired by Miss Hughes, attacked her apollonian nature. "Excuse me a minute, Jacques. According to my French dictionary the word for boy is pronounced garçon with a soft c. Is that what...?"

A cigarette cough that had obviously taken years to develop continued uncontrollably for a few minutes, a handy cover-up Mandolin thought, for these truthful situations.

K-one was concerned. "Aha! A few more days in our frresh air and your cough will be...What's your name?"

My name? Eet ees Jacques like I said."

"I mean your full name. Jacques what?"

"You want my *fool* name?"

Kevin was confused and laughed. "Ah, you are *indeed* a funny one."

Hopscotch spoke up. "He wants your last name, my darling."

"*From*-age. My name is Jacques, Jacques *From*age like the sign on the road," was his response.

"*From*-age? You mean like the French word for cheese, fro-**mage?**" Kevin asked.

Kevin arched his brows and turned towards his grandson. "Meet K-two with whom I am well-pleased. He has wisely been payin' attention to me all these years so's to learn to shepherrd his sheep same as our Lorrd Jesus did in his day."

Jack blew his sick humor into the conversation. "Jesus ees like ze sheep! He tries to pull ze wool over your eyes." Once again he laughed heartily…and then wheezed alone like a *Jacques*-ass thought Mandolin until she spoke up.

"Hi. We're obviously tourists just like you said, and thanks K-two, for getting here faster than we could say superfragil…super…"

Kevin-two had had experiences with *supercallifragillisticexpialidocious.* "That's grandpa's description of almost everything that suits him."

With Mandolin's help, K2 slipped the tire into place and rubbed his hands together. "Good job there, gir-r-l." And with that he hopped up on a post and rail fence, walked along it and challenged her.

She took the bait and they amused one another. "You got good balance there girl."

Mandolin reacted happily to each and every compliment and yet had still never learned to express her appreciation. Nervously she jumped down, flipped out her yo-yo and performed the complicated *brain twister.* Jack had another cigarette while both Kevins watched the yo-yo respond perfectly to Mandolin's wrist action.

"Say, we could use you around here. You're a kick and a half. Was pretty good in my day. I'm rememberrin' you hook the loop around your third finger and spin it out all the way like this." K-one was pleased with himself and handed it to K-two who caught on fast.

Grampa rambled on. "Bet you don't know the yo-yo is the oldest toy second only to the doll. Or that the astronauts took one to outer space. And here's another true fact f'rr ya. *In the Philippines they used sharp-edged metal yo-yos as weapons.* Now y'rr smart as me."

"Thanks for telling us. My dad was smart too and I was supposed to look up the history and tell him."

K-two did a loop behind his back and brought it forward perfectly.

"Holy Pig!" said Mandolin.

K-two smiled "Hey grampa, we'll have to tell my boss about that expression."

"Good idea, boy." He turned to the group and explained that his boss was trying to promote pig farming in Scotland.

K-two was entranced with the yo-yo. Mandolin noticed "I'd like to give it to you but—"

Hopscotch reacted. "What? *Give* it to him? Why? I gave that to *you* years ago."

"Excuse me. My granddad gave this to my dad and he saved it for me. I haven't inherited much and I treasure this because it came from him."

K-two returned the yo-yo. Then came that grating voice. "What are you saying, child? Your grrrandfather would never have played with a yo-yo. Such a foolish toy."

Jacky boy blew a long stream of smoke in Mandolin's face. "Mon Do. Such a foolish toy, only for ze simple-minded."

"If it's so simple, why don't you have a try, Jock?' suggested Mandolin.

"Pay no attention to her, my darling. We must be on our way. This summer sun is positively ruining our skin. Put on your hat and let's say goodbye."

K2 aimed his camera. "Now let's see a smile. Everyone say cider-r."

He admired the results. This is good! I'll send you a copy if you give me your e-mail."

They exchanged e-mails.

"God speed to ya all," said K-Two. "Gotta look after my friends here, or I'll be in a bit of trouble, eh grampa?" He slapped a sheep on its rump and shooed the rest across the lonely road.

Hopscotch looked across the field and pointed. "Before we leave would someone be pleased to explain zis new method of bundling ze hay. I've never seen it before."

Jerk jumped right in with his usual authoritative and stupid answer.

"You do not understand zees, my love? Helicopters drop ze hay bales on to ze fields so ze cows have enough food to make plent-ee of milk."

Mandolin broke up laughing, another reminder that Jacques was un fou or whatever the French call la-la land. Hopscotch looked at Jack quizzically and then quickly raised her chins high. "Come along Jacques and Madolin. *Tout suite.*"

Mandolin had a question. "I understand the Rosslyn Chapel is beautiful."

This from Hopscotch. "Of course it is. I was married there."

"Tis a lovely churrch indeed," said Kevin one. "They've been thinkin' of closing it one day a week and if it's today you tell the guarrrd, a frriend of mine that you met a plonked old git named Kevin and he'll let you pass."

"You're the greatest, you two. Ta, K-one. And Ta-ta, K-two, for *everything.*"

"Good on you. It's clear enoof that you be *diggin' our lingo* here."

"And here's a snog for you." Mandolin blew two kisses to the Kevins, climbed into the back seat behind driver Jacques and signaled a thumbs up through the rear window. Kevin One scratched his head as if to ask what exactly had blown in and so quickly gone with the wind!

Gone with the Wind. Maybe Mandolin had something in common with Margaret Mitchell, more than just their initials. Marilyn Monroe had them too and the thought of any similarity there caused a quiet snicker in the back seat. For many miles of silent hours, she mulled over the events of her life and concluded that maybe her own story could catch on. She had lived south of the border, not during a war but had suffered in a mansion she called Terror, with a horsewoman as egocentric as Scarlett. Mandolin would make up a happy ending to her story.

Restlessness was taking over her body as well as thoughts of Achilles. Constant checks for his call proved fruitless. The French dictionary then became her focus until she heard her own voice.

"Hey, Jacques. What's a province in France?"

"Province? You mean to say providence, ma cherry."

"No I don't. I…"

Hopscotch frowned. "Please let us alone."

"Okay, but you're right, Hopscotch. The Scots are fun like my dad, and—and you too when you—when you feel good."

Her silence was deafening. And then worry took charge again. Where was her mom? Would Achilles call her?

"Do universities in Scotland have women professors, Hopscotch?"

"A ridiculous question."

"No it's not. I'm sure my dad married a smart woman, and it's possible she could be a professor there."

A sneer from Hopscotch. "Do you really believe your mother could be a professor?"

Mandolin took a deep breath, clenched her fists, ready to slug her when Hopscotch went on.

"Oh my, Mandolin, You are proving to be more uncouth and ignorant than I dreamed. Now be quiet. Jacques and I need to figure out where our next stop shall be."

"Rosslyn Chapel, for sure, right?

Jacques frowned. "You want we go to another church, *ma cherie*?"

"Not if you don't want to, my precious darling."

"Please Hopscotch, I would so love to see where you and grampa got married."

"You want, and want, and want more. Please be quiet, read your Harry Sorcerer book."

Mandolin never spoke again while finishing *Harry Potter and the Sorcerer's Stone*. When they pulled into the Rosslyn Chapel complex, relief from Hopscotch's strident voice ended,

"You have fifteen minutes Madolin, and that's all."

"Twenty?"

"Fifteen."

"Eighteen?"

Jacques smiled. "You sound like your grand mare, exactamont."

Hopscotch shot Jack a stern, paralyzing look to silence him. "Thirteen and that's final."

Mandolin quickly hopped out, convinced the ticket taker that she was writing a school paper on the history of the chapel and then let her in for free. She joined a group of tourists headed to the North Wall and entered the Chapel. The stone pillars and elaborate carvings and figurines told biblical stories that intrigued her. She had imagined it well from all of her reading, and knew that the Chapel was begun in 1446, forty-six years before Columbus discovered America, but the stones carvings everywhere amazed her.

All kinds of historical figures were represented and brought

Christianity to life. Mandolin quickly darted down the unguarded stairs below the main Chapel floor. Oh...my...God! Goosebumps broke out again when suddenly she remembered her curfew. Oh, how she wanted to see more!

Back at the car, the lovebirds had been doing whatever they did and she climbed in, breathless with excitement.

"Sorry. You won't believe all I did in just fourteen minutes. Biblical stories were everywhere—I saw angels with musical instruments, Samson destroying the Philistines, David killing the lion and..."

The hairy one spoke. "Mon do! Mon do! All that action, it happens in there?"

Mandolin was too excited to comment on his ignorance, and excited by the many fleurs-de-lis designs she had seen all around inside. She decided to use a detective skill on Jacques. "What is the name of the famous flower of France? I...I sort of forget."

"Flower? Flower? I do not know flowers. That ees a ladeez thing."

Mandolin was not surprised. She noticed a puzzled glance from Hopscotch aimed at her Jock and continued to describe her adventure "The chapel dates back to September the twenty first, 1446."

"Of course. Your fatherr was borrn on that day."

"No. He was born on September fourth. I remember because he came home for his birthday and to register me in school the next day. But then he was called away on business."

Jacques' comment was biting.

"Aha! We call that monkey beezness."

"What do you mean by that, Jacques?" asked Mandolin.

He proceeded to laugh like a mad man. Mandolin wanted to rip him apart. He knew nothing about the good person her dad was. Hopscotch nudged Jacques to get going. He could not find the key. "I theenk I gave theees key to you, my pet-it."

"The key to me? I think not, my darrling. You are the drriver."

He searched his pockets and the floor in vain. "Een your purse poo-tater?"

Poo-tater? Was he trying to say, *peut-etre*, the French for perhaps?

Hopscotch looked in her purse. No key. They bickered back and forth until it showed up on the seat between them "You see, Madolin, you see? If you hadn't made us stop here, we…"

Jerk could not fit the key into the slot. With disgust, Mandolin reached over the seat, asked for the key, discovered it was the wrong one, leaned way over to the ignition and slipped the right one in. This was a *dejas vu* except a miserable experience this time and not the sensation of her first one a few years ago.

During the next leg of the trip Mandolin worked on a new plan. She would invent a hyberspace connection called The Bee. It would somehow make a buzz when something was lost and lead the frustrated subscribers to the proper location. Yes! It would take time, but she could help all those who became bewildered by temporarily missing items and then be considered more than normal. She would be extraordinary.

6

A Welcome Fire

A GRIM SILENCE PREVAILED until they stopped at a vine-covered "Bed and Breakfast", a favorite of Hopscotch's many years ago. The elder two quickly retired for a late afternoon nap. Mandolin made another plan. A crackling fire in a large stone hearth drew her toward as it would any slim, cold-blooded gal on a bitter day. While warming her backside, she opened her backpack and studied her journal stuffed with mementoes. Then facing the fire she took further notes and wrote picture postcards to Sky, Big Mama and Heather. They were ready to go. So was she. The fire had worked its wonders and she posted the cards at the front desk and then checked her cell. Nothing. Crap! Had Achilles led her on?

Laughter from the bar caught her attention. With a jutted chin and erect posture she ventured forth into a pub alone for a first time ever experience. A bearded gent holding a beer mug beckoned her over and delivered another new treat...a lesson in the art of beer drinking. "You gotta start by blowing off the foam or else you get a white moustache."

She found foam just as he said.

"You're from the States, right?" He chug-a lugged his beer and ordered another.

"How did you know?"

"I'm from Canada and get around the world, my dear. Plus that pin you're wearing clued me in."

Mandolin felt the pin with fond memories.

"Cute as you are I bet you have lots of boyfriends."

"Only one and he's not actually my boyfriend. I'm not quite fifteen yet."

"Is that right? You're rather classy already."

"Are you teasing? My dad told me to make sure people are sincere. Are you?"

"I am, I am, I am. And so are you. You talk easily with people. Where are your parents?"

Mandolin bit her lip. "I'm with my...my gramma and her...her *boyfriend.*"

He raised his empty mug towards the bartender. She did the same while he picked up a pack of cards from the bar and began to hiccup.

"Did you know the Queens (*hic*) in the deck of cards are named after famous female figures...all from mythology and actual history?"

"No, but tell me more. I love to learn."

Her beer arrived, she took a sip and the foam went up her nose. Mr. Shaggy Beard set her straight with a hearty laugh intermingled with hiccups. He thought she was cuter and cuter and continued to pick out the kings from the deck of cards.

"Now look here, the king of spades is (*hic*) David, the king of Clubs represents Alexander the Great, the king of hearts is Charlemagne and Julius Caesar is pictured as the king of diamonds. He's the best."

"Why? Because you like diamonds?"

"My wife does, but I have another reason. Caesar was (*hic*) a man big enough to conquer Cleopatra's heart."

"How do you know so much?"

"Not near as much as Speedy, the bartender here. Well, I gotta be on my way. My wife's expecting me to take her to (*hic*) The Mucky Duck tonight, her favorite pub."

"Hold on, I know how to stop hiccups," she offered. "While you hold your breath, I'll push under your ribcage and opposite it in your back. Ready?"

"Ready." He took a deep breath. She pushed. He was ticklish, and let his breath go.

"How are the hiccups?"

He waited. "Gone! I like you, my dear. My wife gets uppity and on my case when I'm *oot* and *aboot,* and you just rescued me from a lot of lip." He blew her a kiss and waved at Speedy.

"Put her next drink on my tab and tell her to watch her Ps and Qs," and away he dashed.

Speedy spoke. "In the states they ask for you ID but judgin' the look of ya I'd say you pass the test."

Mandolin didn't argue, instead asked about "Ps and Qs?"

Speedy served Mandolin a beer while he explained what he knew. Apparently back in the old days, sometimes letters like ps and qs were jumbled on the printing presses. From there Ps and Qs took off to the pubs where people brought in their own pints and quarts and kept 'em in lockers. On occasion, well, they got "a bit blootered, they did, and us bartenders would warn 'em to watch their Ps and Qs."

Mandolin loved the story and her beer as well as a dart board that attracted her competitive spirit. Out of three tries, the bull's eye took only one hit. "Why is it called a bull's eye and not a cow's eye or a pig's eye?" she asked a man at the bar.

"These Scottish bulls, they got wanderin' eyes which makes 'em bigger, I suppose."

Others around the bar chuckled. Mandolin didn't get it.

"Hi Speedy. I'm Mandolin and you seem to know everything."

"Aye, a bartender can be learnin' a pack of trivia if he listens."

"Then maybe I'll be a bartender."

"It might not be your highest callin' Miss," said Speedy with a grin.

"I like history and trivia as well." Following a large swallow of beer, she asked why a drink was named *Bloody Mary?*"

"Easy. It's made of tomato juice, vodka, a squirt of lemon and spiced up with Tabasco…to match temper of the hot-blooded queen."

"Wowzy! It sounds de*lish* and devilish."

"'Tis Miss. A Virgin Mary would suit you better. No vodka in it."

"Can I at least sip a Bloody Mary?"

"I'm a gambler, I am I am." He pulled a shiny tuppence from his pocket and tossed it in the air. "Heads I win and tails you lose. Got it?"

"Heads."

"Aw. Too bad. I win. But y'r a good sport you are, so 'ave a look at the copper tuppence minted only a few years ago while I pourr you a'alf a beerr. "

Mandolin was examining it when a refined looking couple sat beside her. He ordered two bloody Marys, and by the man's accent she knew they were not Scottish.

While Speedy mixed their drinks, he continued his dialogue with Mandolin "The rampant lion on the tuppence represents Scotland, so I'm told."

"According to my gramma, I'm really rampant." She handed the coin back to Speedy who wanted her to keep it.

She was touched and watched Speedy pull on the tap and pour. "'Ere you go, luv, a bit more to see how you well you hold it. Wipe the foam off the top firrst."

"May I ask you something?"

"Ask away. The answers will prob'ly be worth what you pay f'r 'em. Nothin'"

"I doubt that. You guys over here are brilliant and I'm crazy about intelli*gents* spelled g-e-n-t-s, and intelli-ladies too. Have you ever heard of a family named MacDuff?"

"Sure it's common around here and if you're wantin' to hear what MacDuff said in Macbeth, I am your man. Was a Shakespearean actor myself for awhile, a bloody bad one but I got all the lines from the play right up here in me noggin."

"Tell me some of them. My last name is MacDuff." She gulped her beer.

"Okay then, I'll start when a thane opens the gate. Enter MacDuff."

"Excuse me. What's a thane?"

"A thane is a nobleman of low rank who held lands in rreturn for military service to a lord."

"Go on, I'll ask more questions later."

"'MacDuff speaks: 'Was it so late, friend ere you went to bed that you do lie so late?'

"The Porter speaks: 'Drink, sir, is a great provoker of many things.'

Mandolin drank, inciting and exciting her curiosity as well as her balance.

"MacDuff: 'What things does drink especially provoke?"

"Porter: 'Marry sir, nose-painting, sleep, and urine. Lechery, sir, it provokes, and unprovokes..."Sorry 'bout the language, Miss. Forrgot we in the company of ladies tonight."

"No problem. I'd like to have my nose painted like Pinocchio, Cyrano and...preferably Mandolino. Holy Pig, what am I saying? We were talking about MacDuff."

"And somethin' else as well. Remember back when I flipped the sixpence – heads I win, tails you lose? Think about it."

She spun around on her stool. "Wheee! Silly me. I guess you win either way."

She sipped her drink, aimed three darts at the bull with the wandering eye, missed all three and almost slipped off stool. Ouch! She sat up, pulled in her tummy, and pulled her sweater tightly over her bosoms. "Do you like me?"

"Indeed, Miss. You got more razzle-dazzle than we seen around these parts f'r some time."

Mandolin was inspired, swiveled her hips and sang "'*Taint what you do it's the way that you do it, that what it's all about, hey!*

Speedy laughed, "what you doin' here in our neck of the woods anyways?"

Mandolin shrugged, wanted another beer. "Hopscotch is…is… never mind. I'm trying to find my mom or at least all I can learn about her."

""Scuse me, Miss. Gotta check on my other customers. And I think we better start watchin y'rr Ps and Qs."

He took care of the couple beside her. Speedy called her Hildegard and the man Theodore. Their conversation made no sense although they were having a good time and Hildegard fascinated her for a moment until a fish in a bowl intrigued her more. Mandolin took another sip and shared a few words with it. "Hi little fishy. You look so lonesome and sad. It's no fun that way—no fun a-tall. Is it?"

She poured a few drops of her beer into the bowl. "There. Now you can be happy." After another gulp of beer, she emptied the rest into the fishbowl.

"What's wrong with me? How could I be so cruel to a poor little fishy? Crap!"

Her eyes shifted to heaven. "Sorry Dad. Sorry Sky. Sorry fish. I guess…I guess I'm kinda swacked." And then with her head bobbing, she continued "my apologies to you Mister or Mrs. Fish." Then she asked Speedy if he could tell the sex of a fish. You see I'm very, very, *very* interested in sex."

"Betcha haven't eaten," said Speedy." Here, have some fish 'n chips, on the house."

"On the house, under the house, where is the house? Where is *hakka bakka*?" Her head wobbled around and around. "This bar is getting really really hazy…Say, do you like Picasso?"

"Never met him."

"Me neither." Mandolin laughed in her tipsy state. "Picasso and I appleciate…appreciate that art is an abomination of a…I mean this is very very impotent…I mean important. Art is an elimination of the unnecessary. Picasso and I adore deep melancholy blues—like the satiny neck of a blackbird cross-crissed with—whoa–ooo eee! I feel happy, so happy, loose as a goose, but you know what? It's all kind of weird and blue, out there. She waved her arms as if trying to latch on. Am I crazy?…maybe a little sick… maybe I better go to my room, but guess what? I don't know where it is. Can you fathom that?" and she giggled.

With empathy, Theodore escorted her out. "I hear you've had a long trip today, young lady. We'll find your room and you can rest up."

He took her arm. She looked into his eyes.

"You know what else? You have the most gorgeous crossed eyes I have ever ever seen. They remind me of my dad's but his weren't…I want you to be my best friend in the whole wide world forever and ever. Amen. Okay?"

"I should like that very very very much." He guided her to the front desk.

7
And the Curtain Goes Up

Tintinnabulation woke her. As long as she lived, the sound of bells would remind her of her dad. She sat up, a bad idea. Whoa! Her head was pounding. Back it fell onto another strange pillow until a knock on the door annoyed her. She pulled up from under the sheets, sweating. Rain was striking a tin roof or at least it sounded like that...loud, too loud. Another knock. She realized she was still in the same clothes from the day before...her coat, tartan skirt, a pair of leather boots and a long knotted scarf. Phew! It was so hot and she thought of the day she bought it. It was a morning when Jack and Hopscotch were doing their thing and she looked for bargains around Harrod's. They say you get what you pay for and wow! She hit the jackpot with this purchase. She'd never be cold again.

Another knock "Who is it?" Her voice was strained and raspy. She threw off her coat and boots.

A male voice answered. "'Ave a message f'r you Miss. Y'r grandmum says to tell ya to make y'r own plans around here today. Her and Mr. Fromage are chiffed to bits about the rain and decided to stay in."

She thanked him, resolved to tip him later, fell back onto the bed. They may be chiffed about the rain, but Mandolin was more than glad to spend a day on her own—possibly in bed the entire day or at least until her head improved. A deck of cards on the bed confused her and she tried to play solitaire as she often did when sick or alone… to no avail.

Sometime later, she found her way down the hall to the loo, opened the door and under a stall, saw the pants of a man around his ankles. Horrified, she backed out, checked the door. "Dames and Gents." A full bladder, a very full bladder kept her pacing up and down the hall until an elderly man finally emerged, thank God.

Once again in her room, a cool drink of water from a pitcher helped quench a mighty thirst and she reentered the world of the living, yet still hot and bothered by a serious headache. Chopping it off altogether was a thought. Slowly the memories of the evening returned…a bar, hiccups, a bearded man, a dartboard, a fish and an unexplained painful shoulder. A hangover? Was that what she had?

Air! She needed air! She twisted the handle to open the window, rubbed her sore shoulder again and wondered how she had hurt it. She sank into a chair, checked her cell and threw it on the bed. Hell! Look at me!! I don't deserve him. She fell asleep. Laughter in the hallway woke her. Yes! It would be a good day. She would make it happen. A look at Pink Oink Almost five. Food! Definitely!

Another shower sent her in search of a place to eat, When she passed the bar, it was empty and she continued on. Then a man popped up from below the bar and called to her. He looked somewhat familiar.

"Been hopin' to see you again, Miss. Remember me from last night? I'm Speedy. 'Ow's the head today?"

"Oh my gosh, Speedy. I must have made a real mess of myself. My head is not mine and my stomach is growling. Do you serve treacle here?"

"Sure. We also have Spotted Dick."

Mandolin shrank with embarrassment. "Spotted Dick?"

"You got it, Miss. Treacle and Spotted Dick are panaceas."

She was relieved. "Oh. When I was little, I learned panacea and tintinnabulation the same day. Just thinking about that day makes me...I often wonder what we're supposed to learn from tragedies."

"Only the good Lord knows."

She looks heavenward. "Say up there, I've asked for your help before, it's time to ease up."

Speedy shook his head in amazement. "I got a feelin' that God made you special for a reason. Whatever happened to you, made you more curious than most. Some who sit up here and chat with me are full of fluff and hot air."

She giggled. "Thanks, but I don't understand why it's so hard to find the place you belong."

"Tickety boo, Miss. Can't say I belong behind a bar serving drinks meself, but meetin' you is lovely. Now how about some haggis? That's a specialty around here."

"I know. I had it a few days ago. I'd like to give the recipe to Heather, our cook. She's my good friend back home."

"Y'r welcome to it, but firrst some fish and chips should fix you up quick as a wink...so saith Shakespearre."

"Fish? Did I kill a fish?"

"You rrremember that, eh?"

"I hope tickety boo means he's okay because if so, I'll use the expression from now on."

"You got it, Miss. I changed the poor little fella's water and he's good today."

"Thanks. There's an unusual garden out back. Would it be okay to take a dish of haggis outside there and sit under the gazebo? I need some fresh air."

"Comin' right up, Miss."

After many deep breaths, a fresh breeze blowing a few drops of cool rain on her face, her head cleared and her outlook started to brighten. In addition, laughter from the bar attracted her and she hesitantly peeked in to see what was going on. A woman, probably the most beautiful woman she had ever seen shook her up. No star in the movies or on any TV personality had made such an impression.

The more she watched this woman and her graceful gestures, the less able she was to leave the scene. Mandolin imagined herself with clear white skin, sparkling eyes, and straight, silky blond hair that hung neatly around her face. She liked the way she took tiny sips of a drink that looked like orange juice. She didn't chug-a-lug or stick her nose down into the glass. A couple of delicate manicured fingers held the glass and it seemed to float in her hand. Mandolin was watching a *lady*.

And then she gasped. The lady's husband was speaking to Hopscotch and Jacques. Mandolin turned aside and listened again to the lady's soft mellifluous voice. She had heard this voice somewhere. Where? Oh my Gosh. She dragged her thoughts through the cauldron of the night before. Bubbles. Foamy bubbles and lots of troubles… She was remembering it now. It was Hildegard with her husband Theodore who joined her at the bar.

Mandolin held her head in shame and eavesdropped. "Theodore says I am a Gemini through and through. How about you, Jacques? What sign are you?"

"Moi? In Paree we pay leetle attention to gastronomy. I can only say me and m'lady here are about to eat dinner."

"We *are*?" asked Hopscotch sitting unsteadily on the edge of her chair. "Maybe you are." Her eyes wandered around the room and landed on Mandolin.

"I see you over there, Madolin. Nothing escapes me as I have told you overr and overr. Now take your little book back to your room at once! A child does not belong in…where are we…oh…a barr."

Help! She was caught between Hopscotch and the night before. What must Theodore and Hildegard be thinking? Mandolin had had lit up the bar with more than "a skin full", and now here was her gramma flopping around. Theodore quickly sized up the scene and came to Mandolin's rescue.

"Good to see you again, Mandolin. You're a nifty gal."

Nifty? There was that word again. Was she nifty or numpty?

Theodore continued. "I see you've picked up *Cloudspliiter*."

"Yes. I love to read and the title interested me." She quoted as best she could:

"I wandered lonely like a cloud
"That floats on high o'er dales and hills…"

Theodore added

"'When all at once I saw a crowd.
"A host of golden daffodils.'" William Wordsworth was a famous British poet which I'm sure you know."

"Wordsworth? What a cool name for a poet."

She opened *Cloudspliiter* and Theodore synopsized the story. It was a fictionalized account of anti-slavery activist John Brown who helped spark the Civil War with his attack on Harper's Ferry in 1859.

Mandolin clapped her hands. "I can't wait to read it."

"You and I have much in common, young lady."

What a gentleman, thought Mandolin, so like Sky. He always made the other guy feel good. How she missed him!

"Yes sir." Mandolin quickly responded. "Did I tell you that I was able to take an unguided walk through Rosslyn Chapel yesterday?"

"Ah, the Chapel. An impressive treasure of history."

"What impressed *you* the most, sir?"

"Last evening you called me Theodore and I hope you will again. Now to answer your question, the structure of the building in the shape of a cross was inspiring. Did you by chance see the inscription on the Apprentice Pillar from the apocryphal book of Esdras?"

Mandolin had not.

"It goes like this: 'Wine is strong, a king is stronger, and women are stronger still. But truth conquers all.'

"Shoot! I missed it. Thanks for telling me. My dad was big on truth. He could tell the minute I even began to think a lie."

"Ah, a father who understands what matters…and should to us all."

Mandolin turned to Hildegard and tried not to stare, then she caught herself bowing and tongue-tied.

Hildegard rescued her this time. "You are on you way to a great future, dearie. Your intelligence is impressive."

Mandolin was sure she was talking to two gifts from God, watched her own tears drop with embarrassment. And yet they kept coming like when she helped Heather cut up onions. But these tears were different. There was no onion in sight.

"You often mentioned your father last night with great affection. Could we hear more about him?" Theodore asked sympathetically.

Something new was definitely happening and she found the words with a struggle.

"No…no one has ever asked me that before. My dad took me all over when he could, taught me about *hakka bakka*… and then…"

"What is *hakka bakka*?" Theodore and Hildegard asked simultaneously.

Mandolin was thrilled to explain what *she* knew for a change. "It's the greatest. Like you can watch Kishore Kumar, once a popular Hindi comedian enter a room full of bored people, clown around and turn strangers into friends. You see, he sought his comfort zone or his *hakka bakka* and found it. Finding *hakka bakka* and then spreading its meaning has become my goal. But I've a long way to go."

Hildegard smiled at Theodore. "I am familiar with that look from my dear wife. She thinks I need to take more time away from work and open up to *hakka bakka* myself, right love?"

"Not at all, sweetheart. When I met you I knew we were where we belonged."

Suddenly she turned to him with a wink "Holy Pig! Remember

that client you represented in Jakarta? Wasn't Kishore the name of the entertainer we saw there?"

Mandolin was stunned and listened carefully to Theodore's comment. "How in the world did you ever remember that?"

"Because it's the first time you ever kissed me in public."

Theodore grinned quickly and gave her a peck on the cheek. "So let's hear it for Kishore, *hakka bakka* and Mandolin."

He and Mandolin high-fived, then to Hildegard he said softly "what would I do without you?"

"Excuse me, but that's just what my dad used to say to me." Mandolin turned to Hildegard. "I can't believe *you* actually said 'Holy Pig.'"

"I learned it from you, sweetie. It's an…an awesome expression."

After a few seconds of silence, Hildegard put her arm around Mandolin.

"My heart goes out to you, Mandolin. From what I can gather, your dad gave you a great deal of confidence. Never lose it."

In spite of Hopscotch, she *would* find it again with the help of the good people she had already met on this trip. She took Hildegard's hand. "Do you know if Napier University hires women professors?"

Theodore answered. "Several years ago, a woman became the first president ever of a University in Scotland. It was quite an event. And to answer your question, I have little doubt that Napier now hires women professors. Are you looking for someone in particular?"

"Mandolin nodded. "My mom, but it's just a hunch."

From down the row of bar stools came that voice. "Madolin! Madolin. Are you shtill talking about Achilles?"

"Ah, Achilles! The man with the bad heel. He is amazeeing how he gets all over Europe weeth it."

Hildegard looked Mandolin in the eye. "Keep your chin up."

Mandolin covered her eyes and her body shook briefly. Love. She felt loved again. She imagined this couple as her own mom and dad and began to feel that she wasn't stupid after all. She smiled and put her head against Hildegard's shoulder.

"I assume you were very young when you were separated from your parents."

Mandolin gritted her teeth and nodded. Hopscotch fell off her stool, landed in Jacques' arms and they laughed crazily. He then took her arm and walked her around the bar area. She yelled at Hildegard. "You're a lucky one you are, Hildy baby. You and Theodorable can get up and go places without being shaddled with a granddaughter."

Mandolin hung her head. Theodore caused it to rise when he asked if she read Mark Twain.

"Almost everything he wrote."

"There's a great slogan by him that could be helpful to any young woman embarking on a career."

His message affected her. He's talking about me. A career...like an adult. I'll be embarking on a career soon. Yes!

"Please tell me what Mark Twain said."

"'Make your vacation your vocation' was one of my favorites.'"

"How do I do that?"

"Just as I do. I love my work and take my wife wherever I go. She enhances my vacation while I work on my vocation."

"Which is?"

"Investigation. But we all need to leave room for error, especially when we are young. By that, I mean if you find you've made a mistake, be ready to change direction. For example, I started out as a tennis instructor and then switched to a golf instructor and when one of my students was sued, I became interested in law-related activities."

"I like art a lot and read where Van Gogh reached the top even though he was faced with a life of strife."

"Da Vinci as well. He was born out of wedlock grew up more or less alone. Look at his fame."

"Da Vinci was born out of wedlock?"

"Yes. Did I shock you?"

Mandolin could not speak. Out of wedlock. Out of wedlock! In recent years, she had not only learned its meaning, but suspected that she had been as well. Why? Because a conversation in the car with her dad long ago had bothered her.

"So we're happy, but you have a strange look, Dad."

He bit his lip. "Years ago I—I had a—a friend who collected old movies and videos."

"A girl-friend?"

He looked at her, unsure."

And then mesmerized by the moment; another thought struck hard. If a person is born out of wedlock, there is no reason he or she can't rise to the top like Da Vinci. Yes! It was just possible that she could be another sensation like Leonardo. If not that capable, the idea boosted her self-confidence. It was okay. She was okay. Was it her dad and mom's actions that bothered her gramma?

Only the lovely voice of Hildegard could have brought her away from these calculations "Theodore was enjoying you last night until a phone call from Washington called him away."

Mandolin remembered none of this. "I hope it was tickety boo for him."

At that moment, Mandolin was not bothered by the belligerent Hopscotch, not even by her drinking. An inexplicable sense of joy took over and she approached her grandmother as if she was the parent: "Are you okay?"

"What do you mean by that? Of couursh I am."

Mandolin recalled her own situation the day before. "Have you eaten?"

Hopscotch batted her away ferociously, and at last Mandolin pulled away.

"It's time to order some food."

"Food. Let'sh have some Shpotted Dick or Cock-a-leekie shoup."

Her gramma giggled again and Mandolin tried again to offer her help.

"Madolin!" she screamed, "what did I tell you? Go back to your womb—room now!"

The manager appeared, chatted with Jacques, who then escorted Hopscotch away.

In desperation, Mandolin turned to Hildegard, who caught her look.

"We all learn by experiences like these and I'm concerned about your Grandma's boyfriend. I'm positive I have seen him before." She turned to Theodore. "Yes. You were travelin' elsewhere sweetie, and I went with a girlfriend to Merida. The man and a woman were looking at turquoise bracelets in a specialty shop in Merida."

"My wife is amazing. She's on the ball at all times and never misses a thing."

"I so hope my mom is just like you, Hildegard."

Once again Hildegard slipped an arm around her, like a parent. "I've been thinking. Is there a possibility your gramma could be jealous of you?"

"Jealous of me? Oh no. Absolutely no way."

"Do me a favor and think about it. In my experience, unhappy women are often jealous of the happiness or success of other women. Take Scarlett O'Hara for example. I'm sure you have read *Gone with the Wind*."

"Twice, but so has everyone," Mandolin answered.

"Not everyone. Then you're aware of how jealousy destroyed the friendship between her and Melanie."

"Oh yeah! She wanted Melanie *gone with the wind* so she could have Ashley."

Theodore was ready to go. "I hope my wife has helped."

"You both have, very much. It's so hard to grow up right and you've inspired me to stay cool and study criminal justice back in Houston.

I'd like to work for the FBI eventually and see if I can find the answers to questions about my entire family."

Hildegard had a thought. "Sweetie, tell Mandolin about your early work in the Lockerbie Bombing case."

Theodore settled back and opened up. "I've been involved with the CIA for quite some time."

"Wow! Was he a Muslim martyr?" Mandolin asked.

He nodded. "As you may have read, it was earlier in 1988 that 270 people were killed by terrorists in the plane explosion over Lockerbie, only an hour's drive east of here. The cases were ultimately linked and I suppose this as well as my legal background attracted a fair amount of attention in Washington."

"Holy Pig! Then should I be a lawyer and a criminologist instead?"

"In time you'll know."

"I can't wait. But enough of me. I've been monopolizing you both."

"Monopolize. That reminds me of a spelling game." Theodore smiled.

Mandolin was enthusiastic "Teach me, I love words."

"Good. What do you call a game played with a board and fake money?"

"Monopoly?"

"Right. How do pronounce p-o-l-o p-o-n-y?"

"Po-*lop*-ony."

"Aha! Some might say polo pony."

Mandolin hung her head. Hildegard noticed. "Theodore enjoys that game. I always get stuck on symmetry and cemetery."

Mandolin gasped, "Me too, but let's move on. Do…do you think I should try your game on my new friend? He's starting Napier as we speak."

Hildegard responded. "Some of us have trouble with spelling games. What do you think?"

Mandolin was reminded of Crotchy's advice…not to use big words.

"I think you're right. Thanks."

Theodore and Hildegard said goodbye to Mandolin at the door. She had started feeling empty during the game shen she remembered the day Sky took her to her dad's cemetery and she accepted the fact he was gone forever. She took a deep breath and wandered aimlessly around the small lobby, into the store and ended up at the front desk. The concierge, a Crocodile Dundee type, asked if he could help her.

She had a question. "Are you by chance an Aussie?"

"Good on ya. Right you are."

"My dad and I lived in Sydney for a few months when I was little. Everyone was really friendly there. You look friendly and I'm sort of in a bad place right now."

"Sorry to hear, it Miss. I've seen you around. Thought you 'ad it all together."

"I did and now I don't. Do you ever feel lonesome?"

"Lonesome? Guess you can call it lonesome. Just found out they gonna *tike* me old hip *awhy* and stick in a piece of titanium. I'm missin' me old friend already. Now it's your turn. 'Ow come you feelin 'blue?"

"Suddenly, I'm not. Sorry about your hip but you gave me another something to think about, and it helped. Thanks for talking to me."

He smiled; spoke to a new guest while Mandolin skipped back to her room grateful for her hip. She settled into *Cloudsplitter and read* until her eyes began to swim. Out the window she saw fog but no rain for a change when Eliza Doolittle's voice popped into her 'ead. "The rine in Spine stays minely in the pline but in 'artford 'ereford and—and Devonshire, the rine is—is quite a bit drier."

'Appy she was, because this 'ad bean a loverly dye in all whys.

On the front porch of the B and B was a rocker. Every time she saw it, Mandolin was reminded of Big Mama's and this morning the impulse to rock, while she ate her haggis drove her to it. Ignoring her messy room, she walked with pep in her step down the hall.

The rocker was one of the best. It sent her way back and then forward and she wanted to spring out and leap out like she did when she was in school. She looked up and there was Speedy. He hopped off his bike and jumped up on the porch.

"It's my day off Miss, but it come to me that I f'rgot to give you the receipt for haggis last night."

With deep appreciation, Mandolin accepted it.

"Me writin's nothin' great so I'll read it to ya."

They huddled over the receipt, 'First ya put the heart, liver and lungs and onions in water and boil 'em up. Then, when it's nearly all soft, add a few spices, chop 'em up, add oatmeal' and therre you 'av it."

"Holy Pig! I've been eating *liver*! But no matter. This visit from you on your day off is one of the nicest things that has ever happened to me and I mean it. My boyfriend has forgotten me, but you haven't!"

"A boffin, he is! How you doin' with Tweedle Dee and Tweedle Gum if you don't mind me askin'?"

"Tweedle Gum?"

"Been noticing that beau of y'r granmum's beau follows her all over with his mouth chompin away on his gum."

"Oh my God! So I'm not the only one who thinks he's weird."

"I'm off duty so I can be sayin' the truth to you. If you ask me Miss, both of their bums is out the windy., but he out the most."

"What makes you say that?"

"I see his type all the time. They never pick up the chit, speak of forget-me-nots and flutes to their girrlfriends, and be prrayin' that *this* little beauty'll take 'em to fame and glorry."

"Because?"

"Their wheels have fallen off the buggy, if in fact it ever had wheels. These types are lookin' f'r the penthouse."

There's an old sayin' floatin' arrround. Ya can't clearrr up the waterrr 'til you get the pigs outtta the crrreek."

Mandolin threw her arms around him. "Now I know exactly what I have to do, Speedy. And please, no more "Miss" for me, I'm Mandolin, okay?"

He nodded, and encouraged her to join him at The Highland Games where and his girl was showing her herder dog in the Field trials. Mandolin found the invitation unbelievably kind but her plan was to finally straighten out a few things with her gramma.

His warm smile and wink indicated his sincere approval of her. As his bike took him off, she called after him, "Thanks Speedy, for the recipe, the fish and chips, the bevies and for...for you. I'm findin' a wealth of brrains arrround herre."

He sped off with a wave; she felt a touch of *hakka bakka* and headed inside for a serious chat with Hopscotch.

Inside, and outside the bedroom door of Tweedle Dee and Tweedle Gum, it took a few minutes until she found the nerve to knock.

At last she braved it. No response. She put her ear to the door, heard noises and suspected the TV was turned up high. Another knock. The noise inside grew more intense, like the excitement when a touchdown is scored. She knocked hard, waited a moment and opened the door.

Oh my God! Underneath the Jacques in the Box was the Prima Donna... doing it! Yuck! The sight of their bare bodies touching absolutely revolted her.

She froze, and then escaped, fast! She wanted to vomit. Was Speedy right? Was making out with Jacques why she had she invited him on the trip or was it vice versa? Had he somehow discovered she was taking a cruise and charmed her into inviting him? She needed to talk it out, but with whom?

The next day was difficult...extremely. Mandolin sat in the backseat absorbing the varied landscape without a word. How to be fair and try to understand her grandmother occupied her mind. Maybe other old people still did it. Had she found her in bed with Shakespeare, would it have been okay? Was Hopscotch a nymphomaniac? Or was Mandolin a prude? What would her mom think of this? She was trying to let go but this new scene was mortifying and mystifying. And now she would have an even harder time finding things to say to them.

Mandolin's excitement about the Rosslyn Chapel had inspired Hopscotch to take Jacques there as well as to 'drag" Mandolin with them. They wandered around the outside, Mandolin entered the sanctuary for peace and quiet, and to pray for her sanity and direction. What a beautiful place this would be for a wedding, but after what she had seen of love, was marriage really for her?

Why did people marry? Sky was divorced. She wasn't sure whether Hopscotch and her Grandpa were divorced before he died or not. She was never told; uncomfortable with the topic and had suspicions. Was Big Mama's advice to "her girls" correct? Should she remain a virgin until marriage? What difference did it really make? Why not just be average and loosen up? Shoot! Did anything really matter? There was so much to know. How would she ever decide what was right? Again and again the same question plagued her. "Mom, where are you? I need your help!"

The moments in the sanctuary were the most peaceful in her life. It felt like *hakka bakka*? But she had to move on. It was time to take control of her life, concentrate on becoming a private investigator with the courage of her dad.

She expected the trip back to the States to be relaxing. Wrong! The

Captain, a pleasant British Officer with more than a bit of wit, issued them another one of those dutiful invitations to sit at his table. What would it be like this time, Mandolin asked herself.

With the braded pages of the Lockerbie Bombing case from Theodore, along with her sketch pad, she sat as far away as possible from her grandmother and Humpty Jack. When asked a question, she pretended to be too engrossed to respond…almost the truth. The case had hooked her. It was described by Scotland's Lord Advocate as *the UK's largest criminal inquiry and led by the smallest police force in Britain."*

Holy Pig! No wonder Theodore had been sent from the United States to investigate the case. If only she knew enough, she could help as well. Why was she always too young or in the wrong place at the wrong time?

The Captain stood, resplendent in his uniform, welcomed the guests at his table and hoped to make their trip aboard the Queen Mary2, a pleasant one. A Southern gent tapped his glass. He and his wife had played a game on another cruise and wanted to introduce it. The captain had no objection, reminded him politely that dinner manners apply as always and agreed to his suggestion as long as dinner was not delayed.

No one objected, not even Hopscotch.

He rubbed his hands together and then drawled an introduction to his game. "Alrighty then, ah'm Bobby Wilson from Mur-frees-bo-rah Tinnessee, and this is my darlin' little wahfe beside me. Now what we do is to introduce ourselves around the table one by one and then tell what makes us tick."

Jacques had a question. You say teek? Like a clock? Or teek like a bug in a dog's ear? I am not understanding."

The Captain shifted uncomfortably sensing a long evening. The guests seemed willing, except for Mandolin who dreaded talking about herself.

First up were Madame and Monsieur Avizou. Mandolin turned over one of the pages from her material and started to sketch, apparently a caricature of Jacques since her eyes went back and forth from him to the paper.

Monsieur Avizou apologized ahead of time for her husband's poor grasp of English. Mandolin played detective and noticed a tension in Jack's expression as he went for a cigarette in his pocket. In addition, she observed his nervous knee that shook his body and chair. Hopscotch gave him a nudge and the pack shot back into his pocket.

Mandolin continued her sketch while Monsieur explained they were from France and frequent transatlantic air travelers. Madame interrupted and spoke slowly with purposeful diction.

"My huzbun, he speak quickly. He mean to say we like very much to come wiz you often on the ship. We do not fly."

The Captain was pleased.

It wasn't their turn, but Hopscotch waved eagerly at the Captain. He caught her drift.

"I'm sure we have no objection to this pretty red-headed lady goin' next. Go ahead please."

"I am Hopscotch MacDuff, born in Glasgow and I am here with…" she blew Jacques a kiss…"with dear Jacques from Rouen, France. He has been a proud citizen of the United States for quite some time."

Mandolin made deliberate, bolder marks on her pad. No matter how hard she tried to let it go, the sound of her gramma's voice and everything about her set her on edge. Her gramma sought approval from all around the table, and yet she carried on in such a pompous manner it would have revolted even the Queen of England and probably Queen Mary as well. Ugh! What's the point of pretense, she asked herself.

"Houston has *bean* my home for more yearrs than I care to admit."

Madame Avizou listened. "And your friend Jacques. Your last name, Monsieur?"

170

Mandolin lost her cool. "He's Mr. Cheese."

Hopscotch shot her words out of cannon. "Shame on you Madolin!" And to the table she said "Do forgive my granddaughter. She has much to learn." She hailed a waiter. "My granddaughter has upset me miserby...miserably. I need wine and do keep it coming." The waiter blinked at the empty glasses and the one full one in front of her. Mandolin rebutteth not and instead played her old trick and knocked her glass of water onto her gramma. Her scream caused total chaos at the table until a waiter handed her napkins and mopped the table. During this confusion, Mandolin watched Jacques suffer with stress. He faced a *real* French couple which meant something was going to give... at last. Madame Avizou asked again for his last name, and he searched the air for it. "Ah yes, my name. "Boudoir to all. Je swees Jacques...Boudoir!"

Some laughed. Mandolin smiled. At times he was Jacques Fromage, others Monsewer Boudoir. Madame Avizou was stunned. "Boudoir? I have nevair heard of...*a lady's dressing room?* Are you perhaps a comedian?"

Others looked at one another with raised eyebrows, suddenly aware of both the surprise and humor of the scene. To dismiss the tension, the captain quickly turned to Alison and Audrey, a couple who informed the group they had planned their honeymoon to coincide with the voyage of the QE2.

They received a toast with wishes for long lives together. Mandolin hypothesized the feelings of those in the gay world, and then concentrated on her sketching, oblivious of Bobby's voice..."one of the most *de-lahtful* passengers on the ship. Oh, to be young again. Go ahead, young lady."

"Madolin! Madolin. Pay attention. It's your turn." Hopscotch threw back her head and emptied her wine glass.

"Oh. Sorry." She slid her sketch pad onto her lap. "I am Mandolin from Houston. I am here with—"

"Never mind that now. "She is my granddaughter and 'tis quite obvious, my style has influenced her not a-tall."

Bobby responded. "At the same time, she's mighty pretty and lucky enough to have your red hair." He looked around the table. "Seems to me and my wife that these days this generation is makin' some mighty interestin' choices with their own styles."

The table was in agreement. Hopscotch was irritated. "I was interrupted before I finished."

"And I apologize." said the Captain. "However our dinner is on the way."

Bobby took the helm and looked at Mandolin. "And just before it comes, tell us what you've been sketchin' all this time?"

Mandolin clutched the drawing "Oh please! It's awful."

"Now, now, now," continued Bobby. "You and my daughter are just alike. She never likes to show off her art work and she's darned good."

Hopscotch grabbed the caricature and turned it around for all to see. Mandolin's sketch was of "Shield and Protector" Jacques with a grungy moustache, an exaggerated overbite, squinty eyes, and his pinkie up his nose.

Some couldn't see that far, others found her talent as a caricaturist quite amusing. Hopscotch found it shameful. Jacques had no idea who it was and no one dared to suggest it was a remarkable resemblance of him. Mandolin appeared a bit amused before looking into her lap.

"Since I was rudely interrupted," continued Hopscotch with a dramatic change of topic "I should like to add that I volunteerrr at a charrity shop in Houston and spend many hours choosing approprirrate attire for the needy to wear to work". She referred to her outfit. "Unfortunately, she does not have my style."

She took Jacques' hand. "We have done our best to give an ungrrrateful child an exhausting exposurrre to Eurrrope and it is a rrrrelief indeed to know we arre on our war home."

Alison glossed over the tension. "Audrey and I were just discussing this very topic and agreed that from the minute we are born, we are on our way home."

Hopscotch ignored the comment, looked at Jack as if he was her personal Greek God, and planted a juicy one on his lips. Then she tapped her glass.

"Could I have your undivided attention, please?"

Now what? Mandolin looked into her lap. The others appeared half-interested, have bored.

"We have plans. Big plans. You see I have been simply miserrrable indeed for the past eight yearrrs, ever since my husband and son werrre killed in an automobile accident."

Mandolin broke in. "Her son was my dad and I adored him. He..." She struggled for courage. Hopscotch turned to the group. "My granddaughter always insists on having the last word, but I'll have it this time. As soon as we get back to the States, Jacques and I shall announce our plans to be married."

Silent confusion reigned at the table. Then forced expressions of joy..., not from Mandolin who fought frustration, or Jerk who reacted as if the ship had run aground...but from the polite captain.

The Avizous, never ones to allow an awkward conversational pause, hurriedly began speaking French; Audrey and Alison smiled and excused themselves to speak to friends at another table. Bobby and his wife were greatly relieved to see the dinner arrive, and quickly kindled a lively discussion of English history.

After the Hopscotch and Jack escapade, Mandolin could plainly see that none of this behavior was normal for *any* of them. Hopscotch, now set back into her own imaginary world, simply kept drinking and reaching for Jacques, who was trying to smile, yet looked more like he had a serious case of terminal seasickness.

A long sleepless night was finally followed by a sunny morning. With her tablet and The Lockerbie info under her arm, a walk on the deck took her past two boys about her age. One took a look at her, stopped their game of ping pong and called out, "hey, come and join us."

She turned around, looked them over and decided to try a game she had never played. She put down her papers, accepted a paddle and caught on fairly well. But she lost. The other boy asked if she was an artist.

Mandolin was surprised by the question until she saw him looking at her sketch on top of the papers. "Not really, but I can do better than that."

He called his friend over, they studied her drawing.

"Look at this guy, Jace. Does he look familiar to you?"

"Oh, it's *that* guy, the character who was down in the teen room messin' with our favorite waitress."

Mandolin jumped in. "Excuse me. When was that?"

"Last night. What's up? Is he a friend or something?"

Mandolin tried to be cool. "If...if you see him again, will you... actually I'd love to have your full name and address. I'm keeping a diary of all the interesting people I meet on my trip."

"Sure thing. I'm Hal and he's Jason and here's my card. No big deal, but since I finally finished school, my dad gave me a bunch to pass out. We live in Iowa but I'll go anywhere."

"You mean for a job?"

"According to my father. that's what it takes these days."

"I'm going to get a job soon myself."

A gust of wind caught her off guard. As she brushed the hair awkwardly away from her face and straightened her skirt, she lost her balance and the card. Hal helped her find both.

"Man! That wind came outa nowhere."

"You're really good at ping pong," said Mandolin.

"You hate to lose, right?"

"Is that bad?"

He teased with her. "Next time I'll play right-handed."

She teased back "And I'll play left-handed. Thanks for the game."

She picked up the drawings, the Lockerbie papers and headed to the computer room. And realized she had a witness, someone besides herself to prove her gramma was dating her for money first and sex along the way.

What should she look into first? To learn how to put the finger on Jack the Ripper or explore another ancestry site? Settling down was difficult. Her mind drifted to those cute guys until she remembered Achilles and his big fat line. She had read stories about men who let women down, so how could she be surprised that it happened to her?

Back at the computer, a new fear developed. What if one of her ancestors was a criminal; serving time in prison or awaiting the death penalty for trading in drugs. And yet, as an aspiring Private investigator she felt compelled to go forward. Yes! James P. MacDuff was there on the web. He was not an oilman but rather a mail carrier and a beekeeper which confirmed her dad's story. She did not find her mom's name on any site and began to picture her as a victim of the crash of the Lockerbie Bombing, on the ground all mangled and bloody. *No! No! My mom is not dead! I will see her again if it kills me!*

She sat back and read the entire story of the Lockerbie bombing. Her dad would be proud of her and his words returned "What good did you do today, my little maid of the sea?"

She pretended he was beside her and answered "so so much *Dad. I've learned more about Lockerbie Bombing case, that if I could only help get rid of guys like Gadhafi and help the suffering survivors of the victims, I could make you proud.*

She read on about a piece of charred material found imbedded at the crash site that had been identified as part of an electric timer discovered in a Libyan intelligence agent's report. Apparently the culprit had been arrested earlier for carrying materials for a bomb. What? She settled deep into her favorite chair to learn more, unaware of Jacques' entrance until she caught sight of him pulling out a paperback with a wily smile. He slipped it into his pocket, and disappeared.

Was it too late to convince Hopscotch that this guy was not only a mooch but a thief as well? Or would she discover it eventually?

There was no doubt the Lockerbie case had captivated her. The day the Pan Am flight exploded, a man with an Arabic accent had called the US embassy in Finland. He tried to alert them of a plane to the US from Frankfurt would very soon be blown up by a Finnish woman. Why did they allow a person associated with the Abu Nidal Organization slip through customs? The officials had to have paid attention, how could this be?

Jacques returned and slipped another paperback into his pocket. This time she took issue. "Excuse me Jacques, Did you see the sign over there that no books may be removed from the library?"

He jumped. "Mind your own business or I'll tell your grandmother."

"Go right ahead. She may be surprised to hear what I have learned about you."

His face blanched and she continued.

"You may think it's none of my business, but I don't think you're being fair to my grandmother. You are well aware of her wealth and…"

"What ees this? I am een love with her."

"Why do you fake an accent? If you're not from Rouen, where *are* you from?"

He answered without an accent. "I have warned you before to stay out of my business. Who are you to ask me these questions?"

She didn't know who she was but at least she knew she was no phony and had a right to protect her grandmother from strange sex partners. He shook her shoulders, twisted her arm around her body so far she wanted to scream, and when he tied a rag over her mouth and tied it in back, all she could do was whimper,

"Now we are in business. I can throw you overboard you know, and no one will know the difference. Someone, somewhere will see the story on a back page. *Troubled Teenager Lost at Sea* and who will care?"

Oh my God! Oh my God! He could actually be a criminal and he and her gramma could be in cahoots. He let go of her arm and with her other hand she took her yo-yo, performed a *round the world* effort and fired it at his groin. He fell to his knees with a loud moan. Bingo! He was wiped out. She untied the rag and ran to her room breathless and petrified. When there was no knock, she settled down and envisioned the conversation in the dining room that evening."Did you hear that the granddaughter of Hopscotch felled her beau with a yo-yo earlier today?"

But just as she lay on her bed to celebrate, a ferocious knocking hit her door. Her panic returned "Open this door or I'll tear it down."

She peered out.

Jacques reached in and tried to pull her out. She screamed for help. He jammed another rag into her mouth threatened again to throw her overboard if she didn't stop yelling.

She clasped her hands together as if asking for mercy. He kept a tight grip, removed the rag and listened. "You're...you're right, Jacques. It's...it's really none of my business what you or my grandmother do. Maybe I've been reading too many mystery stories. If you love my grandmother, that's good enough for me."

His moustache became his crutch. He pawed it for comfort and to give him time to plan his next move. "That's a...a smart girl. Your gramma will be proud of your behavior. And you will never mention our little to-do, will you, my dear?"

She shook her head.

He added: "Do you understand me?"

"Oh yes! Totally. I'll never say a word."

"A wise decision. Hasta luego."

He exited with the books. Mandolin looked at her bright red

forearm caused by his tight grip and suffered the pain in in it from his brutal twist behind her back. She suspected he probably *had* been in Mexico and was the man Hildegard had seen in Merida. What she now needed was to pursue lessons learned from the Lockerbie case and to stop talking and actually get to work on becoming an exceptional investigator, at least as good as Theodore.

PART III

1

Attacking the Future

At Houston's Intercontinental Airport, Mandolin was the first through customs and at the baggage carrousel. Sky, at the front of an expectant crowd was waving a sign, *Welcome Home*. Mandolin ran into his arms, forgetting her arm had been strained. He pulled back and studied her. What's wrong, darlin'? I hurt you?"

She had tried not to wince because learning that Jacques threatened her life would only upset him. His income depended on her gramma's employ and if she sided with her, all would be over for him. "Tickety boo, Sky!" She looked at his withered arm. "Forget my arm. I am so *so* happy to be back with my friends again."

"Sure. Seems like you changed into a fine young woman just like that."

"Thanks and guess what? I now suspect I was born out of wedlock and it's okay. I'm totally okay with it. Those with far more talent and intelligence than I have survived and become famous. Plus, in a little over a month, I'll have my driver's license." She raised of her good arm. His hand met hers joyfully.

Mandolin never took a breath as she ran through a list events on her trip; New York, London, The Isle of Skye; Speedy; her first hangover; The Rosslyn Chapel; her ping pong game and …

"Hold on darlin', we got lots of time to catch up. Heather be wantin' to hear all this too. Got anything special to tell us?"

She knew what he meant. "Nothing new about my mom, Sky. but everyone I met was rich and I learned that all rich people aren't mean and selfish like I thought. Hildegard and Theodore and others took a real interest in me and taught me things I hope I never forget."

"You? Forget? You never forget a thing baby doll."

"They made me want to find my own mom more than ever."

"Well good. And while you gone, I been thinking that no one 'cept my folks be as sweet to me as you."

"Now Sky… no one?"

"That's the truth. Not no other blacks or whites or yellows or…"

She threw her arms around his neck, kissed his cheek and briefly related other news…about the Lockerbie case, the upcoming wedding, how Jacques wanted it in Houston and Hopscotch had nearly convinced him to have it in New Hampshire beside the lake on his family's estate.

"I'm getting there, Sky. Hopscotch and I can never be close, but I picked up a book in a shop in the Newark airport called *The Great Gatsby*. It's by F. Scott Fitzgerald, a fantastically crafted story that would take me years and years to even begin to equal. It's about the lavish life on Long Island in the 1920s when money was displayed to win friends. It taught me several things; that Hopscotch is cemented into the era of Summer Whites, clambakes, badminton, croquet and bowing on the green, and lives her life in the past with catered events and limos to bring the socialites to her parties. In addition I now believe that she will never change and I'm the one who has to. I've tried but never actually get there. Do you think there's a sort of family sensitivity there after all? Or am I afraid of some sort of retribution from my gramma?"

"Whatever it is, you gonna work it out. Jes be grateful for the home she gives you and the trip you done had."

"Especially for you and Heather."

"She be real glad to see you."

"One more question. Do you think Hopscotch could be jealous of me?"

Sky was puzzled.

"Hildegard wants me to think about it. Will you help me, Sky?"

"I'll sure try."

A headline on a newspaper drew her attention. *Is Gadhafi Responsible?* Of course she thought of Theodore and described their experiences together.

"Now what's been goin' on around here?"

"The news seems kinda shaky. I shouldn't be sayin this but as bad as we had it during 9/11/, I'm missin' that patriotic spirit we had goin' back than. Seems like 'stead of pullin' the world closer, we gettin' more separated every day."

"I agree Sky. Theodore, my newest best friend has inspired me to read all I can about the events prior to the Lockerbie bombing. I now know the facts about how it kinda began. Apparently an FBI agent sent a memo warning that large numbers of Middle Eastern males in flight training could be planning terrorist attacks. I also found out that a separate CIA intelligence asserted that Arab terrorists were planning to fly a bomb-laden aircraft into the WTC (World Trade Center). So that's why I'm signing up in The High School for Law Enforcement and Criminal Justice to learn how to stay alert for things like this in the future."

"Proud of you, doll baby."

"How are Tina and...?

"Tina doin' real good and Lillian and her boyfriend, Joseph well he found a job and him and her moved to New Jersey."

"What about Big Mama?" He quickly asked about Achilles.

"Oh him! He was a huge disappointment."

"Then he's not the one for you, Mandi."

"I guess you're right, but how do you know when you meet the right one?"

"Lookin' back, I thought I found me a sweet little girl, or maybe she found me who knows? Anyways, we jumped the gun, so you be sure to take your time and look 'em over."

Sky checked out the bags and Mandolin asked about Big Mama again. His forced smile clued her into the truth. Big Mama's days were short. She hugged him, relieved to hear that she was not suffering.

Then the "enchanted" couple arrived. "Welcome home. How did things go, Miz Mac?"

"With a willful teenager hanging on, what can you expect?"

Hopscotch, in her supercilious manner handed him the baggage claim tickets, announced they were going to the VIP lounge and to keep an eye on Madolin.

Back again in "Terror", it felt strange…no longer gargantuan. The ceilings seemed lower, the stairway not so imposing and she and Sky now looked eye to eye. She felt…crap…what was the word… sophisticated sounded uppity and wise went way too far. Confident? That was it! More cultured. Her red hair was back to black with a shapely cut, and her scarf was wrapped stylishly around her neck. Caring about her appearance was new to her. Hildegard's grace and style had made the difference.

Could others tell that her experiences at the Met and the Tate Museums had changed her? She hoped to be asked about *Millais's Ophelia;* about the Tate Boat that ran between *Tate Britain* and *Tate Modern,* or about the Rosslyn Chapel and Da Vinci. No one asked and she would be considered a braggart to talk about herself. Odd, she thought that this notion had never occurred to her when she was younger, or giving her gramma and Jacques permission to do as they pleased. And yet…and yet having *him* around with his constant threatening look, avoiding any dialogue and ignoring the voices and sounds from across the hall at night promised to be a huge challenge.

Her imagination played a big part; her gramma perched on a spectacular antique Queen Anne bed; leaning back on her satin pillow in her feathered nightgown and awaiting the *Jock* after his shower. She pictured him drying off, spritzing cologne around his face and neck, slipping a towel around his middle and then Monsieur Boudoir would enter Madame MacDuff's boudoir and…sheet! How could her grandmother be unaware that this nerd was anxious to take over her bank account, or that she already busted a few strings on her money bags to hold on to him. Buster! Aha! From now on she would call him Buster.

Tina called and listened politely to Mandi's excitement before she excused herself to leave for an interview. "You worry way too much about what your gramma thinks. Don't let her piss you off. Just because my family is close, doesn't mean yours will be. Talk to you later."

Piss me off? Now Tina was into the language her dad objected to. Should she let go of her deference to her dad as well? Perhaps, but for now, she felt better continuing her search for her mom *and* enrolling in a new school to develop her career…for the next three years.

She applied, was accepted with two days to go before it began.

While strapping on her well-traveled back-pack, she felt a twinge of pain in her arm and looked at her bruise, now a rainbow of colors. She threw her leg over the bar of an old Schwinn bike traded for a couple of her animal drawings, and headed to her favorite Whole Foods market. While waiting at a light, a bright red Rav 4, pulled up beside her and a good looking guy in blue scrubs rolled down his window.

"Hi. You look familiar. Have you ever worked at the Guild Shop?"

She nodded and when horns honked from behind, he turned the corner and she pedaled on to the market where she locked her bike to a post.

Inside, she was hailed from the Flower Department. "Mandolin. Hi! Wow-a! You are beautiful!"

It was Ginger, her old school friend. Mandolin asked "You really think that? As I recall you were the little red-headed girl who hated me."

"Wow-a! I never thought you knew that. I hated all the attention you got because you wrote good stories. "Are you still writing?"

Mandolin puzzled a moment. "Maybe later on. I found out by reading a book by F. Scott Fitgerald that writing is a hard-earned craft."

"I was always impressed with your brains."

She thanked her and thought how amazed *she* was by the number of those who accepted the fact that she was a writer without pursuing it .But what came out was. "That's crazy. I wanted your straight nose. Isn't it incredible how jealousy throws us off?" She smiled and silently thanked Hildegard for putting the thought into her head.

"Totally crazy," Ginger answered. "In addition, you were a better athlete. Remember how you beat us all by leaping off the swing and landing farthest away?"

"Don't forget I was always in the principal's office."

"I'd forgotten. So what's going on?"

Mandolin's travels and all she had learned interested Ginger, almost as much as her job interested Mandolin. When she revealed her interest, Ginger took her hand and led to an assistant manager where it was suggested that she come back after school started, to see about a weekend job.

It was a start, at least a hope to help pay for her own books, Hopscotch's most recent command. Mandolin and Ginger planned to do lunch soon. On her way outside to pick up a cart, Mandolin caught sight of Hopscotch struggling to park her 1978 convertible VW in a tight space. Each time she stopped, Buster started to get out. Hopscotch's expression spoke to her irritation.

Mandolin definitely did not want to be seen, and when they entered, she ducked down behind her cart and watched.

As if on Broadway, Hopscotch took Jacques' limp hand, held it next to her heart, looked into his cold eyes and blossomed like a fading red rose.

"And so tell me, my darling, do you have horses on your family estate?"

He parodied with a gratuitous complement about her parking job.

She looked pleased ordered her Buster boy to get a cart.

"Now what was it you were to remind me to do?"

He shrugged.

"It was a simple thing. How could you forget?"

Hopscotch looked around, Mandolin turned her back. "*Anne!* That was it! I need a gift for Anne."

Her following question was to an employee who answered he was not sure if they carried *Tamarind Chutney.*

"What? You don't know if you have it or not?"

"Sorry ma'am. We have over 35,000 products in the store, but I'll be glad to…"

With a sigh of disgust, Hopscotch pursued. "Then answer this. I am looking for a gift for an eccentric employee who comes from Verrrmont. Wherre is your Quarrk?"

The employee was bewildered. "Quirk?"

"No, Quarrk."

"How is it spelled?"

"Q-u-a-r-k. Quarrk!"

He puzzled. "Crack?"

Hopscotch threw up her hands. "Oh neverr mind. It is a frresh cheese made in Gerrmany and Rrrussia. All the employees at Krroger's know the location of their prroducts and so I'll go…"

"We do as well ma'am, and if you'll just give me a minute…"

But "of courrse" Hopscotch didn't have a minute and dashed away.

In the meantime, Buster stayed in place and dialed his cell phone. Mandolin pushed her cart closer to him and remained out of sight. He was absorbed and unaware of her approach. She missed the first words and moved closer.

"Don't give me that shit, man. Listen. We're back in Texas and I've made a real coup...Yeah. For the first time I've latched on to into a classy broad...wait...I'm telling you, she's loaded. She wants us to come up there soon and this is our big chance. You gotta ask our friend Karl to let us stay in his place on the lake until I convince her that we belong in Texas...No prob, man. Your cashier's check is in the mail...Fuck off! That *is* the truth! She gives me money for shopping and never asks for the change. Fuck! Here she comes. And let me know if Nathan gives you any shit. I'm a fucking good arm-twister these days and I mean it! I got this whole deal covered."

Mandolin had heard more than enough to crucify this guy when Hopscotch approached with a small plastic bag in her hand presumably the Quark for Anne but who could be sure. Mandolin moved boldly into the aisle well-prepared for her face-to face battle with the truth, but Hopscotch stuck her nose in the air and passed by rapidly. Was it deliberate? In any case, Mandolin had had it and expressed her severe agitation to the row of juices. "You really really piss me off, Hopscotch!"

She felt better and was now prepared to tell her why when the time came.

Outside, Mandolin met a couple of teenagers admiring the VW.

"That is one cool car, a 1978 model and in great shape. Wow-a!"

Mandolin commented with pride. "I know a little about it. It was my dad's."

"Is it for sale?"

"I'll bet you can make a deal with my grandmother for around three million bucks. Just kidding. She's on her way out and you can ask her yourself. See ya."

With a loaded backpack, Mandolin pedaled off with her mind buzzing. Buster's conversation proved her point, another confirmation of her suspicions, that loose mongrels chase bitches. His infuriating mannerisms continued to haunt her. Never once had she seen him show an ounce of affection towards Hopscotch. His dutiful reactions to hers were like a child on probation. Maybe *he* was on probation.

Her travels to New York, London and Scotland had made her realize she had not taken full advantage of the many wonders of Houston. The multiple food perches on the ship had also beefed her up a bit too much and this was her opportunity to get to know Houston and to work off a few pounds at the same time. On her bike she passed The Contemporary Arts Museum, The Museum of Fine Arts and the Rothko Chapel. As she pedaled past the Menil Collection, she was ready to bet that the De Menils would rise from their graves if they heard that a Jacques Boudoir was claiming French heritage and dating one of their of original contributors.

Along the way, Tattoo parlors sorely tempted her. A Scottish tattoo on her arm with bagpipes and various plaids would be awesome. But no. Enough had happened to one arm and besides drawing attention to herself in any way was too Hopscotch-esque. She rode further to Sunset Park, far smaller than Central Park but friendly and crowded with young kids and their sitters or parents playing with them on swings and slides. She had never played with her Mom so far as she remembered. She asked herself if she could be a good one herself when a small girl leaped off a swing in mid-air and proudly landed at her feet below.

It was beginning to feel like *hakka bakka* once again! Before she knew it, Mandolin, that little girl of the past forgot her painful arm was pumping the swing beside *this* little girl. At the count of three; they jumped off and out. Unlike her early years, Mandolin had dropped her "all about me image," and allowed her to win just like her dad had.

They repeated the action until Mandolin took to a bench and motioned for her new friend to sit beside her. Not for her! The swing was where she wanted to be and off she went. Mandolin felt that familiar sense of rejection when another young lass appeared at her side. Mandolin identified with her need for attention. "Hi sweetie, thanks for coming over."

"My name is Vita," she said with an accent Mandolin was unable to detect. "You are lonezum?" she asked.

"Hi Vita. I like your name. Mine is Mandolin."

"I vant to know. Are you lonezum?" Vita repeated with persistence.

"Often. Why do you ask?"

"You are preetee."

"Really? You definitely are. You remind me of *Alice in Wonderland*. Have you ever read it*?*"

"This book, it is silly. See that man over there? He is my Papa and he is lonezum."

"I'm so sorry. Do you know why?" Mandolin asked.

"Because he comes to Russia, marries my Mama and they fall out of luff."

"Sometimes that happens, Vita. In fact it happened to my dad when I was younger than you."

Vita offered Mandolin her hand. "Please, come viz me for to meet him."

"I'd like to very much. But I feel it best not to interfere."

"I do not understand zees."

"Let's see, interference is like… suppose you and your dad are playing ball like those kids are over there, and I run in and steal the ball. That would be called…"

"In-ter-fer-ence."

"Good girl! And you would be mad at me, right?"

"This is not vot I vant to talk of. My Papa, he is very smart and funny also. Please come viz me."

She reflected momentarily. Matchmaking. This is what girls do. They always want to find love. "Let's go."

Hand in hand, they skipped to her dad. Mandolin introduced herself. He put down his newspaper graciously and with surprise.

"Your daughter and I were talking about interference and before we knew it we had bonded. Are we bothering you?"

Not at all. "By coincidence I was reading in the sports pages about interference in a football game."

"Is that right? I live for coincidences. Tell us about the game."

He looked at his paper. "It says here that coach Kirk Martin, of the Manvel Mavericks near Dallas, has led his team to many victories with the spirited cheer, *hoka hey!*"

Mandolin was excited. "What does Hoka Hey mean?"

He read the article "It says it comes from the Sioux Lakota Indians. Before Battle of Little Bighorn, a member of the tribe danced an inspiring dance and their leader Crazy Horse shouted '*Hoka Hey, Hoka Hey.*' He scanned." It says they have all lived good lives, are where they belong, and ready to die in battle if it is God's will."

A shiver shimmied through Mandolin's body. "A-w-w-w. My dad and I call that feeling *hakka bakka*. I can only hope that my dad knew how much I loved him and was ready to go when he did."

Vita's dad spoke. "My condolences." He immediately referred to his newspaper.

"I find this interesting. *Hakka bakka, hoka hey* and *hakkebakkeskogen* mean about the same thing. They relate a happy message, one worth remembering."

Mandolin gulped, waved and slipped away before she cried.

Vita called. "Vait, stay here viz us. We are fun, no?"

Mandolin smiled and called back. "Times spent with your dad are the best in the world, Vita. Never forget that."

"Goodbye Mandolin. We see you zum times."

Mandolin walked away, sat on the other side of the park and reflected. The sun, the breezes and the sparrows chirped happily in the bushes, reminding her of the surprises and miracles that God provides. She thought of her Mum. Would trips to a park with her been as rewarding as Vita and her dad's? Did they have races the beach on Malaysia? Somehow she knew she had to keep searching.

Theodore had intimated that she should read Mark Twain and she had found a copy of his autobiography in her granddad's library published in 1959. She removed it from her backpack and read it aloud as if the sparrows understood: *"Like other children, Susy was blithe and happy, fond of play; like other children she was at times given to retiring within herself and trying to search out the hidden meanings of the deep things that puzzle human existence, and in all the ages have baffled the inquirer and mocked him."*

Hoy Pig! It's as if he is speaking to me. I want to know all about people and to learn why they do as they do like tGig Mama used to say.

Pink Oink caught her eye at 4:44 PM. She was hot and thirsty and before heading back to the mansion, she biked to Gelato Blu for a pistachio smoothie. Yum! She sat by the window licking it and when she looked out, her scream followed her outside with her fists raised. A raggedy man with a crowbar was trying to steal her bike. She yelled again. He was frightened, then ready to attack her. With surprising strength, she wrestled for the crowbar, almost got a grip when he threw her to the ground.

Undaunted she pulled herself up and screamed louder. "Help! What are you doing? Leave my bike alone. Stop! Stop!!!

Two uniformed students with High School for Law Enforcement insignia on their shirts ran to the scene and chased the guy off.

"Look what he did! The wheel is twisted. I feel sorry for him but..."

"You better get inside. Your leg is bleeding."

"That doesn't bother me. But my bike...my bike..."

The guys straightened the wheel with little problem. She thanked them, asked how she could repay them. They declined and one spoke up. "This is what we do for one another. Right?" They continued on, as she did, with blood running down her leg.

Behind the counter at *Bikes ETC.*, the best looking, handsomest, most gorgeous guy she had ever laid eyes on smiled the warmest, most beguiling smile she had ever seen. She looked behind her to make sure it was not aimed at someone else. Then returned to a helmet he was adjusting at the counter.

"Hi! Come on in and look around." She blushed. His voice was not deep but endearing. She couldn't look around. This guy was literally to die for, so so hot! Sure, Crotchy, Ray and Achilles had blown her away, but this guy had a body that needed no clothes although his choice of a colorful orange and blue striped biker shirt with matching blue spandex showed revealed every ripple to the greatest advantage. When she approached, his spiked hair, the rage all over Europe caused her heart to pump faster. He noticed her leg.

"Hey. What happened? Looks like you had a bad fall."

."Not...not exactly, but that's why I'm here. A guy almost got away with my bike."

"Sorry about that. What you need is a Blackburn Angola Cable Lock, but let's take care of your leg first."

Holy Pig! He leaned over close to her and she flushed again, Mr. Cool Guy handed her a first-aid kit, pointed her toward the rest room and on her way she decided it was not only his smile but his sympathetic nature that intrigued her. When she returned with a wrap around her leg, she stood by and watched him arrange biker outfits, padded shorts, shoes and shirts in a nearby section.

She wanted to thank him, but her voice caught in her throat until she coughed it out and finally came to her senses. "Thanks for your help and the first aid. You can call me ex-bloody Mandolin."

His head rose. And I'm 'Wee Willie Winkie.'"

"You mean the same Willie one who runs through the town?"

"Exactly, but not in a nightgown."

"Oh my God, I thought I was the only one our age to know Mother Goose verses."

"My mother read them to me when I was little."

"You're lucky. Remember the one about Peter Piper?" she asked.

"Sort of. 'Peter Piper picked a peck of pickled peppers.'"

Her turn. "'A pick of peckled... pickled peppers Peter Piper picked.'"

"Okay. If Peter Pecker...I mean...Uh-oh! You got me, but you knew you would, right?"

"Who me? Could I kid Mr. Magnificent himself?"

"Easy. I'm a pushover."

"For sure...Willie?"

Her look came flirtatiously. He looked off, nervously, she thought, and definitely not the not the reaction she expected. He was either a modest or shy type.

"I've been away where bikers are big, and had no idea they come with so many accessories."

"We sell a bunch too. Like I'll be reordering these gloves as well as our hats, speedometers, bells, horns and headlights later today."

"I'm hardly what you call a big spender but as soon as I make some money, I want to buy a better bike, along with a helmet and shirt."

"Want to try some on?"

"Not yet."

"We take credit cards, cash and checks."

"Are you kidding? I've never had a bank account or a credit card in my life."

"We're trying to increase the traffic into this place. Maybe the manager will let you pay on time and you can be another model like my friend."

"Seriously!? I'll even attach a sign to my bike somewhere that advertises *Bikes ETC.*"

"Good idea. We have info over there about biking clubs that go to Galveston and around the Hill Country. Want to join up?"

"With you?"

Willie was shaken. "Wow! You get right after it!"

"You're right. I've just been spent a month in Europe with the older generation and after having my every move watched and critiqued. I'm ready to spring loose."

He studied her. "I lived with my grandmother for awhile so I know what you mean, but Europe? Cool. Maybe we can talk about it sometime."

Yes! He sounded really interested and so she asked if he was a Houstonian. "Nope I came here with my mother."

She figured his parents were either separated or divorced. "You okay?"

He gave her a weird look.

"Sorry. I'm writing a story and to build my characters, I ask way too many questions. Let's talk about your tattoos."

"My mother thinks they're disgusting."

"I don't, but why did you have it done?"

"Because I like a friend's. He's been sweet and supportive."

"Your parents aren't?"

"Haven't you heard? We're not supposed to blame our parents for anything? It's up to us to figure out their weirdness."

She laughed. "You're different. Does the rule apply to grandparents too? Oops! Ignore the question."

His interest shifted to the clothes and she followed him around as he refolded a few messed-up biker shirts.

"This is a cool shop. Do you live nearby?" she asked.

"Pretty near. How about you?"

The question troubled her. To many, living in River Oaks meant big bucks and status. She had heard her gramma tell a friend that her husband gave her a squirrel jacket one Christmas instead of a mink and she threw it on the floor.

"You know what? I used to think that rich people were uppity and some are. But in Scotland I met…tell me more about your tattoos. I almost got one, but…"

Willie pulled up his sleeve onto his shoulder. She shuddered. She was right. Beautiful Willie needed no clothes. His muscles were impressive as was his tattoo.

"Wow! That is awesome! You were brave to go through all that."

He explained this was part of what is called a Japanese body suit. It had begun with a picture of his mother, and then an angry tiger when they divorced. "This fish in the surf over here represents me."

"So you're a surfer?"

"Was, in Newport Beach. Get me near the water and I'm on it, in it, or under it."

"California. Cool. When I was little I lived by the sea but—"

"Where do you live now?"

Afraid of this question as well as another about her mom, she veered away like a goose from its gaggle at the sight of water. She studied his tattoo again, found the word Clair and asked if he had a girlfriend.

His lips tightened. His smile disappeared and she hardly recognized him. "I called her Clair for Clair de la lune. She liked the water as much as I do."

He pulled his cell phone from his pocket to show a photo of his pal.

"Holy Pig! She's beautiful but I expected Clair to be white"

He invited her to see other pictures and as he flipped through them vibes from his body against hers caused her eyes to pop and her insides to tumble in all directions. His chatter became a distant thing and all she could think of was having sex with him …until he suddenly flipped his cell phone closed.

She took a deep breath. "I adore dogs but my gramma says dog-owners never talk about people and dog-talk is boring. So I can only imagine how sad losing one would be. The ends of things always tear me apart."

"So you live with *her?*"

Mandolin squeezed her eyes shut. "Yeah, but not much longer, I hope. So if I dress up in one of your biking outfits and ride my bike around to advertise them, can I have one for free?"

"I'll have to find out from Julie, the manager, and she's on a lunch break."

"Oh, well let's forget it."

"No. It's an awesome idea."

She stared at him. "Promise not to think I'm weird?"

He laughed. "Too late for that…just kidding. Go on."

"Well, our meeting this way is what some people call *hakka bakka.*"

"Sounds Indian."

She was ecstatic. "Right. It's like clicking, like finally fitting a key into the lock and opening up the whole world."

Confused, he asked, "So where are we going with this?"

She filled him in on her past and explained that her gramma was too busy for her, was getting married, and that she was definitely anxious to move on to a happier place. "Any ideas?"

He thought for a long moment. "As a matter of fact, there's an unfurnished garage apartment on the next block my friend and I have been considering."

"I'm not even sure what I can afford, but is there room for three people?"

He shrugged. "Possibly. He's not quite ready to move away from home yet, and I am, so I'll talk to him. Okay?"

"Nifty!"

"Nifty? That's original."

"Not really." She argued. "I learned it in Scotland from a fabulous man."

They high-fived cheerily. She headed out until he called.

"Hey wait. You'll need my bike lock 'til you can pay for one."

The lock was in his hand. She accepted it as if it was solid gold.

"And when you speak to your manager, tell her I don't need a big salary. Whatever she can pay for weekend work will suit me. I'll also come for an interview any time...Willie." Another come-on look.

A man in a business suit entered the shop. "Mandolin! Hello! I bet I've asked everyone in this city if they know a Mandolin MacDuff. Great to see you again."

She drew a blank.

"My boys ask for you all the time. I'm here to buy Jason a bike and he'd so like to have you teach him."

"Oh, it's you Gregory with a haircut. We met in Mexico, right?"

Willie stepped in. "I can help you, sir. How old is Jason?"

"Almost six."

"Perfect time for a small two wheeler with training wheels."

Gregory looked around. Willie addressed Mandolin. "Do you have any furniture or anything?"

"Not much. I have a hammock and a few things and know a great place for bargain furniture. How about you?"

"My Mom has a lot of stuff except for a table and chairs. The apartment is really cheap and divided by three, it should work."

Gregory returned and Mandolin spoke first.

"I'm interrupting a sale so I'll leave you guys alone. Here's my name and cell number."

She jotted it on scrap paper left it on the counter and took off with a skip. Gregory copied it. Willie returned to Gregory with an apology for neglecting him, while Mandolin sprung onto her bike with Willie's borrowed lock in hand. She really really liked Willie and could not believe that a guy this gorgeous had agreed to actually live with her. Her! A gawky, sexually naive gal with a twisted past.

Biking along, she thought of Achilles and how she had helped him outfit his college room at the Guild Shop. O—kay…Or was it okay? Had she been used or what? People were often confusing and she fought that feeling of abandonment all the time. But she had a hunch she had a winner this time and so as she headed back to Terror for one of the last times, she sang to the birds, the bees, passing cars and pedestrians. Little by little her body, heart and spirit felt in sync. She was about to make the big escape and turn their place into the hakka bakka she always dreamed of…ASAP.

But perhaps this was the time to slow down, to think things over and not be in a rush to breeze onward as Sky had always advised . Okay Sky. At least for a night, she would forgo a search for furniture bargains at the Guild Shop, even though she was absolutely positive that Willie was her man!

She pedaled off to River Oaks Boulevard in all its moneyed splendor, biked over a few blocks, and passed the prestigious Long Gallery where years earlier she had watched the upper crust entering for an art show. She still hoped that one day her drawings would hang there.

And then riding high as if she owned the world, she biked down the drive to Terror, and found that part of the second story was undergoing major surgery, an indication that Mr. P and her gramma had finally resolved the view from her bathroom window.

The minute she entered the garage her heart sank. Sky's truck was gone. A workman explained that the caretaker had to leave because "his Mother passed like all of a sudden-like."

Mandolin sat on her bike and thought about her and all the ways she should have expressed her love. Why hadn't she? If she was ever going to be a writer she had to try, to try hard and possibly it would help her pass through another tragic time. With a heavy heart, she moved into the Library, felt lonelier than ever, yet she couldn't cry. Big Mama's death had been imminent and it was as if her emotions were all used up. So she was now gone…like her dad …and perhaps her mom. No! She refused to believe that about her mother.

A call came on her cell. It was Sky. He was still with the ambulance and wanted her to know that Big Mama had requested a solo sung by her at the funeral. She gulped. Big Mama's comforting embrace in her kitchen the night she heard the news of her dad's s death would be forever with her. There had been no chance to hug him or say goodbye to him, nor had she taken the time to visit Big Mama before her end came. Tears gushed down her cheeks for, two special people who shined special lights.

2.

An end and a start

As always, Sky, Tina, Lillian and Mandolin sat in the front pew joined by Lillian, now twenty, and her boyfriend Joseph, who had flown in from New Jersey. Tina waved Mandolin over, opened up a spot between Tina and Sky and wrapped her arms around both. A eulogy, given by Joseph was followed by the choir and congregation who sang *God Bless America*. amidst moaning and groaning and handkerchiefs fluttering.

When the preacher signaled Mandolin to come up and introduced her as a loyal family friend, she clutched her hands together to hide her shakes and prayed silently for her dad and Big Mama and all those who had lost a loved one. Influenced by the couple at the Guild Shop, she then sang a resplendent version of *On Eagle's Wings* (by Michael Joncas, a minister).

"And he will raise you up on eagle's wings, bear you on the breath of dawn, make you to shine like the sun, and hold you in the palm of his hand."

She barely heard the many warm and comforting "Amens!" or the compliments on her voice. Affection from many soothed her before she took her seat. The experience was profound and she was reminded of all she had been through since her dad had died. Now she had lost a friend, one who had helped her find her way as well as develop her voice. Big Mama had been the mom she had not yet found.

After a month, her life had taken a giant leap forward. She had started a new school and; Sky Lillian and Tina divided Big Mama's possessions. They generously gifted the Guild Shop with Sky's family's old Ford truck and Mandolin with Big Mama's Singer Sewing machine, her jingly bracelet, and her old Cadillac. Mandolin took a driver's ed class on line, met all the qualifications, and was now allowed to drive with an adult. Yes! She could be seen *Driving* Mr. *Daisy* around town in a fin-tailed 1959 Cadillac. She couldn't remember the make or model *Miss Daisy's* car which bothered her.

As if that wasn't enough action, word came that Willie's friend would not be ready to move in until the first of the year and for them to go ahead. Holy Pig! How was that for a speedy super turn of events and how grateful she was! Her life was good. Soon freed to drive her own "Caddy" as Big Mama called it, alone, she nonetheless preferred her bike since her job hopes were focused on *Bikes ETC.*

One afternoon after school, she ventured into the Guild Shop where good things had happened to her and she was sure she'd find a table. Right away she noticed changes. It seemed to have grown in size or else it was more organized. The good thing was that Gilbert was still there although he didn't recognize her, a common reaction these days. When she told him about Willie and their needs, his subdued reaction bothered her. Why?

"It's nothing against Willie, Mandolin. I don't know him. I'm just one of those matchmakers and been hoping you and Kris would hit it off."

"Kris? Oh, your friend. But he's kind of old as I remember and you'll love Willie." With her fingers crossed, she related the of her working as Willie's his part-time assistant. He wished her the best, pointed to the back where all major donations were unloaded.

At the back door, Quintus and his co-worker, Cisco greeted her.

"Holy Pig! You guys are impressive in your supportive belts."

Cisco spoke out. "Sure beats holding on to the back of a garbage truck on a hot day."

"Aw! You've taught me something."

"Who me?"

"For sure. When I hear about what others go through, it makes me appreciate what I have."

"We all got it different. Don'tcha think, Quintus?"

Quintus was concentrating on his job. "Take your time and look around. "All of us, 'specially you young ones, got more time than you think. Seems like I'm *numero uno* in the furniture these days, and when you're ready, call on Cisco or me for help. He's a good man. We been knowin' each other for a long time."

Cisco led Mandolin to the drop off area in back where donations and consignments were received and she discovered there was zero market for vintage bikes. This came as real disappointment since she hoped to pay for a table. But she found one with a plastic top and two metal chairs in good condition, at a bargain price. While Quintus put a *Sold* tag on all, three. Mandolin asked if he could pick up a few things from Sky's place in the Heights, a few things from Terror and deliver them to her new place.

"Naw," said Cisco, we don't pick up nothin' unless it's comin' to The Guild Shop. Quintus joined them and Mandolin moved up close and looked into his eyes like a begging dog. "Did you know that Sky, a very good friend of mine who works for my gramma donated an old truck to the shop? Since my boyfriend and I are…"

"Sky?" Quintus stepped back and crossed himself. "Well I'll be! You must be that little granddaughter of Miz Mac's all growed up. I'm Quintus, Mandolin, and been knowin' Brown since high school days. You call him Sky but when we was young, we called him Brown, his last name. Your gramma and your papa was good friends of mine too. We useta play poker with her and Jimmy, your dad over at her big place."

It took both hands to hide the impact of his revelation on her. "Whoa! Whoa! Whoa! You played poker with my dad and my *gramma?*"

"Y'r darned tootin. That's what he used to say all the time. Jimmy was good but your gramma, and she beat us like a drum every blasted time. Never did understand why a lady with enough money to air-condition hell liked to gamble for more."

Mandolin was stunned and Quintus invited her into the kitchen where they sat around a porcelain table. "Been wantin' this table myself, but the price is still up at the top number."

Cisco entered in time to hear his comment and gave him a tease. "All you do is want and wait, and then want and wait for the next thing. Sure is a good thing our customers not all like you. We'd never sell nothin' here."

Quintus gave Mandolin a cup of coffee, took a taste and gagged playfully. "Hold on, Mandolin, Cisco musta made this."

"Please guys, I really want more news of my dad and gramma."

She learned that girls were often included in the poker games.

"One could have been my mom."

Cisco had his doubts and discussed the hot relationship of Jimmy and Janie, one of his girl friends. Quintus took over.

"Jim was smart as a whip but seemed the hee-bee jee-bees got to him over and over. Finally, he up and left school and him and what… what was her name, Cisco? You remember her, the one with the sexy voice?"

Cisco had forgotten and Quintus continued. "Jimmy MacDuff. He was The Man! He did way better than me in school. Everyone knew he liked danger. It was like he could sniff it and soon as he did; he'd be off after it to try to help out."

She bit her lip to hold back a few tears and urged Quintus on.

"Always on the go and the girls! They followed him round like he had ice cream in his back pack. Never could figure out how he did it.

Him and what's her face run off to some place in Mexico or South America."

"You mean to get married?" asked Mandolin.

"Married? This one wasn't looking to marry no one, a good thing cuz Miz Mac thought she..."

Quintus poked him. Mandolin noticed.

"It's okay guys. I need to hear everything in order to find my Mom. What did this girl look like? Was she tall, short, heavy-set, skinny? Did she have distinguishing features like a crooked nose or a long neck like mine?"

"She liked to whistle," said Cisco.

"Yeah, and she was always singing love songs," laughed Quintus as he pulled to his feet. It was time to get back to work.

Mandolin asked how her dad could afford all his sailing trips. They explained that he knew about every boat ever made and got jobs with wealthy folks either hauling or skippering or acting as crew wherever and whenever needed. He built a good reputation and nothing was ever too much work or too dangerous for him to try.

"Like what kind of places did he go?"

"All over." And then Quintus sat down beside Mandolin and recalled an adventure in particular. Seems like it was in 1987 when a big storm hit Great Britain and before you knew he got hisself over there and saved eight people in the North Sea. You remember that storm, Cisco?"

"Not as well as you, but I remember hearing stories about how brave our buddy was."

Quintus turned to Mandolin. "Yup! The minute your dad heard that a storm was comin', didn't make no difference where, he got to it faster than you can bat an eyelash."

Mandolin felt her heart beating and asked Quintus "do you ever stop missing someone?"

"Dunno. Guess me and love for a girl back then never got that close. Used to be a clipping about him right on that wall there."

Words did not flow. Her emotions did. "Does…does anyone have a copy?"

"Ask Louise," suggested Quintus. "She weren't here back then, but she's sharp and prob'ly knows about it."

"Bet you're proud of your dad," stated Cisco.

Mandolin shut her eyes tight. "He was forever telling me to be brave and think of others."

"He never talked about himself to us."

She wiped her eyes. "Nor to me. You have no idea how much it means to hear all this. Thanks."

"Yup! He was one true hero."

"What's the definition of a true hero? Is it someone who saves a single life or more than one, like a member of the armed forces? Is it creating Microsoft like Bill Gates; flying the first plane across the Atlantic Ocean, running a two billion dollar operation like The Salvation Army on a small salary, finding the cure for cancer—or like my dad?"

Cisco commented. "Oh my! You way up there with the intelly gents and ladies. My wife called me a he-ro last night cuz I unplugged the disposal."

"Cool. Teach me sometime."

"Sure, but we better get back to work…now!"

She wrote down her address and he agreed to meet her at her new place on West Pierce at 6 sharp. He had another delivery at 6:30. They high-fived. she departed to find Louise. Cisco had a question.

"I know her papa is gone, but never did get the full story."

Quintus divulged the story. Her dad and her grampa had died in a car accident. Skid marks were found on the street with a dead deer on the smashed hood of the car. Jimmy's and his dad's body was huddled together down the road apiece. Blood was everywhere. Seems that Jimmy was dragging his dad to safety and gave out before help came."

"Um-umh! Poor Mandolin. She had more problems then the law allows," Cisco reflected. "And knowin' Jimmy, betcha he got himself a coupla kids by now."

"Get off of it man! You or me neither one don't know the truth. And what good it gonna do Mandolin to know it all?"

"What I'm not gettin' is how come he chose to raise up Mandolin bu himself."

"All I know is he one a the best…never did cheat at the poker games like we did from time to time, was friends with the world and took good care of himself. Remember how he could pull up to a headstand without using his arms or hands?"

Cisco shook his head. "You suppose Hopscotch taught him how?" He broke up.

"She mighta back then, Cisco, but Miz Mac changed plenty after the accident. She's not near the same since she been with this new guy."

Cisco added. "I heard from Gilbert about a missing diamond ring but we not supposed to say nothin'""

"Rumors build up and travel fast."

A call on the intercom interrupted. "Lock the back doors, guys. Please lock the back doors."

It was quittin' time and Quintus and Cisco were outta there in short order.

3.

On the Dot

MANDOLIN ARRIVED AT THEIR new place on the dot of six. The zip code was the same as River Oaks, but the sidewalks were torn up by tree roots, the street was riddled with holes, the gate beside the paint-thirsty bungalow hung on one hinge, and the uneven driveway sections caused her to stumble on her way to the garage. Quintus appeared from the rear of the newly- gifted Guild Shop truck. He was shouldering a heavy box of clothes. Cisco trailed with chairs and the table and followed her up the rickety outside stairway with a curious cat on her heals.

When Willie heard her call, he appeared, topless and sweaty, opened the door and the cat scooted in. "Where did *he* come from?"

"Not yours?" Mandolin asked.

"No way."

With a boost from his bare foot, the cat found itself reeling through the door which shot an arrow through Mandolin's tender heart.

Inside, a few dirty pots sat on top of a gas cook-top that magnanimously could be called a kitchen. A door with a towel hanging on a vintage glass door-knob led to a bathroom and a day-bed loaded with Willie-stuff was the so-called living room. Her look of disappointment was curtailed by Quintus.

"Forgot to tell you about your dad's job at the Happy Hour Club after school. He called himself "Jumpin' Jimmy and his specialty was imitating comedian Jimmy Durante's version of 'Inka Dinka Doo.' It was the best."

"I love it. Hey Willie, how about calling our new place *Inka Dinka Doo*?

From the other room: "Are you nuts?"

She guessed she was and tipped Quintus a few bucks. He refused. She took a tough stance, a fencing position like she had seen in a movie. Quintus was tickled.

"Okay. You got me *this* time. "

Mandolin followed the Muscle guys down the shaky stairs with a glass of water, all she could find at the moment for the cat.

"Thanks, guys. See you back at the Guild as soon as Willie and I earn some money. Oh, by the way, when I was leaving the Guild Shop earlier, a customer told me there was confusion about a stolen ring. Do you know anything about that?"

Both pleaded the Fifth.

She said goodbye, but not to the cat. It seemed it wanted join her as she started a new life with a new friend, in a new place, with a new job, in a new school where she was learning about law enforcement for the first time.

The future worried her as well as her judgment. Was Willie a slob? She looked into the bathroom. Neat as a pin. Phew!

"My mother is sending over her old double bed in a few days."

Oh! A double bed? She had left Terror and all its horrid memories and forgotten her hammock from Mexico. If only she could invent a connection like the bees have that sends word to other bees about where flowers are. Her idea was to invent a program to remind people of the past and find lost items instantly. It would be called the Bee Connection and make her feel she had accomplished something for humanity. She would do it one day, but for now she was biking over the Bayou and through the Woods' to Terror, with bees and butterflies in her stomach…more than bees and butterflies… more like somersaulting elephants. She had not only left her new hammock, but in all her excitement, forgotten to tell Sky and Heather goodbye…which meant facing her gramma in all probability.

More construction materials were piled in the garage and when she entered the kitchen, Sky greeted her eagerly. He explained that Hopscotch had been told that an additional eating area off the kitchen would improve her chances of selling the mansion. Mandolin was stunned. Did this mean she had waited too long to tell Hopscotch about Jacques?

"Are they…are they around, Sky?"

"Yes Ma'am. They packin' up for a permanent move to New Hampshire. Was lookin' forward to you and me bein' together 'til they moved, but when Big Mama closed up the sewing machine, I knew it was over. They be leavin' in a few more days."

This news bothered her, but far less than Sky's frown when she apologized for neglecting him lately. She tried to wipe it away by inviting him to sit beside her on a stair step beside her. When he refused, she understood. He had been taught his place in life and sitting on the steps in the mansion was not where he belonged, definitely not his hakka bakka.

"I been sensing something. What is it?"

"It's so hard to… this is…this is…I…I want to thank you for all you've done for me and to be first to know I have slept here for the last time."

He only stared. She never noticed because her words gushed forth like water from a hydrant. "Willie and I are really really connected. His parents are divorced and since movin' here with his mom, he wants to get away as much as I want to get away from my gramma. Besides, he's found a garage apartment and we're moving in."

Sky looked down and never looked up for what seemed like forever. "What else you know about him?"

"I don't need to know more. We're in the same boat."

His eyes jumped from the floor to her face "So that's gonna make it work? You thinkin' you found a Moses who gonna lead you outta Egypt to the Promised Land?"

"Come on Sky. Gimme a break. I'll be sixteen next month and wouldn't say this to anyone but you, but I've seen more of the world and read more than most my age. Willie will be twenty one on New Year's Day and we know what we're doing. Please understand."

"I'm tryin', tryin' hard but when I was sixteen, I wanted to be the first pres-i-dent of the United States and you can sure guess where that idea ended up. Then I wanted to work for the phone company and climb up the poles. But when they sent me out on a job to repair the wires on a pole the first time, I got a few feet up there, looked down, my stomach threw me a fit and it was all over."

"So then what happened?"

"I found me a job cuttin' grass for people on the ground where I was safe."

"Here, at the mansion?"

"No ma'am. That came later. Word got around that I was dependable and...but I'm sayin' all this, cuz when we growin' up we fulla ideas, a good thing, a real good thing, Then after we try some of 'em we find they was bad ideas or maybe we stepped into the wrong yard."

"I know all that, Sky. All the books are about struggles, it seems."

"Guess so. But think about it like this. God never made things easy for his only son neither."

"Crap! Of all the people I know, I thought you would support me."

"I loves you Mandi girl. What your gramma gonna say about this?"

"Frankly, my dear Sky, I don't give a damn."

Sky rubbed his forehead. "You know Mandolin darlin,' I'm a whole lot older than you is and I'm not always sure what I'm doing. But I been knowin' you for a long time and know for sure you gonna do what you're gonna do."

He enveloped her. "I'm gonna miss my girl same as when Lillian moved off."

Her lip trembled. Was she sure she knew what she was doing? Was she impatient like her dad said? Her challenge was to prove to Sky she was right.

"Will you come over and see us when we're fixed up?"

Sky always wanted what was best for her, and he played along even though she read his misgivings. "You and Tina both makin' changes. She thinkin' of being a nurse and we been listenin' and helpin' her decide."

She cuddled close to Sky. "You're a really good dad and friend. I love you so much, Sky-ball."

He squeezed her tight. She fell back, looked him over and hugged back. It was more difficult than she thought to say goodbye… for him as well. "You go on out there and give the world a fit! I know you won't get into no trouble, but you know where I am if you need me."

"How about if I don't need you and just want to stop by for a visit?"

There was no need to answer. That same old grin pulled his shiny face tight and he held back his tears.

Mandolin was uptight. "Can I ask your advice before I go?"

"Seems like you gone past that now."

Mandolin threw her arms around his neck. "Never say that, Sky. Please take that back. I'll always need you… as long as I live."

"How can I help you, darlin'?"

"What should I do Sky? What would you do? During our trip, I found out that Jacques is an imposter. He exposed himself to me, is no Frenchman, and is after my gramma's money .I know this for a fact."

"I believes you, but sure wish I didn't hafta."

"Should I tell her what's been going on?"

"You know how I feels about Miz Mac and lemme aks *you* something. What if there was talk about this new friend of yours, like he had another girl or was a druggie? You gonna believe it?"

"No. Willie and I have talked out a lot of things and I'm sure he doesn't do drugs and hasn't got another girlfriend."

"So you're gonna defend Willie, same as Miz Mac gonna stick up for Mr. Jack. Still it may be right to tell her 'fore she gets hurt."

"How about if I confide in Gilbert, the security guard at the Guild Shop?"

"Good idea. From what I understands, he's tough on all kinds of crime."

"Thanks."

"Before you leave, Miz Mac left another box of her clothes for the Guild Shop. You might should go through 'em in case… well, they is pretty high end, as my girls would say."

"Let's ask if they want them."

Sky stood still seemingly in deep reflection. "Oh my! It kinda struck me bad to hear about Mr. Jack stealing."

"I'm sure no one will own up. They don't want other gifts or my gramma's money to be cut off from the Guild Shop."

Sky shrugged and watched Mandolin walk up the stairway to her room unaware that a rush of emotion had grabbed her. It was her last climb up the long stairway. She had certainly been made aware that with wealth comes an obligation to keep up with it. Now she was about to return to the simple life she once knew.

Inside, she shut the door as always, sat in the window seat and looked out the window at an imaginary Sky in the Grasshopper. A melancholy smile crossed her face when the door opened. OMG! It was "day-jas voo" as Jacques would say. Hopscotch burst in and demanded an answer. "Why did you take the photograph off the wall, Madolin?"

Her tone as always, attacked her euphoria and ignited her resolve to approach the Jacques issue with her gramma, "Let's talk about that in a minute, Hopscotch. There's something I need to tell you and I hope you understand it's to help you in the future."

"Nothing *you* have to say could possibly be meaningful to me. I have had a long and difficult life and now I am happy. I'd preferrf not be trroubled by your trrifles. But what is it now?"

Mandolin grew tense. It was more than obvious that *little Madolin* was not ever going earn her gramma's respect or ever matter to her. What was the use? Hopscotch repeated the question. "Why did you rremove the picture of Eleanorr Rroosevelt from the wall, Madolin?"

That dug up another issue! Mandolin rose to her full height and looked down at her gramma. "Why did you remove the great portrait of your son, my dad from the wall? And where are the two packages he brought with us when we came?"

Hopscotch frowned and looked around at the emptied room. "And just what is this all about, if may ask."

"You were good to put me up and I thank you, but I'm getting out of Dodge."

"Getting out of Dodge, ar-r-e you? Where is Dodge?"

"Never mind. I'm moving on just as you and Buster are."

"Buster? Are you referring to my darling as Buster? You are an impudent, young…"

Mandolin hopped over her words." Odd isn't it that our lives never meshed and we are both checking out at the same time?"

"What? *You* cannot go! I need you to watch over the house while Jacques and I go to New Hampshire to make plans for our wedding."

"Sorry. I have found another place and a roommate who thinks I'm not too bad."

"You cannot do this to me. I will not leave without a person I know in charge."

"A person you know? That makes me laugh. You don't know me. You don't know 'your Jock' and you sure don't know yourself."

"Your impudence is beyond belief. I shall discuss this with Jacques."

In her usual hardnosed style, Hopscotch barged out and slammed the door. Mandolin talked to her through the door. "I did my best and while you continue to connive against me, I'll find the packages and the painting if it's the last thing I do."

She then pulled on her tight, torn jeans, a snug body shirt, checked The Pink Oink, gasped sadly and scooted down the stairway, without the hammock.

4.
A Cat in the Hat

MANDOLIN DOUBLED UP THE crooked steps, trailed by Mingle, her name for the cat. At the door she tried to keep him out, but Mingle wanted in. She cuddled him when she really wanted to cuddle Willie. In fact she wanted more that a cuddle. She had unloaded on her gramma, was wound up and eager for a new kind of relationship.

"Willie?"

A disgruntled voice came from the closet.

"Hi. It's me. Sorry to be late."

"Are you?"

She hated his tone. "What's going on in there?"

"Nothing. I'm just trying to hang up my clothes."

"Want some help?"

"No."

"You sound mad. Did I do something wrong?"

"No! You did not do anything wrong."

"Something happened, then. Tell me. I'm good at solving problems."

He shot out of the closet. "The boss ate me out because I ordered too many helmets. Okay?"

Mandolin took his hand.

"You told me about that over the phone. Is there something else?"

"Forget it." He rubbed the back of his neck, obviously in pain.

"What's wrong with your neck?"

He rolled his head around. "It comes from tension."

Mandolin reached around and gently massaged his neck. His head fell. It felt good, she could tell. He sat on the bed, leaned over, she climbed on the bed, kneeled behind him and massaged his head and shoulders until he began make sounds of contentment. He lay back on the bed; she went to the foot of the bed, pulled off his jeans and spoke in a quiet lusty voice.

"I love it here, Willie! It's so like the cottage where I lived when I was little except it's not on the beach. And, by the way, I adore you."

She massaged his neck, arms and shoulders until he totally relaxed. She then slipped off her clothes and tried to pull down his jockey shorts until they got twisted. He offered no help which was beautiful because he she had time to look him over and thrill at the prospect of having have sex with Mister Magnificent, a guy who was ready. Slowly manipulating his jockey shorts down his legs, she then threw herself at him. In Biology class as well as and hot novels, she had learned valuable maneuvers, She blew in his ear and bit his lip, both gently and, then pressed her body against his, absolutely committed to making her first time with a guy his happiest memory. They explored all the places where fingers fit; eyes, nostrils, ears and around the lips until led by their emotions, they breathlessly connected, and lost all sense of reality.

In a manner of a few minutes, it was brought back. Mingle leaped onto the bed and Willie jumped out of it.

"What the fuck! How did that cat get in here?" He kicked Mingle out the door." Get lost!"

"I'm sorry, Willie. I let Mingle in. He obviously likes to mingle in good places with good people."

She had hoped to amuse him, to encourage him back to bed.

He had had enough. He had responded, perhaps not as eagerly as she had hoped, but what did she know. Maybe women were just more passionate…or her squeal of pain had upset him more than her expressions of ecstasy. Once again she assured him she had never been this happy and that her lovemaking would improve. But would it? Here came that feeling of inadequacy again.

He slipped into his jockey shorts and spoke his thoughts. "Oh well, maybe it's a good thing."

"What does that mean?"

"Nothing! Nothing. I forget how you like to ask questions."

His words seemed guarded which bothered her. She had done her best, what would Sky say? She had not taken Heather's advice and could never discuss it with either of them. That's when she noticed a drop of blood on the sheet and was mortified. Had he seen it? She hoped not because it might scare him from having sex again. She stayed in bed until the time came to wash out the spot.

From the bathroom, Willie announced that his mother should be arriving soon with more of her things to fix up their place.

Was this a good thing? Mandolin held back her questions about decorating and when he appeared fully dressed, she quickly placed her pillow over the spot and took a turn in the bathroom.

Shortly thereafter wrapped in a new sort of courage and a short red robe, she reappeared with her comment. "O…kay. I can only hope your Mom's gifts are not as ugly as those in the room I moved out of."

"I'd say we take what we get and be grateful."

"You're right. I'm often over-eager to make things right."

"You can say that again."

What? Had she been too eager? All at once she had a feeling she was in the wrong place like Prissy her favorite character in *Gone with the Wind*. When Scarlett asked for help with the birth of Miss Mellie's baby, Prissy clutched. "Me? Ah…ah don' know nuthin' 'bout birthin' no baby, nuthin' a-tall.'

218

Mandolin didn't know nuthin' 'bout babies, livin with a guy and less 'bout keepin' peace with his mother.

But why was she thinking like Prissy? The trip to Europe as well as the support from Sky and Big Mama had boosted her confidence in most areas. Disappointing them would tear it apart. She had to toughen up.

In the kitchen, she watched a cockroach wiggle his feelers through the crack at the top of an open carton of milk, then crawl down the side and scoot towards her. She had seen many bugs before but none so black, so bold or so vile. She held her breath, kept her eyes on its every move until Willie chased it out the door. It appeared that all creatures great and small (*thanks to novelist James Herriot*) the cat, cockroaches and spiders resented this intrusion into their adopted domain. So far, it wasn't Mandolin's world at all, and she was trying hard to keep a positive attitude.

While she was looking around their place for ideas to make it cozy, the sight of Willie with a shiny new omelet pan above his head came with relief. "Wait'll you taste my omelets."

Anxious to please, she exclaimed "Nifty, I love omelets."

"Me too. My uncle taught me how as a kid and I've discovered it's a helluva lot cheaper to eat in, but my friend found a cool, cheap place outside the loop."

OMG. Money! It had never occurred to her that money would be an issue. They talked it over. She promised to be frugal, but not *parsimonious*, the word she felt best described Hopscotch. They high-fived the deal.

"I'm meeting a friend for a coffee."

"Who is this mysterious friend?"

"You'll like him. Need anything?"

"What about your mother? You said she was coming."

"Oh, her. I'll be back before she gets here."

"Do you know when *your friend* is moving in?"

He looked away with disgust.

"Don't ignore me Willie, that's what my gramma does."

He threw his hat on the bed, muttered something she didn't hear and left. Mandolin felt depressed and disoriented. School began on Monday and she had to get settled. But where to start?

A knock on the door surprised her. Was it Willie's friend or his mother?

She opened the door and Tina received a mighty hug. They scrubbed and swept, and when it came to the bare walls, Tina knew just what to hang, anything with color. Willie's gaudy Hawaiian shirts would do as a start. In addition, Mandolin pepped up the place with a few of her animal drawings while Tina wiped the kitchen counters and filled the cleaned cabinets with dishes Sky had sent.

A call came in on Mandolin's cell. It was from Sky and his words flabbergasted her. "What? She's moving in three days?...Help her? Me?...Well I...you're right as usual...Oh no! Not another of those boring farewell parties of hers?...Okay...but only for you...Miss you too...See you there this weekend."

Tina watched her click off the phone and immediately asked herself how anyone in love could give a party just for herself? But that shouldn't surprise her. Big Mama used to tell her that she never understood the marriage of Miz Mac. She never let her husband know what she was doing.

Mandolin was a little shaky on the subject of love and boyfriends. She so hoped Willie and she belonged together and wondered how long it would take to know for sure. An idea struck! Introducing Willie to Sky at Hopscotch's party would help. At least she thought he would say some good things about her. Until then, she had a list of things to accomplish; her test at school; to help Hopscotch pack, and to run the Komen Cancer Cure for Ginger's mother. She was always good to me."

"It seems to me the more you have on your plate Mandolin, the happier you are."

Tina had to leave for a second and promised to be back. Mandolin mulled over the comment. Tina was right. She was always planning ahead. It helped take the ever-present feeling of abandonment away and kept up her spirits.

Was Willie's mother actually coming? Why did Willie seem so distant at times? Had he enjoyed their sex as much as she did? One of her hunches told to stay alert for *hakka bakka*, although she wanted to believe she was already where she truly belonged. If Willie came with her to the farewell party at Terror she was sure their relationship would grow; and if they were together when they found the missing packages her dad had brought, it was possible he would understand more about her parental problems.

The bed was a mess and in the middle of it was Mingle in Willie's hat. Help! She removed Mingle gently, scolded him and when she put him out the door and met Tina and Heather there… each with a heavy grocery bag. They sang happy birthday to her which absolutely delighted her. "What are you doing here, Heather? Did you tell Hopscotch about my Mexican blooper?"

Mandolin learned in a flash that Heather was there because she canceled her doctor's appointment "ta whip up a little surprahse for her birthday." She presented her a container of hearty soup and Rice Krispie Treats as well as a few things she froze for her and her boyfriend.

Tina was touched, and while Tina showed Heather around, Mandolin found the haggis recipe from Speedy in Scotland. They celebrated until noon with Krispie treats and juice when Heather said she had to get back to the mansion to put the finishing touches on Hopscotch's farewell party. Tina took issue. First, she thought the party should be a birthday celebration for Mandolin, and second she didn't understand Mandolin's thinking. "I don't have a boyfriend like you, but if I did I'd never take him to a big party until later."

Mandolin agreed in part.

"At times I feel awkward with him."

"Awkward? Why? Is he into drugs or something?"

"Oh no! "I'd smell it by now if…"

Heather was ready to go. She thought their place was "real nahce" and Tina left to take her back to Terror.

Mandolin was putting away the treats when Willie burst in. Impulsively she plunged onward. "Hey Willie. I'd so like you to meet a couple of my good friends at a party tonight. Some are awesome and if they're not your type, I know a cool game we can play there. Will you come with me?"

He was guarded. "What's the game?"

"It's called the waiter game and it's fun. Let's get dressed. I'll teach you on the way over."

He finally relented. Mandolin pulled down the shade and broke the cord which made it flip open. This meant they now had no privacy. Where were the carols sung around the piano, the mistletoe to stand under for a kiss, and the laughter she had shared with Sky and his family? This day totally lacked pizzazz. Mandolin had grown to expect explosions from Willie when things went wrong. This was one was only minor.

It took some time to remedy the shade and a few hours later, they were ready and arrived in silence at the height of the party. Sky met them graciously at the door in his formal party attire and his usual shine. He told her about a man with a deep voice who had called her several times and left his number.

"That was Gregory. Don't take another call, Sky. He's a real pest."

Willie took note. Sky then handed her two letters.

"Here you go, Mandolin. One is from New Jersey and this one… well I never did see a stamp like this one before."

"I'm psyched. They remembered me. Thanks."

She opened the one with the unusual stamp. "Look Sky and Willie, these are my friends from Scotland. This one is Kevin, this one is his grandson and—"

From behind came that familiar Scottish voice "Madolin, dar-rling. Look whom I have brought to meet you. Isn't he divine?"

Mandolin gave a polite nod to the guest, and then launched her own introduction.

"Hopscotch, my *dar-rling gramma,* look who I have brought to meet you! This is Willie, my new roommate."

Sensing what was coming, Hopscotch's Divine Guy, quickly stepped away and her attack on Mandolin followed.

"What? What are you saying? You never asked my permission to move away."

"You've never cared what I did or didn't do. And besides that, I am sure you would certainly not allow me to live alone in *Terror.* I mean in this mansion when you are gone."

Willie stuck out his hand. "Hello, Mrs. MacDuck."

"Mrs. MacDuff is my name and I bet my granddaughter put you up to that, did she not?"

"Oh no ma'am. My mistake."

"Never call me ma'am. I am from Scotland and I am neither accustomed to nor appreciate being addressed as ma'am."

Willie turned to Mandolin for help. Sky took the ball. "How about somethin' to drink, Willie?"

"Ginger ale, please, but I can get it."

Hopscotch gasped. "Ginger Ale? We have all kinds of drinks but no one ever asks for Ginger Ale."

"What do you drink, ma'am?" Willie asked.

"I…I never touch alcohol, if that's what you mean."

Mandolin's eyes nearly shot through the skylight. Had the disappearing jug of Grasshoppers escaped her memory? Had her gramma been so wiped in Scotland that the…the episodes had not sunk in? Was she trying to hide something?

Willie was unaware of this and with a playful glance at Willie, Sky offered to fix his specialty, a skyball martini. "Yes sir, Willie. Be back right away."

"Pleased to have met you, ma'am. Oh Jeez! Sorry."

"Never take the name of our Lord in vain in my house," announced Hopscotch sanctimoniously. "What is your name again, young man?"

Mandolin ignored the question and took Willie's hand. "On your mark, get ready, get set, here we go into the living room to meet '*the madding crowd.*'" (*a quote from Wuthering Heights, a required novel by Emily Bronte she had read in school.*)

The cocktail chatter was deafening in a room crowded with stylish guests of all ages. The women chose cocktail outfits; the younger men in sharp current suits; the older gents wore bright ties, shirts and blazers, each one clutching a glass of wine, a highball, or a dry martini with the recent inclusion of a twist of apple or orange.

She invited Willie to sit in the same seat as at her first party. It was in the corner where she had once sat against the flowered wallpaper shivering with intimidation. He appeared restless and told her he'd be back in a minute. She wondered where he was headed. He seemed he liked his independence.

What a difference nine years made. She was still often overwhelmed by glitz and glamour and yet had learned from Theodore and Hildegard plus a disputes course at school, that listening rather than speaking inanely was vital for good relationships, as well as for detective work. She absorbed the interplay of a group of young women close by.

"Did I tell you that my Alicia made all A's first semester?"

An interruption. "So then guess what happened?"

Another interruption. "Do you put in the toilet paper so that it rolls out from the top or bottom?"

"How about this? I was telling Lucretia about my Czech friend when she interrupted me with a snotty comment: "Really Florence, the word is chic, not check."

Mandolin smiled and thought it out. Maybe she should check

with the sheik about her sore cheek before attending a chic party of sick chicks.

Then, on the other side of the room as it often happened, the men had formed a group among them Judge Baker, the lawyer who had secured her passport from Malaysia years before. She looked around for Willie and in his absence, joined the men to hear comments of dings in fenders by wives who parked too far from the curb, business deals, traffic, weather, sports and politics.

Willie returned. Mandolin greeted him warmly. "Hi! There's Judge Baker over there. He knew my dad."

Willie elbowed her side. "Let's get out of here. My parents entertained these same kinds of people—full of themselves and boring."

"I agree. It's like they don't see us—but let's not leave yet. I want you to meet the Judge and we haven't played the Waiter Game. See that man over there talking to the woman with the fake boobs?"

"The one that looks like a drag queen?"

Mandolin nodded and waved to Willie to follow her. She addressed the woman.

"Excuse me. I'm Mandolin, Hopscotch's granddaughter and this is Willie, Hopscotch's new waiter."

Willie was stuck. Mandolin took over. "There's such a crowd that if you tell Willie what you want, he'll bring it to you."

"Let's see. What will I have? Oh. I'll have a Cosmopolitan tonight."

Mandolin whispered to Willie and he asked the guest, "Another one?"

Mandolin was delighted he wanted to play. The guest was shocked and asked for Sky who was "polite and knew how to fix a Cosmopolitan exactly to her liking."

Willie looked at Mandolin. "So this is supposed to be fun?"

"Sorry. Last time I only had to pour margaritas for the guests and met all kinds of fun people."

In the kitchen, Mandolin introduced Willie to Heather and raved about his omelets.

"Hi there, Willie. Good for you. Ah've learned a bunch of new things since ah came to work here. Mah real name is Fanny but Mrs. Mac related it to my'"… she grabbed a buttock with each hand "my big bohunkus back here, and Fanny fell outa favor." She laughed heartily and winked. "Come to think of it, that lady called *Fanny* is good spirited. We've had some laughs around here and lots of surprises."

She went out of her way to be cordial to Willie and he took to her immediately. Even with her hands busily slicing up a juicy rare roast beef with "foody hands", she stretched out her arms and welcomed him in. "Our girl Mandi may be a handful, but she's the best of the best and has a real good head on your shoulder." Heather laughed at herself.

"You're precious, Heather," smiled Willie.

Precious? For some reason the word bothered Mandolin. Was it because it was too delicate a word for a guy or because she hated sicky-sweet anything? He raved about Heather's horseradish sauce and Mandolin took a taste. It caught her by surprise; she coughed and choked out the words. "Sorry. This happens every once in awhile. Did you know I don't have a uvula?"

Willie shot her a look of disbelief. "You don't need to tell us all your personal problems, y' know."

Heather burst into laughter. "Willie boy. She's not talking about what you think. Sounds pretty much like it, but a uvala is the little gismo that hangs down in the back of your throat and helps you swallah." She pointed to hers, wrote down the horseradish recipe, gave Heather a farewell hug, tucked the recipe in his shirt pocket and they returned to the entrance atrium. She wanted to take his hand. He went on ahead of her.

A few guests were dispersing. Others, including Judge Baker had congregated around the sleigh.

Afraid of missing something, Mandolin wanted to stay. Willie offered to return for her in an hour and departed. Mandolin joined the group and tagged on to the Judge's joke.

"And then my granddaughter continued: 'Come on Daddy-o, it's the truth. I actually did see the cow jump over the moon last night." And so I asked her if she could jump as high as a cow and she assured me she could jump higher."

Mandolin stepped into the scene. "Good for your granddaughter. She sounds like me when I was young. Whatever you do, listen to her and don't make fun of anything she says. Hi, Judge Baker. You don't remember me but I'm Mandolin MacDuff."

"Well, well, well, Mandolin. You have become a lovely young woman."

Mandolin smiled. "You know what, you're an inspiration. You know how to kid and be serious, play dumb and be smart and say all the right things."

"You should hear me in court, sweetheart. *No* one wants to hear what I say, but that's the nature of most trial lawyers."

"If I hang with you, I'll bet you can help me with all kinds of things, especially finding my mom."

He slipped her his card. She jotted down naughtynauticalnut@ hotmail.com and handed it back to him.

The doorbell rang. She looked at Pink Oink. It was too early for Willie to be back; yet there he was. She waved him over, told him she was ready except for a quick question for Mr. Baker. Willie closed his eyes and sighed.

She explained her interest in being a private investigator and asked about the Lockerbie bombing case. "So, if they found out that Megrahi blew up the Pan AM flight in 1988 and put him in prison, why do they want to set him free after killing American kids and parents over Scotland?"

Willie was about to blow a fuse. Judge Baker continued his dialogue with Mandolin. "Your facts about the attack are astoundingly accurate and you ask brilliant questions. Wars in that part of the world are often caused by tribal factions or misunderstandings between countries and then inflamed by greed and pride. The US supposedly killed the daughter of Gadhafi, and he felt he had to strike back to preserve his honor in the Arab world."

The Judge placed his arm around Mandolin. "You are a woman now, a woman of great character and determination. Let's talk tomorrow about your mother."

She hooked her arm into Willie's and they headed out. "You know what, Willie? If I hang with him, before you know it, I'll be as successful a Private Investigator as he is a lawyer."

Judge Baker called to Willie. "Let's walk out together. It will give me an opportunity to hear about *your* activities."

"I'm into biking, sir."

"He works for *Bikes ETC* and I help him when I can."

"Ho ho! I've been doing my biking indoors at the gym and after my current trial ends, I'll stop by. Maybe you'll fix me up with the works. My granddaughter and I have been talking about taking a bike trip together."

Mandolin explained the shop's location.

"I'll be there."

They arrived at Willie's jeep. The Judge had more to say. "Used to drive one of these myself. In fact I was a sucker for a good looking girl and had a special one, one night. The moon got to us and first thing I knew I missed her curfew which cut that little romance off quick as a hiccup."

His story amused Mandolin more than Willie and while he cleaned off a fender with his shirt sleeve, the judge chatted with him. "So you're Willie, short for William, I imagine. That's a famous name in our country, as you know. Let's see, we've had many men named William in our government. Presidents, like William Harrison, McKinley and

Clinton; Chief Justice William O. Douglas, as well as William Howard Taft who was both."

Mandolin thought he must be lonely because he liked to talk. As for Willie, when he heard that the judge hoped to see them again on New Year's Eve, he had had it.

"Oh no," Mandolin replied." Hopscotch is leaving on Monday for New Hampshire."

"Really? Earlier she told me to save the date for another of her rip-roaring New Year's Eve bashes."

Mandolin jumped in, "I didn't get the word, but it's okay. It's okay." She looked into Willie's eyes lovingly. "We have a big birthday to celebrate that night."

Judge Baker shook Willie's hand vigorously, opened the door to Willie's truck and indicated for her to get in. "Look forward to knowing you better, Willie. And take good care of this girl, she's different and I mean that in the best way."

Willie nodded, made no reply and they took off.

"This is Microsoft age, for God's sake Mandolin. We gotta move on! Is he a full of it, or will he actually come to the shop?"

"I like him…a lot. If he said to count on him, we should. One day I'll tell you about all the things he's done for me…like he helped get me started in school here in the States."

He shrugged "Maybe so, but he's one helluva bore."

Mandolin was really taken back. "Please don't be mad at me, Willie. I like you so much and arguments get to me."

Forcing a smile, he replied "Everything was kinda weird tonight."

"It always is around my gramma. That's why I want to move in with you. Would you rather I didn't?"

"I'd rather you didn't talk about yourself so much, but outside of that, I think what the judge said is about right. You're different."

"Phew! Thanks."

5.

Was the cupboard bare?

Mandolin nicknamed their place 'Ourspace.com.' It was hardly snug, but it was theirs and they had each had enough dissension to last the rest of their lives. They would work around their differences. He was convinced that always winning was not worth the effort, which she needed to hear. If either one wanted to see a specific movie, they agreed that the other would either go for it, or make plans on his or her own.

Mandolin so wanted Willie to fall for her and did her best to make it happen. One night, she kicked off her tennis shoes and in her tight skirt and tank top she danced around and sang her version of one of Big Mama's favorite Cole Porter songs.

"You'd be so easy to love
So easy to idolize all others above
So worth the yearning for
So easy to keep the home fires burning for…"

Willie waved her off.

"I just noticed your crooked toes. Have they always been that way?"

She covered one foot with the other.

"No Willie, no! I'm not falling for this. When I lived with my Dad,

I loved the world and everyone in it. Then I came to Houston and met my gramma who totally destroyed my buoyancy and permeated my life with doubts. Much against her own wishes she included me in a trip to Europe and on my own I met people who cared about me. I returned from that trip with confidence, met you and now I refuse to allow you to destroy it with insignificant comments about my actions or crooked toes."

He looked surprised and she felt she had made an impression particularly when he asked about the letters Sky had given her. Was he jealous? She hoped so and finally replied "Oh, they're friends, one is an ex-boyfriend."

"Don't they have e-mail?"

Shoot! This was not the *hakka bakka* she *had* hoped for. She felt tense and not a bit celebratory. Once again she expected too much too soon. In time she would teach him to tease like her dad…if she took a different tangent.

"Wish you had met the friends I made in Scotland."

"What makes you say that?"

"The love this one couple had for one another after many years depicted her idea of a perfect marriage. They…they were kind to each other and listened to me no matter what I said." She looked at him with an endearing smile. "I suppose they made me feel important. Me! Important!"

"So that's what you care about?"

"Not exactly. My interest in investigative work became stronger because of this prominent lawyer."

"Let's hear the letter."

"You don't act really interested. We can talk about something else."

"I'd like to hear the letter."

He sounded harsh and angry, but she read it anyway. "*My dear Mandolin, Theodore and I so enjoyed meeting you in Scotland. You are an enterprising young woman and you impressed us both. If you have any need for help with your gramma's friend, please contact us at our New Jersey address. We care about you a great deal. Our fondest regards, Hildegard Badenhausen."*

Mandolin put down the letter. "This proves they too were suspicious of Jacques."

"Am I supposed to care about all these people?"

"Sorry, Willie, but I so wish you'd help me. I'm afraid my gramma wants to marry a guy who's after her money and only escorts rich ladies so they'll wine and dine him."

"Many homosexuals like older, wealthy women as well."

"Is that right? I never knew that."

"I...I...there's a helluva lot you don't know."

"True and ever since I was little I've been trying to catch up." She smiled. "So, if I had my toes straightened, would it help our relationship?"

He stared at her. She gave him an impish look.

"Or how about if they replaced my uterus, I mean my uvula? Would that do it?"

No reaction. Not even a smile. Crap! What should she do? He turned his back to leave.

"Don't go, please. That's what my gramma does. The minute we start to connect, she leaves."

"I...I got used to mine. Chill!"

"How did you...?"

He slipped on his jacket and headed out. Was she oversexed or was he lacking libido?

"I'm hungry. Lou and other friends meet at Kimm's Bar every other night after work and so I'm joining them."

"Have a good time. Maybe one of these times you'll invite me to come too."

He smiled a quick one. "By the way, my boss wants you to work for us."

She hugged his unresponsive body. "You must have done a really good sales job."

"Nope, you did. She was in her office and heard our entire conversation."

Thud! How good it would have felt it hear that he had talked his boss into it. And yet her enthusiasm prevailed. "Yes! Yes! Yes!" she exclaimed, pumping her fist in the air. "We'll be working together on weekends and holidays."

Willie moved to the door and waved goodbye. "Toodles, I'm leaving."

Crap! Why can't I love a laid-back kind of a guy, she asked herself? Then her friend Pink Oink caught her eye. It was 6:15 and she had not a trace on an appetite. She threw on her trash jeans, an old shirt and flip flops. She had to get out of there, gathered her books and headed to the school library. An important test on jury duties was coming up followed by two lectures; one on ways to approach a jury and another on how a mock trial works. She couldn't wait to get started on all of this.

At Thanksgiving Willie offered to cook the meal. She invited Tina and Sky. He included his friend Lou who had accepted only an hour before. He was not her favorite person, but she would be good to him and make their first guests at Ourspace.Com a happy experience for all.

An image of her gloomy room at Terror flashed before her. Where was that pastel of the boy Hopscotch had removed, And where were those packages she had left at Terror the day she moved in with Willie? She kept forgetting to ask Sky if he knew and even now she was concerned that it was last day of the church sale and they had no pumpkins. A small donation to the church was gratefully received and the helpers carried the remaining pumpkins of all sizes and shapes to the back of Willie's truck.

Ourspace.Com turned into a colorful pumpkin palace—of which she and maybe Willie were proud. Mandolin made it look special with the many pumpkins she carved into amusing Pilgrim faces as well as hanging several of her colorful tissue paper animal drawings on the wall Unbelievably they were still providing spending money in various cheap eateries.

She forgot to thaw the turkey the night before. Willie kept his cool and at the proper time, proudly paraded his perfect turkey around the room to the ahs and ohs of all. Her food contribution was feeble. The canned succotash was only fair and she managed to scrape just enough overdone rice from the pot to feed the group. Tina and Sky praised their organized efforts while Lou sulked because he missed his cranberry sauce and green beans.

Mandolin placed a bowl of fruit on the table and they finally sat on whatever was available around the glass top table. It seemed that much of what she learned came from conversations when seated at a table. Mandolin bowed her head and said a grace.

"Bless this food, all the hands that prepared it and especially those that are not with us. Amen."

When she opened her eyes, she noticed that Lou and Willie were eyeballing one another. Was it because they were unaccustomed to a blessing or because they knew Willie had prepared most of it? Mandolin let it go and discussed Quintus and Cisco. She was sorry they had other plans. Tina missed Lillian, hated it that she had to be with Joseph's family and not with them, but understood.

"Joseph? Who the hell is he?" asked Lou.

Tina took offense. "He's an Iranian med student and the coolest possible brother- in-law any one could have. They'll make a super team."

Sky and Mandolin showed support by nodding.

The conversation chugged along. Mandolin asked Lou when he was moving in and was told it had been postponed for reasons of his own. Various turkey stuffings such as bread crumbs mixed with onions, chopped gizzards and cranberries; rice with apricots and sausage, and pistachios, apples, and oysters were discussed. Mandolin was reduced to using a packaged one because a certain selfish, Scottish lady interfered with Heather's offer to help her. While they ate heartily and in silence, Mandolin wondered about her mom, her whereabouts and if she celebrated Thanksgiving. Sky and Tina offered to help clean up. Willie waved them away and took Lou home. Mandolin tidied up and fell asleep before Willie returned.

During Christmas break, Mandolin worked daily side by side with Willie at the bike store except for the day she took off for personal reasons.

Sales were brisk in all departments due in part to Mandolin's creative, colorful tree decorations of paper and engaging ways with the customers. When Judge Baker brought in his granddaughter and Harry, his granddog named for him, Mandolin nudged him into a Christmas splurge of bike gear for all of them.

At their place, Willie set up a two foot tree with a few lights by a fake mantel in hopes that Santa soon would be able to find them. Mandolin decorated it with colorful plastic spoons, and forks, a few streamers and a sprig of mistletoe, that she often stood under to no avail.

On Christmas morning, Mandolin woke up first. He faced the wall and she took the spooning position, nothing new. She always woke up excited, cuddled him and began to feel his comfort level improving slowly. She ran her hand gently and adoringly along the contour of his beautiful back. He groaned and turned over. "Merry Christmas dear Willie," she said with tenderness.

"Oh my God! It's Christmas," he said as he jumped out of bed and went to the door. She sat up and watched. He did in fact find presents outside the door from his friends and hers which bothered her since she had none for them. With her arms wrapped around her legs, she watched Willie open his presents with rare enthusiasm, a treat to see. Afterwards they celebrated with hot chocolate before they climbed back into bed. Mandolin studied Willie. He cracked an eye. She wished him another Merry Christmas, and was sorry they had agreed not to exchange presents on this, their first Christmas. But she wanted to make the day a happy one and scurried into her playful mode.

"Remember the day we met, Willie?"

"How could I forget it?"

"I dreamed of this day."

"Well?" he asked in a kind of off-handed way.

"Promise not to laugh?"

"Come on Mandolin, what's on your mind?"

"Okay Wee Willie Winkie, who said it's not too hard, not too soft, but just right?"

"Got it. One of the three bears."

"Wrong." It was Goldilocks and I'm with her. I think *you're* just right."

He tensed and asked if she had anything for his mother.

"Your mother? No sweetie. I wanted to buy you a new shirt, but was afraid you'd think me extravagant and the type who wants to change a guy."

Willie shrugged, folded his hands behind his head and looked her over with an expression she had never seen before. It felt tender.

"Do you ever have unusual ideas?"

She pursued his question. "You mean, like… like when you want to have sex every minute?"

"Not exactly that."

"I have many weird ideas all the time. What do you mean?"

"Just checking you out, I guess."

She pulled her hair down and looked at him with her fetching Marilyn Monroe look. "Um-m-m. Sex in the City—in daylight?"

She took his hand and guided it over her body when her stomach had a fit. She gagged and took a deep breath to collect herself. "I'm thinking I got a bad oyster at the Fish Shack last night."

Willie sat up. "Maybe it's the hot chocolate. We've never made it before."

She barely made it to the loo in time, felt better and when she came out, Willie was waiting by the door with his clothes in hand.

He slipped into the loo without a word. She fell onto the bed and rubbed her tummy. Within minutes he appeared fully dressed and headed to the door. She stood and took his arm.

"Hey Willie, what's going on? I'm not a bad person because I got sick, y'know."

"I didn't say you were. I'm just going out to wish a few of my good friends a merry Christmas while you recover, that's all."

"Fine. But what would you think of putting me in the loop? I'd kinda like to know your plans as well."

"Sure. Hope you feel better."

She watched him leave, listened to his fast pace down the rickety steps and fell back into bed. Actually what seemed important was to re-read "Forever Amber," a lusty historical novel that she found in the Library at Terror. Plus, a look at *101 Sexual Positions,* the book Buster read on the ship could give her new ideas. Her sexual desires had mounted and in order to lure Willie, she needed to learn a whole lot more about provocative moves.

Christmas Dinner at Willie's mother's house was another unusual event. Roxie liked to eat in the late afternoon and greeted them in a severe black dress, with her jet black hair pulled tight into a bun and without makeup. She seemed timid and unsure of herself. The only Holiday décor in her small Heights home was a tiny fake tree set atop a stool in middle of the room, and decorated with Willie's swimming medals.

Mandolin's slim green skirt, red heart-shaped neckline and her every move were designed to stir Willie's interest. Lou's pink pants were way too pink for a guy she thought, but he flaunted them. Willie wore his traditional jeans, paused awkwardly at the tree, and seemed even more unsettled in the dark living room.

Where were the carols sung around the piano, the mistletoe to stand under for a kiss, and the laughter she had shared with Sky and his family? This day totally lacked pizzazz. No one asked questions which so bothered her that she impersonated a mime like the one in London. The guys totally ignored her and she was embarrassed. Finding the wine bottle opener was clearly more important. Why was she the one who always felt compelled to enliven the atmosphere? Was this how Kishore Kumar, the *hakka bakka* entertainer felt? Or was he able to choose the proper moments to turn on? Once she read one of Confucius sayings: "It's better to remain silent and be thought a fool than to open one's mouth it and remove all doubt of it." Was that really important? She tried to visualize her mom. Was she shy or outgoing? Did she have a job? Did she have children? Her thoughts drove her crazy at times and Tina was right. Keeping busy helped.

Mandolin found the opener on the table underneath the Christmas present she had brought Roxie… her drawing of a colorful lady bug on tissue paper. Roxie admired it and showed a sincere interest as a realtor in buying a few others as thank-you is for her clients. Lou struggled to open the wine, Mandolin offered help and, was brushed away just the cork popped loose and wine spewed all over the white carpet.

Lou made no apology. Was he one to refuse responsibility? Her request for a bottle of soda came speedily from Roxie, and while Mandolin scrubbed the carpet, Willie set the table and Lou asked what time they were eating.

"When the goose is cooked, Lou," answered Roxie.

"I think Lou's goose is *already* cooked," said Willie, a remark that sent him and Lou into hysterics. Lou then parodied "*has anyone ever had an Easter goose?*"

Mandolin found none of this at all amusing, empathized with Roxie who was actually serving a goose, and offered to help in the kitchen. Lou moved in ahead of her, filled the "Steu*ben*" goblets with water, and made a point of informing the others that Steu*ben* was a century-old New York company that designed handmade glassware often for royalty.

Mandolin was interested until he toasted Roxie "To you beautiful Roxie, our queen of the day." Roxie nodded sweetly. Mandolin reacted with a silent "yuck" and before all had settled in, Lou offered a blessing.

"God is great, God is good. Good God, God, where's the food?"

Mandolin found this offensive and yet at the same time, wondered if God was really so great, why he filled her life with turmoil.

Willie followed with two plates filled with hunks of goose, sweet potatoes and green beans, along with a dish of a canned cranberry sauce.

"What do you think Roxie? Did Willie and I do a good job or what?"

She was well-pleased. And so was Mandolin when Willie asked about the small heart-shaped tattoo above her left shoulder.

Phew! He had actually noticed it. "I did it for you, Willie." Her tone was alluring.

Lou coughed and Willie quickly asked his plate when it had been done. She reminded him of the day she took off from work. Roxie's face brightened once more and gave Mandolin an endearing hug. "Willie never shares much with me and all this conversation t makes me incredibly happy."

Willie nodded to Lou and they went into the kitchen. It was all so sticky and yet Roxie simply had to know that her son "came into my life at exactly the right time. I think we're learning to be more than just friends."

Roxie called to the kitchen. "What do you think, Willie?"

Something that sounded like a dish crashed in the kitchen, and when Lou and Willie marched in, each had a dessert above his head. They harmonized to *Shoo Fly Pie and Apple Pan Dowdy*.

Roxie listened, thanked them and asked "Which do you prefer, Madolin?"

"Her name is Mandolin, Mother."

Roxie reached for her hand apologetically which touched Mandolin as any and all affection did. The desserts were attacked enthusiastically by all until Lou scratched his chair along the floor. Roxie eyed the floor critically and stood as if it was time to wrap. Willie eyed Lou and told Mandolin to hang back. He needed Lou's help under the hood. Under the hood? Was that a druggie term? Surely not or she would have noticed his habit before. It was obvious that Roxie wanted them gone.

At the truck where she joined them, Willie and Lou were laughing rather stupidly, she thought. Only the seat by the front window remained which totally demolished whatever tolerance Mandolin had left for Lou's obnoxious manners and horse laughs.

"What do you do when you're not sitting between Willie and me?" she asked abruptly.

"What do you mean?"

"I mean do you have a job?"

"Of course. Haven't you heard? I am employed by one of the most esteemed architectural firms in the city."

His chicken wing nudged Willie for a reason she didn't understand. What she *did* understand was that he was absolutely in the way. She had to move him out. She spoke in her in her Scarlett O'Hara voice.

"Don't you lovely gentlemen just adoah lookin' foahwahd to tomorrah? Why somethin' always good happens especially when Willie and I are alone

togethah. It's been delightful bein' with you Lou, and we'll see you soon, darlin.'"

Willie's glance at Lou floated past her. She felt her confidence returning even though no one spoke on the way home.

The After-Christmas sales at *Bikes ETC* were slow until Julie offered to give bonuses to all who made sales above their quotas. In addition, Mandolin's suggestion to keep the Shop open later put them way over the top.

The more she was around Willie the higher her libido climbed. But she was unable to feel that hers and Willie's matched up. She then tackled 101 Sexual Positions and was near the end when a drop-dead beautiful customer told her about her love affair. After three years together, her live-in announced he had stayed with her just to keep house for him. Was this her story? Was that what Willie wanted of her? And why her mom and dad had gone their own ways? Was her Mom shy, boring, unable to help her dad make money, a prostitute, sickly with an undisclosed medical problem or something else? If only she could shake off these unsettling ideas and find her.

There was more. Hopscotch and Jacques's departure was fairly imminent as was her need to expose her gramma to the truth about the imposter. The next day, at the end of a Criminology class, she asked her teacher for her help with a hypothetical question. What if two senior citizens, the female being far older, were in a suspicious relationship and the life of a younger family member had been threatened. Her teacher surprised her. "I suggest you develop this case as an assignment."

Aha! Gilbert might be the perfect resource. When she passed the Guild Shop in her "Caddy" this time, he was locking up and she pulled up to the curb. "We missed you and your gramma at the Volunteer Appreciation Party."

"Oh, shoot! I forgot all about it and have no idea about my gramma's doings."

"Annie came and was seemed surprised Hopscotch brought her some Quark all the way from Europe."

"Me too, but I have a question for you."

Gilbert smiled. "The facts, ma'am. Just the facts."

"What do you mean?"

"Oh. Back before your day, there was a radio series called Dragnet where Jack Webb, spelled with two b's played Sergeant Joe Friday of the LA police force. He was famous for saying "the facts, ma'am, just the facts."

"I want to hear more, but first, you need to know these facts. I never knew my mom, and since the day I found out my dad died, I've been trying to find her here, there and everywhere."

"Here, there and everywhere. That reminds me of *The Scarlet Pimpernel*."

"Pumpernickle?"

" No, one of my favorite fictional characters of all time, *The Scarlet Pimpernel.*"

"I've never read it."

Gilbert was well pleased with himself. "Can't believe I'm teaching *you* something."

"What do you mean? You teach me things every time I see you. Tell me about it."

"Come to think of it, the real reason I went into security work."

Mandolin wanted to get on with her question but he was into The Pimpernel.

"A pimpernel looks like a thorny red primrose."

"I get it. This guy was sharp."

"Exactly like you. With your curiosity, you'll make a super detective."

Gilbert had hooked her. "Tell me more."

During the French Revolution, he disguised himself in order to free the nobility from certain death."

"You've helped me already. I'm not sure about the nobility bit, but know for sure Hopscotch needs the truth about Jacques and soon. What else?"

"The Pimpernel was an illusive soul. A descriptive passage goes something like this: *"They seek him here, they seek him there. Those Frenchies seek him everywhere. If you should see him, do give a yell! That damned illusive Pimpernel."*

"That's Jacques!" exclaimed Mandolin. "You're brilliant! He's exactly like that that blasted mosquito that sings around my ear every night and always gets away."

Gilbert was sympathetic. "Sounds like this Jacques and the mosquito are after blood. But The Pimpernel is different. He's a good guy."

"Okay. "I'm ready to go. Now, Sir Scarlet, I need your help. From time to time things go missing in the shop, right?"

He nodded.

"So what if there's a time when it's an inside job. Would you go after that person or persons?"

His eyes studied hers. "Not unless I had some sort of proof, like a camera shot or an eye witness."

"And if you did?"

"I would speak directly to this person and tell him or her to return the goods or face prosecution. No matter how they try, there's no right way to do the wrong thing."

"Whoa! You're a lot tougher than you look. If that's what it takes, I'm not sure I'll make a good detective, after all."

"Hang in there, Mandolin. It's well worth the pursuit and gets easier."

Mandolin went after it. She gathered names and addresses of her reliable sources and called stores in Merida...a tip from Hildegard One call led to another she finally contacted the most exclusive jewelry store there...*Turquoise de Elegancia*. Did they have a record of a Jack or a

Jacques who made a purchase in late July? If so, it would be additional proof that he was both a flake and a fake and possibly a fluke.

A reply came within a day. An American, Jack Spartacus, had bought an authentic turquoise bracelet on July twenty fourth. And the check? "Eet bounced."

Spartacus! A perfect alias for him. A Gladiator captured during the slave rebellion in the early Roman Empire who spent his life escaping. Maybe she could become "The Clever Pimpernella," approach Hopscotch on her blind side and break the case wide open.

The following morning, a teacher's holiday, Mandolin biked directly to Hopscotch's hair salon. She knew her gramma well enough to know she would be having a roots touch-up and a new do before leaving for New Hampshire. Hopscotch was under the hair drier. Mandolin approached breathlessly and waved at her to take her head out.

She yelled back. "What is it Madolin? Can't you see I'm busy?"

Still under the drier, Hopscotch turned to her manicurist and shouted. "She thinks of no one but herself all the time."

Mandolin pulled up the drier and fibbed a tiny bit. "I have news, Hopscotch. I…I found my mom."

All heads turned towards the two of them.

"Where? I suppose it was in some bar."

Mandolin was shaken and managed to say "um…um…as a matter of fact, that's exactly where I saw her."

"Well I am not a bit surprised," she announced to the room." That's where she picked up my son."

Mandolin's mouth dropped and her eyes widened.

"I met my husband at a bar as well," the stylist grinned. "Can you believe I met a dream machine on a barstool?"

"So what happened, Mrs. Mac?" the manicurist wanted to know.

"They left town and that was the …"

Hopscotch noticed everyone staring, pulled the drier back down and waved her granddaughter away.

Progress. Mandolin hadn't yet exposed Jacques but she had gained additional information that could lead to her mom.

Outside the salon she reviewed the event. So her parents met in a bar. What bar? Where? And then her thoughts jumped to Willie. She had met him in a store. What was up or not with him? None of her flirtations or sexual efforts had worked. He hugged his side of the bed, always facing the wall. Was she crazy to hang in? No. Since moving in together, things had gone well at the Shop and whenever he smiled in direction, she read pride into the look. And besides, she agreed with Thomas Wolfe. *You Can't Go Home Again.*

Her self-confidence was improving. Her teacher gave an A on her presentation of the Jacques vs. Mandolin case and suggested she follow it up with a sequel. Even when Willie pulled out his Basset Hound expression, she was convinced she would eventually win him over. She wanted him and to cheer him as Sky and Heather and her Scottish friend had her.

She and Willie stayed busy in the shop until New Year's Eve, a difficult time since it meant the end of the year. With it came painful memories of her dad's end, and still no progress in locating her mom.

Word came that Hopscotch's party was on hold. Jacques had to be back East to close a deal. Perfect! Willie planned to help fix up a friend's house for their annual New Year's Eve bash, and she didn't feel up to it. That meant she could spend quiet time with Heather and Sky and wish them the best for the New Year.

They sat in the newly remodeled kitchen of the mansion discussing the effects of the changes.

"Before you show me around, Heather, I have a question. Got time?"

"Sure. Ah always have tahm for you."

"Good. After our great trip to Mexico together, I know you can help me. It's about Hopscotch and my Mom." An attack of indigestion struck her. "Do...do you think Hopscotch has this problem with me because she hates my mom? My gramma is not always generous and if my mom stole something from her, she could be taking it out on me."

"Now, now sweet girl, you're lettin' yourself go *haywahr*. Bet she loves you more than know."

Heather opened a huge new two door monochromatic fridge and offered Mandolin the left-over turkey. Mandolin gagged and laughed at herself.

"Sorry. My stomach is sorta screwed up, but I'll take some to Willie. He thinks you're cool and will love it. And by the way has either of you found those two packages I left here when I moved out?"

Heather had not and Sky, the problem-solver, of course offered his help. "The day you came I unloaded 'em from your dad's car and took 'em up to your room. Never seen 'em since."

"I'm sure I slipped the slim one in the bottom drawer with the moth balls."

Together they searched her old room once again. Nothing turned up. Sky suggested the attic. Mandolin pulled down the ladder from the ceiling. Sky removed the rope from her hand with an explanation that he never allowed his withered arm to restrict his duties. His dignity and compassion always impressed her.

"Don't mean to be putting Miz Mac down but it's kinda hard to see her climbing up here by herself. Fact, I hope she never did."

"Hopscotch does as she pleases, Sky. You know that."

They rummaged through a few cartons and she found a dusty photograph of a pretty young redhead on a horse jumping over a fence.

"That there is Miz Mac. Used to hang over the mantle in the old place."

Heather joined in. Sure did. Back then her hair was natural red and she said somethin' ah tucked upstairs in my head. "Sure it's naturally red, and you can be sure, it's gonna still be red when ah die...d-y-e."

Sky chuckled. Mandolin now was assured that Achilles story about her horses was true. They dug their way through an attic loaded boxes and trunks. "I feel as if I'm a character in a Nancy Drew mystery story. Or else a Harry Potter character."

"Look! How about this?" Sky held up a package loosely wrapped in brown paper and a rope.

"Sky! This is the package!"

She shook as she tore off the paper. Little by little a painting of a girl somewhere in her teens was revealed. Her hair was thick and black; her figure athletic; she was and strumming a musical instrument and strolling along a beach. The title was on the back; *My Girl.*

Paralyzed by their emotions, Sky finally found the courage to say what was on his mind.

"If I - if I didn't know no better, I'd be thinking this was you, Mandi."

Mandolin broke down. "Am…am I crazy, Sky? Could…could this actually be my mom?"

"You never been crazy. Her eyes is brown and yours is green, else you could be twins."

Mandolin looked it over. "There's no signature."

"Betcha your dad did it."

"Why, Sky?"

"Seemed like your dad could do anything he wanted and like we been sayin', never did much like to take credit."

Mandolin fought tears. "So…so you're thinking Hopscotch found the painting, didn't want me to see it and brought it up here herself, right?"

"Else Mr. Jack did."

"Why didn't Hopscotch want me to see a painting of my own mom? Why?"

"Got some ideas but don't know about speaking out."

She begged him to tell her. He just shook his head.

"Come on Sky, I know you played poker with his girlfriends. Does this girl look familiar?"

"That was many years ago."

"Come on, level with me, please."

"Your papa did many things without telling Hopscotch or me."

"Whoa! I get it. My gramma hated being out of the loop. She has to know what's going and when my dad didn't tell her, she kept it all inside, just as she's doing with me."

"You way ahead of me, now."

Mandolin sat on the floor gingerly, as if in pain. She studied the painting and smiled. "My dad wanted me to see this, his impression of my happy, beautiful and talented Mom."

"You on the trail, doll-baby, same as good detectives."

She plowed into her mind. "You know what? In Scotland I decided my birth was an accident like Da Vinci's. Hopscotch must know the truth and I'll bet she worries that if word gets around that her granddaughter was illegitimate, her social image will be ruined."

Sky turned aside.

"I'm no bargain, but why didn't she stick around to help me grow up?"

"Who knows, doll baby. You and Miz Mac gotta sit down and talk."

"When? Every time I've tried she scoots off like I have a case of poison ivy."

"Well, now you knows more about her and can talk about horses and then get into the rest. Keep on tryin' and be happy your dad loved your mama enough to want his pretty little girl to know her. That's sure how I woulda done."

Mandolin rolled onto her back and pressed in her stomach for relief.

"You feelin' bad?" Sky asked.

"I'm okay. You knew my dad. I guess he never suspected he'd be a single dad."

Sky fought back tears. Mandolin grimaced and buried her face in her hands. Sky reached out with his good arm, pulled her to her feet and enveloped her like a fledgling.

"Afraid I said too much."

Nestled close, Mandolin choked out, "You never say too much, Sky. But right now...I...I gotta go. Please keep the painting for me until I know what I'm doing."

She tried to break away. He held her arm. "Look at me, doll baby."

Her eyes met his. "You not looking good. Your eyes are bloodshot and you look tired. I'm thinkin' you got too much on your plate; your boyfriend, your gramma, your job, your school and on top of all that, you lookin' for your mom. Let one of 'em go."

"Okay. I'm ready."

She ran up the stairs, stood outside Hopscotch's door and heard Jacques chatting in his accent. She knocked.

Clutching a sexy robe, Hopscotch opened the door. "Well, this is a surprise."

" I came to wish you a safe trip and a happy life with Jacques."

Hopscotch seemed pleased "Really? That's the only decent thing you've ever done. It's about time you approved of me, child."

"Sorry Hopscotch, I don't feel like a child, not with all the experiences you've given me."

Hopscotch spoke back over her shoulder. "Jacques dear, guess who's here? The pest."

Jacques replied. "Then I weel take thees opportunity to play-zure myself in your delicious shower...without you."

"And leave me alone with...her?!"

Mandolin's temper broke loose. "What makes you so angry at me? Is it because I'm illegitimate?

Time stood still. For the first time in all the years she had lived in the mansion, Hopscotch, didn't turn and walk away. Her body took the shape of a frozen mime, a totally shocked, frightened one.

Mandolin went on. "Would you be good enough to answer two questions?"

The Mime unfroze with blatant relief. "Aha! Now we have it. I suspected a motive was behind this visit."

"Why do you say that? I want to tell you…"

Sky arrived at the top of the stairs seemingly to check on Mandolin, heard voices and knocked.

Hopscotch went to the door. Mandolin followed. "'Scuse me Miz Mac. Mandolin's wantin' to keep in touch just in case something happens. I got the number right here." He slipped it into Mandolin's pocket.

Mandolin understood how much Sky wanted peace between the two and listened to her gramma's reply.

"Isn't it a lovely number-r, Sky? Mr. Jacques pulled some strings."

It was those kinds of remarks that embarrassed Mandolin and she shot forth the words of her second question like a string of firecrackers. "What happened to the painting I left in my room?"

"*Your* room? That is *my* guest room."

"Dad sent a painting of my mother for us to enjoy. Is there a reason you wanted to hide it?"

"Madolin! Madolin! Madolin! Must you continue to ask ridiculous questions? I never touched it. Sky does all the heavy moving around here."

Sky left the scene dutifully, yet unhappily. Mandolin got into her gramma's face. "It was not heavy and you know it. Did you know there is a way to learn the truth, Hopscotch?"

"And just what is that?"

"Fingerprints."

Hopscotch renewed her cynical style of putting Mandolin down. "And just how do you intend to get my fingerprints?"

"I have connections through my school… friends in the Police Department."

"Do you expect me to believe that?"

Her gramma had not the least intention of helping her find her mom. Although suffering with nausea, Mandolin was still determined to complete her mission and spoke with courage and conviction.

"Whether or not you want the truth about your dreamy Jacques as you call him, these are the facts. He collects women of all types and ages; and had a relationship with a young waitress on the QE2. He has been seeing a woman in Merida, and still pretends he is chasing *you,* a wealthy aging widow. I wouldn't be a bit surprised if he has many other predatory targets yet to be named."

Hopscotch turned to shut the door. Mandolin grabbed the handle. Hopscotch snatched it away and shrieked at Mandolin. "Now I'll tell *you* the truth. You are jealous because you have no boyfriend, and I do."

Jealousy. There it was, Hildegard's word of warning. For some reason, it made her laugh and a verse from *Alice in Wonderland* spilled out.

"In my youth, I saw an old lady standing on her head.
I feared it might injure her brain.
But now that I know there's nothing there
I'd do it again and again."

Mandolin started down the stairs but backtracked into her previous bathroom, just in time to throw up. Feeling only somewhat better, she said goodbye but never, never to Sky. She climbed into her Caddy, glimpsed him working in the front garden circle and shouted, "thanks for all your advice and don't worry about me, please! I just need to get home."

She drove off while Sky watched until his smile slowly vanished.

Back at Ourspace.Com she climbed up the dilapidating steps two at a time, stopped at the top and looked around. Something was wrong and when she entered she knew. She knew Willie had done away with Mingle, a stray like herself. And not only that, she assumed he had not wanted to face her and gone off alone.

Her heart was broken. Nausea struck again and afterwards, loyal Pink Oink revealed it was just noon. She lay on the bed, so missed a cuddle with Mingle and sobbed. Why do people act like they do?

New Year's Eve arrived. Mandolin's confidence about her future with Willie was dithering. Why? Was it due to the fact that she wasn't at the top of her game? She still loved him but…but did he really love her? When Willie asked her to help finish the decorating, she was astounded by her own reply. "If it's okay, I'll be there after I fix myself up." Whoa! Fixing herself up was something she never found important until she met Hildegard. Memories of that gracious lady inspired Mandolin to carry on…at her own speed.

Willie called from the bathroom. "It's three hours until midnight and there's still plenty to do over there. Are you coming?"

"Later."

"Come as soon as you can."

He dashed from the bathroom, waved goodbye happier than she had seen him since the day they met, and he left. She was encouraged until realizing he had not suggested coming back for her.

Tina! As she suspected Tina had zero plans and agreed to be on the alert for her call. Mandolin lay down for a short nap and the next thing she heard was a horn. She looked at Pink Oink. What? 10:10? She looked down at the street. There was Tina's car. She called her cell and found she had come to check on her because she feared an accident of some kind. It was not like Mandolin to be late.

"Sorry. I'll be ready in ten minutes. Come on up if you want."

Tina declined. Mandolin pulled herself together and while

experimenting with a French twist, began to feel better until she wondered why Willie hadn't called. Or had she slept through his call?

From a pile of outfits on the floor, she chose a slitted black skirt with the hem out. Okay. Big Mama had taught her "a stitch in time saves nine" and so basting the hem was not a problem.

What about a dressy top? Her only choices were the familiar sequined top or one heavily studded with rhinestones given to her by a classmate with a huge bosom. It was a real plunger, *so* not her type, but nothing dressy was or ever had been her type. She balled up two bunches of her thongs, and attached them with Velco inside the top'. There! Now she had a cleavage and became the Marilyn Monroe Willie hoped for.

Reminiscent of the days in Hopscotch's boudoir, she modeled and rearranged her French twist hair-do by pulling her hair over one eye and looking through it provocatively in front of a cracked bathroom mirror. Okay, this was it!

At ten thirty, Tina's horn outside made her jump. With a hoist of her top, she dashed down the stairs into the humid night and climbed into a Toyota Corolla.

Tina took a look at her.

"My God! You look smashing…the best ever. Why can't I pull myself together like that?"

Tina was like her dad. Both had a way of relaxing her. And when she related how she was pulled together with Velcro, they giggled.

They arrived at a house on a corner with country western music blasting from inside. Tina could not be convinced to join her and Mandolin entered alone. The room was dark with strobe lights, strings of balloons and colorful plastic spoons giving it a party-like flavor. A Willie Nelson tape was playing *Always on my Mind* when a cool looking dude dashed over to speak to her. Yes! She couldn't look too bad and chatted with him. His name was Jordan and did not know Willie, *her*

Willie. He spotted a friend, explained with a flipping hand, that he "simply had to meet his friend's new cub" and excused himself.

Cub? Mandolin studied him, moved in closer when the smell of alcohol and marijuana threw her a hard ball, right in the pit of her stomach. She looked around for Willie through the smoke-filled room and when she saw pipes being smoked by many, she tried to be cool. Impossible! She was shocked and sickened. She wanted Willie! If only she could…and then a cross-dresser or so it seemed with a Dolly Parton figure and dripping with jewels…swung her around to accept the bong. She felt a pull under her top. The Velcro had had it. A thong had sprung loose under her left boob. She clutched it just as whistles and horns sounded and strains of Happy Birthday arose from another corner. She wanted a ladies room, looked around, and focused on a gang surrounding Willie and Lou. A tribute, apparently to Lou, ended; he grabbed Willie and they fell into a tight embrace.

Mandolin screamed, ran outside and kept on running down one street and another dark one, until she fell into the street and threw up. In a minute or two, she picked herself up, ran onto a lighted street and into a 24 hour pharmacy, to catch her breath. When a man approached her, she dashed onward until she arrived at Sky's house in hysteria. She threw up again on the large front porch and collapsed against the door.

Exhausted and breathless she screamed. "I'm no good, world! Just forget me. I'm a waste of everyone's time! Nothing has worked for too long and it's New Year's Eve! Go! All of you. Find your perfect mate and have a fantastic life. Sorry Dad. Sorry Mom. Sorry Sky and Heather." And then she passed out.

PART IV

1.

Where am I?

IN AN EMERGENCY ROOM, two nurses were transferring Mandolin from a gurney to a bed with an IV taped to her arm. Sky was fighting tears. Tina's were flowing.

"Poor Mandolin," said Tina in a hushed voice. "Seems like everything bad happens to her. Why, Papa? Why?"

"I got no answer this time sweet girl, 'cept to say we bringin' her home with us."

Mandolin stirred, her eyes slowly opened, took in the room, and focused on Sky and then Tina who held her hand.

"We love you Mandolin. Dad and I are going to take care of you."

The sympathy brought more tears.

Sky took over. "You real special to us and we not forgettin' that, never."

Mandolin tried to smile. "I love you all so very much, but my heart hurts - everything hurts."

"We know. We know."

"My knee - my shoulder - oooo!"

The nurse entered and checked the IV. Sobs began to shake

Mandolin's body. Mandolin asked for some kind of relief. She kept wanting to throw up. The nurse seemed surprised and asked if this was something new. No. Then she disappeared "to talk to the doctor." Mandolin longed for her mom and dad.

The ER doctor entered with her chart. "Hi there Mandolin. Sorry for the wait. I have good news about your shoulder. It's not fractured as we suspected. A bad sprain to be sure. Keep it wrapped around your body as the nurse will show you and have it checked by your regular doctor in three weeks. Any questions?"

Yes. Why was she nauseated again? He checked through her chart history and asked if she had seen an ob/gyn recently. Her eyes widened and she grabbed his arm.

"Why?"

"Your nausea could be morning sickness."

"No! No! Don't say that!! I'm not pregnant! How could I be? I've only had sex once in my life."

Sky's eyes popped. The doctor continued. "We have an ob/gyn here in emergency, would you like me to call her?"

"No. Absolutey not! I'm not pregnant! I'm not! I'm not! I'm not!"

Sky interrupted and explained his position over the protests of Mandolin. The doctor comforted her as best he could, explained the importance of regular exams and left the room. She sat up and looked heavenward. Please God. This is not the way I planned my future.

The next afternoon with her shoulder in a sling, a spiritless Mandolin sat with her head down at Sky's kitchen table. Sky, Lillian and Joseph, her boyfriend surrounded her. The familiar cross-stitching of "Home Sweet Home" still remained as did the piano. The keys were shiny and white; the black key was replaced, and a large pile of sheet music was piled on top. Mandolin bit her lip hard, looked at Joseph at Lillian, tried to speak and then looked out the kitchen window.

Joseph held her hand. "We had an easy flight from New Jersey and we're happy to be here. Lillian added that since Joseph ran a medical clinic, he could recommend the best ob/gyn in Houston."

Mandolin had cried her eyes out and yet here came more tears when she looked up at the portrait of the lovely young woman on the beach. Sky had hung it over a desk between the kitchen and parlor.

"I'm pregnant! I'm pregnant! I'm too young to be a mom. I've never known my own. I don't know how to be a good mom. OhmyGod! Oh… my …God! I'm …"

Mandolin's cell phone buzzed. Unconsciously, she continued her thoughts into the phone. "I'm pregnant!"

"This is Roxie." Mandolin held the phone away from her ear. " I just heard that news, that's why I'm calling. Willie asked me to."

Mandolin was speechless. Roxie continued. "It's all so hard to explain, Mandolin. My son and Lou filled me in. They want you to know that they thought you knew they were gay, and so did I."

"You thought I knew? Then if you knew he was gay, why did you act so happy for me when you saw my tattoo and heard me say I had done it for him? What ever made you think I knew? Did you ever think of my feelings?"

"I – I – I…hoped Willie would not to have to suffer the confusions of homosexuality and when you came with him on Christmas, I was encouraged. I had no idea Lou's dad had forbidden him from coming out until his twenty-first birthday which, as you know, was on the first of January. Of course I supported him and Lou."

"And now that it's out, *you're* the one who's calling me and not Willie. I thought I loved a guy with some spine, but I was wrong."

Joseph tried to take the phone. Mandolin held it tight and listened to Roxie on the offensive. "From what I understand you pushed yourself on my son. Willie told you they would eventually move in together."

"Right, and that was the end of it. He never brought it up again even when I asked."

"That's because Lou got a huge restoration project in Corpus Christi and since they both love the water they're moving down there."

"You mean they're leaving me to raise our baby alone? Excuse me Roxie, but it would seem more appropriate to discuss this in person with Willie rather than over the phone with his mother."

"His dad and I have discussed it and agree that they are very much in love and have no interest in you or the baby."

"What? Willie has no interest in his own child?"

"Lou suspects it is not my son's baby anyway."

"But I've never had sex with anyone but Willie."

"Who's to believe you and not Willie? They wish you out of their lives."

"So not one of you believes me or sees this as abandonment?"

"We've never seen our son this happy."

"Then if he's found his *hakka bakka*, he's one lucky guy."

Mandolin's head fell. The dial tone sounded from the floor. Her position never changed for minutes, until she lay back. Joseph retrieved the phone. She finally sat up with a strange expression. She had always told the truth. Did she really think Willie was a lucky guy? Was he sure where he was headed? Did this same thing happen to my mom and dad? Then she turned to Sky.

"Did my Mom abandon me and force my dad to raise me?"

Tina entered as if she knew she was late and caught up.

"You knows better than that, Mandi girl. Your dad loved you to smithereens."

She had no idea of the definition but the word as well as the message made her smile."

Tina agreed, "You're right, Dad." She then addressed Mandolin with deep affection. "You may not have had him for long, but think of all the kids who are never loved."

"Thanks Tina. He gave me all he could until he died. And now that I'm going to be a mom, I'm more determined than ever to know my mom."

"And introduce her to your child," said Tina as she rubbed her back with tenderness. "Grammas are the best. We all loved Big Mama a bunch, right?"

"I just can't believe I'm pregnant. I've heard of couples who try for years and I get pregnant when I've only had sex once in my life."

Sky had a comment. "'Course we believe you Mandolin, and yet some girls these days have sexual partners long before they're twelve."

"Sky! You make me feel like I'm lying. I swear to God I have had sex once in my life and that was with Willie."

Lillian took his defense. "He's trying to be helpful, Mandolin."

Joseph advised her to have his DNA checked to be sure.

"God, Joseph. I've made some mistakes, but I sure hope I've learned enough by now to know what I'm doing. Willie knows the truth. He's not the man my dad was, and if he doesn't want to share the responsibility of my baby and want us, then we don't want him. The two of us will make it on our own."

Tina and Lillian put their arms around Mandolin. Lillian spoke. "Joseph and I can't have kids and so when the baby grows a little, we look forward to having him for extended visits."

Tina added. "And I'll be a super duper aunt."

It was Sky's turn. "Don't none of you be trying to push me out of the way neither. As they say in Mexico *mi casa es tu casa*, long as you needs it."

Joseph shook Sky's hand. "My house is your house. First I knew you're bilingual."

Sky beamed."*Si, si*, senior."

Mandolin smiled for the first time. "You've always known how to get to me, Sky. Thanks to all of you. "We'll be the best ever Ma/babe combo. Just watch us."

"And tomorrow we'll meet Dr. Churchill, one the best ob/gyns in Houston. He'll get you off to a good start," comforted Joseph.

In Big Mama's bed, Mandolin finally found a comfortable position for her shoulder and drifted off to dreamland. *She and her mom were playing in the surf together and singing a song that Big Mama had taught her. But her Mom was always behind her and she could never see her face.*

When she woke, she was alone and her first thought was about her Mom. Then she felt her shoulder. It was a bit better; her leg had stopped bleeding, and her morning sickness had eased. She patted her stomach with love and looked down at the lump. "Hi Babe."

A knock on the door. She struggled to pull up. Tina cracked open the door and entered. "It's past noon, sweetie."

"Noon?" How could that be? Memories of her first day at the mansion returned, the first time she had slept late.

"Hi Tina." Have you heard the news?" And then with a tiny smile, "in about six months we're going to have a very special person around here."

Tina lay on the bed beside her and kissed her cheek. "Yay, Mandi! Welcome back. You sound like yourself again."

"Remember when Big Mama used to read *The Little Engine that Could* to us?"

Tina nodded. "'I think I can-I think I can-I think I can.'"

Mandolin smiled "You know what? I know I can."

"Good, cuz Joseph made an appointment at one-thirty in the Medical Center."

Mandolin gasped with fear and felt her wrist for Pink Oink.

Tina removed it from the bedside table and handed it to Mandolin. She clutched it lovingly.

The waiting room in the Medical Center was full of women in various stages of pregnancy. Mandolin was one of them. She flipped through a magazine when the receptionist held up forms on a clipboard. Sky started to take it and Mandolin grabbed it.

"I can handle this, Sky."

He was stunned and moved away. She took the form to an empty seat, and after a few minutes Sky moved next to her "How you doin', doll baby?"

"I'm okay, I - I guess."

"You sure? Your hands are shakin' like a leaf on a Pear Tree when one of our surprise Norther hits."

Mandolin smiled. "You're a surprise yourself, Mr. Brown. Any chance you're related to Dan Brown, the author?"

"Now you teasin' with me and it feels good, real good."

When her name was called, she jumped, dropped the form board and papers scattered.

The nurse collected them and waved Mandolin down a hall for a blood test and a pap smear. In a small examining room, she was told to slip on a gown with the open part to back. "What is your approximate date of conception?"

"Late October."

"You're sure?"

"Absolutely."

The nurse wrote this down and informed the doctor and his replacement would be right in to give her a thorough exam. Her offer to help Mandolin onto the table was shunned. The nurse was gracious. "I'm the same way. I like to do as much as I can by myself."

Left alone, she was totally terrified. Exposing herself to one doctor, let alone *two* had definitely not been on her anticipated agenda.

Please God. Help me! I'm aware that doctors see many nude women every day, but this is so far from my comfort zone.

Clutching the robe, she studied her nails and then bit off a ragged one, and then another. Too many minutes later, the doctors and the nurse entered. The younger one showed surprise. Why? Was it because she was young? The lead doctor, white-haired and a proper sort introduced himself.

"Good morning. I am Doctor Churchill and with me is my well-qualified replacement, Dr. Kris Desai. I think you've met Gloria, my nurse."

Mandolin nodded, heard his words of gratitude for the referral from her renowned brother in-law but was anxious to get this exam over. Dr Desai shook her hand but she was too nervous to pay attention to his dark skin, lean build, well-styled haircut, soft-spoken and manicured demeanor, or the twinkle in his eyes. She *did* notice his warm, firm handshake. It was reassuring.

"I consider myself lucky to now work with Dr. Churchill. He's one of the most respected men in this practice in the country."

Mandolin was panicky, she couldn't help it. Could this young doctor possibly know as much as a venerable one?

"As I recall, your name is Mandolin, may I call you that?"

Mandolin wondered. He *recalled* seeing her? When was that? Was he confused?

"Sh-sh-sh-sure. I've never been called Miss MacDuff in my life."

"And please call me Kris, short for Krishna."

Mandolin had relaxed enough to study him. He was not a bit young, probably about thirty with a fatherly smile.

Dr. Churchill explained that he was retiring and after his examination Dr. Desai would take over."

"Oh! Oh! If he's new, has...has he delivered any babies before or is he just learning how?"

Dr. Churchill reassured her that his replacement had delivered many babies. "Under my watchful eye and only a week ago, Dr. Desai miraculously saved both the baby and mother after a horrific car accident."

Car accident? Was this a good or bad omen? Kris patted her shoulder in a pleasant, modest manner.

"Thanks for that Kris. I'm scared to death. And when I get that way, I babble like a verse I learned long ago called *The Brook.*

'I come from haunts of coots and fearns and make a sudden sally.

I sparkle out among the paths and bicker down the valley.'"

A surprised smile crept over Kris' face and he tagged on.

"'I chatter over stony ways in little sharps and trebles.

I bubble into eddying bays, I bubble on the pebbles.' 'It's by Tennyson."

Mandolin frowned. Was it normal to find so many others who shared verses? She held up her palm. "Hey there, Dr. Babbler."

His reaction? His palm met hers, gently. "Good girl. Helping our patients relax any way we can is part of our job."

Their eyes met briefly and he suggested she scoot to the end of the table and put her feet in the stirrups.

"Stirrups? My gramma used to ride to the hounds in England a long time ago."

"How about that? As you probably know, in 1857 the Brits colonized India, the home of my dad."

"I didn't know about your dad, but there was a lot of strife back then. India gained its independence in 1947, right?"

"You amaze me, Mandolin. Not many people these days know history that well."

"I read a lot. What is that odd looking elephant figure over there?"

"He is called *Ganesh*, one of the Hindu Gods, and represents good fortune. It was my dad's and comes along wherever I go."

"Do you know about *hakka bakka*?"

"No, but I'll read up on it, or better yet, how about explaining it to me."

Her reply was simply "later." She was nervous and cold. Both doctors looked over her chart while she cuddled in the blanket provided.

"P-p-please don't hurt me," she begged. "I—I—"

"We'll be gentle. First we take a Sonogram. This will determine how far along you are and if your ETA and ours match. Afterwards you can see the results as you watch them on this screen. Mandolin took deep breaths.

"Excellent. Keep it up." It was Kris.

Dr. Churchill and Kris examined the sonogram. They nodded and Kris turned to his new patient.

"You have nothing to worry about, Mandolin. Every thing is totally normal. So how do you feel now?"

"If I'm normal, it's a first. Nothing about me has ever been normal."

Kris liked this. "Normal is great for pregnancies, but in my opinion those who appear normal in life miss a lot of fun."

"So do goody-goodies."

Kris smiled. Yes! Kris liked to tease as did her dad and his manner was gentle like Sky's. Dr. Churchill excused himself and wished her well. Kris asked her to dress and join him outside.

"But first do you have any questions about any of this?"

Did she! Holy Pig! Here she was in a room alone with someone who at last made her feel mature enough to take responsibility for herself. She replied quickly "So you're not going to ask to meet the baby's father?"

"Only if you want me to."

"No. I made a mistake and it's all over."

He removed his surgical gloves. "You and your baby are healthy and I predict all will go well." His eyes twinkled, "providing you do as your doctor says. See you in a minute." And he left.

It was difficult for her to absorb all that was going on and while dressing, she studied the various framed degrees of Krishna Desai on the wall; one from Princeton and another from Boston Medical University. She decided Kris had to be bright. There were no pictures of his wife or kids which she assumed meant he kept his family and business apart or perhaps a divorce or tragedy like she had experienced.

Should she ask Sky for his advice? No! Absolutely not. She now had enough confidence to trust her own judgment. In a short time, she had developed the same sort of admiration for this Dr. Kris Desai as she had for actor Kris Kristofferson. Both seemed to have a knack for putting spirit into their vocations.

In the waiting room, Kris joined them and she stood to show respect. He looked up into her green eyes with surprise.

"You are taller than I thought," he blurted.

Her immediate reaction was to panic. "Are you saying something is wrong with my baby?"

Kris reassured her. "Not at all. It means a beautiful baby is inside... possibly a tall one."

These were the first words that assured Sky all was well. His eyes filled with tears and pride. Mandolin laughed, at last released from the fright of the exam and turned to Sky. "This is Sky, Kris - my very best friend."

Sky had to wipe his eyes before he shook his hand and hugged Mandolin. "Can you tell us the sex of the baby yet, doctor?"

"No Sky, no. I like surprises."

"Course you do. Sorry Mandi. Got in over my head outta excitement."

Kris smiled at Sky, advised exercise for Mandolin every day, and when possible to take naps.

Naps?! She had never in her life taken a nap. Naps were for the bored, the oldsters, for those without ideas or imagination, or felt no obligation to accomplish. But now she could allow herself some time off because the doctor said to rest. Could she?

An announcement over the hospital intercom.

"Doctor Desai, room Eleven. Doctor Desai, room Eleven. Stat."

He gave her and Sky brief embraces and once again advised her to take caution, and follow the rules in the hand-out. Her head was spinning. He started to ask her something and then he was gone. She thought it odd, the way he looked at her before he left. Was there something he should have said? *Come on, Mandolin. The doc said you're doing well, now relax.*

Sky and Mandolin walked out of the office arm in arm. She was on her way to motherhood and womanhood with faith that *hakka bakka* was ahead. She wondered about her mom's reaction. Would she be happy to be a gramma?

After a sound sleep she dressed and skipped playfully to the hammock. She chatted with the birds, the bees, the worms, and the bounding lizards. While stretched out and staring at the oaks above, she imagined herself in the role of a self-made successful woman delivering an address to her child's high school graduating class.

"Good morning. The opportunity to speak at your graduation, this real milestone in your careers, is a truly scintillating experience. Like me, I imagine you have thought back to those years long ago when you knew little, thought you did, and were absolutely positive this day would never come. I'm remembering my excitement when my dad took me on a mystery trip in a car. When I told him he was innovating he asked me to explain the meaning. I made up an answer that surprised and pleased him. Innovating. I-n-n-o-v-a-t-i-n-g. It means you're the best dad in the whole wide world.'

Well, at the time, I had no clue what it meant but it had the right effect. Since then I have learned that innovating means creating and taking chances. And so to the point, step away from the norm and never be afraid to take a gamble. A great part of life is luck and daring and neither one should ever be underestimated. When you least suspect it, either one or both can brighten your way."

More birds twittered in the trees. She continued to entertain them.

"And so, remember Charles Lindbergh who saw aviation as the key to

trade and growth, and who flew the first solo flight across the Atlantic to Paris way back in 1927. See the world through the eyes of Elisha Otis, who ventured out and developed elevators and escalators which changed the floor plans and architectural design of every building in America. And currently think of Bill Gates and others for opening the world to speedy knowledge and communications through cyberspace. Finally, keep grounded with a keen sense of humor as illustrated by the timeless wit of Will Rogers. He was a simple man from the Midwest with a sage wit 'We can't all be heroes because someone has to sit on the curb and clap as the cars go by."

Actual applause startled her. Kris had come to check up on her.

2.
And Here We Are

TINA TAUGHT HER THE functions of a birthing ball, how it relieved the strain on her legs and back, and that soaking in a warm tub and gentle massages were a big help. Some felt the remaining six months dragged, and yet for Mandolin the time passed quickly. Her classes in law enforcement and criminal justice classes at school as well as her computer searches kept her busy. Then news came that the staff at Joseph's clinic in New Jersey was overworked and Mandolin insisted that he and Lillian return to their duties. She was sincerely grateful for all the comfort they had given… especially for a doctor she respected and one who had a calming influence on her.

Shortly thereafter, in the midst of a mock trial at school, Mandolin jumped, a reaction to a kick inside her. It was for real! An honest to God baby was actually in there and the adventure into the world of Motherhood was on the way. If it was a girl, she would name her Lily after Big Mama and do her best to be as good a mother/grandmother as she.

Her daily walk to the Beignet Shop, for treats for herself and her baby made the long wait more fun. Eating had become an adventure and she always sat at an ice cream table across from a serious gentleman who for the most part kept his nose deep into the *Wall Street Journal*. She had a hunch that on this day, news of her first kick would cheer him.

Wrong! He was concerned about the decline in the economy and his jewelry business just above the shop. Many clients were months behind on their payments and the success of his grandfather's business weighed heavily on him. His grandfather or *de-dush-ka*, she learned, had arrived from Russia in 1940, and had begun a prosperous business in gems, just before the economic slump due to gobal economic fears. Not only was there a reduction in spending but fear of theft as well. His customers gave up wearing real jewelry and turned to costume pieces. She was happy for the Guild Shop because many had already commissioned pieces there, and the current influx of Jewelry sales provided more money than any other department in the store to satisfy its mission: to serve the community by providing partial housing for the needy.

Many days she was too tired to study, and when spotting occurred, she took comfort in the doctor's insistence on rest. During these rest times, Tina often came into her room and they discussed their goals. Mandolin was touched by what she learned. Tina had given up nursing and had begun teaching Pre-K and Kindergarten kids. Why? Because Mandolin's background without a parent and her struggles to find love had prompted her to help other needy kids through their early ages.

Mandolin in turn, often visited her class to gain insight into what comes with motherhood.

What about having her tattoo removed?

Better to wait until after the baby, was Kris's suggestion. Severe pain, like too much coughing, often brought on labor before the due date.

Pain? She knew what that was all about.

Sky still had his full-time job watching over the mansion, and felt it quite enough for his "tired old bones." Heather had a part-time job working at the home of a confirmed bachelor and often stopped over to help with dinner for her, Tina and Sky. When the house filled with the familiar smells of Heather's good cooking, particularly her juicy meat loaf with her own barbecue sauce, she felt she and her baby were safe and well in a happy home .

At the kitchen counter, Heather chatty as always, enjoyed relating stories of the early times in the mansion.

"What happened before I came, Heather?" Mandolin wanted to know.

She chuckled. "Ah thought you'd never ask. Well, Mrs. Mac set me free on a new Chambers Range. You remember, them, don't'cha? They were one of the first three burner stove tops and had a griddle on top of a deep well broiler oven."

Mandolin smiled. "Hmm. So that's what prompted Big Mama to sing that cowboy song *Home on the Range* all the time."

"And she sang that old tune too." Heather cracked a few words. "'Oh give me a home, where the buffalo roam...' Yes indeedy. When ah first went ta work at the Mansion, we wore uniforms. Now on any job, we wear what we damn well please, as long as it's clean."

Mandolin jumped again, rubbed her hands over her soccer-ball belly and offered Heather a feel.

"That baby's gonna be a big one, mark my words. When's it due?"

"In exactly five weeks and two days."

"Then you're over the hump."

Mandolin's hands circled her belly. "A huge hump. So go on, Heather."

"Let's see. We used ta be called upstairs maids or cooks like me, not gourmet chefs and housekeepers."

Sky and Tina entered. "Heather's got it right. We were called yard men, not lawn maintenance operators or whatever the PC got us sayin' nowadays."

Tina giggled and spoke up. "Big Mama told us about the buzzer."

"Oh mah goodness, that was a story and a half too. When me and Sky heard that buzzer in the kitchen, we knew Mrs. Mac wanted something at the table. And she wanted it not yesterday or tomorrow but raght now. So Sky, passed through the swinging door ta the dining room, addressed her quietly, found out her needs and came ta tell me. Then the both of us got it together and he'd serve one dish at a time around the table."

"Where was the buzzer?" Tina asked.

"Generally under the rug at her feet and whenever Mrs. Mac held her foot on it by mistake, we had to correct her quietly or we'd ketch it later. Between the entrée and dessert, we cleared the dishes and put fingerbowls with '*exactly* one and one half inches of water' in front of the mister and missus. Same thing went on when they were entertaining."

Sky took a turn "You sure got that right, Heather. That was so they could rinse off their sticky fingers."

Heather guffawed. "You remember that guest who wet his napkin in his fingerbowl and scrubbed up his face?"

"Sure do Then he dried his hands on the tablecloth. And while all this was goin' on, I was feelin' sorry for you, Mandolin, stuck upstairs all alone with all the laughter down below."

Mandolin joined in. "I hated it at the time Sky, but thinking back from the top of the stairs where I listened in, I discovered old people aren't all that happy. They got one thing wrong after another."

Sky turned to Heather. "Tell Mandolin how Mr. Mac made the guests come prepared with a topic for discussion."

"Cool! I'll do that too with my child."

"Really?" commented Tina. "My topics would be boring."

Mandolin suddenly looked worried. Sky recognized her look and tried to cheer her. "I won't never forget when your Mama got pregnant with you, Tina. She wanted oysters real bad. You got any cravings like that, doll baby?"

"No Sky! And quit worrying about everything I do or say. Sometimes I just don't feel like talking or kidding around. Okay?"

"Now what makes you think I is?"

"Because that's what my dad did. He always tried to keep me laughing when Sunday nights came and I became quiet because I knew he'd be leaving again."

The meal ended, Heather prepared to leave when Mandolin jumped and held her stomach. "Hold on. Something's going on."

The atmosphere became tense, until Mandolin lightened up. "Holy Pig! this little one has the hiccups. Anyone want a feel?"

Of course they all did. While hands took turns feeling around her belly, Mandolin told the story of lawyer's case of hiccups in Scotland.

"Now there's a story for you, Mandolin," said Tina, "The Case of the Hiccupping Attorney."

"You hold your breath, right?" asked Sky.

"Exactly. Turn around." She used him as a model. He was extremely ticklish, squirmed, and she kept after him. He yelped and begged for mercy.

Suddenly, she caught her breath squeezed her fists and breathed deeply in pain. Everyone grew tense.

"Hold on. It's going away, thank God. It's way too soon for the baby."

"We all need to be patient," suggested Sky.

"Excitement can't be put on hold, Sky, and you know what? Whenever I think of having this baby I hear Prissy's voice when she talked to Scarlett O'Hara. 'Ah don't know nothin 'bout birthin' no baby'. The facts are that as hard as I've tried to learn about my mom, I still don't know anything about her. If she ran off with another man and actually lives in India, Australia or a place like Dubai where men dominate women, I'll never find her. And every time I want to ask

Hopscotch why she removed the painting of my dad as a boy from the wall, she's too busy to answer me. Even if it was horrid, why would she suddenly want it gone after so many years?"

"Maybe if we had seen them together we might understand," suggested Tina.

Sky took a turn. "Lemme think how it was the night you and your Papa arrived. What comes to mind is that Mr. Mac was pacing the floor waiting for your papa to join them for a hunting trip up East."

"Go on, Sky."

"Well, he blew into the Mansion with you fast asleep in his arms, was real sorry for being late cuz of bad traffic. Then when Mr. Mac seen you he nearly fell over cuz he was seeing his granddaughter for the first time. He grabbed you and danced you around and around the room whilst he was kissin' and huggin' on you all the time."

"How did Hopscotch react?"

"Miz Mac? Well she didn't say much, never looked at you and left the room. Me? I thought she was tired."

"Do you still think that Sky? Tell me the truth. All I want from here on are the facts, *just the facts* sir, about everything."

"No doll-baby. From what's been goin' between you and her all these years, I'm thinkin' that whatever happened after Mr. Jim went off from Houston years back, was not to her likin'. He was sixteen then, same age as you when you left us at the mansion."

"Please, don't go there Sky! What else happened that night?"

"Mr. Mac, he turned you over to me, and I hugged and kissed you too cuz no one said a word to me about you even bein' born. Then Mr. Jim put his cheek beside yours and says to me, 'take good care of Mandolin 'til we get back. Okay buddy?'"

Mandolin gasped, first in tribute to her dad's love and then in pain. She turned aside, took many deep breaths and held her stomach. Sky never noticed and continued. "Meant a whole lot that Mr. Jim trusted you with me and all I said was 'she look just like you.' Well,

275

Mr. Jim winds up and starts bragging on you. 'You oughta see this little mermaid swim and steer my boat with the tiller. She knows how to tack already. Yes sir. She's my 'little maid of the seas.'"

Mandolin's pains subsided and her emotions took over. A call came in on her cell. She checked it and handed the phone to Sky while she collected herself. "It's Hopscotch."

'Hello Miz Mac. We been talking about you. How you and Mr. Jacques doing?"

Mandolin took the phone. "Hi Hopscotch. It's me, your huge granddaughter. Tell us about you and Jacques...a hearing aid? All the better for him to hear you, Hopscotch."

"What? Speak up Madolin."

Mandolin held the phone away from her ear to avoid eardrum damage.

"Neverr mind. Put Sky on the phone again while I move to the otherr rroom."

Sky took the phone. "Hello again Miz Mac. How the weather up there?" The whites of his eyes expanded. "A house in the Adirondacks. Well, that's real nice."

Mandolin caught her head in her hands.

Sky continued with Hopscotch. "Your furniture?...You mean you movin' for good?...All right then. I'll be back here at the Mansion at eight fifteen in the morning waiting for your call."

He returned the phone to Mandolin who spoke into it. "I guess it's time to admit I was wrong about Jacques."

Her gramma's voice blasted in her ear and she held it away. "Wrrong! I mean rright! He made promises that were absolutely rridiculous. He owns nothing a-tall and lives over a garrrage on the property of a wealthy banker. In addition, there was absolutely no need or any reason a-tall for my couturierr outfits. So last week I sprang loose and met a delightful charrmer who is opening an elite restaurant in New

York City. He thinks I am hotterr than horrseradish. Lovely, do you agrree?"

Mandolin was too shocked to speak. Hopscotch continued. "What? I can't hear you. We must have anotherr one of those abominable connections."

"No," Mandolin replied. "I wish the very best for you both. I'm hoping that this is *hakka bakka* for you and you will settle in with your new beau."

"*Hakka bakka*? Did you say *hakka bakka*? Is that voodoo?"

"In a way. But it's not spooky, it's a time when you suddenly discover you're in a happy place. Now tell us more about this new guy." She held the phone away again and listened.

"He is a gentleman, a scholarr, a chef and his name is Zoum Z o-u m. Zoum from Cameroon. He knows all about you and wants you to bring my grreat grrandchild to visit."

Her thoughts? Her grandmother's taste in men confounded her. Her words? "You're amazing, Hopscotch. I guess our lives are constantly in flux. Good luck."

"My luck is here with me as we speak and perhaps you will find yours the minute you stop assuming you know it all."

The call ended. All stared at one another with their own thoughts until an angel of compassion flew over Mandolin.

"In any case, let's all high five a woman who knows what she wants and gets what she wants."

Sky spoke. "Halleluiah! I been prayin' for you and your gramma to work it out and now this baby anxious to meet us all seems like. How you feeling, doll baby?"

"Tired. Really tired. I'll keep you posted if there's any more action. See you in the morn—"

She was gone before finishing the sentence and in no time returned with a vintage book in her hands and tears in her eyes.

Tina comforted her. "What's wrong, sweetie?"

"I…I noticed my old backpack was hanging lop-sided on my door handle and felt sure I had emptied it my first night at Terror." She wiped her eyes. "Then when I reached in, there was this small package, the one I thought I had put in the bottom drawer in my room."

"You mean it had been there all along?" asked Tina.

"I'm not sure but when I opened it, I found this handwritten note inside a Bible: "For Your Grandmum. Please read the story of The Flood, Genesis 7 verse 12 to your granddaughter. Thank you."

Just inside the flyleaf was a dedication: "This Bible is for you, my dear daughter, on your fourth birthday. It has no pictures because if you're like me, we believe pictures in Bibles are for babies. From your devoted Abba."

Mandolin rubbed her stomach. "I…I never saw this before, ever, ever, ever."

Heather spoke "If you ask me, seems like your gramma never *wanted* you ta see it. You say your grampa and your dad died in an accident the night you came. Ah'm thinking she blames you for comin' here, upsettin' her lahf and she'll never forgive you. So you forgive her and move on like she's doing."

Tina found little sympathy as well. "Sorry, but I can't stand how her happiness comes first no matter what."

"Thanks for your support but it's okay, everyone. Sometimes we never know the answer to why we do what we do. The good news is my Mom wanted me to know that God made us suffer with rain for forty days and forty nights and then when it was over, he gave us a new beginning. She wanted me to understand that life is not easy and was thinking of me and that's what matters. And so as a result I now have four goals…to find my mom, to be a good Mom, to read my child *James and the Peach Giant* and to find *hakka bakka*. It looks as if I'll be giving up school, my story and my other ideas…at least for a while.

Mandolin re-read the note signed 'Abba.' Whoa! "Americans don't call their mothers' Abba. What country does?"

Tina agreed to help her find out. One of her students came from India. She might know. But first came classes in natural childbirth where she learned how to breathe and relax during childbirth and find answers to anything and everything she didn't understand. This had been the story of her life, asking, asking, always seeking. And how good those prescribed naps felt at the end of the day.

She continued her walks to the Beignet Store and ran into the Russian dad of the cute little girl whom she met years ago at the park. They had both made an impression because she had never met Russians before. This time she felt more relaxed and wanted to talk to him. His name was Boris, named for his father. She learned that sons are never called Juniors and the father's first name is incorporated into the last name...like became Boris Borisovich. In naming girls, she would be called Olga Borisova—*Ova* indicates the *daughter* of Boris. What would she name her child?

It was these kinds of cultural differences that fascinated her and helped pass the time...until he asked what her mother's name was. She winced at the question as well as an excruciating pain. "You know something, I think I'd better go. Something feels a little strange."

"My car is right there. Where may I take you?"

She assured him she was okay, that a foot or arm was probably changing position and she would see him later in the week. She never saw Boris again.

It was a Sunday, her due date and in the distance, there was tintinnabulation, just like her first morning at Terror. The first really hard pain attacked and from then on chaos dominated. Everyone wanted to help and time pieces of all kinds were pulled out to keep track of her contractions. Sky informed Kris that the contractions were still mild and nearly an hour apart. Kris told him to monitor the proximity of the pains and when they were 10 minutes apart to call him and head for the hospital.

Mandolin was determined to collect the trash from all the wastebaskets, until she screamed. Sky and Tina rushed her to the hospital. On her way to the delivery room on a gurney she removed Big Mama's jingly *kickshaw* and Pink Oink, the only jewelry she ever wore, and handed them to Tina for safe-keeping.

The delivery was difficult. The baby was turned sideways which demanded the expertise of Kris and his hospital staff. The pain became intense even with the gentle massaging of Tina, her dutiful doula, and tapes of her favorite music were meant to soothe. She pushed and pushed until she could stand the pain no longer. Kris convinced her that many wanted to have babies naturally *more than anything* just as she did. Mandolin continued to push hard until the pain became too intense and she agreed to sedation.

When she came to, the nurse stood over her hospital bed with her a baby swaddled in a blanket. "Look who I have here, Mandolin, your perfect little baby boy."

In a tiny frail voice, she commented "You mean it's over? You mean...I'm actually a mother and we're both alive?" She took the baby from the nurse, placed her cheek next to his and wept like a baby, and she heard laughter and cheers. This was truly hakka bakka ...the same explosion of joy as when Kishore Kumar appeared in the video that she and her dad watched together so many years before .

"Hi, you darling guy. Hi. Before you grow up I want to explain that you, like I, will have questions to answer about your parents. Your dad and I chose different lifestyles and live in different cities, and we're okay with it. You may never meet him but we will have a blast together just as I did with my dad. I'll try to teach you to feel the pain of disappointment when you let me down or I let you down. I promise to always love you and never abandon you – never, never, never!"

Applause from Sky, Lillian, Joseph, Heather and Tina surprised her. She so wished that Hildegard, Theodore, Speedy, Lillian and Joseph could have been there as well. "Hey everyone. Come meet my son."

The excitement continued until the nurse took the baby away to clean him up with a promise to bring him right back.

Mandolin's thoughts bounced around. She had a son. She would teach him to respect women and have him circumcised because God explained to Abraham that all males were to be circumcised. It was a sign obeying the covenant.

When the nurse brought James back, freshly scrubbed, she took her baby in her arms and smothered him with kisses.

"Oh my God, you are, totally gorgeous. I'm your Mom, your Mom! I love bald guys with big ears because they're all the better to hear me with, you good little wolf. But hold on. I'm so excited I forgot what I was going to name you. "Bear with me, gang. Is it Boris? No! Oh! Now I've got it." She looked lovingly at her baby.

"You, my sweetheart, will be named James Brown MacDuff, in honor of two great family men, my dad and a dear dear friend. Welcome to our world."

More applause, Kris arrived to congratulate her with a hug when the nurse taught her how to put the baby to her breast, that it would be a few days before actual milk came in. While the others departed, Kris stayed to assure Mandolin she had done a superb job and would see her again shortly. She was so grateful, their eyes locked and he left modestly.

The next afternoon and two days later as expected, her breasts hardened and filled with milk. James was a happy, yet a hungry little guy and cried often for his mom's milk. Mandolin treasured motherhood and being needed. She sang and read to him, pronounced words carefully for his comprehension and was proud of his first sounds. Each morning they listened to Sponge Bob. She sang the words, he made noises and they laughed.

Mandolin had learned that baby care was a full time job and that being a total mom meant the world to her. James learned to sit up, spit up, crawl, and delight his "Mama" in every way. No more time for animal sketches and law enforcement school. Only time for baths, nursing, diaper changes, nursing, washing, nursing, house cleaning, and naps, if she was lucky.

How needed they were when she could fit them in. And how she loved reading. Kris brought her a book a biography of *John Adams* by David McCullough. He had bookmarked a section about John's wife Abigail, a gutsy independent woman who raised their kids alone while her husband was in France framing the Constitution for a new country, the United States. John Adams was one of many brave men and women who lived hard lives in order to create a great country and she could hardly wait to find time to read both. In the meantime, Mandolin's flag pin would be her first gift to her son.

"You remind me of Abigail Adams," Kris admitted on one of his daily visits to check on them. "I could have lived then. I was a gutsy guy myself and took all kinds of chances. I wanted to fight in Afghanistan but because of a back injury, was never accepted. When my marriage failed, I ended up in the medical world like my dad."

"Don't say ended up. Who knows where any of us we will end up?"

Gutsy. He had guts. She had used the word lightly in the past and realized she had nothing to complain about compared to many. She had never faced death on a battle ground or flown into enemy territory. Or eaten tulip bulbs to survive during the war as some of the Dutch had. She prayed that James would be so lucky, and if not that she would be able to give him the integrity needed to make her proud.

On James' second birthday, Kris came by with a present for Mandolin, a new book called *The Da Vinci Code*. She was thrilled because she had heard it was about unraveling a code involving Da Vinci and his painting of *The Last Supper*.

Kris agreed in part. "It's a real gripper and some of the mystery takes place in the Rosslyn Chapel in Scotland.

"Where I've been!" She threw her arms around him. "OhmyGod! Thanks sooo much. I can't wait to read it."

He stared at her and muttered. "Those eyes of yours! Those remarkable green eyes, They do me in!"

The little guy waddled up, sat on his haunches and opened his arms to be picked up. Kris had a present behind his back, asked James which hand it was in and of course he guessed perfectly. Kris sat on the floor with him, and together they opened the present.

"This is a dump truck, James. Can you say dump truck?"

"Dum fuck" was his attempt which caused guffaws from the celebrants Sky, Tina, Heather, Ginger, and Crotchy, her first beau and a tennis friend of Kris's. Hesitant to encourage this kind of talk at a first, Mandolin then smiled as she fought off her prudish ways around James and assimilated the fun aroused by the two words "dum fuck." Kris held James by his arms and swung him under his legs and back. James loved the game.

Mandolin gasped. "Kris. That terrifies me."

"Doesn't seem to terrify the big guy."

"Hold on, Kris. That comment causes me to think over our relationship."

"Go girl. Go! It's growing everyday, right?"

"We've been together for what… three years and had a good time together. But I wonder if you're kind of making us the family you never had? I mean I'm much younger than you and…and crap…Am I like the daughter you wish you had?"

Kris felt like laughing but managed to choke it away. "Do I treat you as a father?"

"You do."

"All the time?"

Mandolin looked into his eyes with a devilish smile. "No. Not always."

When Kris put James down, he tried to kick him. Kris reprimanded him.

"No James, no. All of us want our way. Never, never kick anyone."

Mandolin absorbed their relationship. "Believe it or not, I find some similarities in you and James. He wants his way." "And you don't?"

She put her hands on her hips in playful defiance and he wrapped her in his arms.

On weekends, she and Kris took James to the beach in Galveston, always careful to cover his pale Scottish skin with sun block and to wear a hat over his head now covered with black hair. He delighted all within hearing range with shrieks of excitement especially when the waves rolled in filling his deep holes in the sand. His increasingly fearless ventures into the water scared Mandolin yet Kris convinced her to be proud, and to have confidence in him as a baby-sitter. They often kicked the ball to one another which James could do for hours.

"We have a good kid here, sweetie."

"Excuse me, Kris. This sweetie stuff pisses me off."

Kris shot her a deep frown.

"What's that all about?" she asked.

"You noticed."

"Sure. It's the same look my dad gave me whenever he was irritated. What did I day that bothered you?"

"I've never heard you say 'pisses me off' before. It sounds common, which you're not."

"Come on Kris. Everyone uses that expression."

"It's a bad habit."

"Okay. How about this? Gee whizzagers, sir. When men assume more than they should about a relationship, it annihilates my pleasant disposition."

He laughed." May we always solve our disputes this easily and by the way I have never assumed, at least to my knowledge that we're not in this as a team."

Mandolin kissed his cheek and then looked directly into his eyes as if, as if…she was afraid to say she adored him in case…in case he changed his mind . She simply asked" you know what Kris?"

"No what, my girl?"

"I'm proud to be your girl." And then her sparkle returned. "Can't promise my disposition will always be pleasing but as long as I'm your girl, I'll best my very do.'"

Kris smiled with a reply "and I'll best my very do to please you every way I can."

The voice of James interrupted them. "Bang! Bang!" He was using a piece of driftwood as a gun, pointing it in the air, and making killer noises.

"I'd say this kid has an impressive imagination like his mother, although it runs along the lines of us crazy guys."

During the next few years, Kris spent many hours with James practicing his ball-kicks through hoops and over various bar heights. They paid off. At the age of five, he was accepted onto a pee-wee soccer team. During the last game of the season, when two teams were tied for the championship, Sky, Heather Tina, and of course Kris and Mandolin came to watch. The game was a cliff-hanger until James scored the winning goal. All the parents and guests on their side of the field screamed with excitement; Kris and Mandolin wrapped each other in arms as if afraid to let the other go and then kissed more than once. James was surrounded by high fivers and was cool. He didn't think he was all that big a deal.

Sky, Heather and Tina went on their way and Kris took the hero and his mom home. James invited him in for a scoop of chocolate fudge ice cream on top of Angel Fool cake, the same cake Big Mama taught

Mandolin to make years before and his favorite. At the table, James asked Kris if he played soccer when he was a kid.

"Wish I had, Cowboy. I know diddly squat about ball games and was never good at them like you."

James laughed. "Diddly Squat! Diddly Squat. That's really funny. What does diddly squat mean, Pop-pop?

Kris shook his head with a smile. "Sorry. I don't know diddly squat about diddly squat."

They were having fun together when an outside noise turned their heads towards the door. It opened slowly held by Tina's foot. Heather entered, followed by Sky with his arms pulled behind his back. Heather cleared her throat.

"Now then, me and Sky are real proud of you for bringin' your team to victory so we bought you a present. Neither of us are nowhere near smart enough to work these dang things but we know you are. Maybe you can teach us a few games, and anyways we know you gonna learn plenty right there as you go along to college."

Sky set a laptop down in front of James and backed off beside Tina.

"Coo- ool! Look Mom and Pop-Pop. It's my very own laptop."

Kris thanked them, "This is huge James, the perfect present." James turned to his mom and Kris. "You know what, maybe we can try googling diddly squat."

They smiled. "I've always wanted to know the origin of that myself, James. Big Mama used to say it all the time."

Mandolin looked at Kris and the threesome gathered around the computer where Kris found a story.

"Uh-oh! This is fairly long and maybe a little complicated. It looks like a kind of history lesson."

James never missed a beat. "It's okay. I love to learn. Read it to us. Okay Pop-Pop?"

Memories of saying those same words to her dad choked up

Mandolin. Kris pulled up a chair beside him and Mandolin and James shared it as he read.

Diddly Squat was born near Philadelphia in 1732. His divorced mother worked as a waitress at a popular tavern, and called him Diddly because they reminded her of the diddle her bow made when playing her fiddle.

Diddly's childhood was lonely. He wandered around the streets, learned to play the banjo and began writing songs when he was fifteen. Many encouraged Diddly to play his songs in taverns for the oppressed colonists.

James asked his Mom if she ever sang there? She simply replied that her voice was never good enough.

Kris continued. *By 1750, Diddly was the answer to the American dream. The King of England wanted to check out his act and George Washington and his friend Benjamin Franklin spent all their money on two tickets to see Diddly.*

Kris turned to James. "When their fathers heard this, what do you think happened, Cowboy?"

"They got into deep doo-doo."

"Not exactly." *Young George went directly to his father to plead his case and asked , "you don't know Diddly Squat?*

Kris and Mandolin smiled and sat back.

"Yay! That's awesome," exclaimed James. "You're kind of stupid if you don't know Diddly Squat because he knows famous people, has good dreams and if Sky and Heather didn't bring this laptop to me, we wouldn't know Diddly Squat, right?"

Mandolin and Kris adored this boy and showed it when they put him to bed, said prayers with him, hugged him tight and then one another.

Thus began their big night out. Kris was excited, dressed quickly and went to get the sitters. Mandolin couldn't decide what to wear since the addition of Big Mama's vintage accessories and many of Hopscotch's couturier outfits now filled her closet. Her choice? A satin sheath with puffed sleeves, an indication that her tastes were changing. She looked through Hopscotch's large collection of earrings, chose a pair of clips that amused her even though she preferred the pierced variety.

Kris pulled up to the restaurant where a valet parked his Acura MDX. He put his arm around Mandolin's waist and led her inside. One of those feelings down below hit with an impact. Oh yes! She was with the right guy at the right time. She was afraid to call it *hakka bakka* yet, but if he were to toss her in the air like a ballet partner she knew for sure she would land safely back in his arms. They followed the hostess to the table outside under the stars and Kris pulled out her chair and took his seat opposite her. He seemed far away. She felt alone.

The hostess lit a candle and champagne was delivered to the table in a silver wine bucket. Oddly enough it had the same shape as the one on Speedy's bar. The waiter produced sparkling glasses followed by the wine steward with a bottle for Kris' approval. He liked what he sampled and was definitely ready to have it poured.

Mandolin studied Kris. "You know something, sweetie?"

He shrugged playfully "Maybe a little of this and a little of that."

"I've never asked about your early years. What made you study medicine? Was your father a doctor?"

Kris smiled. "Not even close. He was a repairman from Jaipur, and my mother was Dutch. Her family owned a barge business which he took over. In fact, my two brothers and I grew up on a barge."

"Wow! That's a first for me."

"Maybe it was my Mother's tender care when we were sick that prompted me to go into medicine, who knows? I've never thought if it before."

Hugo, dressed as the Miraculous Chef came to the table with a flourish.

"Buenos noches, senor and senorita. Is everything good here?"

Kris and Mandolin assured him it was perfect while Mandolin was floored by all the attention. It wasn't her birthday or his, so what was it? Valentine's Day was around the corner but far too soon to hope a pair of Hoody-Footies or a Vermont Teddy Bear for James.

While the plates were cleared, Mandolin took out her cell phone.

"Please, babe. There's no need to call about James. We're lucky enough to have two devoted family members as sitters who want us to have a night on the town."

"Amazing. You knew exactly what was on my mind. You're right. Then you get to hear what happened while you were picking them up. When I heard a commotion in James's room, I peeked in the door and found he had collected all his stuffed animals on the bed, put them on the shelf as you taught him, and was sound asleep with his 'dum fuck' beside him."

Kris reached for her hand and withdrew it. He appeared nervous and distracted.

"Look at me, Mandolin."

Her temples throbbed, her heart picked up the beat and she felt blood surging throughout her body. When she looked into his smiling blue eyes, he gulped.

"Okay, my treasure. The time has come to talk of ships and kids and rings and things."

"Kr – is? What is this?"

"A good thing. A very good thing. I fell in love with you the first time I saw you shaking in Dr. Churchill's office, and I have loved you ever since. You may not have been aware that I witnessed the entire scene at the Guild Shop when you helped the couple who lost their child. I felt your empathy. Besides that, you once said you have never wanted a relationship and yet we've been in one for over five years."

Her pearl-green eyes sparkled and she teased. "You have quite a memory, Dr Desai."

"You bet and I've been thinking that James seems to like me and… and well…I'd like to become his parent."

"By yourself?"

He teased. "Oh you can come along if you want to."

"I can't believe you said that."

"What? That I would tease at a time like this?"

"Not that, I love it when you tease me. You're so, so like my dad."

"You talk about him quite often. Maybe I've picked up…"

"I guess I've never thought people remember what I say."

"What can't you believe then?"

"I…I never believed that a guy as smart as you would ever want me, a younger woman without a single degree and with an illegitimate child."

He took her hand. She did not resist. "Look, when a guy loves a gal as much as I love you, he has already accepted her as she is and hopes she'll do the same. And so with all my heart I ask if you are ready to be my wife?" She covered her eyes and gasped, "Dear, dear Kris! Can we …can live together first?"

Kris sat back with a deep frown. "No way. I'm the original old-fashioned guy. If what you've seen of me in almost six years is not the man you want to marry, then I already have my answer."

Mandolin's eyes now sparkled like a morning sun on a lake. She walked around the table, sat beside him and looked into the eyes. She lifted her hair over her left ear, and showed him her earring.

"It says yes!"

"And the other one says no," she explained.

"So you'll be my wife?"

"I will! I will! I will! But first, an old fashioned kind of gal has an idea for an old-fashioned kind of a guy."

She punched numbers into her cell phone and handed it to Kris. He puzzled until he cracked a smile. "Sky?"

"Yessir, Dr. Kris. How you doin'? It's been too long."

Kris spoke with his eyes on Mandolin as if searching to see if he was on the right track. Her smile grew. "Right. Mandolin and I are here at a restaurant with an important question. We are truly in love and would like your permission to be married."

The sound of a weeping man was all they heard. Mandolin took the phone.

"Hi, my best buddy. It's me, and I have to tell you, I thought I was wise enough to know what I needed, but I was wrong. This guy knows better, and I adore him. What do you think?"

After a long pause, Sky continued. "First of all, you got me all choked because you is callin' to aks *me*. And second I been pullin' for you two what seems like forever. You bet I approve, darlin'. Nothin' gonna make me happier and the sooner the better for all of us. Now you jes get on with the rest of your life. It's been waitin' on you for a long time."

Now was Mandolin's turn to pause, as if reflecting on her entire life. Never had she been so happy, except when she lived with her dad so many years ago. "I love you Sky and thanks."

Kris felt her emotion. He allowed her time until she looked up and smiled. Their eyes locked, then their lips and then their hearts. Dinner was served; neither ate much and toasted each other when the waiter poured champagne.

Mandolin broke the ice. "You once asked me what *hakka bakka* meant. It's like *nirvana*, your word for paradise and peace. When you find it, you know you're in the right place. And sweetie, you knew it way before I did."

Kris grinned, leaned over and kissed her.

"But I have one question. What would you think if I want to find my mom so she can meet you and James, and be in our wedding?"

"The world is a big place, babe. That miracle may never happen. And if you find her, she may be a disappointment."

"I've thought of that, but listen. Two nights ago, Valentina found my name on the web and called. It seems she has been trying to find me ever since my dad and I left on our trip and never came back. I was born in Malaysia as you know but I never knew that Valentina came to work for him in Cancun when I was a baby. We talked for hours and she says my mom hired her to help my dad raise me, and then disappeared.

Kris's reaction wavered between empathy and exhilaration as he listened.

"Remember: 'The world is full of magical things waiting for our wits to sharpen.'"

Kris' eyes twinkled. "You're too much for me."

She took his hand. "No. You've convinced me I'm just right."

They clinked their glasses to forever.

3.
Beach-lovers

A TAXI ROLLED UP to a beach-front hotel in Cancun. Kris hopped out just as the doorman arrived with a baggage cart. With his help, Kris loaded up the cart, led five year-old James and his yo-yo into the hotel and checked in. Mandolin followed with a heavy shoulder bag and stopped to read a sign. "Entertainment in the Shell Room Every Night. 10-2."

In the elevator, Kris lifted James up and pointed to number seven. James pushed it and called out the numbers, "One, Two, Three, Four, Five, Six, Seven."

"Hold on a minute James, Let's count for Mom."

"Oh yeah. *Ek, do, teen, chaar, panch, chhah, saat!* That's Hindi, Mom and yay! We're here."

"And yay for your Hindi too, sweetheart." Kris and Mandolin exchanged proud glances.

Once they and the bags were in the room, James ran to the sliding glass door in front of the balcony and looked out .

"Holy Pig! Look Pop-Pop. We're on top of the world. I can see China way over there!"

Kris started to laugh and then clamped his hand over his mouth.

He remembered that laughing at kids' remarks often damages their confidence and imagination.

"Holy Pig, Cowboy. You may be right. Now, who's ready for a swim?"

"Me! Me! Me! Can I put on my trunks now?"

Kris quizzed him in fun. "Your elephant trunks or your swim trunks?"

"You know what I mean, Pop-pop. But I better pee first. You're not supposed to pee where everybody swims."

"Good boy," complimented Kris. "Let's all go put on our suits."

James thought that was funny. "Me, Mom and Pop-Pop pee in the po-po and sometimes fart too."

Mandolin smiled and asked herself why most kids, including herself in past years, enjoy potty talk. The trip had been long, and after a late afternoon swim and room service, they all fell asleep early.

The next morning Kris took over James while Mandolin enjoyed a morning alone on the beach. Heaven could be no better. She lay on her back with soft breezes wafting over her body, so ready to let every muscle fall limp on the warm sand while laughing gulls, terns and golden plovers periodically swooped down and then up again. She imagined them flying over the rainbow way up high and wondered what they saw.

The clouds overhead were cottony and floated into animal shapes, ones that gave her ideas for her tissue paper drawings. She was on a different beach but the clouds seemed just like those above when she and her dad memorized a poem by Edgar Allen Poe together. It was about a young girl named Anabel Lee who lived by the sea.

"And this maiden she lived
With no other thought.
Than to love and be loved by me"

But she was in the now and future, no longer in the past on a powdery white sandy beach with aqua water lapping onto it in love with a great guy. Way out there waves began to form, grew slowly and then finally arrived with relief against the sand-packed shore.

She felt that relief. It was a peace she had not experienced for many years. And then came a voice, an inner voice that reminded her she was a mom with responsibilities. She sat up and looked up to the seventh floor where Kris and James stood on the balcony. She waved them down, and while waiting, she dug her feet in the sand and let it run through her toes again and again. When they arrived she showed James how she could pick up a pebble with her toes. He tried three times without success. Kris tried too. James was frustrated. "Come on, Mom. Me and Pop-Pop can't do it. Teach us."

Mandolin remembered the jabs Hopscotch had taken at her early grammar, and corrected James in her own way. "It sounds better to put Pop-Pop first…like Pop-Pop and I can't do it rather than me and Pop-pop. What do you think?"

"Yeah. He's cool. Now what about the toes?"

"Look at mine. They're called prehensile because they curl under and can grasp things. Yours are straight and that makes it harder."

"Monkeys can wrap their tails around things," said James.

"So monkeys and your mom have lots in common," teased Kris which Mandolin so enjoyed.

James produced his yo-yo which he spun out confidently. They built sand castles and when the sand got hot; he raced the waves along the shore line and asked why the water was so hot.

"Here's what the walrus said in *Alice in Wonderland*.

'It's time to talk of ships and things
And why the sea is boiling hot
And whether pigs have wings.'"

James thought she was silly. "Holy Pig, Mom? How can pigs have wings?"

Mandolin laughed. " It's fun to use our imaginations, sweet boy."

James continued with his questions just as she did and would be forevermore. "What's a godfather?"

"First, how about a race back to the hotel?" suggested Kris.

"I already know why Mom chose Sky but—"

Kris drew a line in the sand and pointed his toe at it. James followed suit and away they went with Mandolin trotting along beside. Although Kris was winning, he accidently on purpose fell just before the finish line.

"Too bad, Pop-Pop. Better luck next time."

Mandolin put her arm around them both and they walked through the sand to the hotel.

"My dad and I…and then Sky and I…used to have skipping races just like this."

"Sky's cool," said James and by the time they entered the elevator lobby of the hotel, he understood that godparents are good friends who act as back-ups for kids' religious training. Then he saw a sign, stopped and struggled aloud with the words. "En-ter-tain-ment in the Shell Room. Every Night. Ten to Two."

"How about being my date tonight, babe?" Kris asked Mandolin.

"What about the Lizard?"

"I can go too."

"It's a little late for you, big guy," said Kris.

"No it isn't! I don't want to have a babysitter. I want to come too."

They arrived back in their room and Kris took the reins. "Look at me Cowboy, and listen carefully. This vacation is for us all. Sometimes we do things together and sometimes not. We'll find a good sitter and you can stay up an extra thirty minutes to watch TV. The show is just downstairs and we'll be close if you need anything."

"When the sitter comes, promise not to call me love-bug anymore, okay?"

She laughed without an explanation and hugged him as tight as she ever had. He pulled away and made the hakka-bakka signal. She took his hand and kissed it.

"Don't worry, sweetie. We'll find a sitter you'll like so much you may want to take him or her home with us."

"That would cost too much. When I get big, I'm going to invent a new kind of computer and call it The Prune. It'll work much faster than the Apple and make us really really rich."

"Great idea, "encouraged Kris. "But for now how about playing one of your games with the sitter?"

"O…k-a-ay. But can you first read *James and The Giant Peach* to me? You remember, it's the book my great granddad gave to his dad in the old days."

"Oh that's right, your Mom promised. Sure cowboy. Where is it?"

James pulled up his shirt, beside Kris on the floor.

"One summer afternoon when he is crying in the bushes, James stumbles across a strange old man, who, mysteriously knows all about James's plight and gives him a sack of tiny glowing-green crocodile tongues."

This excited James. "Cool. It's fun to use our 'magines."

Kris and Mandolin looked into one another's smiling eyes.

Me and him and my great grampa and grampa have the same name. That makes us sorta special. But you're special too, Pop-Pop. Read some more, *please!*

Kris agreed to read one more page and continued when he noticed James' head nodding. At the end of this busy day on the beach, he was a pooped trooper and by the time the sitter arrived, he was asleep. Kris greeted the lady in a club uniform and carried James into the bedroom while hearing his sleepy voice. "Tomorrow let's read more about the crocodile tongues. Okay?"

While waiting for the show to start, Kris and Mandolin held hands and she shared her thoughts. "When I see how the Lizard takes to you first and then and yo-yos, second it reminds me of my past and

something Sky once said. I can hear his words now. *'Seems like diggin'*
in your past, and findin' what turns you on gonna send you in the right
direction—kinda like that yo-yo a yours. You send it down, it spins at
your feet a spell there and when you brings it back up you feel good about
yourself. " It symbolizes my life in a way."

Kris raised his hand as if to toast with a glass. "So here's to all the
yo-yos in the world."

"Are you teasing me?"

"If I am it's because I never got mine to roll back into position."

"Aha! I can finally teach *you* something,"

"What a gal!"

"What a dude!"

Kris and Mandolin sat close together and enjoyed the calypso
music as well as the Mexican dancers, Ronaldo and Isolda. After dinner
an American band took the stage and an evening of dancing began,
better than they had dreamed. It reminded them that life was not all
about kids and OB duties. They were pumped, in love and thrilled to
see the other revitalized.

Her favorite song "All you Need is Love" began and Kris was
surprised to find her deep in thought again. Mandolin's role as a mother
was one she took seriously and when Kris offered a penny for her
thoughts, she confessed.

"I was wondering how my mom would have raised James."

Just as Kris started to confirm her concerns, her feet started to beat
to the music and a curious question followed. "Will you come with
me?" Mandolin asked.

"Hold on. We just got here."

"No, no. I don't want to leave the hotel yet, silly."

He wiped his brow playfully. "I'll go with you to the moon and
back, any place except the ladies room, my love."

"Aww-w! You're no fun. I'd follow you to the men's room."

The music interfered with their conversation and she whispered in his ear. He nodded, stood, offered his hand they approached Ronaldo and Isolda who were sitting at a table among the audience.

"I only want to tell you both how beautifully you dance together. There are so many things I want to do in my life and being as graceful as either one of you would make me happy."

Isolda and Ronaldo were pleased and Kris felt compelled to brag about Mandolin. "My fiancée has an ear for music and a beautiful voice."

"She weel sing for us? We like so much for the guests to join in."

Kris took her hand. "Come on, Mandolin, you can do it."

Mandolin was considering it when Ronaldo looked at her with surprise. "Your name, it is Mandolin?"

She nodded.

"Dios Mio!" He stared at her. "You are in the family of 'Miss Mandolin and her Magic Mandolin?"

She was too stunned to talk, could only stare. Kris gripped her arm tightly.

"Does…does Miss Mandolin live here in town?" he asked.

"*No, vives afuera,*" Ronaldo answered with a wave of his arm to a distant place.

"Last week *aqui,* now *alla.* She is big-time, sometimes here in Mexico, sometimes in other Caribbean island."

Mandolin was afraid to believe what she heard. Kris detailed Mandolin's past to him and to the musicians. One performer suggested checking other hotels in the area, like Ixtapa. Another informed him most entertainers had gigs in Mexico City, Florida and the West Indies and anyone as popular as Miss Mandolin could be making the circuit.

"I say again my name is Ronaldo. When you see her, please to say hello for me. She a good woman. *Encantissima!* She want we call her Ruku offstage."

Mandolin was anxious to get to the computer, but Kris was patient. "Why Ruku?"

The vocalist laughed jovially. "Her last name, it is Gillian and she tell me it is too long this name, Mandolin Rukumani Gillian. She then act, how you say?—cuckoo—and she say to call her only Ruku. He laughed and added. "You will like her. She bring fun to all. And remember me. I am Ronaldo." He blew a kiss into the air as if to Ruku.

"I'll never forget this night, Ronaldo. Meeting you is—well in my family, we call it *hakka bakka*, a time when you're at peace and where you belong." She watched the sun sinking into the ocean. "Look over there eeryone. It's like a miracle and a bit of magic wrapped up together."

The band tuned up. Mandolin hoped they all could stay around after the show but the music interfered with the answer. Ronaldo smiled, took the microphone and Kris followed Mandolin back to their seats.

"Mandolin Rukumani Gillian. Holy Pig! I agree, that's a mouthful. Is Rukumani an Indian name?" she asked Kris.

"He was one of the wives of an Indian God, worshipped for his youth and pursuance of artistic pleasures.

"I'm not into Indian culture Do you worship many Gods?"

"Sometimes, but I'm open to the religious beliefs of others. Now go to it, babe! We need to get on the trail of your Abba ASAP. I'll relieve the sitter and we'll meet you back in the room. Stay as long as you need to. We'll be fine. "

He kissed her affectionately and they parted.

The portrait of the lovely girl on the beach with the dark eyes and hair flashed in front of her. So where was this girl of more than twenty five years ago?

On the web, she found the name Ruku and learned she had had a successful career as a boat captain. She talked to the computer. "Please let this be my mom. She sounds like my kind of a woman."

The next couple of days were busy ones. Kris and Mandolin took turns entertaining James, checking the entertainers in various popular hotels or resorts in the Caribbean area on the web and making calls.

Kris enjoyed teaching James how to kick his feet as he pushed a float along the shallow water. All at once a dog ran onto the beach chasing a cat, caught the cat, shook it s neck and left it on the beach.

"Pop-Pop! Come on! We need to rescue the cat."

"You stay here James. The cat is dead. I'll go pick him up."

"No he's not. No he's not."

"Yes. Sadly, the cat is dead." Just as they arrived, the cat upped and walked under a stair step.

James jumped with joy. He's good! He's good!"

Kris snapped his fingers. "I've always known you're smarter than me, Cowboy."

"It's okay, Pop-Pop. We don't have to tell Mom you made a mistake."

Kris bit his lip apparently to avoid disillusioning James at this moment.

"When we get home can we get a cat?"

"We'll have to talk to Mom about it."

An excited shout came from down the beach and James pointed to his mom who was racing towards them. Look Pop-Pop! Mom found her Abba on the computer. Yay Mom!"

"If you're right, let's let her tell us the good news, okay Cowboy?"

The back-to-back flights from Cancun were long and bumpy, and the taxi ride from the airport in Antigua to their hotel was at last flat and very calm, which pleased James. He sat in a car seat behind Gagan, the taxi-driver. James thought Gagan was a funny name and asked how come he had a name like that. The conversation was lively. Gagan explained it was common in the West Indies and meant Sky. James told him about his mom's best friend; asked if he had a best friend, when Mandolin interrupted. She wanted Gagan to tell them all the history of the West Indies.

Gagan lit up and explained to James that many from other countries had come to the West Indies as slaves, had raised cane and eventually been colonized by the British.

"Pop-pop says I raise cain too."

"You do, sometimes, but this is different. Your kind of cain originated from a shepherd named Cain, a Bible figure who many believe committed bad acts. Gagan is talking about sugar cane, a crop that is raised here and provides sugar to all the tropical and sub-tropical countries."

"Oh. Do you have some, Gagan?"

Mandolin took over. "Gagan knows the history of his country, James. We are in the West Indies and all should know as much as possible about our birth places."

"I already know about Playmouth Rock, Mom."

"That's a start," said Kris. "And say Plymouth, not Playmouth."

Gagan spoke up. "He is intelligent sir. Very intelligent."

James smiled. "I like you too and how you speak like God with a funny accent."

Gagan asked his name.

"Pop-Pop calls me Cowboy, my mom calls me Lizard but my real name is James."

"I call you smart guy, okay with you?"

James nodded and Gagan continued. "You be good and perhaps your dad and mum will consent we go to Lord Nelson's Dockyard."

"Can we, Pop-Pop? Can we Mom?"

"Do you know who Lord Nelson was, Cowboy?"

"No, but Gagan will teach me."

Without a word, she took his hand and kissed it. Gagan spoke. "If you do not mind me; I speak for all of us Antiguans with pride about Admiral Lord Nelson. This mon of only twenty-seven years won for us the battle of Trafalgar and was based nearby in English Harbour from 1784 to 1787.

"I want to be an admiral when I grow up. I will be Admiral James Brown MacDuff."

Kris had a comment. "I believe you, Cowboy. You're brave and like adventure like your mom."

At last Gagan pulled up to the guard house and was nodded through. In the distance was the beachfront hotel set in the middle of a cove. They finally arrived; Kris tipped Gagan and took his card.

Inside the open-air lobby, a major problem surfaced. The receptionist announced the club was private. Unless they had a guest card from a member, they would not be allowed to stay. Kris began to speak when James interrupted.

"Poor Mom. She doesn't even know her own mother or where she lives or anything."

Mandolin leaned way down to James put her finger to her lips. The receptionist rang a bell and while they waited, she read Gagan's card.

"Gagan is an interesting guy, Kris, you should read…"

A very black, very jovial and very well-dressed woman appeared wearing a nametag that read Manager Rani.

"May I help you, Mum?"

James spoke up. "She's *my* Mom, not yours, and her real name is…"

Mandolin reprimanded him. Rani smiled politely and explained that many American guests found her accent unusual and that she was a mother of two sons who interrupted as well.

James reacted. "Rani is a funny name. Does it rain a lot here?"

She laughed "No. "My name means queen, I am Queen Rani."

"And I am King James."

Everyone chuckled except Mandolin. Rani suggested a trip to the beach while they talked. "Down below we have towels." Kris thanked her and took James' hand.

Mandolin confided in Rani. "My son often thinks he is an adult, and forgets our two rules, to be a good listener and not interrupt. I'm sure you understand. And also you should understand our situation."

Rani heard about the portrait of a woman playing the mandolin, and about her diligent search for her mother. "Even if we can't spend the night here, could you see if it's possible for me to speak to Miss Mandolin?"

"Yes mum. She is a beauti-ful woman from Malaysia and she comes here every year to be with us. She say our beach is pretty like in Langkawi, her island."

Mandolin gulped. Kris and James entered while toweling off. "Sorry to interrupt. James needs the rest room." They headed off when James called to his mom.

"And after, can we climb up in the old mill over there?" He pointed.

"Will you be quiet until we finish talking?" Mandolin asked him.

"Sorry Mom. Sorry Rani. This is a really cool place."

Rani smiled. "I can learn very much about parenting from you, Mum. Your story, it has touched me. We shall be happy to give you a room facing the ocean, where you can wait for Miss Mandolin's call and enjoy our lovely beach. I shall explain this unusual situation to the receptionist and she will give you a three-day guest card. Have a lovely day and please enjoy it all."

Mandolin took her hand and kissed it.

The Rum Punches served on the beach by staff members were powerful and went down way too easily. A waiter brought Mandolin a message from inside and from her squeals Kris and James knew that it was a very very good message Another rum punch to celebrate and soon they were back in their room, much against the will of James. Kris reminded her that a nap would do them all good, especially in the light breezes. The need for air conditioning was unnecessary anywhere in the club.

4.

A Starry Night

MANDOLIN, KRIS AND JAMES ate dinner outside around a dance floor with a calypso band beating out music on steel guitars, bamboo sticks, frying pans and steel drums. Their table was close to a sign that read *Miss Mandolin and her Magic Mandolin from 8 to 10.* The time was 7:22 PM according to Pink Oink, her treasure from Heather.

The mood jockeyed from excitement to apprehension.

"Hold my hand, Kris. If she's my mother and we don't like one another, then what?

Kris looked around anxiously when he spotted a stylish woman somewhere in her fifties, carrying a mandolin. She was heading towards them from behind Mandolin and James. The steel band finished a number; she stepped onto the bandstand, and hooked the Mic to the back of her outfit. The leader made an announcement.

"While we take a break, we are hoppy to introduce our next attraction of the evening. Miss Mondolin and her Mahgic Mond-o-lin."

James asked if he could call Miss Mandolin, Ruku.

"Not to her face unless she asks," answered his mom.

Ruku began. "Good evening to you all on this beautiful starry evening." She held her hand to her ear as if awaiting a response and repeated. "Good evening."

James shouted. "Good evening."

Miss Mandolin waved at him. "I am happy you are here."

"Woo! Woo! Ruku!" James whispered in his mom's ear. "Ruku likes me, Mom. And looks kind of like the pretty girl in your picture when she was younger."

Mandolin studied her. Ruku waved for silence. "I have just completed a series of shows in Jamaica where my version of Abba's *Dancing Queen* brought everyone to their feet.

Mandolin whispered to Kris. "Who is Abba?"

"Actually Abba is found in the old testament, the son of the father who believes everything is possible for us. The word has been adopted by a famous Swedish Pop Band and taken on meanings like mama as well. It shows tenderness."

Mandolin slowly nodded as if she had learned something important.

Ruku unhooked the Mic from its stand danced happily and sang.," I can dance I can sing. I'm having the time of life:" At James' table, she handed him the mic. Without encouragement he sang, "*It's not what you do it's the way that you do it. That's what it's all about. Hey!*" And then he clapped his hands.

Ruku laughed at his enthusiasm and spoke into the Mic. "I like that song. What does it mean to you?"

"That's easy. To treat people the goodest you can."

Ruku turned to Mandolin, smiled and returned to the stage slowly. Mandolin sensed something was coming when Ruku set her mandolin in position, strummed and sang her own words to *The Start of Something Big.*

"You're walkin' along the street, before a party
You're with a gorgeous guy and suddenly dig,
He's what you really want and then you realize

That this could be the start of something big."

Is this for real? Mandolin asked herself. She had heard this song before and for some reason, avoided Ruku's eyes. She dug into her past and it suddenly hit her. This was her dad's favorite song. She looked up. Their eyes connected. Without words, only tears, they knew they belonged. Within seconds they were in one another's arms.

Kris took the mic and softly announced that the show would resume in a few minutes. The audience sensed something special, and applauded.

"Is she my Mom's Mom, Pop-Pop?" James asked.

Ruku had to collect herself from the stunning revelation and then answered James. "I am. And I hope you will call me Ruku."

"Sure. My name is James."

"And you are…you are my handsome…my very handsome grandson."

"Am I Mom?"

The question affected Mandolin deeply. Kris took over "very much so, Cowboy. And you are all together at last."

James was excited and had a question for Ruku. "Do you know how to yo-yo?"

Ruku threw her head back and laughed. "Not at all. Perhaps you will teach me."

Back on stage, Ruku positioned her mandolin and switched on her mic. "Please forgive us, but this is a joyous time for me and my… my family."

Mandolin's eyes equaled the size of tennis balls and her voice carried. "Oh! Oh! It's *hakka bakka*! We are all where we belong."

Ruku hugged her "So you know about that. Your father and I watched the video of Kishore Kumar many times."

Tears gushed from Mandolin's eyes. Ruku sang show tunes, James and Kris danced and then the time came for James to go to bed. He fussed at first, looked at Kris's face and understood like a big guy. Then he kissed his mom and hugged his gramma.

"My mom said her gramma was sorta weird sometimes. You're *my* gramma and you're not weird at all. We live in Texas. Will you come and see us?"

Her vigorous nod indicated there was no doubt of it. "And I want you and your mom and her friend to come to Malaysia to visit me. You will have a good time. We play a game with a straw ball called *Sepak Raga*. You will love our life there."

James was dubious and turned to Kris. "Let's read where Huck and his dad move to the backwoods and he's kept locked inside his father's cabin, okay Pop-Pop?"

"We'll see, Cowboy. That part may give you nightmares."

"No it won't, promise. Mom taught me to stand up for myself." He looked at Mandolin. "But not in cars, right Mom?"

Mandolin was rapt with emotion. Kris led the group out while the band continued playing "The Start of something Big."

Mandolin and her Mom went to the quiet open air lounge decorated with seascapes on the walls and sat at a table surrounded with barrel-like Caribbean chairs she learned were called equipales. Neither one knew where to begin. Finally Ruku reached out for Mandolin's hand.

"You are a beautiful woman, Mandolin. I hope you have been happy."

Mandolin was surprised at her mother's formality, and before revealing her reaction, she sat back. She had been warned their meeting could be awkward. She already felt her Mom's sincerity and even more when Ruku opened up. She had met Jimmy, James' father during a spring break many years ago. He was a crew member on a race from Hawaii to Port Dickson in Malaysia. They had stayed together for several months until she was sure it wasn't a lasting relationship... especially when his Mom came to visit."

"She likes to be called Hopscotch," offered Mandolin.

"Interesting," said Ruku. "She was not a-tall like I expected. I talked about Jimmy's sense of humor and that he had taught me to sail and…and…actually my problem had nothing to do with her. I was…I was…"

Mandolin identified with her struggle to express the next part.

"If I can make a guess I'd say you were pregnant."

They stared at one another. "I've been there, Mom. So then what?"

Ruku took her hand and looked her in the eye. "Your dad was happy about it. Unfortunately, I wasn't. I was young and not ready for him or our baby and he did the honorable thing. He *willingly* took full responsibility."

"James father was different, but we're good. So…so…Oh my God! So…so that's why my dad had never brought me to meet Hopscotch until…until…"

"What happened? Tell me, dear."

Mandolin covered her eyes. Ruku went to her side and stroked her back.

"I'm so sorry for whatever I said, darling."

"It isn't your fault. We all do what we have to do, but I have so many questions for you. Like have you ever looked for me?"

Ruku was quiet and then said. "I have thought of you every day."

Mandolin uncoiled her frustration, the same frustration that she had about James' dad. "How could you give up your own child?"

"That will take some time to explain. My agent keeps me going and I'm afraid my career has taken over my life. But nothing would make me happier than to arrange a visit in Malaysia for you, James and this gentleman so you can see where I live."

Kris arrived in the lounge. "James fell asleep and I came in search of you guys when Rani stopped me and volunteered to stay with him so we can have time together."

Ruku stood. "I should have thought of that myself. Living alone and out of a suitcase much of the time has kept me in my own world. We should talk again tomorrow. This has been an emotional day for us all."

She hugged them both and left them alone.

Mandolin looked at Kris. "You know, babe, I was sure the ultimate *hakka bakka* would be the day I found my mom."

Totally surprised, he asked. "It's not?"

"Not exactly." She studied him seriously. "In a way, yes—But I—I—"

"Never forget this. if your mom had aborted you, I'd never have met you...or The Lizard."

"You constantly amaze me, Doctor."

"Forget about that. How about marrying me on the beach, tomorrow?"

She looked at pink oink. "Let's see that means we have to wait twelve hours?"

Their eyes and hearts locked and they embraced for eternity.

The following afternoon, as the sun was setting over the Caribbean at low tide, a bare-footed wedding party began to gather. Mandolin and James with his flag pin on his sailor-boy suit waited at one end of a roped off portion of the beach. It was shaded by a thatched lean-to.

Dressed in a floral cover-up with a crown of multi-colored bougainvilleas, Mandolin began to pace. James did too. "You're shaking, Mom. All brides are nervous, I guess. But it's okay. Pop-Pop gets nervous too sometimes."

Reverend Gagan entered with Kris who had chosen a white shirt, white shorts and scarlet tie as his wedding suit. They stood in the sand, facing the Reverend, all members of the staff as well as variously clad guests who had joined the festivities. It was a dream-like like setting for the occasion.

The grounds around the stucco clubhouse were beautifully manicured and the setting sun reflected on the ocean. Ruku entered in a sleek strapless fuchsia gown and stood off to the left with the steel band. She looked over the group and bit her lip to avoid a break-down. With the portable mic up to her mouth, she sang her own words to *The Start of Something Big.*

"You're watching the sun go down with all of us around
"And a life you've dreamed of, all ahead
"We wish you love and joy—perhaps another boy
"Because this will be the start of something big."

The band then began the wedding march with a calypso beat, Reverend Gagan motioned for James and Mandolin to come on down. James stretched up his arm as far he could. Mandolin smiled at him, reached down as far as she could and down the aisle they went hand in hand.

Reverend Gagan asked "Who gives this woman to this man?"

James waved his gramma to his side and in a rehearsed calliopean voice replied "my gramma and I do."

The vows went smoothly and after the Reverend pronounced them Man and Wife, their long kiss caused titters among the guests and a yuck from James.

Gagan made an announcement. "The Management of the hotel would like to invite everyone to meet on the patio for light refreshments starting immediately.

James shouted "Yes!"

His gramma took his hand, whispered something that made him jump up and down and then run to his mom. She nodded her approval and he skipped back to gramma Mandolin.

'Mom says I can come to your room for twenty minutes and no more." They left the scene hand in hand." Later, dancing to the music, the bride suddenly pulled back from the groom. "Will you come with me?"

"To the Po-po?"

Mandolin jabbed him in fun. "Nope. Not this time. Let's call Sky and Heather and tell them our news."

They left the patio and on the way to the lobby, Kris commented.

"Without Rani, all this may never have happened, right?"

She smiled. "I'm not so sure, but she was a big help."

He put some cash in an envelope, wrote her name and left it on the counter. "It's only a small token of our appreciation."

Mandolin called Sky, and left word to tell Heather the news.

They looked at one another in an adoring way.

"If you're thinking what I'm thinking, my favorite doctor and husband, I'm ready when you are!"

"Why Mrs. Desai, are you trying to seduce me?"

"Every chance I get."

EPILOGUE

Sky, now more bent and white-headed with a cane hooked on his arm, paced slowly around his living room. Red-headed Heather rocked in an antique rocker.

"Did ah tell you ah met up with Mandolin and her daughter over ta Walgreen's this mornin'?"

"No Ma'am. How they all doin'?"

"Fahn and dandy. Lily got a scholarship to UT and they were pickin up a few supplies before drivin' up to Austin in our Mandolin's brand new convertible. Would you believe that girl was flippin' a yo-yo around?"

Sky nodded "Course I would. Her Mama hardly never let hers outta her sight. Kinda like me and this here cane Dr. Kris gave me awhile back. What about James. He's a senior now, right?"

"Nope. He dropped outta college after one year to perfect his Mama's Bee Connection, that memory thing. They say he almost got it ready to go to market."

"Good for him. Sure will help me. Lotta times my glasses and pill box make me guess where they gone to."

"Same with me. Haven't heard much about Dr. Kris.lately. Is he still teaching?" Heather asked.

"Sure is. He's teaching over at Baylor and travels to the poorer countries once a year to explain how we deliverin' babies here."

"How about our Mandolin?"

"With all she been through she made me real proud. She got two degrees, one in psychology and one in anotherapology."

"You mean anthropology," corrected Heather.

"Yup. She's still fixin' to teach us all how all our different ways gonna matter to our future."

Heather chuckled. "To tell you the truth, ah got this funny feeling some of us are not goin' too much further."

Sky struggled to sit. "And it's okay, cuz we know *'tain't what we do it's the way that we do it'* that counts."

"You got that right. And we're lucky too. Ah believe we both got our arms wrapped around that hakka bakka jubilee the first day Mandolin showed up at the mansion."

Sky took Heather's hand and they rocked contentedly as the late afternoon sunlight gradually moved onto the keys of Big Mama's piano.

THE END